My name is Cassidy Porter...

My father, Paul Isaac Porter, was convicted twenty years ago for the brutal murder of twelve innocent girls.

Though I was only eight years old at the time, I am aware, every day of my life, that I am his child, his only son.

To protect the world from the poison in my veins, I live a quiet life, off the grid, away from humanity.

I promised myself, and my mother, not to infect innocent lives with the darkness that swirls within me, waiting to make itself known.

It's a promise I would have kept . . . if Brynn Cadogan hadn't stumbled into my life.

Now I exist between heaven and hell: falling for a woman who wants to love me, while all along reminding myself that I must remain . . .

Unloved.

Unloved

a love story

KATY REGNERY

New York Times Bestselling Author

UNLOVED, a love story

Cover Design: Katy Regnery
Developmental Edit: Chris Belden
Technical Edit: Melissa DeMeo
Proofreading: Nom de Plume
Formatting: CookieLynn Publishing Services

First Edition: October 2017
Katy Regnery
Unloved: a novel / by Katy Regnery – 1st ed.
ISBN: 978-1-944810-19-1

For George, Henry, and Callie.
You are <u>loved</u>.
xo

Prologue

Brynn

My car wouldn't start.

That's how it all began.

With something as ordinary as a dead battery.

Turning the key again and again, I was rewarded with silence and finally texted Jem that I wouldn't make it to the concert. I told him I was sorry. I told him to have a great time. I told him not to wake me up when he got home.

He didn't.

Because he never *came* home.

A million times, I've returned to that night, to the simple, nothing decisions that started a chain of events in my life leading to today. I think of Jem checking his phone, wondering why I was late. I picture him getting my text and grimacing in disappointment. I see him in my mind, considering whether or not to leave the club and come home to me—or to stay.

He decided to stay.

Twenty minutes later, he was dead.

The shooter left a note saying that he didn't love or hate the music of Steeple 10. What he hated was the idea of all those people in a club for the same reason: having something in common that they all enjoyed. He didn't enjoy anything with anyone and was jealous of their communal happiness, their shared appreciation for noise pop. So he opened fire on three hundred people packed into the crowded club, killing thirty-one. Among them, my fiancé, Jem.

Sometimes, in my dreams, I'm back in my car on that rainy night, and the engine turns over. I drive to the club. I park outside. I see Derrick Frost Willums get out of his 2011 Toyota Corolla, his black trench coat too heavy and too hot for an unseasonably humid August night in San Francisco. In some versions of my dream, I imagine myself intercepting him, talking to him, befriending him, and inadvertently letting him know that he's not alone. In others, I race into the club, looking frantically over the hot-pink and indigo-blue lights to find Jem's blond, spiked hair in the crowd. I imagine running to my love and telling him to lie down on the floor with me, since those who quickly dropped to the floor mostly survived. I imagine us huddled together on the filthy, beer-slick floor as bullets rain around us and terrified concertgoers slowly realize what's happening, darting chaotically in search of cover, slipping in pools of blood, trying desperately to dodge Willums's relentless rounds of open fire. But mostly, in nine out of ten dreams, I am too late. I see myself sprint, in slow motion, from my car to the club, swinging open the door just in time to see Willums turn the gun on himself, pull the trigger, and fall backward.

I stand there frozen: a lone, paralyzed figure, unable to help anyone, way too late to save Jem, who probably died instantly from a clean shot to his heart—to his strong, beautiful, bursting-with-love-for-me heart.

When I wake up, my pillow is drenched with tears and I reach for Jem, hoping that the dream I've had is somehow just a horrible nightmare, not the truth, not an actual, outlandish, and still-incomprehensible part of my life. But Jem's side of the bed is always empty now, as it's been for almost two years.

The rest of the world moved on from the Steeple 10 Shooting, ever more numb to the news of similar events, out of sympathy for nameless strangers who meet the same tragic end.

But *I* can't seem to move on.

I had someone in the crowd that night who had a name, who was dearly loved. Those of us who survived are the walking wounded. Or the walking dead.

And some of us, even if we never set foot in that club that night, are still somehow there, facing the spray of Willums's fury with our lost loved ones, and uselessly wishing that everything could have turned out different.

Chapter One

Brynn
Present Day

Brynn, any chance you'll be able to complete the website by today? Was hoping to go live this weekend. Please advise. —Stu

I stare at the e-mail over the rim of my coffee cup, rolling my eyes. When I quoted Stu (of Stu's Pools) a price of $1,200 to build his website, I was clear that it would take up to three weeks to complete. It's been ten days and he's already bothering me to finish?

"I hate people," I tell Milo, my four-year-old Siamese cat.

Purring, he paces back and forth on my desk, between my forearms and the warm keyboard, before falling dramatically atop it. The screen quickly starts to fill with line after line of question marks.

"I can't work if you stay there," I say, taking another sip of coffee.

"*Meow*," he answers, licking his paw. *Oh, well. Too bad for you.*

Milo has always been chatty. It was the reason that Jem chose him for me from all of the other kittens at the pet store that day.

"Now you'll have someone to keep you company while

you work," he said, handing the cashier his credit card.

"I don't need anyone to keep me company," I pointed out. "I like working alone. Besides, litter boxes aren't my gig."

"I'll keep it clean," Jem promised.

"I don't *want* the responsibility of a cat," I insisted, whining a little.

"Just let him be your friend. I'll care for him," he said, his New England accent strong on the word *care*, which sounded more like "cay-uh."

In the end, that's what had swayed me—the way his sweet lips said *care*. It made my toes curl. I'd always had a thing for accents, and as a born-and-bred San Franciscan, I'd fallen for his at the first hello.

Jeremiah Benton was from Bangor, Maine, a place so far from the Bay area, it may have well been a different country altogether.

"What are you drinking?" I asked him the first time I ever saw him.

I was working behind the bar, blown away by the aqua blue of his eyes when he looked up at me, and determined to be nonchalant about how insanely, ruggedly hot he was.

"Whatever you have on tap there." *Thay-uh.*

"*Thay-uh?*" I repeated, raising an eyebrow, my lips quirking up.

"Did you lose an *r*?" he asked, grinning at me through a scruffy beard.

"I think *you* did," I teased, pulling him a pint of Go West! IPA.

He chugged down half the beer and swiped at his beard before speaking again, those aqua eyes darkening just a touch as they captured mine. "Sweet girl, I'll wager I'm gonna lose more than just an *r* to you by the time this is over."

Just like that . . . I was a goner.

He told me he'd just spent a month hiking in the Sierra National Forest on assignment for *Backpacker* magazine.

I told him I'd never been on a hike in my entire life.

He called me a city slicker and asked me when I was free to take one.

I had never dated a customer before that day, despite many offers, but I told him I was free the following Saturday.

He lost an *r*. I lost my heart.

"*Meow?*" asks Milo, pausing in his bath, his blue eyes demanding I return to the present day, which, unfortunately, includes building a website for Stu's Pools.

I push Milo gently off the keyboard and delete four pages of question marks, toggling back to my e-mail account.

No, Stu. I'm sorry, but if you'll recall, our contract gives me three weeks to build the site. It will be ready on June 26, as promised.

My fingers fly over the keys, my eyes always slower than the words I'm typing. When they finally land on the date, my fingers freeze and my breath catches.

June 26.

June 26. Jem's birthday. Jem's thirtieth birthday.

The sudden lump in my throat is so big and so painful, it almost feels like choking, so I reach up and massage it, pushing my rolling chair away from the desk, away from the date, away . . . away . . . away . . .

"Would. Have. Been," I say aloud, the words more bitter than my coffee.

Would have been . . . would have been . . . would have been Jem's thirtieth birthday, I force myself to acknowledge.

My therapist, Anna, told me it was like this when you lost a loved one in a violent or unexpected death: for years— or sometimes, in extreme cases, for the rest of your life—

you might still keep track of the important days and milestones. It was because you never got to say goodbye or prepare yourself to say goodbye. Even if you are someday able to make peace with their passing, part of you may not be convinced that the loved one is actually gone. Some secret, hidden, yearning part of you might stubbornly hold on to the unconscious, irrational belief that they aren't actually gone at all, just missing, just away. And when your brain forces you to realize that they are, in fact,

Dead

. . . for a moment—for *that* moment—you will lose them all over again.

It doesn't happen to me as often now as it did in the first year . . . but it still happens occasionally, and it knocks me on my ass every time.

"Lean into it," advised Anna. "Take a few minutes to remember Jem—what he meant to you, how much you loved him. And then take the time to say goodbye again. Ignoring it won't make it go away, Brynn. Ignoring it will only keep you from healing. Leaning into it may help your mind, eventually, accept that he's really gone."

With burning eyes, I stand up from the desk chair and leave my office, listening to my slippers scuffle against the hardwood floor of the hallway as I walk past the bathroom and hall closet. Entering the bedroom I shared with Jem, I head for the walk-in closet and step inside, reaching for the shoe box on the top shelf.

Anna was also the person who helped me come to terms with donating Jem's clothes to Goodwill and sending his books and albums back to Maine for his parents to keep. I'd sent his beloved backpacking equipment, maps, and guidebooks to his twin sister, Hope, who was also a hiker. I'd kept for myself only what could fit in a small box: a

7

matchbook from the bar where we'd met; letters and postcards we'd written to each other during the two years we were together; pictures from the various hikes we'd taken, mostly in Yosemite; my engagement ring, which I'd stopped wearing on the first anniversary of his death; and his cell phone.

His cell phone.

It lay, as it had for almost two years, in a Ziploc evidence bag, uncharged, on the bottom of the box, his dried blood still caked in the crevice between the screen and the plastic body. It had been found several inches from his hand, under the hip of a Stanford undergrad who'd been at the concert with her sister.

Milo wanders into the bedroom, his face inquisitive and vaguely accusatory, as I sit down on the bed and open the box.

"Anna said to," I tell him, wiping a tear from my cheek.

"*Meow*," he answers, winding around my legs before lying down in a patch of sunlight on the carpet and giving me permission to grieve.

My eyes settle first on the matchbook, a shiny, fire engine red with "Down Time" emblazoned across the top in silver. Pushing it aside, I find a picture of Jem and me—a selfie taken at the Vernal Fall Footbridge in Yosemite. Wincing, I lift the pile of pictures and letters gingerly from the box and set them gently on my bed. Generally, I go through the photos at this point, crying as I remember good times, then tearfully replacing them and whispering, "Goodbye, Jem" as I recover the box and put it back in my closet.

But today, for whatever reason, I turn away from the photos and look back in the box at the two items remaining: my ring and his phone.

Impulsively, I reach for the phone and pull it from the box. Unsealing the evidence bag for the first time since it was given to me a year ago, I do something that makes my heart race so rapidly, my head feels light: I lean over my bed and plug Jem's phone into the charger on my bedside table. After two years, it springs to life within seconds, the outline of a battery taking shape on the black screen.

And though the speed and ease with which I am able to bring it back from the dead strikes me as almost obscene, my tears have receded, and I bite my lower lip as a rare feeling of anticipation washes over me. I have no idea what I'm hoping to find on Jem's phone, but it's been so long since it felt like something mattered to me, I lean into the feeling of excitement just a little.

Two years ago, before the Steeple 10 shooting, I had lived a full and rich life. Engaged to Jem and planning our wedding, I got together with my parents in Scottsdale regularly and went out with friends all the time. Soon after meeting Jem, I finished my course of study in website design and started picking up jobs right away. It wasn't long before I quit working at Down Time and spent most days working from home. I liked being on my own. Even though I was alone, I never felt lonely or isolated.

Two years later, however, that same job had become an easy way for me to separate myself from the world.

I rarely leave my house, have my groceries delivered, and exercise on a treadmill in my bedroom. My trips to Scottsdale are infrequent, despite my mother's worried invitations to visit more often. Long ago, the friends that predated Jem grew tired of my ignoring texts and voice mails. They eventually stopped reaching out, finally telling me that when I was ready to hang out again, I should let them know.

I am a hermit, except for my twice-monthly visits to Anna. And while part of me knows it isn't healthy, more of me doesn't care.

Beep.

I look over to see Jem's iPhone light up, an old picture of us filling the small screen, and a polite demand for his passcode.

With trembling fingers, I key in 062687, and the screen changes immediately, his apps lining up in five neat rows.

Calendar. Clock. Weather. Messages.

Voice Memos. Contacts. Safari. Mail.

Maps. Settings. Notes. Camera.

Photos. TV. iBooks. Kindle.

App Store. iTunes Store. Music. Shazam.

Though I've had the phone in my possession for almost a year, only now do I realize there is a smudge on the top corner of the screen, so faint it's only visible because of the lit-up screen now shining through it. Brownish-red and slightly smeared, it's all that remains of a bloody fingerprint, and my breath catches as I stare at it.

Slowly, so slowly, I run my finger over it, wondering when and how it got there, blinking at the screen in surprise as my unintentional keystroke opens Jem's final text message.

The top of the screen reads "Brynn," which means he was writing to me.

An unsent message reads simply, *katahd*

Gasping with the sudden, overwhelming realization that Jem had spent his last moment on earth trying to write me a message, the screen blurs as my eyes fill with more burning, useless, punishing tears. To anyone else, *katahd* might look like gibberish, but I've seen the full word too many times not to recognize it.

Katahdin.

Mount Katahdin.

The highest peak in Maine.

The place where Jem said his soul had lived until he'd given it to me.

Pressing his phone to my heart, I curl into a ball on my bed and weep.

***

"What do you mean you're going to Maine? Brynn, if you need to get away, please come to Scottsdale. You can stay as long as you like."

"Mom, please . . ."

"This doesn't make any sense, sweetheart," she says, her voice wavering between concerned and impatient. I picture her at my parents' lavish mansion, sitting on a lounger beside the pool in a floppy hat, her youthful face marked with consternation. "We know how much you loved Jem, but it's been two years—"

"Stop," I demand softly.

Of all the things people say to you after you lose someone you loved, being told that you should "get over it" is not only unhelpful, it's hurtful and infuriating.

She sighs, but her voice remains gentle. "Brynn, sweetheart, please. Come to Scottsdale for a week."

How can I help her understand what finding Jem's final message means to me?

After these painful, wrenching twenty-four months of grieving him, in the past two days I've felt something new galvanizing within me—a plan, a purpose, a reason to get up and actually leave my apartment. In a way I never saw coming, Jem is showing me, from the grave, how to say goodbye—he's giving me a chance to bury him and move on—but I have to battle my comfortable inertia and start moving to make it happen.

"Mom, he was writing to me. His last thoughts were of me . . . and Katahdin. I know that because he was texting me. He was trying to type the name of the mountain in the last seconds of his life. Don't you see? I have to go. I have to go there for him."

"A few hiking trips with Jem several years ago doesn't prepare you to walk up a mountain clear across the country!" she cries, all pretense of calm disappearing as her voice pitches to a level of near panic. "There are *bears*, Brynn! It's the woods. I doubt you'll have a cell signal. It's so far away! If something happened to you, Daddy and I couldn't get there for days. I am your mother, and I love you, and I am *begging* you to rethink this plan."

"It's already done, Mom," I say. "Jem's sister is picking me up at the airport on Sunday evening. I'm staying with her. She knows the mountain like the back of her hand."

I hadn't spoken to Hope in over a year when I called her last night, and I worried about opening up deep wounds when I dialed her number, but she was as warm as she'd been the two times she'd visited me and Jem in San Francisco.

"Brynn! How are you?"

"I'm okay, Hope. How are you?"

"I'm okay too. Good days and bad," she admitted. "You?"

"Same." I paused, breathing through my deep desire to weep. "I miss him."

"Me too. Every day."

"I, um . . . " I cleared my throat. "I found something. In Jem's things."

"What? What do you mean?"

"I sent almost everything to you and your parents after

it happened . . . but one thing I kept was his cell phone. By the time the police returned it, almost a year had passed. I put it in a box and kept it. I don't know why I never turned it on, but two nights ago, I did."

"My God," she said. "What did you find?"

"Not much. But I think . . . I think he was trying to message me as he died." I bit my lip, willing my voice to stay even. "There was a fragment of a message. K-A-T-A-H-D—"

"Katahdin!" she cried.

"Exactly," I said, that feeling—that get-up-and-start-moving feeling—making my stomach flutter.

"He was writing to you?"

"Yes."

"You think . . . you think he wanted you to go there?"

"I do."

"Just to see it?"

"I don't know for sure," I said. "I just know I need to go."

"Oh. So you're coming East?"

Her voice, which had been pretty warm until then, had cooled a touch, and I wondered, for a split second, if I was welcome.

Though Jem's parents had hosted a small memorial service for their son, I hadn't flown out to Maine to attend. At the time, I'd been staying with my parents in Scottsdale, taking significant doses of Valium just to get through the day. But in the two years since the service, not attending is one of my fiercest regrets, and I've always wondered if I inadvertently offended his parents and sister by not being there.

"Mm-hm. On Sunday."

Hope was silent for a moment before saying, "You're

welcome to stay here. Do you need a ride from the airport?"

My shoulders relaxed. "That would be really great. I get in at 6:20 in the evening."

"Writing it down so I don't forget." Hope paused, but her voice grew cautious when she spoke again. "No offense, Brynn, but Katahdin isn't for beginners."

"Which is why . . ." I bit my bottom lip, then plunged ahead. "I'm hoping you'll go with me?"

"I wish I could," she said, "but I leave for Boston on Monday morning. I'll be gone for a week teaching at BU. How long are you staying?"

"Only three days," I said, wondering if I should have booked an open return, but I didn't want to lose clients like Stu's Pools who'd be expecting their finished work soon after I returned from Maine.

"You know what?" said Hope. "You'll be fine. I'll map it out for you. Saddle Trail to Baxter Peak. Sign in at the ranger station first. Take your time. There'll be tons of AT hikers—"

"AT?"

"Appalachian Trail. I mean, if you need help, someone will be around to give you a hand. I'll make sure you're outfitted too, okay? I'll lend you some of my stuff and get whatever else I think you'll need so you're all set."

I'd really wished for Hope's company, but even alone, I knew there was no turning back. I needed to do this. For Jem. And for me.

Sighing, I push my conversation with Hope from my mind and segue back to the conversation with my mother in which I'd just implied that Hope would be hiking *with* me.

"Stop worrying, Mom. This is a good thing. I promise. It's going to be okay."

"I don't like it, Brynn. You were medicated for months.

Your father and I—"

"Mom, I need your support right now. For the first time since Jem died, I feel . . . I don't know . . . kind of excited about something. I feel . . . like I have some direction. A purpose. I promise I'll be careful, but I have to do this. I *need* to."

My mother's silent for a while before asking, "Do you need spending money?"

"I'm thirty years old and you still treat me like I'm eleven," I say, smiling down at Milo, who's weaving in and out of my legs.

"I love you," she says. "You'll always be eleven to me."

"I love you too."

We talk about my dad's latest golf tournament win, and she updates me on my cousin Bel's new boyfriend. We end our conversation laughing, which hasn't happened in a long, long time. And as I place the handset back in the cradle and head to my room to start packing, I feel grateful.

I feel ready.

Chapter Two

When I was six years old, I happened upon my father in an old shed, back behind our house, dismembering a raccoon.

Lying spread-eagled on its back, it was affixed by its paws with nails to a wooden table taller than I was. Rivulets of blood ran from all four paws and dripped softly onto the concrete slab floor below.

After looking on with curiosity from just inside the shed's open door, I didn't make a peep as I approached the workbench, watching my father stare down in fascination at the dead animal, holding up what I have retrospectively identified as a bloody scalpel.

It was only when I was mere inches away from the animal's face that I made eye contact with it and realized that it wasn't, in fact, dead. Its eyes, glazed over in agony, stared back at me and blinked. I gasped loud enough to distract my father, who turned to me, his face furious.

"Get the fuck out, Cassidy!" he screamed at me. "Get out, boy! I'm working!"

I fell backward in my haste to leave the shed and scrambled to my feet, racing through the woods to get back to the house, back to the safety of my mother.

"Cass!" she greeted me as I ran, out of breath, confused and terrified, to where she stood in the backyard, hanging freshly washed laundry on a line. "Where you comin' from, snow baby?"

Way-uh you comin' from?

From somethin' horrible, I thought, launching myself against her, burying my head in her skirt and wrapping my skinny arms around her slim waist.

Even at six, I knew something was terribly, terribly wrong with what I'd just seen. But instinctively I knew not to mention the incident to her. Some secrets, especially the darkest ones, were too black to verbalize, too awful to share.

"The woods," I said, smelling the sweet goodness of her denim skirt, which was warmed by the summer sunshine.

"You know yore daddy is leavin' tonight, right, honey? Won't be back for 'bout a month, don't you know." She sighed. "Stay close, Cass. Don't go wanderin' off again. We'll have supper together. He'll want to say goodbye."

My father was a long-haul truck driver. His normal route, he'd once shown me on a map, was from where we lived, in northern Maine, down the Eastern seaboard, to Florida, and back again. Up to 12,000 miles a month on I-95, on three back-to-back trips, in a rig he owned himself.

Which meant that we didn't see him very often. He was home for two or three days a month between drives. The rest of the time, Mama and I lived alone in our farmhouse, on the outskirts of Crystal Lake, and spent our summers with my gramp, who had a cabin in the north woods, in the shadow of Katahdin.

As a result, I didn't know my father very well, though my mother always prettied-up when he was home, wearing skirts instead of jeans and her hair down, instead of in a ponytail.

Humming with happiness for those few days every month, she said my father liked his woman to look like a woman, and she was only too happy to oblige. For the two or three nights he was home, I wasn't allowed in Mama's room, but I heard all sorts of noises coming from under the door at night: low-toned moans and groans and the rhythmic squeaking of Mama's bed. It took me years to figure out what that meant.

By my eighth birthday, I'd probably spent less than a hundred days with my father. In my whole life.

My eighth birthday.

He happened to be home that day.

It was the final day of three before he was supposed to hit the road again.

It was also the day the Maine State Police knocked on our door to arrest him.

Chapter Three

<u>Brynn</u>

"Brynn! Over here!"

I look up to see Jem's twin, Hope, waving at me from baggage claim as I descend the escalator at the Bangor airport. She has the same cheekbones as Jem, the same aqua eyes, the same unruly golden-blonde hair that tumbles over her shoulders in sun-kissed waves. Her easy smile, so much like her brother's, makes my heart clutch.

I hope that coming here isn't a giant mistake that will set me back in my progress toward normalcy. *Then again,* I reason, *I'm living like a hermit with only my cat for company.* There isn't much space in which to backslide.

"You're here," she says with a smile.

Hay-uh.

"Hope," I say as I step from the escalator and into her arms, "it's so good to see you!"

As she hugs me, tears spring to my eyes. *Useless.*

When she leans back, her smile has faded. "You're skin and bones, Brynn."

I shrug. "It's the dead-fiancé diet."

She cringes, jerking away from me, a shocked gasp escaping from her lips.

Fuck.

"I'm sorry," I say, shaking my head frantically. "I'm so sorry, Hope. I don't know why I said that. Fuck, I'm sorry. I'm not fit to be around people. God, Hope. I am so, so sorry."

"It's okay," she murmurs, though my thoughtless words have erased her smile completely. She takes a deep breath. "Any checked bags to pick up?"

"No."

"Then, um, let's head to the car, huh?"

I want to say something to make it all better as we walk in silence toward the parking garage, but nothing can take back my thoughtless words, and besides, I don't really want to whitewash the way I feel. Not with Hope.

Jem's gone. I know this. I know he's never coming back. But sometimes my sadness and my anger still feel as hard as ice; that's how I saw them for a long time, in fact. Sadness and anger, an infinitely wide, infinitely thick casing of frost around my heart. Many days, I didn't know how my heart kept beating. And there were days, I'm ashamed to admit now, I just wished it would stop.

But it kept throbbing with life, like it knew that someday the ice would melt. I both dread and welcome the idea of that day. Loving someone new will hold such immeasurable risk for me—how could I bear losing someone all over again?—but living like this for the rest of my life? In a constant state of grief? It's the only thought *more* unbearable than moving on. Because this isn't living. This is barely existing. And since I found Jem's phone again, I've started to wonder if maybe I'm ready to start living again.

"I'm over here," says Hope, pointing to a black SUV. She pops the trunk, and I lift my rolling bag into the back.

"Hope," I say, placing my hand on her arm after closing

20

the hatch. "I'm truly sorry."

"I know," she says, giving me a half smile, half grimace. While searching my eyes, she covers my hand with hers. "I haven't seen you since he was alive. You look a lot different, Brynn. You sound different too."

The words sting, but she's right. That's the thing about losing someone you loved as much as I loved Jem: I can never be the person I was before. Never. I'm still trying to figure out who exactly I've become.

I take a deep breath. "I'm hoping this trip will help."

Hope's eyes brighten a touch. "He would've loved it, you know—climbing Katahdin with you, sharing it with you."

"I know," I whisper, gulping over the lump in my throat.

"Come on," she says, her hand slipping from my arm. "Let's get you back to my place, and we can talk about the best way to get you to the top."

For most of the plane ride to Maine, I read about Mount Katahdin in a tour book of New England I'd purchased in San Francisco.

Katahdin, named by Native Americans, means "the greatest mountain," and for Jem nothing could have been closer to the truth. He'd climbed it the first time when he was ten, and if I asked Hope, she'd have no idea how many times he'd climbed it after that, because he'd practically lived there. During high school summers, he made money as a guide, leading hikes up and down the granite face almost every weekend and on weekdays for church groups and summer camps.

Hope buckles her seat belt, and I do the same, turning to her.

"What do you think about me trying the Knife Edge?"

She had shifted into reverse, but as she jerks her head to face me with a shocked expression, she pushes the gearshift back into park. "I'd ask if you have a death wish."

Jem's favorite way to summit the mountain was on a trail called the Knife Edge. And yes, parts of the trail were only three feet wide, with a steep drop-off on either side. And yes, the trail had claimed twenty-three lives over the past five decades. But I am *here*. And I am desperate to walk as closely in Jem's footsteps as possible.

"Have *you* done it?"

She nods, her face stony. "Yes."

"Then why can't I?"

Hope turns away from me and backs out of the parking space. "Because, like my brother, I've been climbing Katahdin since I was ten."

"I did some challenging climbs with Jem," I say. "He took me to Yosemite every other weekend. I climbed Glacier Point."

"Via the Four Mile Trail?"

"Yeah."

"Right. That's a strenuous trail to a peak under a thousand meters high."

"And . . .?"

"What comes after strenuous on a trail rating?"

"Very strenuous."

"Uh-huh. Then what?"

"Um . . .," I hum, trying to remember. "*Very, very* strenuous?"

Hope rolls her eyes, then pays the garage attendant and drives into the night. "Do you know what the Knife Edge is rated?"

No. But I feel like I'm about to get an earful.

"Bat-shit crazy," says Hope, stopping at a red light and

turning to look at me with irritation and worry. "That's what it's rated. It's only recommended for expert climbers." She takes a deep breath, pressing on the gas as the light changes. "Brynn, should I be worried about you?"

"No." Leaning my elbow on the windowsill, I blink back the sting of tears. "I just . . . I just want to—"

"I know," says Hope, sighing as she turns onto the highway. "You want to feel close to him. But you've got to be smart if you're going to walk the Greatest One. As opposed to Glacier Point, Baxter Peak is at 1,600 meters. An additional fifty percent to climb, Brynn. You're going to be tired by the time you get to the top. Weary like you won't believe. And definitely not strong enough to take on the Knife Edge. No offense. Anyway, Jem would come back from the dead and kill me if I encouraged you to do it. It's one of the most dangerous trails in New England. In the world."

"Okay," I say, reaching up to swipe at my eyes. "No Knife Edge."

"Phew. Thought you might fight me on it."

"Nah. I get it." I nod my head, but my disappointment over the change in my hiking plans makes me change the subject. "How are your parents?"

"They've aged a lot, you know, after . . . it happened," she shares with a heavy sigh. "But they're salty New Englanders. They'll probably outlive us all." She glances over at me. "Will you have time to see them while you're out here?"

I know I won't. Besides, I wouldn't know what to say to them. But Hope glances at me, so I try to give her the answer she wants.

"Maybe on Tuesday, on my way back to the airport. I'll definitely try," I say. "How are you? Still loving your job?"

Hope is the youngest biology professor at the University of Maine.

She nods, her face relaxing. "Totally."

"Any good stories?"

She grins. "Well . . . I met someone."

I smile with her, surprising myself because I feel a rare wave of genuine happiness to hear her news. "Shock me and tell me he's one of your students."

Chuckling softly, she shakes her head, blonde waves undulating. "Sorry to disappoint you. He's a professor of environmental studies at BU. Came up to Orono to teach a class, and luckily, I sat in."

"Love at first sight?" I tease.

"It was the way he talked about land preservation," she says, sighing dramatically before winking at me.

"A biologist and a preservationist. You sound perfect for each other."

"I hope so," she admits, her voice wishful.

"Hey!" I say, pieces of information clicking into place. "Didn't you say you're going to Boston tomorrow?"

"Yep."

"And how long have you two been together?"

"Ten months, give or take."

"Do you think he's going to—"

"Don't say it! It's bad luck."

"—propose?" I whisper over her warning.

"Oh, see what you did? Man, I hope you didn't jinx it!"

"Sorry," I say, cocking my head to the side. "But now that it's out there . . . *do* you?"

"Like I said . . . I *hope* so."

For just a moment, my brain flashes back to Jem on one knee, his aqua blue eyes outshining the sky behind him as he opened a tiny white velvet box in his palm.

Brynn, will you marry me?

I clench my eyes shut just for a moment and take a deep breath, then open them again as I exhale, bracing for the wave of panic that always accompanies an especially poignant memory.

Maybe it's being away from the place where I'd lost him, or being with his sister, who'd loved him as deeply as I had, or this plan to climb Katahdin and bid him farewell, but instead of panic, a wave of peace washes over me, and the tears recede.

With a sigh of relief, I roll down my window and breathe in the Maine air, grateful that memories of my own proposal warm me instead of destroy me.

"I hope so too," I say, looking over at Jem's twin sister and praying that her future holds all the happiness stolen from her brother. "I really, really do."

Chapter Four

Cassidy
Nine years old

The elementary school secretary, Mrs. Hughes, peeks at me over the counter with cold eyes, and I slink down farther in my chair, staring at my beat-up sneakers, which are covered in drying puke.

After lunch, two kids trapped me in the bathroom, the smaller of the two standing in front of the door while the bigger one asked me if I was a "raping, murdering fuck" like my father. When I didn't answer, he pushed me so hard that I stumbled backward into the sink, crying out as the thin flesh covering my hip met the smooth, hard, unforgiving porcelain.

"One eye blue and one eye green," he sneered, spittle collecting in the corner of his mouth as he advanced on me. "It's weird as fuck. You're a goddamned freak, killer."

He pushed me again, and I whimpered softly.

"You gonna cry?" he asked.

I *wanted* to cry.

Heck, I wanted to cry just about every day of my life, but instead I sucked in my cheeks and clamped my teeth around the warm, wet flesh, willing the pain of the bite to overwhelm my tears as I stared down at the tiled floor.

"You don't belong in this town no more," he said. "You and yore mama give everyone the creeps. You got to move on."

"J.J., we gotta go. Someone's gonna come."

"Shut up, Kenny." J.J. turned back to me, smacking my cheek twice, hard, forcing me to look up. "You look at me when I'm talkin' to you, boy."

His eyes were brown and mean when I met them.

"You heard me? No one wants you here, killer."

I gulped down the rising bile in my throat.

"No one wants yore tainted blood here."

"J.J.—"

"No one wants the reminder of who yore daddy was and what he done."

I tried to swallow again, but it felt like the muscles of my throat had frozen and I couldn't force them to work.

"No one wants—"

A sharp, unavoidable heaving sensation lifted the contents of my stomach, and I opened my mouth just in time for my regurgitated lunch to splash all over J.J.'s Patriots sweatshirt, blue jeans, and Nikes.

"Fuuuuuuuuuck!" he screamed, jolting back. "What the *fuck*?"

Tears streamed from my eyes, more a result of the puke than a reaction to the meanness. Vomit dripped from my lips and chin, onto my red T-shirt, onto my scarred Wal-Mart sneakers.

"Screw this!" yelled Kenny, opening the bathroom door and disappearing into the hallway.

"You're gonna pay for this, you little shit!" bellowed J.J., turning around to follow Kenny.

My shirt and shoes were covered in throw-up, and without a change of clothes, I couldn't go back to class. So I headed to the nurse's office instead. She took one look at me and gasped without sympathy, giving me a pair of sweatpants and an old T-shirt from the lost and found. While I was getting dressed, I heard her tell the school secretary to call my mother.

Mama arrived forty minutes later, her eyes worried as she looked into mine. I mumbled something about being sorry, but she told me to stay put as she hurried into the principal's office. Sitting on a chair outside his half-open door, I can hear just about everything he's saying to her.

"This school simply isn't a good fit for Cassidy, Ms. Porter. I'm sure you can appreciate how uneasy the other children are around yore son."

"But why?" she says softly, her voice emotional. "Cass is a good boy. Kind."

Mr. Ruggins clears his throat. "We've never had a problem with Cassidy, per se, and to be clear, I can't *make* you pull him from school, ma'am. But I can tell you that episodes like today will not be isolated. I imagine it'll just get worse for yore son as time goes on."

"I don't understand. He wouldn't hurt a fly," she says. "He's gentle and—"

"No one here is disputin' that, Ms. Porter. But I think it would be better for Cassidy, and for you, ma'am, to think about homeschoolin' him."

"Homeschoolin'! But I'm not a teacher. I don't know *how* to teach him."

I imagine Mr. Ruggins leaning forward as his chair squeaks. "Don't need to be. You can buy a book from the Wal-Mart over in Lincoln that'll tell you how to teach him everythin' he needs to know. We can even order it for you if that would help. Or I can ask Mrs. Hughes to make a recommendation for you."

"But what about friends? He'll be lonely with no one but me for company."

"Ms. Porter," says Mr. Ruggins gently. "Cassidy doesn't have any friends, ma'am."

"Of course he does," she says, "Joey Gilligan. Sam White. Marcus—"

"No, ma'am," says Mr. Ruggins firmly. "He doesn't have any friends anymore. Cassidy sits alone at lunch, alone on a bench at recess. He walks through the halls alone. No one speaks to him unless it's to give him a hard time. He minds his business—yes, ma'am—but trouble still finds him."

My mother sobs, and it tears at my heart a little because I'd been keeping it a secret, how the other kids had been treating me since my father's arrest and conviction. I didn't want her to worry about something else. Now she knows, and I can tell it's hurt her. I clench my fists, and, even though my cheeks are still raw and bleeding from chewing on them in the bathroom, I bite down anyway.

"Mr. Ruggins! Cassidy didn't do anythin' wrong!" says my mother, her voice breaking a little.

"But his daddy sure did," says Mr. Ruggins. His chair squeaks again, and this time I imagine him leaning away from my mother. "Ask the families of those poor girls. *He* did wrong, all right."

"Paul is . . . well, he is a very sick man. We didn't . . . that is, we had no idea what was goin' on. He was away all the time, and . . . and . . ." She pauses before speaking again. "But Cassidy's just a child. He's only nine years old. He's *not* his father."

"Cassidy is his son, ma'am."

His son.

I am the son of the man one reporter called "the

bloodiest serial killer the state of Maine has ever known." My mother tried to protect me from the truth, but there was no hiding it during the trial and sentencing. It was on the TV and in the newspapers at the grocery store. It was everywhere.

My father, Paul Isaac Porter, raped and murdered at least a dozen girls along the I-95 corridor between 1990 and 1998.

It's a fact.

And now it follows me wherever I go.

Rapist's son.

Murderer's son.

Freak.

Killer.

Since his arrest, and especially since his conviction, I've been called every ugly thing you can think of. People cross the street when they see me and Mama coming. They egg our house and throw rocks through our windows. They move out of our pew at church when we sit down. The waitresses at the town diner pretend they don't see us even when Mama asks if we can place our order. Even good people—like my teachers, like the pastor and his wife, like Mr. Ruggins —can barely look us in the eye.

Mama cries all the time. She calls herself stupid and naive and says that she should have known. She doesn't sleep much. She jumps at the slightest sound. And lately, when she doesn't think I notice, she stares at me hard, like she's puzzling through something. If I catch her, she looks away quickly like I would if I was caught doing something wrong.

Cassidy is his son, ma'am.

But I'm not *him*. I'm *me*. A separate person.

There's a long and painful silence as I wait for my

mother to say something—anything—else to try to explain that my father and I are individual people. I didn't rape anyone. I didn't murder anyone. I didn't hurt anyone. Not ever.

But she doesn't say anything.

And her silence is chilling.

"You take him on home today, ma'am," says Mr. Ruggins after a long and awkward silence. "And you think on what I said . . . okay, now? I'm certain it would be best for everyone."

When Mama emerges from Mr. Ruggins's office a second later, her face is white and her eyes are red and weepy, shell-shocked, and defeated.

"Mama?" I murmur, feeling worried as I take her hand and look up into her bloodshot blue eyes.

She looks down at me and lifts her chin. "We're leavin'."

I walk beside her out of the office, down the hallway, and out the double doors to the parking lot. I'm silent as I get into the backseat and buckle my belt, silent as my mother starts the car and silent as she cries quietly all the way home.

Chapter Five

When we get to her place, Hope opens a bottle of good Merlot and barbecues steaks for us, telling me climbing stories about her and Jem while the steaks sizzle and the stars come out. She tells me about how Jem saved the life of a little girl who'd gotten separated from her family during a camping trip. None of the rangers could find her, but Jem, who knew every nook and cranny of Katahdin, managed to find her near one of the waterfalls on the Hunt Trail.

"He was only fifteen, but that's when I knew that climbing mountains wasn't just a hobby for him," says Hope, sipping her wine while fireflies light up her backyard like a chain of blinking Christmas lights. "It was the look on his face when he walked into the parking lot where they'd set up a triage center. He was covered in trail dust. She looked even worse. But he . . . well, I knew we'd never get him out of the woods after that."

"He never told me that story." I take a sip of my wine. "God, I miss him."

She sighs from where she stands beside the grill, putting a hand on her hip. "Promise you won't get mad if I say something?"

My eyes widen. "Are you going to say something

mean?"

"Not mean, really . . . just frank."

I gulp. "Okay."

"I didn't really get you two."

"*Get* us?"

"Don't get me wrong: you made him happy, and I'm a hundred percent certain that he loved you."

I take another sip of my wine, looking up at her from where I sit on a picnic bench near the grill, waiting for her to continue.

"But . . . I think I always thought he'd end up with someone who loved the outdoors—you know, hiking, climbing, camping, all of it—as much as he did."

"I . . . *liked* it," I mumble.

"No," says Hope, and though I've never seen her teach, I have a sudden taste of her in professor mode. "You *tolerated* it. Because it was part of his job, and because you loved him. And maybe even . . ." She pauses for a moment, nailing me with her eyes. ". . . because you thought you could change him."

"You're assuming a lot."

"Am I?" Her voice trails off, and I suspect we are getting to the part that has the potential to get me mad. "I worried about it lasting. You and Jem. I worried that you'd eventually make him choose."

Her words suck the air from my lungs, and my vision blurs.

"Oh."

"Brynn," she starts gently, shutting the lid of the grill and coming to sit next to me. "I don't mean to hurt you. I swear I don't. But I just wonder if, over time . . . if maybe you would have gone to the woods less. You didn't grow up hiking and climbing. You couldn't tell me, here and now, with any conviction, that you loved it. But he did. It wasn't even selfishness—it was *instinct*. It was *need*. It was in his blood, and there was no way you were ever going to get him out of the woods."

"I wasn't *trying* to get him out of the woods. I loved him just the way he was."

"I know you did," she says, wincing as she tilts her head to the side. "But would you have wanted to hike and camp for every vacation? Would you have wanted to raise your kids in the woods every weekend?" She pauses, shaking her head. "You lived in the city. In the middle of San Francisco, Brynn. Going hiking was an excursion for you. A day trip. For Jem it was a way of life. His job was to write about hiking and climbing, and I suspect that's the part of him you tolerated and tried to accept by joining him from time to time. But you must know, even when he was with you, he was subjugating part of his nature by living in the city. He longed to be in the wild constantly. All the time. Every weekend. Every moment."

"He told you that? That he was selling himself out?"

"I knew him better than anyone," she says quietly. "I was watching it. I was worried for him. And for you. For both of you."

Hope's eyes are sad as she looks back at me with a level gaze, and it pinches my heart. Part of the reason her words hurt so much is because they address a truth I ignored, that I never fully admitted to myself: that, over time, I may have gone to the woods with Jem less and less because I didn't love it. And Jem wouldn't have been able to stay away because he did. And maybe I would have resented his precious woods for stealing him away. I might have even started to resent him too.

"You shared your worries with Jem?" I ask, rephrasing

my previous question. I want to know if they discussed this behind my back.

She lifts her chin and nods. "He was my twin."

"What did he say?" I ask, my voice a rasp.

"That he could love you both. That you'd figure it out together."

"We *would* have," I say, looking into her eyes, feeling confused, angry.

She stands up, crosses the patio, and lifts the lid of the grill to flip the steaks.

My righteous indignation mounts as I finish my wine. How dare she question the strength of our love? How dare she doubt a relationship that never even had a chance?

"Why did you tell me this?" I ask. "What's the point?"

She turns around, her expression sympathetic but not sorry. "Because you've been grieving for two years."

"So what?" I ask with a bite.

"So it's easy to idealize someone who's dead, to make your life a shrine to them."

"Do you think it was *easy* to lose my fiancé?" I ask, leaping to my feet. "To lose the love of my life?"

"No," she answers softly. "I think it was excruciating."

"Then . . .?"

"Jem wasn't a god," she whispers, tears brightening her own eyes. "He was beautiful and pure . . . but he was as flawed as anyone else. He offered his heart to you, but his soul already belonged to the woods, Brynn. Always."

My soul belongs to Katahdin . . . Well, it did anyway, before I gave it to you.

I remember the words now, hear them in my head—the way the first half of the sentence was said with reverence, while the second half was said lightly and sweetly, as he chucked me under the chin.

"He loved me," I whimper.

"Yes, he did."

"We would have made it."

She stares at me, her eyes sad, her silence speaking volumes.

"We would have figured it out, like he said!" I insist.

"Okay," she says softly, but something unspoken has already passed between us, and it is a tacit and terrible understanding:

We *might* have figured it out. But then again, we might *not* have.

***

We eat mostly in silence, and it occurs to me at some point that Hope is saying things I'd only say to someone I was never going to see again. And that's when I realize it: tonight is our swan song. We haven't been friends, really—only connected by our mutual love of someone now gone. When she leaves for Boston tomorrow, she will move on with her life, and I believe she expects me to move on with mine. After tonight, we probably won't see each other again.

"Is there anything you want to know?" I ask. "About Jem?"

She looks up, her eyes softening, her lips tilting up in a sad smile, and I know I am right about our farewell. But she shakes her head. "There's nothing I didn't know about him."

"I'm a painful reminder of him," I say without bitterness. "It must have been hard to let me come here."

"Brynn," she says, wiping her mouth before continuing, "I loved Jem. But beyond that, he was my *twin*. He was *part* of me—more than any other human being on the face of the earth. On the night he died, did you know that I passed out at the same moment his heart stopped beating? One minute I was standing in front of my microwave, popping popcorn for a movie. Two hours later, I woke up on my kitchen floor because my phone was ringing. It was you, telling me that he was dead." She reaches for the bottle of Merlot and refills our glasses. "You were good for him. I mean that. He was *really* happy with you. He had high hopes. And I will always be grateful that he experienced true romantic love before he died." She takes a swallow, looking at me over the rim of her glass. "Believe it or not, everything I'm saying to you tonight, I'm saying *for* him." She pauses, letting her words sink in. "Do you understand me? I'm saying the things he would *want* me to say, to help you move on."

I clench my teeth, staring at her, bracing myself.

She continues gently. "He's gone, but you're still here. You have to let him go or you'll never find out what—or who—comes next."

What—or who—*comes next.*

Here is something I feel guilty admitting since I lost Jem: I long for someone. In my loneliest moments, I *long* for someone so fiercely, it aches. I want someone to hold me, to whisper in my ear, to braid their fingers through mine and breathe against my skin. I want to know love again. In fact, I actively *yearn* for it, though I can't actually imagine accepting it.

Why?

Not just because loving again would be terrifying, but because loving someone else would mean betraying Jem.

Reading my thoughts, Hope shakes her head. "Saying goodbye doesn't mean forgetting. Moving on doesn't mean you never loved him. I'm telling you to let go. I'm telling you that you're allowed to be happy."

A sob trapped in my throat escapes, and my hands tremble in my lap, though the evening is warm.

Hopes takes my hands in hers, warming them as she

repeats softly, "Brynn, let him go. You're allowed to be happy again."

A helix of sorrow and relief shoots through me like a high-speed bullet. Sorrow and relief both, but mostly relief. Mostly a beautiful, terrible, long-awaited *surrender* to relief.

My shoulders slump.

My head falls forward to Hope's waiting shoulder.

And I weep.

Chapter Six

Cassidy
Fourteen years old

Five years ago, after my father's conviction, when life in town had become unbearable, Mama and I moved in with my grandfather Cleary, who lived in a cabin in the woods, way off the grid, in Northeast Piscataquis.

In this unorganized territory of northern Maine, with no local government and about 340 people living in 1,800 square miles, my grandfather lived on acres and acres of unbridled, untamed wilderness. The closest road was a dirt logging road, about four miles away from his cabin, accessible only by unkempt ATV trails in the woods.

I was nine years old when we moved here.

I was ten years old when my father was killed in a prison fight.

I am fourteen now.

Before we moved here, Mama and I had visited my grandfather every summer. We were picked up by a puddle jumper at Dewitt Field near Bangor by an Army buddy of my grandfather's, and dropped off on the grassy meadow by his solitary homestead.

I'd grown up understanding how his unusual home functioned.

The original structure was built by my grandfather, Frank Cleary, and great-uncle, Bert Cleary, when they returned from Vietnam. At first, it was only meant to be a hunting cabin, small and tidy at 800 square feet, with a rainwater-collection tank, a diesel generator, and an outhouse.

But as my grandfather, who had lost his arm in the war, became disillusioned with the world he'd returned to, he made adjustments on the property little by little, adding on a kitchen, a sitting room, and two more bunk-style bedrooms. His brother came to help him every summer, and they managed to add a wraparound deck, a root cellar, and a small, glass-enclosed greenhouse. They cleared trees and planted a garden, then built a small barn to hold half a dozen chickens, one rooster, a cow, and a goat. That same year, they winterized the buildings so someone could stay year-round and tend the livestock. And when spring rolled around, my grandfather decided not to leave at all and made the homestead his permanent dwelling.

A couple of years later, at a conference on solar panels in Nashua, he purchased enough cells to cover the roof of his cabin. He also met my grandmother, an ex-hippie from Seattle, who'd been thinking about taking the plunge to sustainable living herself.

After a quickie wedding in Boston, they returned to Maine, and together they fixed up the original cabin, a woman's touch raising its general quality to that of a comfortable, if very basic, suburban home. The solar energy absorbed by the panels was enough to power one appliance at a time, lights, and other small electric devices.

And they were happy.

Until my grandmother discovered she was pregnant with my mother.

At first, my grandfather argued that raising their child off the grid was the best gift they could give their offspring, but my grandmother, whose sensibilities had changed with impending motherhood, found off-the-grid living less palatable. Without any formal medical training between them, she was uncomfortable being so isolated. Plus, she insisted, for proper mental development, their child needed more social interaction.

Grudgingly, my grandfather sold the cow and the chickens, closed up the cabin, and moved his family to the closest proper town, Crystal Lake, which still had a pretty good view of Katahdin.

There, he survived, not lived, waiting for the day his daughter graduated from high school, and he and his love could return to the woods. Sadly, my grandmother, who died from ovarian cancer before I was born, never returned. After her passing, however, my grandfather quit his job, sold his Crystal Lake home, and returned to the Northeast Piscataquis cabin, vowing to never, ever leave again.

Mama homeschooled me from fourth grade onward, and Gramp taught me everything else I needed to know to take care of myself. By the age of twelve, I was capable of managing most of the property: adjusting and cleaning the solar panels, checking the rainwater tank, minding the livestock, and tending the indoor and outdoor gardens.

The furnishings my grandmother chose in the 1980s are probably outdated now, but I don't really care.

This cabin, with its outbuildings, gardens, and meadow, is my home. It's far away from prying eyes full of hate and biting voices that call you names you inherited but never earned.

It is my sanctuary, and I love it here.

"Cass, come and help yore ol' gramp in the garden a

spell. I need to talk to you, son."

"Sure, Gramp," I say, flicking a glance at Mama, napping quietly on a window seat in a beam of summer sun. In the past few months, she's started napping more and more, leaving me to direct my own high school studies.

Last week, Gramp radioed for a plane, and it took my mother to a doctor in Millinocket, where she remained for four nights having tests. She returned yesterday evening looking even sadder and more frail than before she'd left. Last night, I fell asleep listening to the soft murmur of her voice as she sat across from Gramp at the kitchen table, both of them talking in urgent, emotional whispers.

Here is what I know:

There is something wrong with my mother. And it's bad.

And as I stand up to follow Gramp outside, my chest fills with dread.

I don't want to know. I don't want to know. I don't want to know.

Sometimes you just don't want to hear the words.

"Cover yore mama up, then come meet me in the greenhouse, eh?" he says, gesturing to a blanket with his prosthetic hand.

"Sure," I say again, watching him trudge out the kitchen door, leaving me alone.

For most of my life, even when my father was alive, my grandfather was the most important father figure to me. I never felt very close to Paul Isaac Porter, never felt the sort of love for him that a child is supposed to feel for his father. It's possible that his extensive travel schedule had stunted the emotional growth between us, but I know that was only part of the reason. I never felt comfortable around my father the way I did around my grandfather. Maybe it was the memory of that suffering raccoon. Maybe it was a sixth sense about who my father really was. But my father had been a nebulous figure on the fringes of my life at best. My grandfather, bigger than life, with a booming voice and the best bear hugs, had lived inside my heart.

As I unfold the blanket on the windowsill and pull it over Mama's chest, the book she'd been reading slips to the floor, but I manage to grab it just before it falls. Tucking it under my arm, I finish covering her before taking a look at it.

The cover of the book has a grainy picture of Adolf Hitler and what appears to be black-and-white high school pictures of several young men. *The Last of the Hitlers.* I turn it over and read the blurb on the back: *At the end of World War II, the man Adolf Hitler called "my loathsome nephew" changed his name and disappeared . . . the British born William Patrick Hitler, by then settled in the U.S.A., remained anonymous . . . until now. William Patrick's story so fascinated British journalist David Gardner that he spent years attempting to find the last relative to bear the Hitler name. Gardner found . . . that his four sons had established a pact that, in order for Adolf Hitler's genes to die with them, none of them would have children.*

I know who Adolf Hitler was. Mama and I dedicated quite a bit of my schooling to World War II.

Turning the book back over, I look at the young men on the cover, next to the picture of their great-uncle Adolf. They were his nephews, right? Men who'd decided, apparently, never to marry, never to have children, so that the genes of a madman would die with them.

Inside my chest, my heart starts racing, and I drop the book on the small end table beside Mama, staring at it as if it were a coiled snake.

Hitler's nephews had tacitly agreed to kill their

bloodline.

My mind segues without preamble to me and my father, and to those twelve girls he raped and killed.

And I wonder—*gulp*—I wonder if Mama's reading that book because she thinks that I should do the same . . . that I should *also* make a pact to—

"Done in there, Cass?"

Jumping at the sound of Gramp's voice, I turn away from Mama and hurry to join him at the back door. "Yes, sir."

His blue eyes, older and sadder than usual, look into mine. "Let's pick some tomatoes, eh?"

I follow him to the greenhouse, pulling the door shut behind me and picking up a wicker basket from the floor.

"Ain't no good at sugarcoatin' things, Cass," says Gramp, gently pulling a tomato from the vine and putting it in my basket.

"No, sir."

"Yore mama asked me to talk to you."

I clench my teeth and hold my breath, blinking my suddenly burning eyes, as he places another tomato in the basket.

"Sir," I whisper, but his words come quickly:

"She's dyin', son."

The room spins and I hear myself gasp sharply, the quick intake of cool air hurting my chest as the basket slips from my fingers.

"Easy, now," Gramp is saying as he takes the basket from me with his prosthetic hand. His other hand lands on my shoulder. "Easy. Breathe in, Cass. You knew somethin' was up."

"Yes, sir," I manage with a ragged breath as the hot tears crowding my eyes begin to fall. His craggy face blurs in

44

front of me.

"Ain't been well for years. Turns out cancer was eatin' away at her . . . just like her mama."

"There's medicine. Chemotherapy," I say, swiping at my eyes so I can see him clearly.

"Too late for all that."

"Gramp. No!" I sob, leaning forward to rest my forehead on his massive shoulder.

He holds me close, occasionally patting my back as I weep.

"Git all that out, now," he says in a choked-up voice after I've cried for several minutes. "I'll ask you to be strong for my Rosie. For my li'l . . . Rosemary."

His voice breaks as he says Mama's name, and it wrings another round of tears from me until I am hiccuping and spent.

Gramp releases me, walks to the back of the greenhouse and returns a second later with two pails, which he upends across from each other so we can sit and talk.

"She's always been there for you, son."

"Yes, sir," I say, staring down at my hands and forcing myself to stop crying. Mama doesn't need to see my tears; she needs me to be strong for her.

"After what yore daddy did, some folks, well, they thought you might be a bad seed too."

I look up at him, swallowing past the lump in my throat.

Cassidy is his son, ma'am.

". . . thought maybe she should find a home for you somewheres, change her name, and start a new life for herself."

"*What?*" I am appalled by the idea of this parallel existence from which I was spared. "When . . .?"

45

He waves my question away. "Point is, she didn't. She stuck around. She stuck by you." His face softens, and he says more to himself than to me, "Her snow baby, born on Easter Day."

My mind slides back to the book my mother's reading, and it occurs to me that she always seems to be reading books about DNA and genetics, and about people who've done evil in the world.

"Does *she* think I'm a bad seed?"

He winces, looking away from me. "She worries 'bout you."

"Do *you* think I'm a bad seed, Gramp?"

I want him to say no quickly, but he doesn't, and a chill races through my body, pinging off my bones and making me cold. He searches my face for a long while before saying, "You're Paul's son, Cassidy."

"But I'm *me*," I insist, "not him!"

"I ain't know what's inside of you, Cass," he says, reaching out to cup my cheek with his weathered palm. "I've prayed to every god that ever was that whatever was inside Paul ain't inside of you too, son. And you're a good boy. Seems impossible that you could go down such a dark path one day. But the reality is, well, there ain't no way to know for sure."

I know! I want to scream, but the truth is that I don't. The foremost terror in the furthest reaches of my mind is always there . . . always, always, *always* there: the possibility that I could somehow turn out like my father. To know that my mother and grandfather share this fear makes it real to me, makes me feel sick, makes me feel like I'm living with a ticking bomb inside me.

Even after we'd left town, Mama mostly refused to talk about my father. The way her face would seize up whenever

I mentioned him made me feel bad, and anyway, I gathered that she hadn't known him all that well.

"He said he was from Indiana," she told me once. "He said his parents were dead, and he'd used the money from sellin' their house to buy his rig."

My parents met while my mother was waiting tables at a café in East Millinocket. He'd pull off I-95 every few weeks and sit in her section, staying for hours and tipping her way too much. Over time, he started bringing little gifts, like pieces of jewelry—items that we discovered, years later, were trophies from his victims.

Mama was beautiful to me, but compared with a few of the much prettier teachers I'd had in school, I knew she was homely. But based on my thin memories and the one photo I'd kept, my father was handsome enough. I imagine the attention of a good-looking, flattering trucker was enough to sweep a naive country girl off her feet.

Once I asked her why he'd never hurt *us*. She stared at me a long time before replying that she didn't know.

I guess he'd lived two lives.

"Gramp," I say, looking up into his weary eyes. "What happens now?"

"Be strong for yore mama," he says, patting my knee. "She don't have much time. A handful of weeks. No more."

Another sob escapes my throat, and I gnaw on my cheeks until I taste blood.

"After she's gone, we'll continue on here together, Cass. You're safe here with me for as long as I'm alive. And I'll teach you everythin' I can to be certain that you'll be able to protect yoreself after I'm gone."

I cannot bear the thought of losing Gramp, so I push it from my mind. When I do, the grainy image of Adolf Hitler from the front of Mama's book takes front and center in my head.

"What should I do about . . . the rest?" I ask, wondering about the possible demons that lie dormant inside me, that could spring to life at any time, making me into a monster like my father.

"I know it would ease her heart to know you'll be careful, son."

"Careful?"

"Live quiet," says Gramp, using his preferred terminology for our isolated, off-the-grid lifestyle. His blue eyes hold mine like two life rings, and he nods sagely, comfortingly, patting my knee again. "Live quiet, and no matter what happens inside of you, you won't never be able to hurt someone, Cassidy. It's what yore mama would want."

Live quiet.

Live quiet.

Live quiet.

"I promise," I say.

"Good boy."

I nod at him, vowing that the blood in my veins will never, ever infect another life.

I will live quiet.

And Paul Isaac Porter's terrifying genes will die with me.

Chapter Seven

Brynn

Hope had instructed me to arrive at the parking lot by six o'clock and told me that before hiking Katahdin, I'd have to stop at the ranger station to:

> 1) declare my intention to hike,
>
> 2) share the route I planned to take, and
>
> 3) give my contact information, in case I should go missing on the trail.

An ominous thought.

Hope left for the airport at five thirty this morning, and ten minutes later my Uber car arrived at her house, ready to take me to the Roaring Brook Campground. Roaring Brook served as the trailhead for the Chimney Pond Trail, which would take me three and a half miles up to Chimney Pond. From there I could take the Saddle Trail, another two and a quarter miles, to the summit of Katahdin. It would be eleven and a half miles round trip and a hard climb for skinny, out-of-shape me, but Hope had promised that it was the route Jem would have chosen for me.

Staring out the window at early morning, misty Maine, I wonder if I will ever see Hope again, but something—no doubt the same feeling of farewell I experienced at dinner last night—tells me that I probably won't. Our friendship had always been an extension of our mutual love for Jem. With his loss, so breaks our connection.

I also think about her words last night about letting go and moving on. The same sentiment I so abhor from my mother and various well-meaning friends struck a different chord with me coming from Hope, almost as though Jem himself was giving me permission, by proxy of his twin, to live again. To say goodbye.

Spying signs for the Roaring Brook parking lot, that feeling of farewell surges within me again and I reach into the outside pocket of my trail pack to touch Jem's phone, safely inside the evidence bag.

Today I will bury that phone, still bearing his dried blood, somewhere on Katahdin, somewhere that feels right. I'm hoping that the mountain, or Jem's spirit, will guide me to the right place.

While I acknowledge that burying a cell phone in a state park is an ethically gray area, I hope the universe will forgive me for leaving the small, thin, electronic device buried deep in the mountain woods. Some part of Jem needs to join his soul on Katahdin. And when I return to Roaring Brook this evening, I will bid farewell not only to Katahdin, but to Jem, who, I want to believe, would be happy to know that his final thoughts had led me full circle.

"Here we are," says the driver, pulling over on the side of the road at the parking lot gates. "I don't have a parking permit so this is as far as I go."

"Thanks," I say, stepping from the backseat. I zip up my windbreaker, heft my pack onto my back, and trudge into the surprisingly crowded parking lot. Inside the pack that Hope helped me organize last night, I have day hike essentials: a Katahdin guidebook, a twenty-ounce water bottle, water-purification tablets, a first aid kit, a change of clothes, two pairs of thick socks, gloves, an extra waterproof windbreaker, a Bic Lighter, a Swiss Army knife, a small flashlight, rope, sunscreen, sunglasses, bug spray, wet wipes, two apples, a banana, and a six-pack of energy bars.

When hiking with Jem, I always noted a certain feeling of esprit de corps at trailhead parking lots. People from all over the world, from all walks of life, from all experience levels, come together in one place with one goal in mind: to summit a chosen peak. I understand why these were Jem's people. Clusters of hikers gaze at maps together, spread out on the hoods of cars, glancing up at the bright blue sky and speculating aloud about whether the Knife Edge will be a possibility today. Others share food, water-purification tablets, or advice. Still others keep themselves separate from the group, their faces focused and intense as they plan to add another epic walk to their roster.

Knowing that this is likely the last arduous hike I will undertake for a long time, another wave of farewell melancholy washes over me as I head to the long line at the ranger station. Hope was right last night: I won't miss this part of my potential life with Jem. I can admire the beauty of nature as much as the next person, but hiking and climbing? No. I like my creature comforts too much.

I get in line behind two girls, younger than me, who are chatting excitedly about the Appalachian Trail. Checking out the size of their packs—about four times bigger than mine—I realize that they are probably southbound through-hikers.

"Are you AT hikers?" I ask.

One of the two women, tall and fair, with a long, blonde French braid that drapes over her left shoulder, glances back at me.

"Sort of," she answers with a warm grin, her English lightly sprinkled with what sounds like a German accent.

"We're sort of doing it our own way."

Her friend, a petite brunette with short hair and a similar accent, chimes in. "If we were AT purists, we'd take the Hunt Trail, but it's a Class 2 day today, so Saddle's safer."

"Class 2?" I ask.

The girls exchange a look.

"High wind up top. Possibility of rain later," explains the blonde.

Ah. So not an ideal hiking day, despite the blue skies and bright sun.

The brunette gestures to my pack. "You should tighten the straps. Want a hand?"

"Oh," I mumble. "Sure. Thanks."

"Hey, you're not hiking alone, are you?" asks the blonde, her perfect eyebrows squishing up.

"Yeah."

"You're welcome to walk with us," says the brunette, stepping away as she finishes my straps. "We're doing the summit today, and tomorrow we'll take on the 100-Mile Wilderness."

"Wow," I say as I look back and forth between the two girls. "That's brave."

The 100-Mile Wilderness is the most challenging, and arguably the most dangerous, part of the Appalachian Trail, mostly because, once you start walking, there are no towns or supplies for a hundred miles. No stores. No police. No hospitals. Nothing but the trail, lean-tos, and the woods.

The blonde laughs at my expression. "We figure it'll take us about ten days. And then another twenty to get back to Williams."

"Is that where you go to college?"

The girls nod in unison.

"We're studying abroad this year."

"This is our summer project."

"The effects of long hikes on friendship?" I joke.

The brunette chuckles. "Two women on the AT. A firsthand experience."

"I like it," I say.

"So join us today," says the blonde. "I'm Carlotta. This is Emmy."

I hold out my hand, shaking theirs as we move up a few places in line. "Thanks. I appreciate the offer."

"Room for one more?" asks a male voice from behind me.

I turn around to face a dark-haired man wearing a baseball cap and glasses, an olive-green T-shirt, and camouflage pants. His expression is eager, and when he leans forward, I can smell stale tobacco smoke caught in his unkempt beard.

"Huh?"

"I overheard you lovely ladies makin' plans to walk together today. I'm solo too," he says, his dark eyes lighting on Carlotta's chest. They linger there for a moment, wider when he lifts them. "Maybe I could walk with you?"

Emmy darts a quick glance at Carlotta, then turns back to the man, her expression caught between wanting to be nice and not wanting some random man following us around.

"Umm, I think we're all set."

"I have lots of candy to share," he says, opening his bag and dragging out two Snickers bars. He smiles and I note that his teeth are a medium-yellow color. "They call me Wayne."

"Candy's not a good energy source, Wayne," notes Emmy.

Slowly, he puts the candy bars back in his pack, his smile fading.

"Thanks for the offer, but we're having a girls' day," says Carlotta, taking a step forward in line and putting her back to Wayne.

"But I *know* this mountain," he says, his tone taking on a wheedling edge. "I'm local, born over in Millinocket. I could help you."

"We don't *need* help," says Carlotta, exasperation creeping into her voice, making her words clipped and more German. "We're sort of doing our own thing."

"Oh, yeah?" His expression changes from cajoling to cold in an instant. "But you invited *her* to go with you."

"She's a woman traveling alone," explains Carlotta, crossing her arms over her chest, her eyes narrowing.

"And I'm a *man* travelin' alone." He cocks his head to the side, narrowing his eyes right back at her. He points a stubby finger back and forth between the girls. "You know what you are? Sexist."

"Pardon me," says Emmy, "but you don't know us."

"No! Pardon *me*!" he yells, thumping his palm against his chest. "*Pardon me* for thinkin' that you'd include another single traveler in yore happy fuckin' group. Fuckin' bitches come to my mount—"

"Hey," I caution. "There's no need for—"

His eyes flick to me dismissively. "Shut up, *Grandmaw*. I'm talkin' to the kids."

I put my hands on my hips and step to the side, blocking the two teenage girls from him with my slight body. "You're being a total jerk."

"And you're a bitch."

"We're done here, Wayne."

"I just wanted company!" Wayne cries, raising his voice

loud enough to attract some curious glances from other hikers in line.

"Then you should have brought your dog," mutters Emmy under her breath prompting a giggle from Carlotta.

"Did you just call me a *dog*?" Wayne bellows, his face reddening and eyes bulging behind his glasses as he lurches toward tiny Emmy.

"I said you should have *brought* your dog!"

"Can you leave us alone, please?" asks Carlotta from behind me, her face unfriendly, her voice direct. "We're not bothering you."

"That's for *me* to decide," he yells, prompting more hikers to look over. "I'm just tryin' to make friends, and this *cunt* called me a *jerk*!"

"Whoa, whoa, whoa! Everything okay here?" asks a tall, blond, college-aged guy in front of us.

"It *will* be," says Carlotta, hooking a thumb at Wayne, "when this creeper leaves us alone."

The blond guy steps between Carlotta and Emmy, towering over them. "Hey, man. I think the ladies want you to back off."

"Stay out of it," hisses Wayne. "It's none of yore goddamned business, junior."

Blond College Guy steps between the girls, standing next to me, directly in front of Wayne. He spreads his legs and crosses his arms over his sizable chest. "I'm *making* it my business, pal. Shove off."

"I'm not yore fuckin' *pal*!"

"Got that right," says Blond College Guy with a sneer.

"Motherfuckers like you are the problem with this country!" rants Wayne.

"Like *me*?"

"You think you own the whole goddamned world!"

"Dude, I'm about to get the ranger over here and have your ass hauled out of the park. He takes a menacing step toward Wayne, lowering his arms and cracking his knuckles one by one. "You're seriously annoying people."

Wayne's face reddens to the point of fury, and he bunches his fists by his side.

"*Fuck you*," he snarls. "You're just *tourists* in my *dreams*. Bear bait. Shit with legs. I hope Katahdin eats you up and spits you out in motherfuckin' pieces!"

Then he turns and leaves the line, trudging back into the parking lot until I lose sight of him between a couple of SUVs.

"Wow!" says Carlotta, shaking her head in disbelief. "What a freak!"

Emmy chuckles, on tiptoe, still looking for traces of weird Wayne. "*Heiliger Strohsack!* What *was* that?"

"Just some crazy local," says Blond College Guy, turning to face the girls. "By the way, I'm Kris."

"Carlotta, Emmy, and . . ." She looks at me and giggles. "Oh, my God! I'm so sorry! I don't know your name!"

"Brynn," I say, shaking Kris's hand. "I'm Brynn."

He gestures to two guys in line ahead of the girls. "That's Chad and that's Mike. We go to Bennington."

The guys turn around, offering grins and waves.

"My cousin went to Bennington last year!" says Emmy with a big smile.

"Small world," says Kris, grinning down at her like she's the cutest thing he's ever seen. "Where are you girls from?"

"Düsseldorf. But we go to Williams this year," says Emmy.

"This is going to be fu-u-u-un," says Carlotta, looking

back and forth between Kris and Emmy before winking at me.

And suddenly I feel like I'm about one hundred years old instead of thirty. Maybe I should tell them to go ahead with the boys, without me, and let them enjoy the rush of meeting people your age—and as beautiful as you—on a sunny summer day.

But then I remember the look in Wayne's eyes when he called us "tourists in my dreams."

I nod at Carlotta and smile back, grateful not to be alone.

"Yeah. Totally fun."

Chapter Eight

<u>Cassidy</u>
Present Day

"Hey, Mama," I say, placing a cluster of mountain laurel on the large, smooth stone Gramp and I used to mark her grave. She's buried about half a mile from my cabin, not far from Harrington Pond, where she used to take me for summer picnics. "Miss you."

Beside her grave, there is a slightly larger stone marking the spot where I buried my grandfather, ten years ago today. He died three years after my mom, leaving me alone when I was only seventeen.

"Hey, Gramp. Miss you too."

I take a deep breath and sigh, placing my hands on my hips and looking back and forth between their graves, longing for them with a breath-catching ache.

"Been keeping up the gardens, Gramp," I tell him, squatting down to brush some leaves off the stone marker. "Your tomatoes are still coming in strong. Bess died a while ago, like I told you, but I bought a goat off a guy in Greenville last month with some of the savings."

The "savings" is paper and coin money that Gramp collected from the VA until his death. Gramp had all the checks sent to a mailbox at the post office in Millinocket.

He'd go over there every few months to get the checks and cash them at the local bank. Because he'd spent very little money over the years, and had received $1,000 a month until his death, there is still plenty left for me, though my home is so self-sufficient, I have little reason to spend it.

I have Gramp's old Honda FourTrax, which can get me out of the woods when there's a need, but I try to stay close to home. Truth be told, I don't like dealing with people very much and seek them out only when I have to. My experiences with townsfolk following my father's arrest, trial, and death were scarring. I'm not interested in drawing any attention to myself or making anyone uncomfortable with my unwanted presence. It's just better if I live quiet at home, like I promised Mama and Gramp.

"She should be a mule," I say, "she's so stubborn, but I like her company. Named her Annie. I talk to her about history, Mama. And I swear she likes the Beatles 'cuz she's quiet when I sing. I can milk her for about six more months before I'll let her dry. Then I'll have to buy a male and breed her if I want more milk." I sigh, the thought of going back to town in six months making me feel anxious. I guess I'll deal with that when the time comes.

"I still keep the chickens. One rooster and the six hens. They keep me in eggs. Since you been gone, I haven't had the heart to, well, you know."

Every Thanksgiving, Christmas, and Easter, Gramp used to slaughter one of the chickens for dinner. But I can't do that. Besides the fact that the chickens and Annie are my only company, and therefore elevated to a status closer to friend than animal, killing *anything* leaves me cold. Even more than that, it worries me. I don't want to believe that I am capable of killing anything. It seems like an awfully slippery slope, given my genetics.

I remember studying the Salem witch trials with Mama and reading about how some women were condemned to death for having a mole on their chests that resembled a third nipple. It was called the devil's mark, and the common thinking of the day was that evil women had such a mark on their bodies to nurse the devil.

I don't have a third nipple on my body, but I have convicted serial killer Paul Isaac Porter in my blood and bones. That's condemnation enough not only for me, but surely for the rest of the world.

Most of the time, I feel damned.

Live quiet.

Live quiet.

Live quiet.

Sometimes I pray to a God I barely know that, regardless of my parentage, whatever chaos and evil lived inside Paul Isaac Porter doesn't live inside me. That somehow the gene that made my father kill those girls was a mutation within him that wasn't passed down. Or, even if I inherited the gene, it will never be turned on. Or better yet, that even if Paul Isaac Porter had a "kill" gene, that the corresponding gene from my mother overruled his. I want to believe that she was so good, it would be impossible for anything evil from my father to overpower what I received from her.

In the years after my father's conviction, Mama amassed a library of books about hereditary evil and genetics, and over the past decade I have read all of them—some several times, adding to the collection now and then when the Millinocket Library has their annual sale.

A Swedish study of Finnish prisoners found that the majority of violent criminals studied carried the MAOA and CDH13 genes, a combination also known as "the huiman warrior gene" or "kill" gene. The study revealed that a monoamine oxidase A (MAOA) low-activity genotype (contributing to low dopamine turnover rate) as well as the CDH13 gene (coding for neuronal membrane adhesion protein) can result in extremely violent behavior.

In 2009, an Italian prisoner's sentence was reduced on appeal because he showed proof of carrying this gene in his DNA. And in 2010, an American man named Bradley Waldrop, who also carried the combination of MAOA and CDH13 genes, was able to convince a jury that his crime of passion (shooting his wife's friend eight times in front of the couple's children) was manslaughter, not murder. Why? Because his genes made him do it.

For every story of a serial killer's child becoming a police officer or a teacher and living a normal life, there's another story that supports the idea that evil *can* be inherited. And each one chills me through:

Two of Albert Fish's siblings were hospitalized for mental illness, and at least three more relatives going back two generations had a history of mental illness. Aileen Wuornos's biological father was a psychopathic child molester who hanged himself in prison in 1969. The grandson of one of the Hillside Stranglers ended up shooting his grandmother and killing himself in 2007.

The unfortunate net result of my reading is the knowledge that, even if I somehow sidestep my father's insanity, the "kill" gene could still be a part of me, inactive within me, waiting to be passed on to the next generation. It's well within the realm of possibility. And it's the terrifying fact that makes it impossible to imagine what I crave more than anything else in the universe:

Companionship. Love. Family.

While having children is physically possible for me, it is

ethically *im*possible.

Which means that, despite my urges and longings, loving a woman is impossible too.

Because it would be wrong to deprive a woman of children, and it would also be wrong to risk infecting the world with the terrible legacy I might carry in my DNA.

Not to mention, by virtue of my genetics, I could be a danger to a wife and children someday.

As a concept, I accept this truth.

It's a little harder in practice.

My body, which is hard and strong from years of work, longs for a woman's touch. I dream nightly of what it would be like to be kissed or held.

My fingers, which haven't touched another human being since Gramp's death, probably shouldn't remember the soft texture of skin anymore—the warmth of it, the way it felt pressed against my own. But they do. All ten of them remember. And sometimes I wish I'd never known the miracle of touch, the beauty of skin against skin, of my hand clasped safely within Mama's, or Gramp's warm, raspy palm on the back of my neck. You can't miss something you've never known. You can't long for something you never had. Once I knew the glory of human touch. Now I miss it.

Generally I'm pretty good at keeping my loneliness at bay.

But it's been ten years today.

So today, it hurts.

Glancing at the graves one last time, I look up at the clear blue of the sky, at the high sun of midmorning. Perhaps it would be a good day to be around other people the only way I feel comfortable: from a distance, in the woods, staying off the actual paths, but walking up the same steep mountain as the rest of them.

There is a detached camaraderie that I experience by hearing their voices and listening to the crunch of their hiking boots over the leaves and twigs littering the many trails.

I don't want to be around people directly, per se. I don't want to talk with them or share my name or expose myself to questions. But slipping easily through the woods on the mountain, seeing without being seen, a part of and apart from humanity, making my own way to the summit?

Yeah. Today, I want that.

Slowly turning my glance to Katahdin, I wonder how busy it will be today. Baxter Peak is an eight-mile walk from where I presently stand. Five miles from here, I'll find the Saddle Trail, and I could shadow it to the top, listening to the hum of human conversation from the safety of the parallel woods, and pretending I'm a part of the human race. For a few precious hours.

"I'll stay out of sight, Gramp," I promise, backing away from the stones. "Won't draw any attention to myself. Won't talk to anyone. Nobody'll even know I'm there, Mama."

I promise.

***

Three hours later, I'm sitting on a boulder in a heavily wooded area several yards from where the Chimney Pond and Saddle Trails merge, catching my breath. Earlier I saw a lot of walkers through the trees, but more and more are turning around now, due to the cloud cover rolling in. The wind is whipping up too, and the temperature's dropping.

A group of six hikers—three women and three men— come into view, and I focus on them, quickly assessing their ages as best I can. Having lived most of my life isolated, I'm challenged by one of the three women. While the other two look younger than twenty, she appears to be older—in her late twenties, possibly even thirty. I can't tell for sure.

Why she captures my attention, I'm not certain, but maybe because she's closer to my age than the others. I watch her carefully through the trees, tracking her movements as she sits down on a bench while the other five remain standing, laughing, and talking as they take out their water bottles.

My gaze shifts back to her.

She wears sunglasses, but as she sits down, she pushes them on top of her head, taking a deep, weary breath and letting it go.

And the

> world
> stops
> spinning.

And all the oxygen made by every tree in that forest is sucked away, leaving me light-headed.

Because I have never seen such a beautiful woman in my life. Not in real life, when I was little. Not in books. Nowhere.

Her eyes.

Her eyes are the same green as ivy leaves after a rainfall. Deep and alive. Bright and unforgettable. The sort of green that heralds spring and promises rebirth. Glorious, vibrant, and wide, with sweeping, dark lashes, those eyes steal my breath away.

Her hair is a rich, dark brown, held back in a ponytail, and her lips, which she licks after drinking, are red. Her face, with a smattering of freckles concentrated on the bridge of her nose, is shaded with a quiet melancholy that reminds me of my mother.

Everything about her calls out to me, captivates me, makes me long to speak to her and hear her voice, to watch those eyes up close as they look back into mine, to know something about her . . . to know *everything* about her.

As she leans her head back against the bench, I wish I was the sun so I could shine down on her, so I could examine every peak and valley of her face until I have it memorized and can recall it at any lonesome moment: the sad, beautiful, green-eyed girl from the forest.

"So what do you guys think?"

My attention shifts away from the woman on the bench to one of her friends, a tall blonde woman with her hands on her hips.

"Weather's definitely changing," says one of the men.

"It's colder—"

"—and windier," adds a small brunette woman standing beside a tall, good-looking blond man.

"I think we should skip the peak," says one of the guys, and I can hear the disappointment in his voice. "Saddle gets gnarly in the rain. Can't hardly scramble up the boulders."

"Yeah," his friend agrees. "Instead, we could take Dudley to Helon Taylor. Change up the scenery on the way down."

"Let's do it," says the third man, the tall blond guy, who grins at the brunette staring up at him. His voice becomes playful as he gazes back at her. "We have a site at the campground. You're welcome to stay with us for the night. We can try it again tomorrow."

"You wouldn't mind?" she asks, her smile wider.

They're attracted to each other, I think, watching their body language. The girl puts her hands on the back of her waist, which pushes her small breasts forward. I see his eyes drop down to glance at them for an instant. His smile widens when he looks up at her, and she cocks her head to the side and bites her lower lip. *Yep. Attracted.*

"Nah," says the guy, winking at her. "We've got beer and cards. It'll be fun."

The brunette turns to her friend, her face expectant. "What do you think?"

"*Ja.* Fine with me." She nudges the woman on the bench with her knee. "How about you? What do you think, Brynn?"

Brynn.

Brynn, sighs my heart.

Her name is Brynn.

She lifts her head to look up at her friends, and my entire body braces for the sound of her voice. I still my breathing, straining my neck to hear her as clearly as possible.

"I can't stop," she says, hooking her thumb toward the peak. "I have to go on."

Her voice is deeper and richer than I would have guessed, more mature than either of the other women's, which tells me I'm right about her being older.

"Brynn," says the blonde woman, "we can come back. I promise we'll reach the summit tomorrow."

Mesmerized, I watch the play of emotions across her face—the moment of hesitation that is quickly chased away by something stronger. She stands up and adjusts her pack. "I'm halfway there. It *has* to be today."

The blond guy steps toward her, dropping a hand to her shoulder, and I am immediately up on my feet, every muscle tense, ready to pounce if he should threaten or hurt her, and wishing like hell that he'd take his damned hand off her person.

"Brynn," he says, towering over her, his voice imperious. "You shouldn't climb alone. Come back down with us."

She sighs, and somehow I know that her reason for being here today goes far beyond adding another summit to her list. She's small and thin, not muscular like a career hiker, like the others. Yet she practically hums with purpose, and whatever her reasons, they won't let her climb down until she reaches the top. Today.

"I'll be fine. When I get back down, I'll come find you guys, okay?"

"Suit yourself," says the man, stepping away from her and walking toward the start of the Dudley Trail.

A low growl of thunder sounds, and a light sprinkle of rain starts falling. I look up at the sky, then back at Brynn, feeling tense again, split in my hope that she'll turn back with the group for safety . . . but wanting her to keep going, because it is clearly so important to her. I hold my breath, wondering what will happen next.

"Brynn," says the brunette gently, reaching for her hand, "it's raining. And the higher you go, the colder it will get. Come down with us."

"I wish I could," she says wistfully, pulling her hand away, swinging her pack off her back and setting it on the bench. She unzips it and pulls a raincoat from within. "But this is something I need to do."

"You sure you'll be okay?" asks the blonde woman, looking over her shoulder in the direction of the three guys hovering close by.

I can see it like a play upon her face: fear overpowered by determination. She forces a smile, nods at her friends, and slips into her rain jacket. Her voice is higher and sounds falsely cheerful when she insists, "I'll be fine! I'll come find you in a few hours, okay? Be safe getting back down. Go on now."

The two girls share a quick look, then lean forward and

hug Brynn before waving goodbye. They run to catch up with the boys, the sound of low, manly voices and high-pitched giggles fading as they disappear from view.

And Brynn?

She watches them go, standing quiet and alone for several long minutes as her smile falls with the rain. And when her friends and her smile are gone, my heart clutches, because she looks so small, so sad, and so alone.

And though I wish I could join her on the path, walk with her, talk with her, find out what's compelling her to walk through a storm, I know I can't.

Live quiet, and no matter what happens inside of you, you won't never be able to hurt someone, Cassidy.

She lifts her chin, and I watch with admiration and a little bit of awe as she takes a deep breath, glances up at the sky, and hoists her pack.

"I'm coming, Jem," she says to no one, turning her body in the direction of the Saddle Trail. "I'm coming."

Chapter Nine

<u>Brynn</u>

With the wind at my back and the rain whipping my hair into my face, I continue alone, all but blinded, slowly trudging up the challenging Saddle Trail and wondering if I am being foolish. Should I have returned to Roaring Brook with Carlotta, Emmy, and the Bennington boys? Is it madness for a novice hiker to continue alone?

During our companionable walk from Roaring Brook to Chimney Pond, I'd seen a lot of hikers, but Saddle has considerably less traffic, many walkers likely opting, as the rest of my group had, to return below and save the summit for another day. But I have the heaviest feeling in my heart that if I don't get to Baxter Peak today, I never will. So I push forward, despite Kris's warning, Emmy's sweet concern, and my own trepidation.

My thoughts turn inevitably to Jem as the near-howling wind pushes at me and icy raindrops pelt my face, and I try to take some small comfort in the notion that his feet walked this trail dozens of times. I try to feel close to him, but to my immense frustration, I can feel my connection to Jem fading, even here, in this place that he loved so well. The trail is rocky and winding, and it impedes my slow progress. As the sky darkens and the rain falls harder, I have to concentrate wholly on forcing my body forward.

As two hikers approach me, descending from the summit, one of them shakes his head in warning. "Bad up there! You can't see a thing."

His friend nods in agreement, squinting his eyes against the rain. "Not worth the walk up!"

I wave at them weakly. "Thanks."

"I mean it," says the first guy as he passes, both of us turning slightly so our bodies won't touch each other on the narrow trail.

"Turn back," says his friend, making eye contact with me for a nanosecond as he walks by.

I clench my jaw as their footsteps fade, pausing for a moment to tighten my hood. My hands are freezing, but I don't want to take out my gloves yet. I'm not certain they're waterproof, which means they'll be sopping wet in two seconds if I put them on now, and my hands will be that much colder.

Underneath the gloves, in its sealed Ziploc bag, is Jem's phone, still smeared with the fingerprint of blood. It's that smudge that makes me keep moving through the punishing conditions. Picturing it, tears flood my eyes, and I look up at the steep, rocky trail, wishing I was anywhere but in these godforsaken woods in the middle of nowhere.

Sniffling pathetically, I reach up and swipe at my nose before trudging forward. I promised Jem that I'd bury a part of him at the top of Katahdin, and that's exactly what I aim to do . . . no matter what.

"Coming up on the left!" I hear a voice call from behind me, and I glance back to see two men with walking sticks making their way briskly toward me.

As they pass by, I feel a renewed sense of purpose. *They* aren't letting the rain get them down. Nor am I.

Lifting my chin, I soldier on, trying to ignore the weather, though my pants and socks are drenched and getting heavier and colder by the minute. To comfort myself, I softly hum one of my favorite songs, an old Beatles tune my mother used to sing to me as a child.

There are places I remember . . .

I wish I'd thought to call her this morning before setting out; no doubt she's worried about me. Once I get home on Wednesday morning, I'll take a couple of days off and go see my parents in Arizona. I'll tell them all about my treacherous climb up a mountain, and how I'd been able to finally say goodbye to Jem. And maybe I'll cry a little. Maybe they will too. But they'll know that this trip wasn't in vain— that it was a necessary step toward living my life again.

Living again.

What does that mean, exactly?

Hmm.

I guess it means calling my old friends to see if they still have room in their lives for me. I know that my closest friends will be happy to have me back in circulation. And though it will take courage and strength to say yes when they invite me out for drinks or to a BBQ, I'll finally have the will to say yes. Even though my heart might still ache for Jem, it's time to start saying yes again.

Maybe I'll take my bike out of the shed behind my house, wipe off the cobwebs, and oil the chain. I could join my old biking club. I don't know if there will be anyone I know still there, but it wouldn't be the worst thing in the world to meet some new people, I guess.

I don't know if my friend Mona still works at the Petal Salon and Spa near the bar where I used to work, but I could stop in and see. After two years, I could use a cut and color.

Maybe I'll get some paint and repaint a few of the

rooms in our house—*my* house—too. Freshen it up. Make it new. Make it mine. Start over.

Live again.

"Gah!"

I'm so engaged in my thoughts of home, I trip over a tree root in the path and fall to my knees with a cry. Gasping at the pain in my palms and knees, I push up from the ground and stand gingerly. My palms are bleeding, and my pants have ripped open at one knee. I wince at the mix of dirt, debris, and blood seeping from the tear.

"God!" I yell, looking up at the sky, fresh tears of rage mixing with raindrops. "Can you cut me a break? *Please?*"

He answers with a loud crash of thunder, and the rain starts falling sideways.

"Thanks a lot!" I sputter, crying as loudly as I please in heaving sobs.

My palms are a mess of mud-covered, bloody scrapes, so I use the back of my hand to push wet tendrils of hair from my face and let my tears fall freely, the warm saltiness mixing with the cold rain and slipping between my lips.

"It's not fair!" I cry, fisting my broken hands at my sides. "He was good! He was young! I *hate you* for letting this happen!"

Another crash of angry thunder makes me cower a little, but I straighten my spine a moment later, turning my face to the onslaught of rain.

"I don't *want* to be alone!"

Lightning brightens the dark sky for an instant, a jagged burst of white-hot light followed by a crack of fury.

"Please! Help me!" I say in a broken voice, my shoulders slumping as my strength is sapped.

I sigh heavily, a drowned rat, drenched and muddy, and shield my eyes to look up ahead.

The path is empty, but another strike of lightning draws my eyes to a structure of some kind off to the right. I squint. Yes. A cabin? No. A lean-to. A dark-brown painted clapboard lean-to. I cry even harder with relief as I approach. One of the many lean-tos placed strategically along the trails in Baxter State Park, it's the ideal place to sit down, clean my knee, and wait out the worst of the storm.

"I take it back," I mutter at the sky. "You came through. Thank you."

Wiping my tears away, I move purposefully toward the little hut, only noticing, when I am a few feet away, that there appears to be someone else inside. Though I can't see very well through the wind and rain between us, it looks like there's someone sitting on the bench in the back.

Stepping up onto the floor of the lean-to, I almost sigh with relief as the loud patter of raindrops on my jacket ceases, but my heart flips over when my vision clears and I realize who's sharing the tiny space with me.

Wayne.

You're just tourists in my dreams.

He stares at me as I stand on the edge of the platform, his eyes slipping to my chest, then down to my ripped pants and bleeding knee.

A chill races down my spine as his lips tilt upward just a touch.

"Well," he says, looking at me square in the eyes, "if it ain't Grandma."

Grand*maw.*

I know he's calling me that because I'm ten years older than my companions, but truth told, he and I are probably right around the same age. He grins at me and my skin crawls, but I force myself to hold his gaze, trying not to look intimidated, though he is easily twice my size and we are very

73

much alone.

"Looks like you got a li'l scraped up there, huh?"

"It's, um . . ." I gulp. "It's Wayne, right?"

I don't take another step into the lean-to, just stand on the edge, staring at him, trying to figure out whether to stay or go.

"Ayuh," he says, pursing his lips. "It's Wayne, all right. Ol' Wayne, walkin' all by his lonesome." He cocks his head to the side. "You lost or somethin'? Thought you was walkin' with friends."

"They, uh . . . well, it started to rain, and I . . . well, they . . ."

As I mumble, he drops his eyes to my chest again, lingering there as he adjusts his glasses. I glance down quickly to find my windbreaker is plastered to my breasts, my freezing nipples clearly outlined through my T-shirt and the thin Gore-Tex slicker.

I cross my arms, and Wayne slowly raises his glance, his eyes darker now.

"All them fine friends got washed away, huh?"

"Um, no. They're waitin' for me," I lie, hoping he'll buy it. "I hurt my knee. Just wanted to clean it quick, and then I'll be on my way."

"Don't matter nohow to me," says Wayne, reaching into his bag. I brace myself—for what? I don't know—then relax when he pulls out an old-fashioned thermos. He tugs the cup off the top with a *pop* and unscrews the canister, pouring some steaming, amber-colored liquid into the cup. "Tea and syrup and scotch. Nectar of the gods."

I nod, edging into the lean-to a little more. I want to sit on the bench and tend to my knee, but there's only one place to sit, and I don't especially relish the notion of getting closer to Wayne.

"Want some?" he asks, holding out the cup.

I loosen the straps on my pack. "No, thank you."

"Ha! Lookit that. You got some manners, after all."

He lifts the cup in cheers and grins at me, showing off his yellow teeth. He winks before throwing back his drink, his eyes locked on mine the whole time.

There is something about the way his eyes seize mine and hold them that makes me feel trapped, that makes me feel like . . . like his prey.

Get out of here. Get out of here. Get out of here.

I look away from Wayne, glancing quickly toward the trail, hoping to see some hikers coming or going, but there's no one in sight. By now, the guys I passed before I fell are probably well out of earshot.

"See yore friends out there, waitin' for you in the downpour?" he asks, his voice mocking.

I turn back to him and I can see it on his face. He knows I was lying. He knows that I am alone.

"Want me to take a look-see at your kneesie?" he asks, placing his empty cup on the bench beside his fatigue-style pants. Hunting pants.

My stomach flips over at the cajoling tone, and I look out desperately at the still-sheeting rain.

"Um," I say, starting to feel breathless from the increased pounding of my heart. "No, um . . . I think I'll just—"

"No, huh?"

"No, thanks," I say, turning back to him.

"No, thanks," he mimics, snickering softly as he leans down to rummage through his bag again.

I reach up and tighten the straps I've just loosened. No rain is bad enough to spend another moment alone with Wayne. He creeps me out way too much.

"Um . . . I'm just going to, uh, keep going . . ."

I don't want to take my eyes off Wayne, but I need to turn my back to him to step off the lean-to platform, so I pivot quickly, taking a step forward when my feet fly out from under me and I am suddenly yanked backward.

I am thrown to the far left corner of the lean-to, landing on my battered knees, my hip bone slamming into one wall, which causes my forehead to crash into another. My head whips back from the force, and the left side of my face scrapes against the filthy wooden floor. The wind is knocked from me, and I blink rapidly, sucking in a sharp breath. A flash of panic—of pure, visceral dread—sluices through me with such velocity, the adrenaline rush numbs my pain.

"You ain't goin' nowhere," says Wayne from behind me. "Yore friends ain't waitin' for you."

I flatten one hand on the floor and brace the other on the wall in front of me, trying to right myself in the tight space. My fingernails curl, clawing at the dirty planks on the floor, but my movements are sluggish.

"Please," I mumble, my voice hoarse. Weak. Breathless.

"Please?" repeats Wayne. "*Please* let me walk with you! *Please* be kind to strangers! *Please* have a sip of my goddamn motherfuckin' drink!"

I am still trying to sit up when his boot slams into my left side. This time, the pain is so sharp, I scream, my head lurching forward where it slams against the wall again. Bright flashes of light—lightning? fireworks?—blur my vision as I mewl in pain, tears spilling from my eyes. Every movement hurts as I maneuver into a half-kneeling, half-fetal position, facing the corner of the lean-to, hunching over in an attempt to protect myself.

I'm dazed and disoriented as I glance back to see

Wayne squat down behind me.

"There we go," he says. "You lookit me when I'm talkin' to you, Grandmaw."

I keep my arms clasped protectively, pathetically, over my chest as I suck in shallow breaths in sharp spurts. My hip throbs in pain as it twists slightly so I can face Wayne.

That's when I see it—the glint of metal in his hands—and my heart, which is already racing, starts skipping beats, making me even more light-headed.

Oh, my God. Is there any way out of here? Away from whatever he has planned for me?

"P-please," I sob, vaguely aware of something wet and warm trailing down my forehead. Am I bleeding? I want to reach up and wipe the blood away, but I pull my knees closer to my chest instinctively. My eyes stay trained on the shiny blade of the Bowie knife.

"You don't look so good," says Wayne, leaning forward.

I smell his breath—a mix of stale cigarette, scotch, and syrup—and avert my face. But he doesn't like this. He reaches for my chin and grabs it, forcing me to look at him.

He holds the knife up to my face, using the blade to lift a strand of my hair. And though I am repulsed by the fact that he is touching me, I don't move. Each breath I take feels perilous, but I can't control the jerky rise and fall of my chest.

Releasing my chin, he takes one stubby finger and slides the digit across my forehead. When he withdraws it, smeared in my blood, he draws it to his lips, licking the red slick slowly. "You don't look good . . . but you *taste* just fine."

He pulls the straps of my pack away from my back, and I hear the blade slice through the thick nylon. The weight of the pack falls from my shoulders, slumping against my backside, the only thing between me and Wayne.

"Turn around," he says.

I squeeze my eyes shut.

"*Turn around*!" he yells, his hand landing roughly on the base of my neck. "*Now*!"

I pivot awkwardly to face him, my back to the corner of the lean-to, Wayne about six inches away. He grabs my backpack and throws it over his shoulder so there is nothing between us but air.

"Drop yore arms."

"P-please," I sob.

He plunges the knife into the wood to the right of my ear, and I gasp, my breath wheezing and loud in my ears.

"Do it!" he yells, yanking the blade out of the wall.

Slowly, shaking uncontrollably, with tears and blood slipping in streams down my face, I lower my arms.

"Yore titties is like headlights," he says, a high-pitched giggle following this observation.

His tongue darts out, and he licks my blood from his lips as he stares at me from a few inches away.

Oh, God. Oh, no. Oh, God.

"P-please, Wayne. P-please—"

"Shut the fuck up," he growls, still staring at my breasts. "Yore ruinin' it."

Oh, God. Oh, God. No. No. Please, no.

"W-Wayne," I say, shaking my head. "P-please. P-please d-don't—"

"What?" His eyes slide up from my breasts, angry, affronted. "What? You think I'm a fuckin' rapist? Fuck no! I ain't want yore cootie pussy, Grandmaw."

Why his words comfort me some tiny bit, I have no idea. But I whimper "thank you" as I stare up at him, literally backed into a corner, completely at the mercy of a madman.

Is it possible that I can live through this nightmare?

"*Thank you*," he mimics, so close, his vile breath dusts my face with every word. He giggles again. It's childlike and feminine and turns my stomach. I vomit into my mouth, gagging as I swallow down the bile. Wayne doesn't seem to notice—he's smiling at me like he's on autopilot. "Ask me what I *do* like. Ask me! Come on! It'll be fun!"

"What?" I say, tears blurring my vision as he passes the knife back and forth from one hand to the other.

"No. Not like that. That's not fun!" he says, frowning, the knife stilling for a moment. "You gotta ask me, Grandmaw. You gotta say, 'Hey, Wayne, what do you like?'"

His eyes are wild with excitement, his lips stretching into a terrifying smile.

I swallow. "W-Wayne . . . what . . ."

I can't speak. No more words will come out because I am sobbing softly, my body quaking with terror.

"You're wreckin' it!" cries Wayne, his face turning furious. His hand raises the blade over his head. "Ask me what I like!"

"No!" I wail, dropping my head to my knees and wrapping my arms around them. I hold myself as tightly as possible.

Jem. Jem, I'm so sorry. Mommy. Dad. Oh, God. I'm so sorry.

Wayne roars his fury just as I feel the steel point slice my skin open, forcing its ugly coldness into my side, the pain so intense and so unbelievable, I scream. I know I scream, though the sound feels like it's apart from me, not a part *of* me. It sounds far, far away.

I list to my other side, still clutching my knees to my chest as the blade rips through my hip a second time.

I scream again, but this time it isn't about Wayne or the knife or even the pain.

It isn't about losing Jem, or Derrick Frost Willums, or never hearing my mother sing the Beatles to me again.

It isn't even about living the last two years in unimaginable, freezing darkness, every waking moment a nightmare that I couldn't escape from.

I am not screaming for my past or my present.

I am screaming for my future.

I am screaming because I know I want it and someone is taking it away from me.

I am screaming because my eyes are closing and the steel blade keeps landing and my arms can't hold on tightly to my knees much longer.

I am screaming because the stabs don't hurt anymore, which means I must be dying.

Again the blade.

Again the sound of my scream, weak and soft, torn from my fading soul.

And then . . .

Darkness.

Chapter Ten

Cassidy

My first, and strongest, instinct, upon watching Brynn separate from her group and start climbing alone, is to follow her.

Follow her. Follow her. Follow her.

It is a chant in my head. A mantra. And it takes only a few seconds for it to chill me to the bone.

Is this what it had been like for my father?

Would he see a beautiful girl and think to himself:

Follow her.

Talk to her.

And then, suddenly, and maybe without any warning:

Touch her.

Rape her.

Kill her.

Could it really be that simple? The escalation from admiration and interest to evil and destruction?

And if I follow her, will I be walking in his footsteps?

Inhaling sharply with the horror of it, I sit back down on the boulder, close my eyes, and count slowly and carefully to one thousand, seeing the numbers in my mind and acknowledging every single one before moving on to the next. I have no idea how long it takes me—over fifteen minutes, I assume—but when I am finished, I'm thoroughly soaked. I open my eyes, and the trail before me is empty.

Brynn is gone.

And something inside feels suddenly hollow.

Empty and longing. Aching, almost to the point of pain.

Slicing through my fog of yearning, my mind presents a simple question:

Why?

Why do I feel so empty?

Because I am a normal twenty-seven-year-old man who saw a pretty girl and wished to know her?

Or because somewhere deep, dark, and murky inside—somewhere I can't feel and almost can't fathom—I don't just want to know her—I want to hurt her?

What is it that would bring me satisfaction? That would fill the emptiness?

Knowing her?

Or hurting her?

To my shame and fear, I don't know. I'm not certain. I can't answer these simple questions of meaning and intent, which makes me growl softly in frustration and despair.

Pushing off from the boulder, I survey my surroundings. Rain still falls in sheets, pelting and angry, and even from where I stand under a thick canopy of trees away from the trail, I am getting drenched.

I had set forth this morning with two goals in mind: the first, to reach the summit and admire the vast beauty of my world; the second, to feel like a part of humanity for a few harmless hours, to listen to the voices of other people, see their faces, watch them communicate with their words and bodies.

No issues with the first goal. But I grimace, rubbing the

scruff on my chin with my thumb and forefinger, as I review the second. Is it bad that I'd wanted to be around people? To feel human—like a part of the human race, the collective community of man—for a few precious hours? Or was it breaking my word to Gramp and Mama?

I see two men walking quickly down from the summit, heads down, clearly on a mission to get back to their car below.

Hmm. So it's still passable, despite the rain.

I want to see the summit today—even as rainy and cloudy as I know it will likely be. I may have failed or bungled my second goal, but I can still meet my first.

No doubt Brynn is far ahead of me by now, I think, the idea comforting and sad at once.

But even if she isn't, I could use seeing her as a test. Even if I catch a glimpse of her out of the corner of my eye, I won't allow my gaze to linger. No matter how drawn to her I feel, no matter how lovely her face and sad her eyes, I can fight against the temptation. I can force myself to look away, to stay away, to keep her safe from me, and then I'll know that I am stronger than my father—that, given the opportunity, I won't yield to weakness or temptation, that I won't indulge even my longing to look.

A test. Yes.

And so I start loosely following the trail through the woods, not on it, but nearby, climbing through brambles and over rotting logs as the rain beats down on my bare head, bathing me in heaven's tears.

Up and up. My breath is steady because I am accustomed to such exertion, my long legs carry me surely over the uneven forest floor, and I guess it'll take another hour or so to reach the cloudy top. But I will make it. I will—

That's when I hear it break through the thrumming of my heart, the crunching of my boots, over the roar of the wind and the rain . . .

A scream.

I stop in my tracks from the singular awfulness of it, frozen in place, waiting to hear it again.

A hawk, I try to convince myself, hoping against hope that it wasn't a human sound. But rationally, I know that no bird of prey would be out in this rain. They're waiting out the rain in their nests, beaks tucked under feathers.

Again I hear it.

And now I'm certain it wasn't an animal screech; it was definitely a human scream. Piercing, tormented, and high-pitched over the wind, it is the sound of intense distress.

My feet move suddenly, racing toward the sound. They are stealthy over the brush, running fast. My calloused hands reach for thin tree trunks, and I use them to propel myself forward like slingshots. The rain bites at my face, but I run in spite of it, everything within me rising up against the genesis or provocation of this sound.

Again the piercing scream, closer now, but weaker, and I do something I've never done before: I leave the woods and allow my feet to touch down on the path. With my eyes closed and body still, I freeze on the path, waiting for the sound again, willing for it to find me and guide me.

Heeeeeeeelp!

Through the whipping wind, through the angry rain, I hear it, and my whole body jerks to the right as if obeying its command. Crossing back over the path, I run as fast as I can toward one of the brown-painted Appalachian Trail lean-tos set along the path.

I race to it, shocked by what I find.

A man squats in the left corner of the lean-to, hovering

over something on the floor. Unaware of my presence, he lifts his arm, a bloody, dripping knife suspended over his head for a moment before he brings it down with the whole force of his body, the sound of a slice followed by the squish of blood as the knife is withdrawn and raised again. Dark red drops drip down onto the man's head as he adjusts his grip and plans to lower the blade again.

Noooooooooo!

I am in motion, my body surging forward, up and onto the platform, my hands landing under his raised arms and yanking him back. His body, the first human form I've touched in the decade since Gramp's passing, is easy to lift because I have surprised him. I throw him across the small space with all my might, into the wall to my left, his legs knocking into a bench as he flies through the air. I watch his head slam into the wall with a sickening thud. He falls to the floor, and I stand over his body, waiting for him to stir, but he is still, knocked unconscious.

Turning back to the corner, I recognize her hair and jacket immediately.

"No!" I cry, fisting my hands helplessly by my sides as I shake my head. "No, no, *no!*"

It's Brynn—*small, brave Brynn*—curled up in fetal position, her face battered, her jacket ripped and bloody.

The instant, and almost blinding, mix of panic and rage should paralyze me, but it doesn't. I reach down and scoop her small body into my arms without thinking, moving her away from the corner and onto my lap. Gingerly pushing up her jacket and shirt, I can see several stab wounds concentrated on her waist and hip. None are gushing blood, so it appears—by the grace of God—that her attacker didn't hit a major artery.

She whimpers as I hold her, turning her head into my

chest, and a slight scent of sweetness rises up between us. Vanilla. The beautiful, injured woman on my lap smells like sugar cookies, which makes me sob for no good reason, except that this shouldn't have happened to her, and I am furious that it has.

Her injuries bleed slowly, in pools of crimson that slide in garish red streaks over her creamy skin and drip onto the floor. I need to stop the bleeding as best I can, so I reach for her backpack and open it. Inside, I find a T-shirt and a couple of pairs of thick, cotton socks, dry inside a Ziploc bag, and a first aid kit. I use her dry T-shirt to wipe at the stab wounds, counting six. Because they are close together, I am able to cover all of them with her clean socks, and then I use an Ace bandage from the first aid kit to affix them, wrapping the tan, stretchy bandage around her waist and hips and securing it with a double pin.

I can't be sure that the wounds aren't immediately life-threatening, but based on what I learned in the paramedic correspondence course that Gramp forced me to take, I don't believe they are. Still, they need to be cleaned, sewed, and dressed as soon as possible.

I pull her shredded, bloody shirt and jacket back over the improvised dressings and gaze down at her face, gently pushing wet strings of hair from her forehead and trying to figure out what to do now.

Not that I am intimately familiar with the smell of alcohol, but Gramp indulged in bourbon now and then, and I can smell it strongly around me. Glancing around, I pause my eyes on the man's still-unconscious body. Hmm. If he'd had enough liquor to make the whole lean-to smell, he'd probably be out for a while.

Perhaps I should leave her here, scramble down the mountain to a public telephone, and call the Chimney Pond ranger station to come and collect her?

I look over at her attacker again, feeling a storm of fury rise up, swirling within me. *No. You can't leave her with him. What if he wakes up and tries to finish the job he started?*

You could tie him up, my brain reasons. But I rebel against this notion stubbornly. If he woke up before her, he could have a couple of hours to free himself and hurt her again before I am able to find a phone and make a call.

Besides, what if I am wrong about the severity of Brynn's wounds? What if one of the stab wounds *is* fatal?

I can feel the weight of her body on my lap, and I know she doesn't weigh much. I could easily carry her to the ranger's station.

But . . .

Once there, I will have to give my name. They might even suspect that I am the one who hurt her. What if, in the time it took for me to take her to safety, her actual attacker woke up and ran away? *I'm* the son of a convicted serial killer. No way they'd believe I was innocent in all of this.

She mewls softly, and I scramble to come up with another plan.

I could . . . well, I could carry her a little ways down the trail, closer to Chimney Pond, and then prop her against a tree, hoping someone would find her.

But I glance out the open front of the lean-to at the dark sky, sheeting rain, and empty trail. She could end up sitting against that tree all afternoon and into the night. And if an animal didn't get her, drawn to the smell of her blood, what if someone else—like the human animal lying to my right—tried to hurt her again?

My arms tense at the thought of her being hurt anymore, and I hold her closer, wincing at her faint moan as I shift her hip. She is in pain. Even unconscious, she is in pain.

I can't leave her. I have to take her with me and get her to safety.

The incisions will need to be sewn shut once I get her home, but there I have antibiotic ointment and pills, plus a full stock of first aid items to tend to her. It's still raining like hell, but I am young and strong, and she needs me. I can do this.

"I'm gonna get you down from here," I say, looking around the lean-to as I figure out how to carry her.

I'll have to leave her backpack here. She probably weighs a little over a hundred pounds, and it will already be slow going through the woods.

At least we're going down, not up, I think, shifting her carefully to the floor.

She whimpers softly and murmurs, "Help me," so quietly, I almost could have dreamed it.

I kneel down beside her, leaning my head close enough to smell sugar cookies again. I savor the sweetness of the smell as I whisper, "I'll help you, Brynn." I add, more out of hope than certainty, "You're safe with me. You're safe now. I won't hurt you. I promise."

Her furrowed brows relax, and I hear her sigh softly, which tugs at my thrumming heart. Though I would happily stare at her forever, I force myself into action. I have work to do.

Reaching back into her pack, I find a ten-foot rope and double it, tying a secure knot at the end to create a large double loop. I hoist her on my back, one loop of the rope holding her against my back, and the other acting as a sling for her butt. I reach for her legs, putting my arms under her knees to carry her piggyback-style.

With one last look at the piece of human excrement

who hurt her, I turn from the lean-to, into the pouring rain, and start back down Katahdin.

I don't know if I'm doing the right thing.

I hope to God, praying with every heavy step I take, that any evil that lived within my father doesn't live within me . . . but there is no way to be certain.

The only thing I know with any certainty is that I couldn't leave her.

So I carry her.

Seven miles on my back.

All evening and into the night. Rain pelts me from every direction. Wind whips my hair into my face and debris into my eyes. More than once I lose my footing and stumble, my sheer desperation to bring Brynn to safety the only thing that rights our bodies before a dozen disastrous falls.

My back feels, at times, like it will break.

My legs ache. My arms burn.

And still I carry her.

All the way home.

Chapter Eleven

Brynn

I don't know why-y-y nobody told you . . .

Pretty.

So pretty.

I try to open my eyes, but they are heavy and sluggish so I stop trying, concentrating on the soft music that is coming from somewhere nearby. A clear male voice sings the old Beatles ballad. The gentle strains of a guitar are so ethereal, I don't know if I am awake or dreaming.

Dreaming, I decide, drifting back into a deep sleep.

I'm only dreaming.

***

"I don't want to hurt you, but I need to put a little more ointment on here, okay, Brynn?"

Okay, I think, whimpering when I feel the pressure of a finger tracing a painful line on my hip. There is a moment of relief, and then the pressure resumes in another spot. Groaning in pain, I force my eyes open. They don't want to focus, but it appears that I am lying down, staring up at a ceiling made of wooden beams. I clench my eyes shut as the pressure returns, but hot tears escape, slipping from the wells of my eyes, scorching a trail down my cheeks.

"I know it hurts," he says, his deep voice thick with

regret. "I promise I wouldn't do it if I had another choice."

I close my eyes, sinking into his voice and anchoring myself to it at the same time. Though the voice is intimately familiar to me, I can find no face in my mind with which to identify it. Had it not been for a sixth sense telling me that I am in a safe place, I might become panicked . . . because how can his voice be familiar when I have no idea what he looks like?

"You're okay now," he whispers close to my ear, the warmth in his voice like a lullaby. "Sleep, Brynn. Heal. I'll be here when you wake up."

Who? I want to ask. *Who will be here when I wake up? Who are you?*

But sleep is already pulling me under.

And I don't fight it.

***

My eyes open to a dimly lit room, my ears aware of someone singing softly to a guitar. *I know this song. I've heard it before.* Closing my eyes again, I listen for a moment, licking my lips and finding them dry and painful.

"Water?" I manage to croak.

The guitar stops instantly.

My eyes flutter open to find someone walking toward me, his form tall but hazy as he comes closer, finally standing over my bed.

Do I know you? How do I know you?

"Brynn? Did you say something?"

His voice is familiar—*deeply* familiar—though it is not my father, and it is not Jem.

"Did you say 'water'?"

"Please," I murmur, my throat so dry and scratchy, the single word hurts.

The mattress beneath my body depresses a little as he

sits next to me. Placing his hand behind my skull, he lifts it, and I find cool glass pressed against my lower lip. I drink greedily as he tips the glass. Some of the water dribbles down my chin in my haste to hydrate.

Where am I? And . . . .who . . . ?

The glass is removed, and a moment later, a washcloth wipes the drizzle from my chin and neck.

"Who are you?" I ask, my voice soft and raspy. "Where am I?"

"I'm Cassidy," he says, shifting his body from the bed to kneel beside it. His eyes are now level with mine.

I don't know him.

If I had ever met him before, I wouldn't have forgotten him. Why? Because his eyes are unforgettable, otherworldly. Surrounded by long, thick lashes that curl up at the ends, his left eye is green and his right eye is blue.

"Your eyes . . .," I murmur.

"It's heterochromia," he says, blinking self-consciously. His lips flinch slightly, like he wants to smile but doesn't. "Weird, but not contagious."

I let my eyes skim over the rest of his face.

His skin is clear, though deeply tanned, and he has three moles—beauty marks—on his left cheek: a tiny one under his eye, a larger one in the middle of his cheek, and the largest of the three a bit lower, covered by the dirty-blond scruff of his beard.

His hair is unkempt, as though it hasn't been cut professionally in a while, standing up at odd angles, a combination of bed head and owner apathy. It is a dark blond with copper highlights, the ends almost flaxen, and curled at his neck. Like his eyelashes, it gives him a youthful, disarming look.

"How do I know you?" I ask.

"You don't, really."

I stare into his eyes, the different colors slightly jarring. "Where am I?"

"My home."

"Umm . . ." My heart starts beating faster because I know I am forgetting something—something very important that would explain why I am here. "Why . . . What . . . what happened to me?"

"Breathe in," says Cassidy, his voice firm but gentle.

I take a breath.

"Deeper."

I inhale enough breath to fill my lungs but cry out in agony as they expand. Sharp, shooting pains from my hip and side force me to exhale slowly. Blinking at Cassidy, I see him wince in sympathy before nodding.

"Do you remember?"

"I hurt," I moan, my eyes shuttering closed from the pain.

"Brynn," he says, his voice farther away now, like he is calling my name down a well. "Brynn, stay with me . . ."

"I hurt," I whisper again, surrendering to darkness.

***

The next time I wake up, I remember things right away:

I am in Cassidy's house.

Cassidy's eyes are different colors.

I don't know how I know Cassidy.

Cassidy doesn't want to hurt me.

My body hurts.

Don't breathe too deep.

I am lying on my back but turn my head to the side, finding a man—the same Cassidy that my brain remembers—asleep in a rocking chair beside my bed.

I recognize his face from before (minutes ago? hours

ago? yesterday? last week?), but I still study it for a few minutes.

His lips are parted and slack, full and pink, and I have a sudden image of kissing them, which shocks the hell out of me since I haven't had a hot thought about a man since losing Jem. Tugging my bottom lip between my teeth, I find it tender to the touch. Reaching up to finger it, I find a scab on the upper right lip and another on the lower, as though both were split. Touching the rest of my face gingerly, I find a Band-Aid on my forehead and wince when I press down on it. Another anonymous wound.

I remember Cassidy telling me to breathe deeply the last time I woke up, and I slowly move my fingers down my body, grateful to discover I am clothed, wearing a T-shirt and underwear. As my fingers near my waist, I feel the pain of my touch. And when I try to move, to test the soundness of the area by shifting my body, I feel it even more sharply.

Sucking in a breath, I cease my crude examination, removing my fingers and flattening them on the sheets by my hips as tears fill my eyes.

I am hurt on my face and my body. Someone has hurt me.

You're just tourists in my dreams.

I look over at Cassidy, who snores lightly in his sleep, but instinctively I know it wasn't him. I don't know how I know this so certainly, but I do. I know that I am safe with him.

"Cassidy?" I whisper.

I have so many questions, and I am too awake to go back to sleep.

His eyes flinch, and he changes his body position just slightly, but otherwise he remains asleep.

"Cassidy?" I say a little louder.

"Mama?" He grunts softly, his eyes blinking open.

"Brynn," I say, watching him reach up and rub his eyes.

"Hey." He leans forward. "You're awake."

"How long have I been here?" I ask, trying to sit up, but the pain in my side reminds me that I need to move slowly.

A crease appears in his forehead. "Three days, I guess."

"I've been asleep for three days?"

"You've been in and out," he says, resting his elbows on his knees as he looks back at me with one green eye and one blue.

"My face . . . my hip . . ."

He nods but otherwise remains still. "Do you remember anything?"

"Not much." I take as deep a breath as I dare. "I only know it wasn't you."

I have never thought of relief as a palpable, visible, living emotion before now. Joy is exuberant. Grief is oppressive. Fear is constricting. But I see relief transform Cassidy's face, delivering it from doubt and shedding layers of worry with its arrival. It tugs at my heartstrings just as surely as it makes me wonder.

"Did you . . . save me?" I ask.

He grimaces, his jaw tightening. "Wasn't there in time to save you."

Thay-uh.

The way he says "there" pinches at something inside me because it sounds so much like Jem. A Mainer accent. How I've missed it.

"I'm sure sorry for that, Brynn," he says.

"But I'm alive," I point out, maneuvering ungracefully into a semi-sitting position and reaching for the glass of water on the table beside me.

95

"If I was even a few seconds later . . .," he mutters, a note of disgust in his tone.

I sip the water, grateful for the coolness sluicing down my dry throat, trying to recall what happened. And suddenly—*a flash*—metal over my head. Another *flash*—the squishing sound of something hard sinking into something soft.

The glass starts slipping from my hand, but Cassidy reaches forward lightning fast and grabs it, pulling it from my limp fingers.

"You're remembering," he says, nodding at me with wide eyes.

"I was stabbed," I murmur in a rush. "Someone was . . . s-stabbing me."

"Yes."

"Who?"

"I don't know," says Cassidy. "Didn't wait around to find out his name."

"But you called the police? The . . . the rangers? Did they arrest him? Do I need to . . . I mean, should I make a statement about the attack or . . . or . . ."

"Police'll take your statement when you're better. Don't worry about it for now."

He's been holding my eyes steadily, but now he looks away, placing the glass back on the end table and standing up.

"Are you hungry?" he asks, rubbing his stubbly chin between his thumb and forefinger.

Am I hungry? I blink up at him. "I don't know."

"I'll heat up some soup, okay?"

Before I can ask another question, he's turned and slipped out of the small bedroom, pulling a curtain shut behind him.

Chapter Twelve

<u>Cassidy</u>

Shoot. Shoot. Shoot.

Now what?

I stand at the stove, reheating the chicken noodle soup that I made for her yesterday, looking over my shoulder uneasily at the curtain that shields me from her view.

She's asking about rangers and police and . . . *what're you going to say to her, Cass? "I carried you here to my house in the woods because I'm the only son of a serial killer and I wasn't about to show up at the ranger station or the police station with a stabbed girl in my arms."*

I run my free hand through my hair, clenching my jaw and shaking my head.

I shouldn't have brought her here.

I should have figured out something else.

But what? I considered my options back up on Katahdin and came up with the best possible plan for both of us. Perfect? No. But I didn't have time for perfect. She was hurt and I was panicked. I did my best.

After carrying her home and placing her on the bed in Mama's old room, I undressed her so I could tend to her wounds. Never having taken off a woman's bra and frustrated with the closure, I finally cut it off with scissors. I considered leaving her underwear on, but it was caked with dried blood. I closed my eyes as I pulled it off, then covered her privates with a washcloth and her breasts with a towel, determined not to leer at or linger on the swells and curves of her body. Setting to work, I flushed her incisions, cleaned them with iodine, sewed them up with fishing line, and covered them with sterile pads and gauze.

In Mama's bureau, I found a soft, clean T-shirt and some underwear folded neatly where she'd left them. I redressed Brynn and carried her to the living room couch, then I made Mama's bed with the softest sheets I could find, moved Brynn back in there, and tucked her under a down comforter. Every twelve hours or so, I changed the dressings over the incisions, reapplying antibiotic ointment and making sure that they were seeping pink or clear, not yellow.

On the afternoon of the second day, I smelled urine. Lifting Brynn from the bed to the sofa, I stripped off her underwear and T-shirt, and sponge-bathed her with my eyes closed. Then I re-dressed her in clean things of Mama's, changed the bedsheets, and resettled her under the covers.

Under oath I'd have to admit that I peeked once at her breasts while she was naked.

Maybe twice.

But I swear I feel guilty about it, and my penance is that no matter how hard I try, I can't stop thinking about them now.

While she slept, I sat beside her bed in Gramp's old rocker, picking out the chords to "While My Guitar Gently Weeps." Mama used to sing it to me when I was sick, and it always made me feel better. I hoped that it might soothe Brynn too.

The soup starts to boil, and I turn off the burner, pulling the pot from the stove and tipping the contents into a mug.

What're you going to tell her?

How're you going to explain how she ended up here?

I have no talent for lying. There's been little need for evasion in my quiet life, and suddenly I feel a little helpless as I stare down at the contents of the steaming mug. How much do I have to tell her? I remember once reading a quote about lying. The gist of it was, if you lie, you must remember your lies. If you tell the truth, you don't have to keep track of your words. Resolving not to lie, but to share as little as possible, I grab a spoon from the drying rack beside the sink and head back toward the bedroom.

With no door on which to knock, I pause outside the curtain, uncertain of etiquette. "Um, I've got some soup."

"Okay."

"Can I come in?"

She pauses for a moment before answering. "It's *your* house."

"It's *your* room," I say, still standing on the other side of the curtain, though I am starting to feel a little foolish.

I don't expect to hear the soft sound of her chuckle. Honestly, it's been so long since I heard someone laugh at something I've said, it takes me a moment to register her reaction, but once I do, I replay the soft sound in my head, carefully placing the precious sound bite in the growing mental file labeled "Brynn."

"So, um . . ."

"Yeah," she says quickly. "It's fine. Come on in."

Pushing open the curtain, I take a step into the small room, trying not to look her in the eyes and hoping that my presence doesn't make her feel uncomfortable. I have grown accustomed to having her here over the past three days. I mean, I marvel at her presence, but I am no longer startled by it. But she has not had the same amount of time to accustom herself to me, and I am twice her size. I am aware of all this as I place her mug of soup on the bedside table, then step back, looking around the room uneasily.

"I've, um, had the shades drawn so you could sleep. Want them open?"

She is reaching for the soup but stops to look up at me thoughtfully. "I assumed it was night."

"They're blackout shades," I say, hooking my thumb toward them. The mug of soup scrapes the tabletop as she pulls it closer. "Shouldn't be too hot."

She takes a sip, watching me from over the rim of the cup before lowering it to her lap. "It's good."

"Thanks."

"You made it?" She seems surprised.

I nod, putting my hands, slick with nervous sweat, on my hips.

"Are you a chef?" she asks, offering me a small, uncertain smile.

It so transfigures her already pretty face, my breath catches, trapped in my lungs, while I stare back at her.

"Are you?" she asks, as she lifts the mug to her lips again.

"No," I say, forcing my lungs to compress and exhaling deeply. I glance at the windows, then back at her. "The, um, shades?"

"Okay."

I move quickly, pivoting around and crossing the small room. Across from the bed, there are four pane-glass windows, and as I open the four shades I hear **Brynn** gasp behind me. When all are opened at once, they offer a panoramic view of Katahdin.

"Wow!" she breathes, and, because the awe in her

exclamation sums up how I feel about the view too, I can't help turning around to see her expression.

Her face was badly battered by her attacker, and there are still visible reminders of his assault three days later: her lips are puffy and scabbed from where they were split, and a medium gauze pad and tape covers a contusion on her forehead. But to me, she is so beautiful, it hurts me to look at her, and I turn away sharply.

"Yeah. My, um . . . my mother loved the mountain."

"Is this her room?" she asks.

I swallow. "Was."

"Oh," she murmurs. "I'm sorry."

Nobody other than Gramp has ever shared condolences for Mama's death, and I'm not sure how to respond. I nod, still staring up at Baxter Peak.

"Are you alone here?" she asks.

"Yeah," I say. The silence between us grows heavy, and without approaching her, I turn around. "Well, I mean, *you're* here."

"But . . . we're alone," she says—a statement, not a question.

I nod once.

She blinks rapidly, then drops her eyes, lifting the soup to her mouth again.

Have I made her uncomfortable? I didn't mean to do that.

"You're safe here," I say.

She stops drinking and looks at me carefully, her expression hawkish over the rim of the cup, like she's trying to decide whether or not this is the truth.

I place my hand over my heart, like we used to do before ballgames when they played a recording of the national anthem. "Brynn, I promise—I swear on . . . on—"

101

On what? "——on the memory of my mother——I will not hurt you."

As she lowers the cup, her face relaxes. "Were you a boy scout?"

"For a little while," I say, searching her face, hoping for her trust while knowing I don't deserve it. My voice is a whisper when I repeat, "I won't hurt you."

"Okay," she says softly, nodding at me. She places the cup on the bedside table and looks around the room. "Do you have my backpack? I should charge my phone."

I shake my head. "No. It's still, um, up there. I couldn't carry it."

She looks upset about this, dragging her bottom lip between her teeth, then wincing as she is reminded of her injuries.

"Why not?"

"Because I was carrying you," I say simply.

Her eyes widen. "You carried me down the mountain?"

I nod.

"By yourself?"

I nod again.

"How?"

"On my back."

She gasps, the sound ragged and shocked. "On your . . . *back?*"

"There was no other way to get you down."

She looks beyond me, out the windows, to Katahdin in the distance. When she catches my eyes again, hers are filled with tears, and her voice breaks when she asks, "How f-far is that?"

I shrug. "Seven miles. Or so."

"You carried me . . ." She pauses, her eyes searching my face while tears slide down hers. ". . . s-seven miles? On your b-back?"

"Couldn't leave you there."

"*Thay-uh*," she repeats softly. She sucks in a choppy breath, her face contorting as she sobs, "Y-you s-saved m-my l-life."

I move to the side of the bed, taking the mug from her hands before the contents slosh out. Tears stream down her cheeks, and it hurts me—*hurts me*—to see it, but I don't know what to do. I think about Mama, who barely ever cried. But when she did, Gramp would lay a hand on her shoulder and say, *There, there. There, there, Rosie.*

I reach out and lay a hand on Brynn's shoulder. "There, there."

I am surprised when she reaches up to place her hand over mine. It's the first voluntary contact she has initiated between us, and it sends my body into chaos to feel her touch. My blood rushes; my heart pounds. Her palm is soft against the back of my hand, her fingers grasping.

"H-he was k-killing me," she sobs. "S-stabbing me. I was . . . I w-was s-so . . . s-so . . ."

She is full-on weeping now, unable to speak anymore, and I don't think before sitting down on the edge of the bed beside her. I'm not sure what to do next, but it turns out I don't need to know. She scoots forward, turning into me, moving my hand from her shoulder to her uninjured hip and letting her forehead drop to my chest. I realize that she wants me to hug her, so I gently wrap my other arm around her, careful of her wounds, pulling her as close as I dare.

She flattens her hands on my chest, and her body trembles in my arms. Her tears wet my T-shirt as she sobs, murmuring unintelligible words.

"There, there," I whisper every few seconds, keeping one hand flat on her hip, where she's placed it, and the other on the tangles of her hair, which falls down her back. I run my hand over the hair gently, trying to soothe her, desperately wanting to be of use to her.

"I w-was so s-scared," she says through hiccups, as she fists my flannel shirt in her hands. "I th-thought I w-was going to d-die. He w-was t-trying to k-kill me."

She's right about this. If I hadn't arrived when I did, she would surely be dead by now. From what I observed, her attacker didn't plan to let up, and he eventually would have hit her iliac artery. She surely would have bled out in that little lean-to.

"Did you know him?"

She shakes her head. "N-no. His n-name w-was W-Wayne. He w-was b-bothering some g-girls at the r-ranger station b-before we started h-hiking. I-I th-think he w-was c-crazy."

"Yeah. I don't think that's debatable."

She snorts softly, and I realize that she's laughing, which kind of startles me since she's also still sobbing. I didn't realize until now that people can laugh and cry at the same time.

"Y-yeah. D-definitely c-crazy," she says, her sobs starting up again.

She turns her head slightly so that her cheek rests on my chest, and she feels so small, so vulnerable, nestled against me, I can't help but hold on to her tighter. I have no idea what I'm doing, so I'm going on instinct, and every instinct says that holding her, comforting her, is right.

"How d-did you f-find me?" she finally whispers against my chest.

"I heard you scream."

She nods, her body shaking with another sob. "I remember s-screaming."

"I'm glad you did," I say, still stroking her hair. "Or else
. . ."

"I'd be d-dead now."

"Yes," I whisper, the word bitter on my lips.

She takes a deep breath, but it's ragged.

"Breathe again," I say. "Slowly, now."

She does, and it's a little easier this time.

"One more time," I say, rubbing her back.

This time it's deep and smooth and slow.

"I'm so tired," she says, her tears subsiding bit by bit as
her weight falls heavy against me.

I shift a little in the bed, so that my back is against the
headboard. She nestles closer to me, but her rhythmic
breathing, intermingled with soft, leftover sobs, tells me that
she's fallen asleep.

I think about Annie, who needs milking, and the eggs
waiting for me in the henhouse. The garden should be
fertilized, and I religiously chop wood for two hours every
day from May to October so that I'll have a pile large enough
to last throughout the cold fall, winter, and early spring
months. Now that it's summertime, I should be fishing every
other day and freezing or drying my catch. There are little
repairs I should be making on the cabin, and crops that need
tending in the garden.

But this human being—the beautiful girl asleep on my
chest, her ear over my heart—needs me right now. So I hold
her close and let my eyes shut as the sun lowers over **"the
greatest mountain."**

I don't really know her.

I don't have any right to her.

I shouldn't get attached to her.

In a handful of days she will be gone.

But right now, there is simply nowhere else on earth I'd

rather be.

Chapter Thirteen

Brynn

Thump-thump.
   Thump-thump.
   Thump-thump.

My eyes open slowly to the rhythm of Cassidy's heartbeat, and I find the room cast in a pink glow. Turning my head slightly, I realize it's dawn. The black outline of Katahdin stands majestically in the distance, with pink and orange light in parallel streaks behind it. The sun is still hidden by the mountain, where my backpack, holding Jem's phone, has been abandoned.

When Cassidy told me that he'd left my backpack behind, its loss was a stab to my heart.

But when I discovered he'd carried me seven miles—an unimaginable distance over rough ground in torrential rain—on his back to safety, it disarmed me completely. The walls behind which my tears and fears were held crumbled and fell.

His chest is solid and warm under my head, and his arms still hold me as they did when I was falling asleep. We've slept like this all night, I guess, and it surprises me that sleeping a whole night in Cassidy's arms—an intimate act that requires so much vulnerability and trust—feels so organic to me. Especially since I haven't slept with anyone in a long time.

I lift my head and peek up at his face, at his pillowed lips slightly open in sleep and the three beauty marks on his otherwise rugged cheek. His beard has grown in from last night, and I can see a pulse beating in his throat, a little beacon that pronounces his strength every few seconds.

This man saved my life.

Several times.

Once on the mountain, when he stopped Wayne.

Twice when he carried me to safety.

Three times when he cared for my injuries.

I am in awe of his selflessness, grateful for such profound kindness and care from a stranger.

I lean back down and close my eyes, breathing in his scent. The smell of his cotton flannel is familiar and comforting, and I long to drift back to sleep in his arms, but one thing is stopping me: my bladder is so full, it hurts. I need a bathroom.

I roll onto my back and pull myself up into a sitting position beside him with a grimace of breath-catching pain. On my left is the wall; on my right, Cassidy. And for the first time, spread out beside me, I realize how big he really is—he is sitting up in bed, but his bare feet still hang over the edge. I don't want to wake him, but I don't know how to maneuver my body over his when my hip screams in pain every time I move.

"Cassidy," I whisper, shaking his shoulder. "Cassidy."

"Mmm?" He sighs in his sleep, murmuring softly, "Let it go. *Please* let it go."

I don't know what he's talking about, but he must be having a pretty intense dream because he's frowning.

"Cassidy?"

"Hm? What?" He jolts awake, blue and green eyes opening wide. "Huh?"

"Where's the bathroom?" I ask, keeping my voice soft.

He scrunches his eyes shut and scrubs a hand over his forehead. "You gotta get out of here. You gotta go."

"Exactly," I confirm, nodding emphatically. "I gotta go. Now."

He lowers his hand and opens his eyes, blinking at me for a moment, as though confused by our conversation. "What?"

"I have to go!" I say, worried that if he doesn't help me out of the bed, I'm going to pee in it.

"To the bathroom?"

"Yes!" I nod, glancing down at his legs, which take up more than half of the twin bed. "Can you . . .?"

His legs slide off the bed, and he sits up as I push down the covers and pull my bare legs out from under the sheets. For a split second, I'm aware of how naked they look. *He took off your clothes.* The thought passes through my head, but I put it aside. I'll ask him about that later.

"You know where?" he asks, then quickly answers his own question, his voice still sleep-disoriented. "No, she don't know where. You have to show her, Cass."

Cass. As a nickname, it's perfect, and I find myself wanting to say it, just to see what it feels like falling from my lips.

He stands up, stretching his arms over his head before offering me his hands. "Move slow."

I scoot to the end of the bed and take his hands, leaning heavily on them as I drop one foot, then the other, to the floor. As I stand up, my hip throbs with such intense, searing pain, I cry out, and Cass squeezes my hands.

"It's okay," he says softly. "No hurry."

Easy for you to say, I think. I'm about to pee on his floor.

It takes me a second to adjust to the pain of standing, and though my bladder is throbbing with a different sort of discomfort, I force myself to stay still for a second. I don't want to move too quickly and pull the stitches.

"I know you're hurting," he says. "I'll get you a painkiller while you, you know, do your business."

I nod gratefully, following his lead as he pulls me slowly from the bed to the curtain.

"It'll get better," he says. "I promise."

We've entered a living room, and I want to look around, to find clues about where I am and who he is, but there's no time to linger right now. I follow him into a dark hallway, and he drops one of my hands to push open a door. I step inside. The bathroom is dark, lit only by the rising sun filtering through the window and a night-light on the sink.

My fingers search for a light switch on the wall inside the door. "Where's the light?"

"Isn't one."

I blink at this odd answer as he pulls the door shut, leaving me alone.

My eyes adjust to the dim light as I brace one hand on the sink and pull down my underpants. As I lower myself to the toilet seat, I endure a whole new wave of unforgiving pain, but after I'm finally seated, my bladder empties quickly, and for a moment my relief overrides my discomfort.

Not in a hurry to stand up again, I look around. It's the tiniest bathroom I've ever seen—just enough room for the toilet, the small sink beside me, and a shower stall across from me. Behind the door is a hook that holds a solitary yellowish-gray towel. Cassidy's, no doubt, since he lives here alone. The sparse room is clean and very tidy, with a hand towel on a rack beside the sink and no other decoration. In other words, nothing else to look at, and no clues about my host.

I take a deep breath and hold it as I reach down for my panties, but as I pull them up, my stomach flips over. They're grayish and frayed around the edges, like they've been washed about a hundred times. But more important, they're not mine. Which means Cassidy undressed me all the way and helped me into these panties.

My cheeks flush with heat as I imagine being completely naked while I was unconscious. I mean, I know that he saved my life, and I'm grateful. But realizing that he's seen me naked makes me *uncomfortable* . . . like he took something that didn't belong to him.

Trying to shake off the feeling, I force myself into a standing position, gasping at the pain, and pull the granny panties up over my bandages. I'm further creeped out by wearing someone else's old undergarments, but I tell myself not to be stupid. I'm lucky he found me, lucky he carried me somewhere safe, and lucky there was extra underwear to be borrowed at all.

Turning to flush the toilet, I find there's no handle. I look to the left and right. Nothing.

"Um, Cassidy?" I call.

"Yeah?" he answers from outside the door.

"I, um . . . how do I flush the toilet?"

"Don't worry about it," he says. "I'll take care of it."

Um, no. No, you won't. "That's okay. I'll do it. Where's the handle?"

"It's a composting unit," he says.

A *what* unit? I stare at the toilet, feeling annoyed with it, then turn back to the door. "I'm sorry. What?"

"It's not a regular toilet. You don't flush it."

Huh. Okay. I *am* from San Francisco, so I have

obviously seen low-flow toilets. But a composting toilet is new to me. I sigh and decide to fight the flush-my-own-pee battle another time.

Reaching for the sink faucet, I find there's only one lever, and when I turn it on, my hands are jet-blasted with a rush of freezing-cold water. I yelp with surprise, quickly turning off the water and staring at the tiny sink like it has hidden fangs.

"Okay in there?" he asks.

"Your water's very . . . cold." *Like, Arctic cold.*

"It comes from a cistern on top of the house," he explains. "Gets chilly at night."

Hmm. No electricity and no plumbing. Is he Amish? Where the hell am I anyway?

"I see," I say, though my questions are piling up like crazy. I'm about to ask one, in fact, when I look up to see the face looking back at me in the mirror.

Oh, sweet Jesus.

It's me.

My lips part, and for a second I feel dizzy, looking back at a stranger.

My face is bruised, with cuts and scrapes, and my lips are puffy and scabbed where they were split. On my forehead there is a white bandage. I pull on the corner to find an ugly gash beneath and quickly re-cover it with the dressing.

Taking a shaking breath, I lift the T-shirt I'm wearing and count six separate bandages on my left side. Some are stained with blood that has seeped through and dried. Tears start falling as I realize how badly battered I am. It's too much to process.

"Brynn? You okay?"

"I'm . . . I'm . . ."

"Hey, um, can I come in?"

I can barely speak from crying but manage to croak, "Okay."

He opens the door carefully, looking in without opening it all the way. When he sees me looking at myself in the mirror, he sighs. "Aw, Brynn."

"He . . . he really h-hurt me."

Cassidy nods in sympathy, but his eyes narrow and his jaw flexes. I think he's controlling his anger for my benefit, and something about witnessing his restraint makes me feel safe, makes me feel stronger.

"I . . . how long will it take for them to heal?"

"Stitches can probably come out in two weeks."

I take a shaking breath, anxious to change the subject. Looking down at the underwear I'm wearing, I slide my eyes back up to Cassidy.

"You changed my underwear. I was . . . naked."

His eyes widen as he stares at me in surprise, his Adam's apple bobbing. "I had to."

I need to know that he didn't abuse the power he'd had over me. "*Had* to?"

He nods.

"*Had* to. Not . . . *wanted* to?" I ask, holding his eyes.

"I didn't . . .," he whispers, his cheeks flushing, his breathing quickening. "I didn't hurt you."

That's a weird thing to say, I think.

"Hurt me? What do you mean?"

He shakes his head vigorously. "I would never hurt you."

He's so focused on this notion of "hurting" me that he doesn't seem to understand what I'm asking him: I want to know why he took off my underwear. Because I wasn't conscious when it happened, and I don't know him well enough to trust him with my naked, unconscious body, I need for him to tell me about it now. I don't want a black hole in my memories.

"Cassidy, *why* did you take off my underwear?" I ask him directly.

"Because it was bloody," he says. "You'd been stabbed through the fabric."

My heart drops. Of course. "Oh."

Then he blurts out, "And then I had to take them off again when you soiled yourself. I couldn't just let you . . . let you . . . lie in . . ." He gestures with his hands, dropping his eyes to the floor as his cheeks flush with color.

I blink at his chest as I process his words.

Oh, my God.

I shit or pissed myself, and he *had* to change my underwear. When he said "had to," he meant it literally. And now I am ready to die of embarrassment. If a huge sinkhole suddenly opened up in this tiny bathroom and swallowed me whole, I'd be okay with that.

Alas, no sinkhole. Just Cassidy, who dealt with my bloody, shredded underwear once, and a disgusting mess in them later. No doubt he was trying to preserve my feelings by not mentioning either.

"Oh," I say weakly, my cheeks aflame. "You *had* to."

"That's what I said," he muttered. "Now come out of there and let me deal with the toilet."

For the first time since I've met Cassidy, his voice is cool. I've offended him, and I couldn't be more sorry. He carried me down a mountain to his home, sewed up my stab wounds, changed my soiled underwear, made me soup, slept beside me so I'd feel safe . . . and the first chance *I* get, I essentially ask him if he'd treated himself to a free peep show.

I'm ashamed of myself.

I reach for the doorknob, opening the door completely and taking a step toward him. Placing my hand on his arm, I squeeze gently and say, "Cass, I didn't mean to accuse you of anything. I . . . I had no right to question you. I'm sorry."

His eyes search mine with an intensity I can barely stand.

"You had a right," he finally mutters.

"I trust you," I say, surprised to discover I mean the three words without conditions or reservation.

"You probably . . . shouldn't," he says, his voice soft, low, and gritty, like he's straining for control. Then he sidesteps me, into the bathroom, and closes the door.

I stare at the door, my mouth open, wondering what he means. He's shown me nothing but kindness: *why* shouldn't I trust him? What has he done that merits my distrust? Nothing. And yet I am unsettled by the comment.

My head aches as I make my way back down the hall, and I'm breathless by the time I reach the living room, winded by just a few steps. I place my hand on the hallway wall, looking around the living room as I catch my breath.

Like the rest of Cassidy's house, it's small but tidy, clean, and comfortable. A couch with an outdated pattern sits against the wall to my left, facing six picture windows like the ones in the bedroom. The view of Katahdin is just as spectacular.

In front of the sofa, there is a coffee table on top of a braided rug, and the wood planking on the floor is clean and shiny. I realize that the fireplace to my right accounts for the wall of brick in my room—it's the backside of the chimney. On either side of the couch are end tables with lanterns, and over the couch is a large picture of an older man standing behind a young woman in her thirties. She sits on a stool, holding a little boy on her lap who appears to be about five or six.

I take two steps closer to the picture, to look at the faces, grateful for the sun breaking over the mountains, shining like a spotlight on the portrait. There is no doubt that the little boy is Cassidy, and the date on the bottom reads 1995. I do some quick math in my head and estimate his current age at about twenty-seven, which surprises me a little because he seems younger to me.

"Need some help getting back to bed?"

I turn to see Cassidy standing beside me.

"This is you?" I ask, looking back up at the photo.

"Yeah."

"Is that your mom?"

When he doesn't answer, I turn back to him. He nods but doesn't offer any additional information. His face is tight, almost like it's closing up before my eyes, which is strange, because the portrait isn't hidden or anything. It's right out in the open where anyone could see it. That makes it free game for conversation, right?

I turn back to it. "Is that your fath—"

"How about we get you back to bed now?" he says quickly, a sharpness to his voice.

"I'm not trying to pry—"

"I know," he says, holding out his hand to show me half of a blue pill. "But if you're going to take a painkiller, you should be lying down."

"Yeah," I say, looking at the pill longingly. "You're right."

He helps me to the bedroom and into the bed, giving me a fresh glass of cold water to wash down the pill.

"Sleep a while," he says. "When you wake up, I'll make you some eggs, okay?"

I nod. "Thanks, Cassidy. For everything."

He gulps, his eyes darting away from mine before returning to rest on them. They are so warm, so tender, my stomach flutters in a way I'd almost forgotten it could. I have a quick flashback to falling asleep in his arms, to waking up with my head resting on his heart.

"You're welcome, Brynn," he says in that low voice that sings Beatles songs like lullabies. Then he turns and walks over to the curtain. "I'll be here when you wake up."

Hee-uh.

Just like Jem.

Which makes me realize that I've been awake for a while now, and this is the first time Jem has even crossed my mind.

Chapter Fourteen

As soon as she is asleep, I take down the portrait of me and Mama with Gramp, wrapping it in a plastic garbage bag and placing it on the top level of the barn, where we store things we don't need but aren't ready to throw away.

Then I go back into the house and take down all the pictures of me and my family, grabbing a photo album on the coffee table on my way back to the barn. Though there are no pictures of my father in the house, I still don't want to talk about my family, because questions about my parents will inevitably arise. Heck, I couldn't even let her finish the word *father* before the pressure in my chest had me so panicked and light-headed, I'm surprised I didn't pass out.

And in the bathroom, before? When she lightly accused me of taking a peek at her naked body while she was unconscious? The guilt I felt . . . the fear . . . my God, I don't know how I remained standing.

The truth is, yes, I needed to change her underthings, but I also peeked. And worse, I wanted to. I desperately wanted to look at her—to see the tender, vulnerable curves and valleys of her body.

I want to look at her every minute she's in my presence. Drinking her in is quickly becoming an addiction.

Does that make me bad? Does that make me like Paul Isaac Porter?

I promised Mama and Gramp that I'd live quiet so I couldn't hurt anyone, but here I am with a woman living in Mama's room, and my heart feels bleak when I confess to myself that I like her. I feel myself growing attached to her.

I pull the curtain to her room aside and feel my whole body recharge just from the simple act of checking on her. The covers rise and fall as she sleeps with her dark hair spread out on the stark white cotton of the pillow. My heart swells until my chest feels tight, and I rub the place over my heart with my palm, wondering if—I mean, if there were a parallel universe in which I was allowed to consider a future with her—one day I *won't* ache with reverence at the very sight of her. I wonder if I could ever take her for granted, and somehow I know I never would.

Not that it matters. My dreams of devotion are pointless.

I remind myself that during a human being's lifetime, their DNA methylation, or how genes are activated, is not static. For instance, a change in DNA methylation patterns can turn on a gene that should have stayed off, and cause cancer. Should my methylation change over time, the wrong gene could be turned on, and I could become a serial killer. I have no way to know and no way to prevent such an outcome.

But . . .

Live quiet, and no matter what happens inside of you, you won't never be able to hurt someone, Cassidy.

I close the curtain to shield Brynn from my view and turn to face the living room. A low bookcase is built into the wall under the windows looking out at Katahdin, and the shelves are full to bursting with books about heredity, DNA, nature versus nurture, neurobiology, coding and decoding, gene expression and regulation.

I have read every single one, but the answer I want—the answer my mother so desperately searched for—isn't in any of them. There are no guarantees, and only a monster would gamble someone else's life when the possibility of a tragic outcome is so much higher than average.

My fists clench by my sides in frustration.

I need to *do* something. I need a release.

Shrugging angrily out of my flannel, I throw it on the floor, then pull my T-shirt over my head and step outside, into the cool morning. I cut down two trees the week before last, and both need to be chopped for firewood.

It feels good—relieving—to swing the ax again, the physical exertion welcome after three days of sitting by Brynn's bedside and sleeping semi-supine last night beside her. As the steel blade splits the wood, I let myself think about last night for a few minutes.

The way it felt to hold a woman in my arms, the overwhelming feelings of protectiveness and gratitude that I have now experienced—it's something I never want to unknow. She will leave someday soon, but I will hold on to those memories forever. I will be grateful for them, for the opportunity to relive the night I fell asleep with a woman, with Brynn asleep against my heart.

I flick a glance at the house as I lean down to lift another large, circular log.

She's as weak as a kitten right now, and I'm still not sure she's out of the woods in terms of infection. If all goes well and she manages to escape infection, the stitches can come out in seven or eight more days, but I wouldn't trust them on the back of my ATV for another two or three weeks after that. Which means that we still have about a month together.

A month.

I swing back and bury the ax in the chopping stump, then reach down to collect what I've split, relishing the punishing texture of the bark against my bare forearms and chest. It's a reality check I need. Walking over to the six-foot-high pile of logs behind the barn, I lift the tarp that keeps it dry and add the pieces I'm carrying.

A month with Brynn.

Why this hasn't occurred to me yet is beyond me—probably because I've been totally consumed with her survival and haven't had time to map out the immediate future.

If I feel like this about her after three days, how in the hell am I going to feel after four weeks? Lord, I need to come up with some strategies to ensure I don't become any more attached to her. I need to figure out how to keep my distance.

I flex my muscles in the morning sun and reach up to the sky, appreciating the burn caused by an hour of chopping.

Hmmm. That's one thing I can do: I can stay busy.

Really, I can't even afford the time I've already lost sitting by her bed. The garden and animals need daily, constant tending, wood needs chopping, and I should be making those summer repairs to the house. The windmill behind the barn could use some maintenance, the solar panels need a good cleaning, and I should tinker with the brakes on the ATV a little. If there's no time to sit and gaze at her like a lovesick pup, it'll be easier not to develop feelings.

Another idea: I can stay out of the house. She can have the house for the next few weeks; it'll be her domain. I don't even have to sleep in my bedroom, at the end of the hallway, just past the bathroom. I can sleep in the sleeping porch back behind the house, piss in the woods, and use the outdoor shower. I'll stay out of her way when I use the kitchen once or twice a day, or maybe I'll go the extra mile, pack up meals for myself all at once and keep them in the root cellar under the barn. Then I won't have to go inside the house more than once or twice a week unless it's raining real hard. And even then, I suppose Annie wouldn't mind a night of company in her small, leaky barn.

"You don't want to get more attached," I tell myself aloud as I head back to the stump. "Intense feelings can lead to changes in behavior, so stop being stupid. Does she need to be here? Sure. For now. But she's not your houseguest. And she's certainly not some potential love interest. She's just a girl who got into some trouble and needed your help. Soon she'll be gone."

I'll still have to interact with her, of course—especially over the next three or four days. She'll need help cleaning and changing her dressings. And while she's recovering in Mama's bed, I'll need to bring her food and drink. But once she's well enough to tend to herself, I'll make myself scarce until it's time to take her down to Millinocket.

Feeling stronger, though undeniably melancholy, I pull the ax from the block and place another full-size log on the stump for chopping.

***

I shuck off my jeans and stand under the outdoor showerhead, grabbing a bottle of Dr. Bronner's liquid soap from a small shelf affixed to the side of the house and pumping a handful into my palm. I work it into my hair, then rinse. It doesn't make a lot of bubbles because it's biodegradable, but it still does the job.

I'm still working through the last few cases of gallon bottles that Gramp bought. If I mix the concentrated Castile soap with water in a foamer bottle, it lasts ten times as long, and I only end up needing to use two or three gallon bottles a year. Sometimes it feels like I'll never run out, and I wonder if that was Gramp's intention—to stock me for life so I'd never have reason to leave.

I run my hands over my soap-slicked pectoral and abdominal muscles, which are hard and well defined. As my fingers slip over my nipples, I have a sudden mental flashback to Brynn's, which were dusty pink and delicate. I only saw them for a moment before I forced myself to look away, but they were perfect, and seeing them with my own eyes was the most erotic moment of my life.

Suddenly, the blood in my head races down to my pecker, making it stiffen and grow. I close my eyes and flatten my hands against the house, letting the cold water run down my back while I give into the feeling of sexual excitement. It's not something I experience regularly, and even when I do, I try to control it.

My father's hobby of raping his victims prior to murdering them makes me cautious in my approach to my own sexuality. Even when I allow myself to feel some brief physical pleasure, I rarely allow myself to totally surrender to it.

Mama and Gramp never sat me down and discussed reproduction with me, though I had a crash course when I came across two of our goats—Hector and Dolly—one fall morning when I was thirteen. I watched in fascination as Hector mounted Dolly over and over again, sticking his pink, pencil-thin penis into her rear. I had no idea that Dolly's kids the following spring were a result of this exercise, but I understood that the act of sex was something that happened naturally among living things.

A larger share of my education came when I was sixteen. Gramp returned from his monthly trip to the Millinocket post office with three magazines in a brown paper bag and handed them to me.

"I know you ain't goin' to meet a girl out here, but I figure every man should at least know what his pecker's for."

Inside the magazines were pictures of naked women— some in sexual positions with men and other women, and plenty of accompanying narratives about what was going on between them. I masturbated for the first time staring at the pictures in those magazines, though I felt guilty afterward, uncertain if what I'd just done was right or wrong.

I still have an ambiguous relationship with my own sexuality. I know I am heterosexual, and there are parts of me that long to be sexually active with a woman, but at this point my personal desires are so tangled up with my fears about turning out like my father that it's a love-hate relationship.

Right this second, though, as cold water slips down my back, and my rigid length strains against my stomach? It feels more like love than hate. As I remember Brynn's body while stroking my own, it feels like its own kind of worship, and I allow it. Letting my head fall back, I think of the gentle weight of her body on my chest, the sound of her laughter when I "knocked" on the curtain, and the touch of her hand on my arm when she apologized to me this morning . . .

I cry out, closing my eyes and coming in hot spurts against the side of the house, breathless and panting.

I don't want to open my eyes.

I don't want to feel bad about something that feels so good.

I don't want to feel ashamed for touching myself and

drawing pleasure from my body.

I don't want to feel guilty about thinking of Brynn as I climaxed.

More than anything, I don't want to be Paul Isaac Porter's son . . .

. . . but I am.

I open my eyes, cup water in my hands, and throw it against the side of the house to erase any traces of my orgasm. Then I turn off the water, wrap a towel around my body, and head back inside the house with a heavy, unsettled heart.

***

After I chop wood, milk Annie, and shower, I go back outside to collect eggs from the girls—Macy, Casey, Lacey, Gracie, Tracey, and Stacey—avoiding a peck to the hand by Tyrannosaurus Rex, the lone rooster, who is protective of his hens.

I get eight eggs in all and bring them inside to the kitchen. The clock over the sink says it's ten o'clock. That's four hours from when Brynn took half a Percocet. Although the pills are supposed to have a three-year shelf life, I've kept the bottle in the cellar, where it's cool and dark, and they appear to be managing her pain, though the pill should be wearing off right about now. I'm hopeful that when she wakes up she'll be ready to eat something substantial. She hasn't had a proper meal since I found her.

I crack all eight eggs into a bowl and add some of Annie's milk. She's a LaMancha goat, so while her milk isn't creamy, it's a decent approximation of whole cow's milk in consistency and sweeter than milk from Saanens or Oberhaslis, both of which we've kept in the barn at different times.

Whisking the eggs, I add a little salt and pepper, then

place Gramp's old cast-iron skillet on one of the burners. The twenty-inch stove has a battery ignition but cooks with propane, and if I'm sparing—using it once a day—I can go for months without needing to refill the tank.

I pour a drop of olive oil in the skillet, then add the eggs, inhaling deeply as they sizzle and scramble. Taking two plates from the cabinet, I place them side by side on the counter, marveling at them for a quiet moment. I am cooking for two people today, something that I haven't done in such a long, long time.

"What's for lunch, Mama?"

"Fetch two plates for me, Cass. I'm makin' grilled cheese."

I pull a chair to the sink and climb up so I can reach the cupboards.

"Mama, when am I goin' back to school?"

It's been a year since the incident with J.J. and Kenny in the bathroom, and I keep waiting for her to tell me we're moving back to town.

I open the cabinet and pull out two stoneware plates, holding them in my hands as she inhales sharply enough for me to hear.

"Never," she finally says, buttering the four pieces of bread on the cutting board roughly, angrily. She clears her throat, looking up at me. Taking the plates from my hands, she lowers them to her sides, which makes her hands look like big white Frisbees. "You remember yore . . ." She pauses, looking at my face carefully. ". . . daddy?"

"Not so well," I say.

I have some memories of him, but they're few and far between, and none of them makes me feel happy. He was just someone who appeared every so often and then left again. I never knew him. Not really.

She nods, looking down at the floor. "Come on down from there."

I hop to the floor and drag the chair back to the table. When I turn back to the counter, Mama has tears running down her face.

Suddenly she raises the plates over her head and drops them to the floor with a furious scream.

Openmouthed with shock, I stare at her, wondering what to do. Shards of broken white ceramic are scattered across the floor, and she sobs softly, her shoulders trembling, her lip quivering.

"He's gone, Cass," she whispers, raising her eyes to mine. "Someone . . ." She whimpers softly. "He's gone now."

I know that my father was arrested and found guilty of hurting some ladies me and Mama never met, and I know that he was set to die at some point. I figure that point has now come and gone.

The thing is? I don't much care. I don't care that he's gone. If anything, I'm glad. He scared me more than I ever loved him, and I much prefer living here with Mama and Gramp. But seeing Mama this upset makes my guts tighten.

"Mama?"

She turns to me, placing her hands on my arms and looking deeply into my eyes. "Am I the stupidest person livin' on God's green earth?"

I shake my head. "No, Mama. You're the best person livin' on God's green earth."

She yanks me into her arms, hugging me tightly as she presses her lips to the top of my head. "You're good, *Cass. Remember that. Always remember that. You're a* good *boy. Be good. Stay good, Cassidy . . ."*

". . . Cassidy? Cass?"

Someone is calling my name.

"Coming!"

I turn off the burner, pull the eggs from the heat, and go check on Brynn.

Chapter Fifteen

<u>Brynn</u>

When I wake up, my hip hurts. Sharp pains alternate with a dull, burning throb, but I suppose pain is to be expected when you're healing from injuries like mine. *Don't be a baby, Brynn. Be strong.* To distract myself, I breathe through my nose, and my mouth waters. Someone is making food, and it smells *beyond* delicious.

"Cassidy?" I call as my stomach growls loudly enough to wake the dead. "Are you there?" No answer. "Cassidy? Cass?"

"Coming!"

I brace my hands on either side of my hips, lift my head, and slide back a little into a sitting position by the time he pushes the curtain aside.

I have seen his face several times now, but I am struck by its singularity all over again. It's not just his fascinating mismatched eyes, or those three beguiling beauty marks that tease me. It's not even how tall and strong he is, though he's wearing a T-shirt that shows off his insanely toned arms, with the muscle definition of a lumberjack.

It's a lot more than how he looks. It's that my heart has been moved by his kindness to me—by the fact that he has saved my life multiple times and continues to take care of me, a stranger. When I think of him carrying me on his back for hours and hours on end through that unforgiving rain, I want to cry until all the tears in my body are spent. I can't remember the last time I met someone so selfless. It makes my heart ache a little.

"Hi," I say softly.

"How're you feeling?"

I take a deep breath, and the burning in my side flares to an almost unbearable place. I hold my breath until it subsides a little. "It hurts . . . but I'm okay."

"I guess it'll be sore for a while." He tilts his head to the side. "Up for some eggs? They're fresh."

"Sure," I say with a grateful smile. "They smell delicious."

He disappears, only to return a moment later with a plate covered with scrambled eggs. My mouth waters as he sets the dish on the end table beside me, but I stop him as he turns to leave.

"Wait! Aren't you having some?"

He hooks a thumb toward the kitchen. "Yeah."

"Do you want to bring yours in here?" I ask, my voice hopeful.

He holds my eyes for a second, then looks away. "Thought I'd just eat quick. Lots of work to catch up on."

"Oh," I murmur, surprised by how disappointed I feel.

"Hey," he says quickly. "Sure. I can . . . I can take a break. I'll bring mine in here with you."

His jeans are worn, and he wears them low on his hips, I notice, as he walks back toward the kitchen to grab his plate. When he moves, I can see a strip of tanned skin between the jeans and his shirt, and I feel my cheeks flush as he turns around and catches me gawking, though there's no look of teasing or triumph on his face. It's almost like he didn't notice, or that he's so modest, he didn't correlate my ogling with his muscular body.

I pick up my plate and am digging into the eggs when he returns and takes a seat in the rocker on the other side of the end table.

"This is, oh . . . mmm," I say, swallowing a mouthful.

"The girls do good work," he answers, taking a smaller and more polite-size bite of his own.

The girls? "What girls?"

"Macy, Casey, Lacey, Gracie, Tracey, and Stacey."

My fork freezes halfway to my mouth, loaded with fluffy yellow goodness. *"Who?"*

"Macy, Casey, Lacey, Gracie, Tracey, and Stacey." He chuckles softly. "The hens."

My brain acknowledges that he's talking about chickens, but my heart is completely distracted by the soft, low rumble of his laugh. *Do it again. For the love of all that's holy, please laugh again.*

"The girls rhyme," I observe, taking another bite.

"Yes, they do," he agrees, but he doesn't laugh and I feel cheated.

"Did you name them?"

He nods.

"Very interesting."

"How so?"

"You don't look like the type to name your chickens all rhymey and silly."

"Are you saying I'm no fun?"

I shake my head, grinning at him. "Just serious."

"Is that bad?" he asks, looking at me closely, like he expects an honest answer.

"Not to me," I say. "I like serious."

He turns back to his food, but I think I see the corner

of his lip twitch like maybe he approves of my answer, though he doesn't say so. I shovel the last of my eggs into my mouth and put the plate back on the table.

I think I've been here for about four days now, but I'm not sure. Either way, I should probably call my parents and let them know I'm not dead.

"Cassidy, can I use your phone?"

He jerks his head to look at me. "Telephone?"

I nod. "Landline or cell. Whatever you've got handy. I want to call my parents and let them know I'm okay."

He shakes his head. "I don't have a telephone."

I feel my face go slack. *No phone? I've never heard of such a thing.* "What do you mean?"

"I don't . . . I mean, I don't have anyone to call," he says simply, spearing another bite of egg.

"No family?"

"Might still have a great-uncle over in New Hampshire, but we lost touch a long while back."

No family? No friends? I'm about to pry, but force myself not to. Maybe he's taking a break from the world for a good reason. *Didn't I live like a hermit in my apartment for two years? Pot, meet kettle.* I have no right to pick at him.

"Okaaaaay," I say, working to control my curiosity. "Can I use your laptop?"

He stops chewing and stares at me. "You want to use my . . . lap?"

"Your lap*top*. Your . . . computer? I could e-mail them."

"Oh," he says, looking relieved as he swallows. "Computers. Right. Um, they have computers in the library over in Millinocket, but I never tried them."

"You don't have . . ." I'm staring at him, and I know it's rude, but I'm in such a total state of shock, I can't help it. "You don't have a computer or a cell phone or a landline?"

"What is that?"

"A landline? It's a phone on, um, you know, mounted to the wall? With a . . . a cord that—"

"Oh," he says, nodding. "A *regular* phone. Nope. No phone. Telos Road is four miles away. But there's no telephone line on Telos Road, because it's mostly just for logging access." His eyebrows furrow as he thinks about something. "Closest phone is at the Golden Bridge Campground and Store."

"How far away is that?"

"About fifteen miles. Three or four miles of bushwhackin' and another eleven or twelve on logging roads. Telos and then Golden."

"*Bush* what?" I ask, almost feeling like we are speaking two different languages to one another.

"Bushwhackin'. You know, riding through the woods. Rough trails. Not on roads."

"How do you drive if you're not on a road?"

"I have an ATV," he says, as if that explains it.

"You have what?"

"An *all-terrain vehicle*," he says, enunciating each word like I should know what he's talking about.

I stare at him, ignoring his tone, my mouth catching flies and my eyes likely turning like pinwheels as I put the facts together.

"Oh, my God," I murmur. "No phones. No computer. No roads. You're *totally* isolated here."

He nods at me. "Pretty much."

"Why?" I ask softly. "Why do you live like this?"

The question surprises me, especially because I've already resolved not to pick at him. It's indelicate, and I grimace at the vaguely judgmental note in my tone. I'm sure Cassidy has his reasons for living apart from society. It's

132

absolutely none of my business, and yet I'm leaning forward, staring into his eyes, my curiosity so sharp, I can taste it like metal.

He stares back at me, his unusual eyes locked on mine. Finally he licks his lips and looks down at his almost-empty plate. "It was my gramp's place."

"Oh . . . like a summer place?" I ask.

His cheeks flush, and he shrugs. I've made him uncomfortable when I really didn't want to.

"Are you a prepper?"

"A what?"

"Someone *preparing for the end of the world*?" I ask, enunciating every word because I figure turnabout is fair play.

He grins at me—caught—before looking back down at his empty plate.

"No, ma'am," he answers politely.

His smile, born of chagrin, is so beautiful, so welcome, I decide to keep the mood light and tease him into another. "Hey, you're not on the run from the cops, are you?"

My plan instantly backfires.

His head jerks up, and his face visibly blanches, his smile gone, his eyes wide and unsettled. It's such a complete transformation from a moment ago, I lean back, a chill slithering over my skin as I process his reaction.

"Oh, God," I murmur, my hands fisting in the quilt that covers me from waist to toes. "Are you?"

"No!" he says, shaking his head vehemently. "I'm not . . . I'm not in trouble with anyone. Not the authorities. Not anyone. I stay *out* of trouble. I live quiet. I . . . I can promise you that."

I know he's telling me the truth—don't ask me how I know, I just do—though I sense there's a *much* larger story behind his words. Maybe he was accused of something he didn't do? Or maybe he had a run-in with the cops that ended badly for him? I feel like I'm looking at the tippy-top of a massive iceberg, and my curiosity is so sharp, I'm going to bleed inside from all the questions I want to ask. I opt for one:

"Are you hiding from someone?"

"No. Not really." His eyebrows crease and he sighs, the color returning to his cheeks. "I just . . . I just like living out here, is all. I won't . . . I won't hurt you, Brynn. I'm not some psycho. Not yet, anyway. I promise."

Again the assurance that he won't hurt me.

It has to be the fifth or sixth time he's said this.

Maybe it's more than a fear of authority—maybe he's misunderstood. Maybe he has Asperger's or a social anxiety disorder. He's smart, and he's obviously skilled in living out here. He's kept himself isolated for a long time.

He's different, I think, remembering that he carried me to safety on his back. And kind. And beautiful. And I'd like to pull him out of his shell a little, which almost makes me laugh. Me, Brynn Cadogan, self-isolated for two years now, eager to pull someone else out of their shell. Oh, the irony.

I look up at him, and I'm sorry that his face seems troubled. I've touched a soft spot, and I'm anxious to make amends.

"Hey, Cass," I say, reaching out to nudge his knee with the back of my hand. "I know you won't hurt me. Why would you go to all that effort to save me if you just meant to hurt me again? You don't have to keep saying it." I pause as he looks up at me, an inscrutable expression brightening his eyes. It looks like hope, and I have a notion that my words are like the sun and Cassidy is like a sunflower after ten straight days of rain. "I trust you. You've been really good to me. Really *amazing*. I *trust* you, Cassidy. Okay?"

I'm not sure, but I think he's holding his breath as I finish speaking, and it's so touching to me, I feel my heart pinch a little. My words *mean* something to him. Something important.

"Thank you, Brynn," he whispers, averting his eyes as he collects our plates. He stands from the rocking chair and looks down at me, his eyes searching mine. "Do you need me to call someone for you?"

"You'd have to drive fifteen miles each way to make a phone call."

"I'll do it," he says, his voice earnest, his face serious, "if you need me to."

"I can't ask you—"

"You didn't. I offered."

"You don't mind?"

He shakes his head. "I can pick up a few things while I'm there."

Relieved, I nod. "I'd really appreciate it, Cass. I'll write down my parents' number."

"I'll bring you a pen and paper," he says, turning to leave. Just before he disappears through the curtain, he turns back to look at me. "Would you like a book or two to pass the time? There's a lot."

"Sure," I say. "I'd love one."

"What do you like to read?"

Instantly my cheeks flush. My favorite kind of books are romances.

"Um . . ."

His lips twitch again, and I have a sense he's on to me. "I'll bring a few to choose from." And then he's gone.

A minute later he returns with half a Percocet, a glass of water, paper, a pen, and three books: *Then Came You*, by Lisa

Kleypas; *Potent Pleasures*, by Eloisa James; and *Welcome to Temptation*, by Jennifer Crusie.

He sets the obviously well-loved novels beside me on the table, and I eye them as I swallow the half-moon blue pill. Oh, he's *definitely* on to me.

"Will that cover you?" he asks with a small grin.

"Mm-hm," I say, taking the paper and pen he's offering me and quickly writing down my parents' phone number. I refuse to be embarrassed about loving romance novels. Anyone with half a brain loves romance novels, and the rest are lying. I hand the paper to him. "Their names are Jennifer and Colin Cadogan. Tell them I'm okay. I'll call them as soon as I can."

He nods, taking the paper from me, folding it three times and putting it in his back pocket.

"See you soon?" I ask, realizing, for the first time, that I'm going to be all alone, in the middle of nowhere, for the next few hours.

He nods, grimacing, as though he's just realized it too.

"See you soon."

Chapter Sixteen

<u>Cassidy</u>

I think about her as I ride over the rough terrain between my homestead and Telos Road. It's not a ride I enjoy most of the time, and I like it even less today. I don't relish leaving the safety of my hidden homestead, and I'm not fond of dealing with people in general. Plus, leaving Brynn all alone at the cabin makes me uncomfortable, but letting her parents worry about her doesn't feel right either.

The ride is physically demanding, and I use my whole body to stay balanced on the old quad as I dart through the woods, going faster than I should be because I'm anxious to get where I'm going and then back home.

Over the years of coming and going from my place to Telos Road, a trail of sorts has developed, though, to discourage visitors, I purposely never filled it with gravel or trimmed back the overgrowth. I want it to be hidden.

During the bumpy ride, my conversation with Brynn weighs on me. It illuminates how isolated from the world I have become. Heck, when she asked to use my laptop, I thought she was asking to sit on my lap for some reason, and imagining her there made my adrenaline rush so fast and furious, I felt weak for a hot minute. But apparently, a laptop is some sort of computer. And a landline is a regular phone, like the one we had in my house when I was little. And I know what e-mail is, because I spent a few hours at Millinocket Memorial Library last fall, and I saw signs about it over by the computers, but I wouldn't have the first clue how to use it.

What really jarred me, however, was her asking me if I was on the run from the law or in hiding. I know she was kidding. I could tell by the tone of her voice and by the fact that she was smiling when she said it, but it still felt a little too close to home. I mean, I'm *not* on the run, but I surely am hiding.

I dodge trees and brace my body for roots as I race through the woods, hating the very thought of . . . *hiding.*

Like I've done something shameful when I haven't.

I haven't given much thought to the way I live my life; I've just accepted it as a truth. I made a promise at age fourteen to live quiet, and I never really reconsidered that plan.

Now a part of me—the part that desperately hates being the son of a madman—wonders if there is any option other than hiding.

Loving a woman? Being loved by her? Having a family with her? Absolutely not. All impossibilities for me if I have any sense of morality, which I do.

But do I *have* to live alone in the middle of nowhere? Do I *need* to hide?

Maybe—just maybe, and I'll have to give the matter a lot more thought after I've said goodbye to Brynn—I could use some of Gramp's money to move away, to set myself up somewhere different, somewhere new. I could change my name, couldn't I? Sure I could. Legally, I don't *have* to be Cassidy Porter. I could go to the courthouse and change my name to Cassidy . . . Cassidy . . . *Smith*. Yeah. Cassidy Smith. If I was Cass Smith, I could move to Boston or New York or North Dakota or China. Heck, I could move *anywhere*. I'd be someone new, with a last name that meant nothing, far away from Maine, where no one would ever make a connection between me and my infamous father.

For a moment, *hope*—like I've never felt before—fills my chest. I can almost feel the shackles on my wrists cracking open from the force of it. *I could be free. I could be free. I could be . . . free.* My heart swells so big, it just about aches with longing.

There is a problem with this plan, whispers a voice in my head. I recognize the tone and texture of this voice. It's my conscience, and we're old friends. *The problem is . . . you're not Cassidy Smith. You're Cassidy Porter, Paul Isaac Porter's son. And you can never, ever forget it.*

As I near Telos Road, all that marvelous hope disappears like smoke from a pipe dream, because my conscience is right.

What if I somehow tricked myself, after a time, into believing that I actually *was* Cassidy Smith? What if I decided that Cassidy Smith was allowed to live his life in ways that Cassidy Porter was not? What if Cassidy Smith became the very person I have fought my entire life not to become?

Being me—*being* Cassidy Porter—is, in part, what keeps me in check.

My blood is my father's, and so is my name. And I am my father's son.

I am also my grandfather's grandson and my mother's son.

And if I become someone else, it will be a different sort of hiding: instead of hiding from the world, I'll be hiding from myself. Sure, there would be a certain type of freedom in leaving this life behind and starting another. But it would be a life built on nothing—on air, on wind, on nothing substantial, on willful self-deceit. Such a fake, impermanent freedom would betray the promises I made to myself and to those I loved—to those who loved me.

Only a man without character would build his life on a lie.

Only a bad man would risk the lives of others for his own pleasure or cheap-bought freedom.

I pause about six feet from the road, hidden by thick brush, letting the engine idle. I listen carefully for oncoming traffic. I want to be sure the road's empty when I pull out.

After several minutes of silence, I give the FourTrax a little throttle and engage the clutch, shifting into first gear and making my way up the sharp embankment and onto the dirt road.

I look behind me as I shift quickly into second, third, and fourth, heading south toward Golden Road. I should make it to the store in twenty or thirty minutes. I glance over my shoulder at the thick forest I've left behind, hoping I'll be back home in about an hour.

***

When I see the bright green roof of the log cabin–style Golden Bridge Store up ahead, I get butterflies in my stomach, like I always do.

I try not to come here more than once every two or three months. And when I do, I always wear my hat low and try not to call attention to myself. I don't buy anything out of the ordinary. I don't make conversation. I don't want them to remember me. I want to blend in with every other transient hiker on the AT. Nameless. Faceless. A wanderer.

I pull the quad into the dirt parking area and cut the engine, taking off my helmet and placing it on the seat. I grab a nondescript ball cap out of my back pocket and mash it on my head with the brim low.

When I open the door to the store, it's a mini assault to my senses.

It's jarring, as always, to be here.

To be anywhere that hums with humanity.

Inside, the air conditioner is blasting, and it smells of French fries, which makes my mouth water. This is how it is when I brush elbows with the world sometimes—it makes memories from my childhood come rushing back, and I remember little things, like sitting in the back seat of Mama's car while we go through the McDonald's drive-through. *McNuggets and fries.* It's been two decades, and my stomach still groans wistfully at the memory.

Grabbing a shopping basket by the door, I step quickly to the left and into a grocery aisle. I wasn't lying when I said there were a few things I wanted. Butter is a luxury I don't have very often, so I grab some from a dairy case. I get a six-pack of beer too. I don't use deodorant, but now that Brynn's staying with me, I probably should, so I grab a small canister that says "Old Spice," like the one Gramp used. They have a good stock of batteries, and I buy six packages of D's. Sixteen D batteries will power the portable TV and VHS player through two movies, and though my selection isn't great—*Jurassic Park, Forrest Gump, The Sandlot, Groundhog Day, Home Alone,* and *Toy Story*—and I've watched each at least a hundred times, maybe Brynn would like to watch one sometime while she's staying with me.

I sigh heavily, pausing to stare down at the deodorant and batteries, and remind myself that she's not my girlfriend, and we're not having some kind of demented courtship in my off-the-grid homestead while she recovers from stab wounds. Christ.

Don't start acting like Cassidy Smith, I tell myself, reaching into the basket for the deodorant so I can put it back on the shelf. But at the last minute, I drop it back into the basket, grab her a toothbrush, and move on to the next aisle.

I pick up some Crisco and olive oil for cooking.

I browse the aisle that has cooking supplies, but don't end up getting much. I have flour and sugar, which I use sparingly. Mixes that make brownies and cake are expensive luxuries I don't need.

Looks like Doritos has some new disgusting flavor that I need to try, so I grab a small snack bag and toss it into the basket.

They have a good selection of fishing supplies, and I decide to gift myself a new lure. I'm behind on my fishing and need to get up to Harrington and McKenna Ponds over the next week or two. I try to eat a lot of fresh fish in the spring and summer since ice fishing, though a skill set I have developed, is not one of my favorite activities. I'd just as soon go vegetarian every winter than sit on a frozen pond hoping for a bite.

I go back to the aisle where they have the deodorant and toothbrushes, and although I am well stocked with medical supplies at home, I pick up a few more things: a large bottle of alcohol, iodine, some nonstick bandages, medical tape, and a small bottle of ibuprofen. I figure Brynn should stop taking the Percocet in another day or two, and she might be glad to have control over her own painkillers.

My basket is pretty full by the time I get to the cashier. Luckily, it's a man working. I find women are much more likely to try to make conversation with me, while men just want to check me out and keep moving. Impulsively, I add two candy bars to the pile, pay up, and take my change.

As I'm about to lift my two sacks from the counter, I

remember that the entire point of this trip was to call Brynn's parents and I've almost forgotten.

"You have a phone?" I ask.

"Ain't you got a cell?"

"Um. Broken."

"Hmmph." The cashier turns toward the restaurant and yells, "Maggie, this guy's cell's broke, and he needs t'make a call."

Dang it!

All I want is to stay inconspicuous, and now everyone in the store is glancing over at me.

"To where?" yells Maggie.

"Where you callin' to?" asks the clerk.

In normal circumstances, I would tell him to forget it, grab my groceries, and run. But this isn't normal. There's an injured girl lying in my mother's bed, and I promised to help her.

"Um . . . Arizona."

"Arizona? Dang. *Long* long-distance. That's gonna be pricey, son."

"I, um, I'd really appreciate it if I could just . . ."

"Arizona!" he bellows toward his boss.

"No way!" she yells back. "Tell 'im to get his phone fixed!"

I flinch at this refusal, feeling frustration rise up within me. Looking up at the cashier, I say softly, "I'm willing to pay for the call."

"How much?" he asks.

"Ten dollars?" He looks at me curiously, but doesn't say anything. I add desperately, "Twenty?"

"Twenty bucks to make a phone call?" He reaches behind and pulls something from his back pocket, holding it out to me. "You can use mine."

I've seen people on hiking trails using their cell phones, of course, but I've never actually held one in my hands, and I have no idea how to use it. It's a little bigger than a credit card, but when I touch the screen, it lights up with little pictures.

"Thanks," I say, staring down at it.

"You can go over there," he says, gesturing with his chin to a bench between the restroom doors. "I'll watch your stuff while you make your call." As I turn to leave, he asks, "Ain't you forgettin' somethin'?" I stare at him. "The twenty?"

I reach into my pocket and take out a twenty-dollar bill, placing it on the counter between us, then head to the bench.

I sit down and touch my finger to the screen again.

It lights up with lots of colorful squares with a picture on each. Hmm. Oh. Okay. Maps. Weather. Clock. Contacts. Right. Okay. I look at each picture for the one that looks right and finally find it: a phone.

I press on the green box, and a keypad comes up. I quickly take the note from my back pocket and dial Brynn's parents' number, holding the phone to my ear. Hearing the sound of ringing is strangely familiar, though I haven't used a phone since I was nine.

"Hello . . ."

"Oh, hello!" I say, my heart racing with nerves. "I'm calling about—"

". . . you've reached the Cadogans. Jennifer and Colin are not here right now. Please leave your name and a message, and we will get back to you ask soon as possible. Thank you for calling!"

Oh. A message machine.

Beeeeeeeeeep.

"Yes. Hello. I'm calling about your, um, your daughter.

144

Um. Brynn. That is . . . I have your daughter. Well . . ." I gulp. I am not good at this. "Brynn is staying with me, um, here in Maine. She is, well, she was injured climbing Katahdin. But don't worry. I patched her up, and now she's on the mend, um, so you don't have to worry. She doesn't want you to worry. Um. Yes. That's all, I guess. She'll, um, call you when she can. Okay? Okay. Goodbye, then."

I pull the phone from my ear and stare down at the keypad. Beneath the numbers is a red End button, so I press that, and the main screen, with all the colorful little squares, returns.

So easy. Almost insanely *easy.*

Looking up at the clock on the wall across from me, I realize I've been in the store for over half an hour, which means I've been away from Brynn for well over an hour now.

I jump up and return the phone to the clerk with a hasty thanks. Then I grab my bags, tie them to the back of the quad, gas up, and head north for home.

***

Two hours later, I finally arrive back at my cabin.

It shouldn't have taken so long, but I got cocky on the return trip, anxious to get back, and instead of going around a bad mud bath, I tried to go through it. Unfortunately, I also got stuck, which meant I had to use the winch, fastening it around a tree and pulling the quad out of the muck. Now I'm covered with mud and so are at least half the things I bought. But heck, I guess it can all be rinsed off, including me.

I park the ATV in the unused stall beside Annie, put the muddy grocery sacks on the front porch, and head to the outdoor shower. I strip down and wash off the mud, soaping up and rinsing quickly because I'm anxious to check on

Brynn. I'm sure she's asleep, but I'll feel better when I see her chest rising and falling easily under Mama's quilt.

Slipping naked back into the house, I race through the living room and down the hallway, to my room. I throw on clean jeans and a T-shirt, then head back to Mama's room.

I know something is wrong—*very* wrong—right away.

Brynn's been living with me for four days now, and I know she doesn't talk in her sleep. But as I approach her room, I hear her mumbling.

"Jem. Jem. Oh, nooooo," she mutters, her voice breathless with panic, breaking on tears.

Pushing open the curtain, I find her in bed, lying on her back. But her face is bright red, and the hair around her face is damp, sticking to her glistening skin.

"No," I mutter, lurching forward to press my hand to her forehead. "Shoot! No!"

Her skin is hot. So hot. *Scary* hot.

"Jem?" she says, opening her heavy eyes. "I should . . . have . . . been there."

"I'm getting you a cold cloth," I say, leaving her to run to the bathroom. I grab a hand towel and douse it in cold water, then hurry back to Brynn.

I shouldn't have left her. *Damnation*, I shouldn't have left her.

Kneeling beside her bed, I press the towel to her forehead.

One of her wounds must be infected. I need to take a look at them, then get some ibuprofen into her to fight the fever.

"Jem," she mutters as her eyes flutter closed. "My . . . battery. Oh, noooo . . ."

I don't know who Jem is, but the profound sadness in her voice makes my insides clench with sympathy. Her voice sounds like mine after I lost Mama. Bereft. Lost. Alone.

"Brynn," I say gently, close to her ear. "It's Cassidy. You're safe. You're not alone. I'm looking after you, remember?"

"Jem," she sobs softly as tears trickle down her cheeks.

Leaving the icy compress on her forehead, I run to the kitchen and open the cabinet over the refrigerator, where I keep medical supplies in a plastic tackle box. I grab it and place it on the counter. I'm going to need to boil water too, which I generally do in the fireplace or outside, over the fire pit, but I don't have time to make a fire. I decide to use the propane stove instead. It'll use a lot of gas to get the water hot enough, but I don't care. I'll go back to the Golden Bridge Store next week to stock up on more propane if I have to.

I fill a pot with water, place it on the stove, and ignite the burner.

Uncertain of whether or not she'll be able to swallow pills, I crush four ibuprofen tablets between two spoons and mix them with goat's milk.

When I return to Brynn, I prop up her head and give her the milk, which she, blessedly, drinks without issue. Then I pull down the covers and lift her T-shirt to take a look at her incisions.

I see the problem immediately: around one of her many bandages is an angry-looking redness, and seeping through the bandage is a yellowish-brown discharge. I lean closer. It smells off too.

It hurts. . . but I'm okay.

Why didn't she say something this morning? She had to have been uncomfortable. Maybe the Percocet masked the pain? No. I'm only giving her half doses. Maybe she was trying to be brave by not saying anything?

147

She's your *responsibility, Cassidy. How did* you *miss this?*

And then I realize: I fell asleep beside Brynn last night before changing the dressings, and I was so distracted by my attraction to her this morning, I raced out of the cabin before I could tend to her. She's had the same dressing on for almost twenty-four hours, when it should have been flushed and disinfected last night or this morning. I'm lucky more of them haven't soured.

By fighting against my feelings like a self-centered, self-absorbed teenager, I've put her in danger.

That stops now, I tell myself. *You put her first. You take care of her. If you develop feelings for her, so be it. You can* un*develop them later, once she's gone. But as long as she's under your roof, she comes first, Cass. You hear?*

Furious with myself, I take the compress from her head, run to the bathroom to resoak it in cold water, and replace it on her forehead before checking on the boiling water. If the sutures have to be removed and the wound flushed with saline and resewn, I'll have to sterilize any instruments I need to use. Including a syringe. She's going to need a shot of lidocaine before I do anything.

When I return to her side, she's mumbling about Jem again.

Jem. Who is Jem?

I squat down beside her.

"Shhhh," I whisper. "Brynn, listen to me . . . you're going to be okay. You've got a little infection, and it started a fever. I'm sorry I wasn't here. I promise I'll make it better."

"Jem. Jem, I'm sorry," she murmurs. Then, so softly, I almost miss it, "Cass."

My heart stutters, and my breath catches as I stare at her face, at the tan freckles against her red skin. She has remembered me, even in her feverish state, and it makes something happen inside me. Something that I've never felt before rips through me at the speed of light. It is strong and true and heavy in such a good, light way that for a moment I feel like I could float away from the force of it. My lungs burn as I suck in a deep breath. My eyes water and I blink them rapidly.

I vow that I will never, *ever* let anyone hurt this woman again. Not Jem. Not Wayne. Not anyone. And definitely not me.

"Brynn," I say, my voice gravelly and shaking with emotion as I reach up and adjust the cloth on her forehead. I thread my fingers through her hair, smoothing it away from her hot face. "I'm here. I'm here with you."

"Casssssss," she sighs, drawing out the *s* in my name until it's just breath.

I can hear the water boiling, so I return to the kitchen and put two needles, a spool of fishing line, a syringe, scissors, tweezers, and several cloths into the water. Then I bring it all, along with the medical box, back into Brynn's room.

I've known the devil in my lifetime.

I'm fairly certain that a part of him still lives inside me.

But I'll gladly do battle with him now to make her well again.

Chapter Seventeen

<u>Brynn</u>

I'm so sorry, Miss Cadogan, but we need to speak to you . . .
Is there a Jeremiah Benton residing at this address?
Can we come in?
Can you sit down, miss?
A band called Steeple 10 was playing tonight at the . . .
We regret to tell you that Mr. Benton . . .
Is there someone we can call for you?
Miss Cadogan? . . . Miss Cadogan? . . . Miss . . .

Why my brain forces me back to that night, I don't know. I wish it didn't.

There are so many other times of my life I'd rather revisit, but this one always seems to win out. The well-intentioned female detective. The male officer in his dark blue uniform with a seven-sided star over his heart. The black-and-white squad car outside, on the street in front of our house, blue and red lights swirling, painting garish shadows on the walls.

But breaking through my memories, I hear another voice telling me that I'm safe, that I'm not alone, that I'm going to be okay.

It's new, but I trust it.

It's like the voice of God breaking through the cold,

dark hell of my worst nightmares. And suddenly I am warm again. I am *so* warm. *Should I be this warm, Cassidy?*

Cassidy. Cass.

In my mind, I search for the face that matches the voice, and I see a clear stream with a blue stone and a green stone sitting side by side, glistening on the sand just beneath the still water.

I'm here. I'm here with you.

"Cassssssss," I whisper, my voice light-years away. *Help. Oh, Cass, please help.*

There is a soft ripping sound, like someone pulling tape from skin. Under the sound of my scream, I hear him groan.

Something's wrong.

I open my eyes, and his face is turned away from me, but his unkempt blond hair is familiar, and it comforts me.

"Cass?" I murmur. "Help."

He turns to me, those glistening stones blinking at me. "I will, angel. I promise." He exhales. "This is going to pinch."

I cry out as I feel a fresh stab of pain in my hip near the burning.

"That was lidocaine," he whispers, wincing like it hurt him too. "It'll numb up the area. I have to take out the stitches, flush it, and resew it."

I close my eyes and try to breathe through the pain.

"I'm sorry, Brynn. It got infected. But I'll fix it. I promise. Won't take long. A few minutes."

But in reality, it takes only a few seconds, because— thank the Lord and Baby Jesus—I pass out from the pain.

***

If I trust in you, oh, please, don't run and hide . . .

He's singing the Beatles to me again.

I open my eyes and find Cassidy in the rocking chair on

the other side of the end table, guitar in his lap, fingers gently strumming, eyes closed, lips moving softly.

"Cass?"

His hands freeze. His eyes open and slide to mine. "You're awake."

I nod. "Can I have some water?"

"Yep."

He places his guitar on the floor, reaches for a glass on the end table, and holds it to my lips as I lean up to drink. When I'm finished, he puts the glass back down and squats beside my bed.

"How you feeling, Brynn?"

"Like I've been through something," I mutter, letting my head fall back on the pillow. "What happened?"

"One of your incisions got infected," he says, his eyes heavy. He grimaces, looking down at the mattress between us. "I had to open it, clean it, and re-suture it."

"Doesn't hurt," I say, surprised to find I'm telling the truth. I don't feel it. I don't feel much of anything, in fact.

"I gave you a full Percocet," he says.

Percocet is a weird and funny word, I think, trying to focus my eyes on his face.

"Cass?"

"Hmm?"

"Are you a doctor?"

"No. But I'm as good as a certified paramedic."

"As good as?" I ask, turning my head slightly to look at him. The movement is sluggish, like my head's encased in molasses.

"I studied hard and took all the tests. I mean, I took them here from the back of a textbook, but I did good. I would have aced them in a classroom."

"Your eyes are . . . different colors," I note aloud.

His lips twitch like he wants to laugh, but doesn't. "Yes, they are."

Cocking his head to the side, he stares at me hard, like he's trying to figure something out.

"What?" I say, working hard to keep my eyes open. "Ask."

He clenches his jaw, and I don't see his hand reach up, but I feel it resting gently on my forehead, and I don't mind that he's touching me. "You're cooler."

"Is that what you wanted to ask?"

"Don't do that again," he blurts out in a rush.

"Do . . . what?"

"Be sick." He looks away, his jaw clenched and tight. "You *scared* me."

"You called me angel," I say sleepily, my eyes starting to close.

When did he call me angel? I can't remember.

His head jerks up and his breath catches. I hear it. I hear it . . . catch.

"It's . . . okay," I say on an exhaled breath, closing my eyes because I am just too damn tired to keep them open anymore. "I don't care . . . if you call me . . . angel."

"Brynn," he says. "I should have . . . I mean, I shouldn't have left you . . . I should have been here. I'm sorry. I'm so dang sorry."

"I was hot," I mumble. "Scared. Jem . . ."

"I'm sorry."

"Hold me," I whisper, "while I sleep."

I am drifting off, but I don't surrender until I feel the mattress dip under his weight and his body slide onto the bed next to mine. One arm slips under my pillow. The other falls gently just under my breasts.

"Good night, angel," he murmurs.

I breathe in the smell of Cassidy.

And then I sleep.

***

When I wake up, the sun is rising through the windows, and Cassidy is lying beside me. He's on his right side facing me, while I'm on my back. But in my sleep, I have turned my neck to face him, our noses almost touching. It's warm and intimate, and I am fully aware that we don't know each other very well, but it doesn't feel like that. I feel . . . I feel . . . I feel like I *trust* him, like I *need* him, like I *want* him.

Not sexually, although he is definitely a hot-looking guy, but *viscerally*. Like, for survival. He has become my lifeline, and without him I would have died too many times to count.

Suddenly, I have this existential notion that there can't be a me without a Cassidy. This thought isn't romantic or poetic. It just . . . is. But it's solid and real, and I don't mentally recoil from it. In fact, I lean into it . . .

There is no me without you.

. . . and it's not like anything I've ever felt before.

Unfortunately, I can't lie beside him and savor the feeling because my bladder is full again.

"Cass?" I say.

"Mmm?" he mumbles.

"Cass, I have to go to the bathroom."

"Yeah. Okay."

I lean back a little so I can look up into his face, and his eyes open slowly.

"Angel," he breathes, his eyes slowly focusing on mine.

Angel?

I hear myself chuckle softly. "No angels here. Just me. Brynn."

His eyes snap open now, fully aware, fully awake. "Oh.

154

Right. Yeah. Sorry. I just . . ."

"The bathroom?" I prompt.

He rolls to his back, swings his legs over the side of the bed and stands up. He rakes a hand through his hair, then offers me his hand.

I sit up and take it, surprised that the pain in my left hip is less than it was yesterday morning. Not that I feel great, but I don't hurt like the devil anymore.

"I feel better," I say, sitting on the side of the bed for a moment, bracing for the pain I'll undoubtedly feel when I stand up.

"Five of your incisions are looking really good. One's a problem child. I need to take a look at it after you . . . go."

I nod. "Okay."

Today I move to the bathroom a little faster, and it's not as strange to me as it was yesterday. I lower myself carefully to the toilet seat, remembering that I don't need to flush when I get up. As I am washing my hands in the sink, I look up at my face. It's still battered, and maybe I'm just used to it now, but I think it looks better than it did yesterday morning.

Good night, angel.

The words hum through my head.

Hmm. When he called me angel a few minutes ago, I assumed it was part of a dream he was having. But now I wonder—did he call me that on purpose?

"Cassidy?" I call as I open the bathroom door, but there's no need. He's in the hallway, across from the bathroom door, waiting for me.

"I'm here."

"What exactly happened yesterday?" I realize that there's a sizable gap in my memory, but during that time, apparently, I was given a pet name. *Angel*. But when? How did I earn it? What did *I* do? What did *he* do?

"What do you remember?"

I lean against the wall in the dim hallway, staring up at him. He's wearing jeans and a T-shirt, and I'm wearing his dead mother's underpants and T-shirt. It should make me uncomfortable, since we barely know each other, but it doesn't. It doesn't bother me at all.

I cut to the chase. "Why are you calling me angel?"

His eyes widen and his cheeks flush. "You said . . . I mean . . ." He rakes his hands through his hair.

"Here's what I remember: we had eggs, then you offered me some books while you went to the store," I say slowly, trying to create a timeline. "I was reading one . . . and then . . ."

"And then . . .?"

I finish quickly. "And then we wake up together, and you're calling me angel."

He sighs, dragging his bottom lip between his teeth before releasing it. "You had a fever yesterday. A really bad one. When I came home from the store, you were burning up."

Jem, I'm sorry.

Fuzzy memories start bobbing up from my subconscious. Intense heat. Memories of Jem. Cassidy taking care of me.

"I . . . I was pretty out of it?"

"You were. The fever didn't break until after midnight."

"I don't remember much. What . . . what was I doing?"

"You were talking about someone named Jem when I got here. Upset. You had an infection. I had to open one of the incisions, clean it, flush it, and resew it."

"My God." I am not uncomfortable that Cassidy tended to me, because he's given me no reason not to trust him, but I really don't like not being able to remember. "Are you a doctor?"

His lips twitched. "You asked me that last night. The answer is no . . . I'm, well, I'm sort of a paramedic."

"Sort of?"

He grins. "You asked me that last night too."

"And . . .?"

He grimaces. "I'm not actually certified . . . but I took the test and aced it."

Another strange Cassidy-ism. I'm starting to get used to them.

"Huh. Okay. So I was feverish and out of it, and you fixed me up . . . again."

He shrugs but nods, still standing across from me in the hallway. I suddenly realize that this is the longest I have been out of bed in days. It feels good too. The pain in my hip is achy, but not sharp and burning like yesterday. It's a dull and constant throb, and I know instinctively that this is good news, not bad. I'm healing.

"Thank you," I say.

"I shouldn't have left you," he says, frowning at me, his gaze intense. "I won't do that again. I promise."

His eyes, so intriguing, nail mine, and I feel the gravitas of his promise meet my body like something actual, like something . . . *physical*. It makes me so aware of him, I backtrack on my earlier thought about not wanting him sexually. I think maybe I do.

"It's okay," I say, my voice a little breathless.

"It *isn't* okay," he insists. "You're my patient, my . . . my guest. I should have been here for you."

I take a deep breath and can feel some of my stitches pull a little. "Seriously? You were doing me a favor. Stop beating yourself up."

He looks down at his bare feet, eyebrows furrowed, lips straight and thin.

"Cassidy," I say sharply. He looks up at me. "You saved me. Again. Thank you."

He gulps, staring at me hard before nodding. "I'll do better, Brynn. I promise."

I'm about to say that he's already doing great, but I sense we'll just keep going around in circles, so I don't. Speaking of circles, as much as I like being out of bed, I'm starting to feel a little dizzy now.

"I think I better get back to bed."

"Do you need help?"

"No," I say, starting back down the hall, toward the bedroom. "I'm good."

"Want half a Percocet?"

I shake my head, blaming part of my memory lapse on the strong painkiller. "I think I'll tough it out from now on, okay? I don't like being out of it."

"Brynn," he calls to me, just as I'm about to turn the corner.

I stop to face him. He's still standing across from the open bathroom door.

"You asked me a question."

He takes a few steps toward me, his bare feet silent on the carpeted floor. I try not to check him out, but the way his jeans are slung low on his hips almost gives me the shivers. He's tall and lean and muscular, beautiful in a messy way, and I don't know if this is some sort of fucked-up Florence Nightingale–style crush on him because he's taking care of me, or if it's more, but my heart skips a beat, and my stomach fills with butterflies.

"I called you angel at one point last night," he says softly, like he's confessing something to me. "I don't know why. I was . . . I was about to give you a shot of lidocaine, and I knew it would hurt. I called you angel just before I stuck you."

I don't have a memory of this, but it *feels* right, *sounds* right.

"I don't care if you call me angel," I say softly.

He grins at me thoughtfully, and I feel my whole body warm up in reaction to the small smile.

"That's what you said last night," he says lightly.

"I did?"

He nods. "And just so you know, I was in your bed because you . . . you *asked me* to hold you."

I don't remember asking him to do this either, but I know it's true. Not just because I trust Cassidy to tell me the truth, but because there is something so natural, so nice, so potentially addictive, about sleeping beside him that I long for it even now, after a whole night spent together.

"Thank you," I whisper.

His eyes are forest green and navy blue when he nods at me slowly.

I turn back to my room and crawl into bed, leaving the curtain open, and wishing he was next to me as I close my eyes and fall back to sleep.

Chapter Eighteen

<u>Cassidy</u>

After I make Brynn some toast with butter, sugar, and cinnamon, I spend the morning outside, milking Annie and mucking out her stable, and collecting eggs from the girls and vegetables from the greenhouse. I spray organic pesticide on the indoor plants, and change out the tray in the composting toilet, dumping what's been cultivated about a quarter mile from the house, in the fertilizer heap. I decide to leave wood chopping, cistern filter changing and treating, and solar panel cleaning for the afternoon.

At about noon, I head back inside to make some lunch and check on Brynn.

The curtain to her room is open, which must be her doing, since I've been careful to leave it closed, and I peek in to find her sitting up and reading *Then Came You*, by Lisa Kleypas.

Like most of the other books in the house, I've read it at least a dozen times, and though I prefer science fiction and fantasy to romance, it's among the better choices in Mama's old love story collection, which is why I offered it to Brynn.

Well, *that*, and because there is a quote in the book that I should keep in mind while Brynn is visiting: "Sooner or later everyone was driven to love someone they could never have."

A good reminder . . . especially since my thoughts are increasingly—heck, *constantly*—of Brynn. And my feelings for her? Growing exponentially. After last night's fever scare, I know that losing her will hurt. When she returns to the world, I will grieve the loss of my angel.

And you know what?

So be it.

All morning I have, more or less, resigned myself to that fate. I'll have a lifetime to get over her once she goes. I'm determined to enjoy her—her company, her smiles, her occasional chuckles, her warm body sleeping beside mine—while she's here.

Although, if I am honest, my warm and happy feelings for Brynn are compromised by another, darker, feeling that I haven't known in a long, long time: jealousy.

And one question has circled relentlessly in my head since yesterday:

Who.

Is.

Jem?

"Hi."

"Uh . . . oh!" I stutter. "Hi."

"How long have you been there?"

"Just a minute. Came in to check on you."

She holds up the book, then grins at me. "I like this one."

"Me too."

"Wait. What?" She smiles so wide, I wonder if it hurts her healing lip. "You read this?"

I shrug. "When you live out here, you read everything you can." *Five, six, seven, twenty times.*

"Huh," she says, still grinning. "It's good. He wants to marry her."

I cross my arms over my chest. "Should she marry him?"

"I don't know yet." She looks back down at the book. "I mean, I know she will because they're the main characters, but . . . I don't know. I'm not sure they'd be good for each other yet. She's wild and crazy. He's . . ."

"What?"

"Will he be happy with a wild woman? Or does he want some prim society girl?"

"I guess you'll just have to see what happens."

"I guess so."

I am so curious about Jem, I use this moment of speaking loosely about fictional relationships to try to figure out who he is.

"Were you ever married?"

"No," she says softly, her smile quickly fading.

Part of me feels like I should apologize and slink away for violating her privacy, but my jealousy, hot and low in my stomach, boils up, refusing to back down. I want to know. I *need* to know who he is and if he has a claim on her.

"Who's Jem?"

Her eyes widen, and she takes a soft, jerking breath. "W-what?"

"You mentioned his name yesterday when you were . . . out of it."

She nods distractedly, still staring at my face with sad, surprised eyes. "Oh. Right."

My arms are still crossed over my chest, and though I don't take pleasure in her distress, it's the collateral damage of assuaging my curiosity and, therefore, jealousy. Negative emotions like envy, anger, and greed frighten me because I feel sure that the seven deadly sins are even deadlier for someone like me, who has the blood of a murderer in his veins. Part of being Cassidy Porter means handling such feelings head-on and quickly, lest they become a gateway for behavior. I won't let them fester. I won't let them guide me into darkness if I can help it.

Realizing that I'm patiently waiting for an answer, she furrows her eyebrows, then says, "I was engaged to Jem. But he . . . he died."

Later I will feel ashamed of the sharp relief I feel at hearing her words. But for now? I let that relief cover me like a blanket, soothing the beast within me.

"I'm . . ." I uncross my arms and clear my throat. "I'm sorry for your loss."

She nods, reaching up to swipe at her eyes, which I now notice are glistening. "He was a good man. He was from here. Maine. Bangor, but we met in California."

"How long ago did he . . .?"

"Two years," she says, sniffling, then offering me a brave smile. "He was shot. He was, um, he was at a concert. He was caught in one of those mass shootings."

"Mass shootings?" I've never heard of such a thing.

She takes a deep breath. "It's when, um, someone goes to a crowded place and shoots a bunch of people. That's called a mass shooting." She exhales slowly, like she's forcing herself to let go of memories that hurt worse than any of her healing injuries. "I lost him."

My shame doubles as I realize I have forced her to talk about something incredibly painful just to satisfy my jealousy. Before now, I have never heard of a mass shooting, but for me, with only history as context, it conjures images of Nazi soldiers firing on innocent people wearing yellow stars pinned to their coats. The mental image horrifies me.

When I search her face, I see that same elapsed horror in her eyes. She has had to come to terms with this mass shooting concept—something so unspeakable, it should be impossible.

My heart aches for what she has endured.

"God, Brynn. I'm really, really sorry."

She gives me another brave smile and nods. "He was a good person."

"I'm sure he was, if *you* loved him."

"I *did* love him," she says softly. "I didn't want to live for a while after I lost him."

"I lost my mother to cancer," I hear myself saying. "I was close to her. It was . . . awful."

"How long ago?"

"Thirteen years," I say, though the number surprises me because it feels much more recent.

"How old were you?"

"Fourteen."

She winces, and a small sound of pain escapes her lips. Leaning to her left, she places the book on the bedside table, then reaches her hands out to me.

Gramp wasn't much for grieving. He loved my mother, and I know it hurt him to lose her, but he poured his grief into work, keeping busy and exhausting himself before bed every night. Me? I had no one to talk to, no one to hold me or let me cry about the parent I'd lost.

Except now . . . now here is this angel-woman holding out her hands to me in sympathy and compassion. I take them in mine, lowering myself to the bed beside her, drinking in the soft kindness of her eyes as she squeezes my hands.

"I'm sorry," she says. "You were so young. I can't imagine losing my parents. They've . . . I mean, they were

164

everything to me after I lost Jem." She gasps softly. "Hey! Did you manage to call them?"

"Your folks? Yeah. I left a message. I said you'd been injured, but you were okay and you'd call them when you could."

"You're very kind, Cass." She breathes deeply and nods, still holding my hands. "Your mom must have been amazing."

She's always been there for you, son.

Gramp's words from our talk in the greenhouse come back to me so fast, you'd think he just said them yesterday.

"She was," I say, wondering how bad it must have gotten for her in those years after my father's arrest and conviction. She never really talked about it, but it must have been hell. She would have been a pariah, and yet she protected me the very best she could.

"You okay?" asks Brynn, her voice gentle.

I look up at her and nod. "I don't talk about her much. It's . . ."

"I know," says Brynn. "It's sad. And it hurts."

I nod, amazed by her empathy, by her ability to understand how I'm feeling. Somehow it lessens the sadness in that moment. And the pain. As I look into her eyes, she smiles back at me, and the miracle of it is that it's possible I might be doing the same for her. That, by sharing our pain with each other, we aren't doubling it, but halving it.

"You know?" she says, squeezing my hands again. "He would have . . . he would have loved it here. Jem." She turns to the windows and looks out at the mountain. "Oh, man, he would have really loved this place."

"Yeah?"

"He loved Katahdin." She sighs softly, facing me. Her eyes drop to our joined hands, and she gently untangles hers from mine, pulling them away. "Can I tell you something?"

"Sure. Anything."

"The whole reason I was here was to bury his cell phone on the mountain. About a week ago, I took it out of an evidence bag for the first time, and I realized it had a smudge of blood on it. I came here to bury that small part of Jem up on Katahdin. I thought I should do that."

"That's what you were doing? When you were attacked?"

And suddenly I realize that last night wasn't the first time I heard Jem's name. I remember the first time I saw her—the way her friends kept asking her to turn back with them and the way she kept refusing:

I wish I could. But this is something I need to do . . . I'm coming, Jem. I'm coming.

"You were *burying* him," I whisper, running a hand through my hair as the pieces come together.

"Sort of," she says, unaware that I'd been watching. "His body was already buried, of course. But . . . I don't know. I guess I just wanted to say goodbye in my own way."

I think of Mama and Gramp buried side by side by Harrington Pond, and I understand exactly what she's saying. Saying goodbye to those we've loved and lost isn't just about burying them, but also about having a special place to remember them. Brynn wanted that place to be Katahdin.

"The phone was in my backpack," she says. "Didn't work out the way I hoped it would."

And now I understand completely.

She wanted to bury her fiancé on Katahdin, and the chance to make that happen had been stolen from her.

I feel anger bubble up inside me.

She should have been able to say goodbye to this Jem,

who meant so much to her, who was taken from her so brutally. Instead, she herself was attacked while pursuing that end.

My rage toward her attacker intensifies by the second until I'm practically shaking with it.

"Cass?" she says, cocking her head and looking at me curiously. "You okay?"

I jerk my head in a nod. I need to get control of myself. An emotion like anger stewing inside my body is no good for anyone.

"Want lunch?" I ask gruffly.

She nods and I stand up, looking out the windows at Katahdin's jagged peaks.

Don't sit on your anger, Cassidy. Don't let rage manifest inside you.

First chance I get, I'm going back up there for that phone so that Brynn can finish what she started.

***

Brynn's fever hasn't returned, and I've made it a priority to flush and re-dress her wounds every twelve hours. Though she still sleeps for long stretches, she's definitely on the road to recovery now. I figure I'll be able to remove the stitches in another week or so. We'll see.

Because she likes the company, most nights after dinner, I read in the rocker in her room while she reads in bed. Occasionally we share some funny bit of writing with each other, or some pretty turn of phrase. I've come to treasure these quiet moments together, reluctantly leaving her around midnight, once she's fast asleep and the uncomfortable spindles on the back of the wooden rocker start digging into my spine. She hasn't asked me to hold her while she sleeps again, though I silently long for the words, willing them to issue from her lips night after night. I don't know what it is I want from her—I don't allow my mind to wander to carnality, but have to fight against it heading there on its own.

I've never been with a woman, of course. I've never even kissed a woman. And despite those old magazines from Gramp, I'm not totally certain I'd even know what the hell I was doing, given a chance. But I'm a man, not a child, and I can't help my longings. When I head back to my cold, dark room after a warm evening in hers, it feels punitive somehow—much lonelier than it actually is. An ache rises up, and I have to fight the desperateness of my yearning to be near her. It's a certain kind of torture, but I wouldn't trade this time with her. Not for anything. I have a terrible feeling that these moments will be all I have one day, so I am very careful not to jeopardize them.

This evening, however, I'm not headed back to my room.

After I pull Brynn's covers up to her chin and dim the light in her room, I put on my hiking boots and grab Gramp's old miner's helmet from the closet in my room, placing it on my head. I fish his watch from the back of my underwear drawer and slip it onto my wrist, grateful that it winds because I wouldn't have the slightest clue how to get my hands on a watch battery. I set it to the correct time, then head quietly out of my room.

There is a closet in the hallway, and I open it. Inside are three rifles—mine from childhood, Mama's, and Gramp's—all of them oiled and ready. I take out Gramp's, which is the only one made for a full-size man, and sling it over my shoulder. It's unlikely that I'll need it, but I'll be in the dark forest, and Baxter Park has a good share of wildlife. Night hiking has its risks.

I look in on Brynn one more time, fairly certain that

she'll be asleep for the next six to seven hours. But just in case, I write out a note:

Went for a night hike. Back by dawn. —Cass

I leave it on her bedside table, then take a long look at her. Her chest rises and falls easily, and her closed lids flutter in the throes of REM sleep. She's peaceful. And I haven't a second to waste if I want to be back by sunrise.

"Sweet dreams, angel," I whisper, backing away silently from her bedside.

The last time I left her, she was in bad shape when I came home. But I know she's healing now. I don't have to worry about her fever coming back. And I know she sleeps pretty soundly once she's asleep for the night. No tossing and turning. No waking up at three a.m.

Besides, I need to do this for her.

And for me. Letting that rage sit and simmer isn't smart. And the only way to mitigate it is to do something about it. Something real. Something good.

I take a deep breath and sigh, hoping her backpack is still there to be recovered and knowing it's going to be a long night.

Chapter Nineteen

<u>Brynn</u>

When I wake up, the first thing I do is check for Cassidy in the rocking chair, but he's not there, and the house is quiet. The sun is higher than usual, so I'm assuming it's about seven o'clock, but I don't smell coffee brewing or eggs frying.

Stretching my arms over my head, I take a quick inventory of my body.

Face? Not hurting at all anymore.

Hip? Not hurting as much, though a dull ache persists.

Gingerly, I sit up and swing my legs over the side of the bed. Bracing my hands on the mattress, I lift my body, wincing a little at the pain. I know how to move around now to keep my discomfort at a minimum, but big movements, especially standing up or sitting down, still hurt.

As I steady myself for a moment, I realize there's a note on the bedside table. I pick it up. Hmm. Cassidy went out last night, but it's well past dawn, and I don't think he's home yet.

"Cass?" I call.

Nothing.

I walk to the doorway and call again, a little louder.

"Cassidy?"

Not a peep.

Trying not to blow his absence out of proportion—he *is* entitled to his freedom, after all—I make my way to the bathroom, pee, wash my hands and face, and walk back into the living room.

Up to now, I've always just returned to bed after using the toilet, but the house is so still, I pause in the living room, looking around.

Over the couch, the portrait of Cassidy and his parents is gone, as are any other framed pictures, which I find curious. He must be really protective of his past, and I tell myself not to pry, no matter how much I want to.

Taking a few steps into the room, I pass by the coffee table and check out the books lining the three long shelves under the picture window, starting at the far left and scanning to the right.

The top shelf is nothing but books on biology: *Your DNA and You, The DNA Files, Heredity and Genes, Tracing Your Genealogy, The DNA Challenge, Nature vs. Nurture: The Eternal Showdown, The Secret of Life, Untangling Your Genetic Code*, and on and on. A whole shelf, maybe twelve feet long, with every book on genetics that you could possibly imagine.

Are these Cassidy's books? His mother's? His father's? Was one of them a doctor? Or a geneticist?

I let my eyes drop to the next shelf, which is just as long and packed with books, but this time, it's all fiction. Romance is on the left, with a small space open where three books—no doubt the three in my room—are missing. Science fiction. Fantasy. General fiction. The shelf ends with a collection of hardcover books by John Irving, including my favorite, *A Prayer for Owen Meany*. Reaching forward, I take it from the shelf, flipping through the worn, dog-eared pages.

There is so much wisdom—so many beloved quotable lines—in this book. I hold it against my chest, determined to read it again.

The bottom shelf is not as organized as the top two. It's covered with a mix of genres—some poetry and hiking books, a few *Old Farmer's Almanac*s, and half a dozen books about Maine. And at the far end, there is a collection of videocassettes in puffy plastic boxes. When I was little, we had a VCR, and I had all the Disney Princess movies in similar boxes. I check out Cassidy's small collection, wondering which is his favorite. One of mine, *The Sandlot*, sits on the very end. I tug it from its place, flipping it over to read the back of the box.

But tucked between the clear plastic covering and the back cover beneath is a faded newspaper photo. The caption reads:

Seven-year-old Cassidy Porter, son of Rosemary and Paul Porter, of Millinocket, Maine, is carried on the shoulders of his teammates after he hits the winning run, leading the Millinocket Majors to the Maine State Little League playoffs.

I tilt my head, drawing the box closer, looking at the face of the little boy raised high above the heads of the others. He is smiling joyfully, arms over his head in triumph. He seems well liked by the other kids in the photo, which contradicts my possible theory that Cassidy lives out here because he suffers from social anxiety or awkwardness.

So why does *he live out here?* I wonder for the umpteenth time.

Why does he keep himself so isolated from society? From the rest of the world? What is he hiding from? Or running from? Or—

Wait.

I think about my words: Why does *he* keep himself so

isolated? What is *he* hiding from? Hmm.

I've been assuming that Cassidy moved here on his own. He told me this was his grandfather's place, and for whatever reason my mind decided that he inherited it as an adult and moved here.

But now I back up in my mental process, piecing together what I know to create a timeline of Cassidy's life.

First, there was the portrait that Cassidy removed. I recall that it was taken in 1995, when he was five. It was of him, his mother, and his much-older father.

Second, there is the photo of his Little League triumph, when he was seven. And the caption mentions his parents living in Millinocket, so they hadn't moved here yet.

Third, I know that Cassidy's mother died thirteen years ago, when Cassidy was fourteen. Since I'm staying in her room and wearing some of her clothes, I think I can safely assume she lived here when she passed away.

So he *didn't* move here as an adult. He moved here when he was still a child—sometime between the ages of seven and fourteen—presumably with his parents, but *definitely* with his mother.

Which means . . .

Cassidy wasn't the one who chose this lifestyle.

He just chose to *stay*.

Still hugging *A Prayer for Owen Meany* to my chest, I turn away from the books and head back to my room, wondering why he never returned to the world . . . and wondering why his mother left it.

***

I am on chapter four when I hear the front door open and close, and I'm surprised by the shot of adrenaline I get. I'm so happy, I feel like a firefly at dusk, bright from the inside.

Cassidy's home.

I hear him place something on the coffee table in the living room before appearing in my doorway, his body covered with dust and dirt, a mining helmet on his head.

"You're awake," he says.

"I am. You're back."

"I am," he answers grimly.

"How was your hike?"

He sighs. "Okay, I guess."

"What's the benefit?" I ask.

"Of what?"

"Hiking at night."

"It's quiet. Peaceful. I don't know." He shrugs off the question, looking irritated. "How're you feeling?"

"Fine. Better every day." But *he* seems out of sorts. "Everything okay with *you?*"

"I need a shower," he says, turning away. "Then I'll make you some breakfast."

"I'm feeling better. Really. I can help."

"Don't worry about it," he says over his shoulder, already walking away.

I watch him go, but I don't get the usual thrill from watching his tight ass saunter away. He's upset about something, and I find that bothers me a lot more than I would have expected.

Then something terrible occurs to me:

Maybe I've become a burden to him. Maybe he wishes I wasn't here.

Having to care for me means he doesn't have the freedom to come and go as he wants. He has to be back here every few hours to check up on me, and I've been here for a while now. How long? Four days? Five? Hmm. Three days unconscious. Three more since the fever. Plus today . . . Seven. Seven days. I've been here for a *week*, which means that today is—

"Oh, God," I murmur.

Today is June 26.

Today is Jem's thirtieth birthday.

I close my eyes and breathe deeply through my nose, filling my lungs as much as I can without pulling the stitches.

When I open them again, Katahdin stands tall and strong before me, and I am surprised by the deep sense of peace I feel staring back at it. Yes, my eyes are teary, but my breath doesn't catch and my heart doesn't ache.

Jem is gone. But I am still alive.

What happened with Wayne was horrifying, but being in a life-threatening situation made me realize that I want this life. I want it very much.

And I am grateful to Cassidy for preserving it.

I feel tears slide down my cheeks, but I let them fall.

Goodbye, Jem, I think, staring at the soft peaks of his favorite mountain. *I wish I could have left a part of you up on Katahdin, but I know there will always be a part of you there. Your spirit will find its way back to the place you loved above all others.*

"Brynn?"

I turn to see Cassidy—wet hair, bare feet, and a clean change of clothes—standing in the doorway. He scans my face, and his instantly registers distress.

"What's wrong?" he asks, covering the distance between us in two steps, his mismatched hawk eyes scanning mine. "Why are you crying? What happened? Are you okay?"

"It's Jem's birthday today."

"Oh." He sighs, sitting down slowly beside me, careful not to nudge my hip. "I'm sorry."

"Me too," I say, tracing Cassidy's face with my eyes.

He clenches his jaw, his gaze stormy as he turns away from me. "I went to look for it. The backpack. The phone."

"What?" I say, leaning forward a little, my breath catching, my heart racing.

"That's what I was doing last night," he mutters. "But I . . . I failed you."

My chest is so tight, so full, as I process this knowledge, I don't know what to do. My fingers dig into the sheets, curling like they're trying to keep themselves from . . . from . . .

"You *failed* me?" *By doing something so insanely kind and thoughtful?* "How did you *fail* me?"

"It was gone," he says softly, looking up at me with bleak, haunted eyes. "I looked all over—all over the lean-to and in the woods surrounding it. Underneath branches and leaves. I . . . I wanted to find it for you. I wanted you to be able to—"

My fingers fly from the sheets, and I lurch forward, flinging my arms around Cassidy's neck and pulling him against me. I am undone by the hugeness of his heart, by the unselfishness of his spirit.

"You w-went b-back?" I sob, close to his ear.

His arms wrap around me, holding me close, and I lay my cheek on his shoulder. My breath fans his neck as I cry.

His throat rumbles close to my lips, and I feel the vibrations of it as he speaks. "I . . . I went . . . I mean, I climbed back up, but it wasn't . . ."

"Oh, Cass," I whisper, closing my eyes, because now I am crying in earnest, my tears wetting his T-shirt. "You didn't have to d-do that!"

"I wanted to," he replies.

"Fourteen m-miles?"

"No. About twelve, round trip. I had to go a safer way when I was carrying you, and that added miles. The way I went last night was steeper. But faster."

"T-twelve m-miles," I say, my voice breaking. "For m-me."

His arms tighten around me, and we hold each other as to a lifeline. His face shifts slightly, and I think he is pressing his lips to my head, but I'm not sure. The thought makes a sharp sensation rip through me, and I clench almost-forgotten muscles deep inside, a wave of pure, carnal desire for him making my head spin, making me dizzy.

I want you. Like I've never wanted anyone before.

"You *didn't* f-fail me," I say, the words breathless and emotional.

"I didn't get the phone. It was gone."

"Cassidy," I say, leaning away so I can look up at his face. My eyes get caught on his lips, and I stare at them, timelines converging. If he came to this cabin when he was so young, has anyone ever kissed them? Has anyone ever loved them? The thought of being his first kiss is so arousing, I whimper softly before skimming my gaze to his eyes.

"You okay?" he asks.

I swallow as I nod. My breathing is rapid and shallow.

If he is truly that inexperienced, he doesn't need me kissing him right now while we're discussing Jem. Cassidy's first kiss shouldn't be shared with memories of another man.

I take a deep breath to calm myself, but it makes my breasts rasp against his chest. I feel my nipples pucker and bead under my T-shirt, scraping against his rock-hard abs through two layers of cotton. Can he feel them? Does the touch of them affect him like his body is affecting mine?

"Thank you for trying to find it," I say, reaching up to cup his cheek.

His eyelids flutter for a moment, then open. He is staring at me so intensely, it should make me pause, but all I want is more. More of this look. More of Cassidy.

His jaw tightens as he sucks a whistle of breath through clenched teeth. "I'm sorry—"

"No," I interrupt him. "I won't accept an apology for kindness."

"*Failed* kindness," he says, flinching like he's done something wrong.

"Cassidy, listen to me," I say earnestly, my palm still flush with the dark blond bristles on his cheek, savoring the warmth of the skin underneath. "No kindness is ever wasted. Not on me."

"But how will you say goodbye?"

"I already did," I whisper. "I didn't need to *bury* him here. I just needed to *be* here."

Hope's words come rushing back to me:

Saying goodbye doesn't mean forgetting. Moving on doesn't mean you never loved him. I'm telling you to let go. I'm telling you that you're allowed to be happy.

I run my knuckles over Cassidy's cheek, and he lets his eyes close this time, leaning into my touch, his breath shuddering as I touch him. I can't help running my fingers through his thick, damp hair, but when he opens his eyes and they're so dark with desire, I let my hands fall away from his body and lean back a little so he'll release me.

Something intense and exciting crackles between us. It's chemistry. Intense, combustible chemistry. But now isn't the right time to test it.

Not here. Not now. Not during this conversation.

His arms, which have been holding me close, lower, and he nods. "I understand."

The strangest thing is, I know he does.

Even though he doesn't have the experience I do, I know he understands why we have to stop touching each other right now. And even though I lost my lover and he lost his mother, I know he understands exactly what I'm saying about my farewell to Jem.

What surprises me is the peace that starts in my stomach and warms my whole body like the summer rays of the sun. There is such profound relief in being understood—in finally being known in the inexplicable way that can come only from empathy, from one broken person fathoming the grief of another.

It binds us together in that moment as the sun crests over Katahdin, illuminating his mother's room—*my* room—with warm, golden light. As my lips tilt slowly up into a smile, his do the same, and I feel like I am looking at my reflection, except Cassidy isn't me and I'm not him. We are bound through understanding. We are bathed in grace.

Finally he looks away from me, taking a deep breath. He sighs, leaning his head to the left, then the right. He must be exhausted after walking all night, but when he looks at me, his face is easy for the first time since our emotional conversation began.

He's still smiling at me. "Hungry?"

I nod, wiping away the last of my tears and smiling back at him. "Yes."

"I'll make us some breakfast," he says, standing up from my bed.

"Cass," I call to him, just before he leaves my room.

He turns to look at me.

"Thank you for doing that for me," I say. "It means . . . it means the world to me."

He looks like he wants to say something, but instead he nods.

As I hear the sound of cracking eggs and a whisk, I turn my eyes back to Katahdin.

"Goodbye, Jem," I say softly. "Goodbye."

Then I close my eyes.

And for the first time since that terrible night so long ago, I breathe easy.

Chapter Twenty

<u>Cassidy</u>

I'd do anything *for you.*

The words circled in my head when she thanked me, and I thought about saying them, but something held me back. Something, but . . . what?

As I whisk eggs for the skillet, I decide that it's *confusion.*

My emotions are in a tangle, and I need to unravel them before I say things I *don't* mean, *can't* mean, *wish* I could mean.

So what, exactly, *are* my feelings?

Well . . .

I was jealous of Jem when she called out for him in her fever, but then I knew a fierce longing to give her what Wayne had taken away—the chance to make peace with Jem's loss, the opportunity to say goodbye the way she wanted to and needed to.

So I was deeply frustrated by failing in my mission to her. I wanted to find that phone and deliver it safely to her. I was angry with myself when I returned home this morning; ashamed to look her in the eyes, lest she see the full extent of my defeat.

But my heart changed direction again when I saw her tears because I cannot bear to see her unhappy, and I ran to her bedside, desperate to right whatever wrong was hurting her . . . only to learn that she wasn't crying out of pain or unhappiness. Not in the way I'd assumed. She was crying because, despite my unsuccessful efforts, she'd managed to say farewell to Jem on her own.

And then?

Then I knew only desire.

Near paralyzing.

So strong, I should have burst into flames while I held her.

When she touched my face so tenderly, placing her hand on my cheek, part of me wanted to die . . . because I knew my life would never get any sweeter than it was in that moment.

But even that moment was surpassed by another—by the communion of two hearts that have broken and kept on beating. By the keen and consummate sympathy that is born only from surviving something that almost broke you and recognizing that journey back from hell in someone else's eyes.

And that's when I learn something new about myself:

My feelings for Brynn are only deepened by the way she makes my blood run hot and my heart beat out of my chest with desire. My body aches for hers, but I am fairly certain that the crux of my growing affection for her is less physical and more profound. The essence of it, despite the chasm of differences between us, lies in understanding. And that meeting of hearts and minds makes her feel far more familiar to me than she should after only a week's acquaintance.

I don't know that I've ever mulled the idea of God custom-making one person for another. But if I had wondered, meeting Brynn would almost be enough for me to turn the corner from conjecture to conviction.

The sound of screeching brakes in my brain makes me flinch.

Porter!

Your name is Cassidy Porter.

Your father was Paul Isaac Porter.

I blink at the eggs, which hiss and pop in the frying pan.

She was not *custom-made for you, Cassidy.*

No one *was made for you.*

My heart lurches in protest, wanting so desperately to refute this dark claim, but my mind, carefully conditioned for decades, won't allow it.

You cannot love her, I remind myself sternly. *Because no matter how strong your connection or how deep your feelings, you cannot have her. Ever.*

Especially if you actually care for her.

My chest aches with the terrible injustice of it as I slide the eggs onto two plates. Then I brace my hands on the kitchen counter and force myself to lean into the bleak truth and accept it before I pick up the plates and walk back into Brynn's room.

***

I close my book and set it on the coffee table before us, picking up my mug and taking a sip of tea.

For the last two evenings, Brynn has insisted on reading in the living room instead of in her bedroom. At first I protested that she needed to stay in bed, but she argued that she could relax and heal just as well on the couch. Envisioning us without an end table between us made me give in a lot faster than I probably should have, but my misgivings weren't warranted. It's worked out fine.

I insisted that she still lie down, and she asked if I minded having her feet on my lap.

I think there will be very little in my life that I mind less than Brynn's feet on my lap. While I am supposed to be reading, I study them: the delicate lines of her bones and the light blue rivers and tributaries of her busy veins.

Since my mental reminder in the kitchen, two days ago, I've worked hard to reframe my feelings for her into a more manageable context. She is my guest. She is my patient. She is recovering at my house, and when she is fully recovered, we will say goodbye. When I think of things in this way, it's not that it's necessarily easier to accept them, but it's tidy packaging that forces my mind to move on from fruitless wishes for what can never be.

"Did you finish already?" she asks, looking up from *A Prayer for Owen Meany*, which she has almost finished.

"Yep."

"Wow! You were on page one last night!"

"It's a fast book."

"How was it?"

I've read every story in Kurt Vonnegut's *Welcome to the Monkey House* at least a hundred times. "Good. As always."

Her face is thoughtful as she places Owen on the coffee table beside Kurt.

"Can I ask you something?"

"Anything."

She glances at the bookshelves under the window, then back at me. "One whole shelf is devoted to genetics."

I nod. I already know I don't like where this is going.

"Was one of your parents a geneticist?"

"No."

She stares at me, and I know she wants to ask more questions, but I'm hoping if I don't volunteer any more information, she'll choose a different topic.

"When did you move here?" she asks, switching gears.

"When I was nine," I say.

She nods. "I figured."

"*How* did you figure?"

"That portrait of you? The one that used to be over the couch? With your mom and dad? That was taken in—"

"The man in the picture was my grandfather," I blurt out, my voice sharper than I intended. But something won't allow her to believe that the face of a man I loved was my "dad."

"Oh," she says, leaning back a little, her eyebrows furrowing. "You lived here with your grandfather?"

I don't want to talk about this. Truly I don't. But I get the feeling that if I keep hedging her questions, they'll only multiply.

"I moved here with my mother when I was nine. My grandfather already lived here. My father was . . . gone."

"Gone?"

"Passed away."

It's a slight falsehood. He wasn't killed by another inmate in prison until I was ten, but she doesn't need to know that.

Her face registers instant shock. "Oh, no! Cassidy, I'm so—"

"It's fine," I bite out, standing up and placing her feet back on the couch cushion. I run a hand through my hair before catching her eyes. "Do you want more tea?"

"I shouldn't have asked," she says, screwing up her face, feeling sorry. "I'm just curious about you."

"Why?"

"*Why*?" she repeats, looking up at me in surprise. "You saved my life; you nursed me back to health. You live alone here, in the middle of nowhere. You're kind but quiet. You're well-read but soft-spoken. You manage this whole place with a little solar power, some propane, and batteries.

You're interesting. I . . . I don't know. I'm *curious* about you. I want to know more about you."

I gulp, my heart unaccountably swelling from her words. From her interest in me.

"I tell you what . . . I'll get us some more tea, and when I come back, you can ask me some questions, okay?"

She grins up at me. "*Any* questions?"

"I don't promise to answer them all," I say. "But you can ask."

I leave her for a moment, stepping into the kitchen to pull the still-warm kettle from the stove and add water to our cups. I don't know why I decided to answer some questions for her, but maybe it's because I *want* her to know me. Not all of me, of course. Not who I really am. Not whose son I am. But she's still going to be here for a couple more weeks. I don't blame her for wanting a few answers from her host.

When I sit down again, I pull her feet back onto my lap and look at her expectantly.

"What do you want to know?"

"Okay, first, why did you and your mother move here?"

I breathe deep. "After my father was gone, my mother didn't feel comfortable living alone in town. We moved here to be with my grandfather."

"She didn't want to remarry?"

"It wasn't really an option."

She looks curious, but doesn't pursue this answer, and I'm grateful.

"Why did your grandfather live all the way out here?"

"He was . . . disillusioned with society after fighting in Vietnam. He wasn't treated well when he returned. And, well . . ." I grin, just a little, remembering Gramp's fiercely independent nature. "He didn't want to be told what to do. He wanted to be . . . free, I guess. He wanted space and peace. He found it here."

"I get that," she says slowly, her eyes locked on mine. "After Jem died, I just wanted to be left alone. It's . . . it's hard for people to understand that, isn't it? They want to help. They want to be there for you. But sometimes all you need is quiet. Space and peace. And time."

I reach for my mug and take a sip of tea, silently agreeing with her.

"When did your grandfather pass?" she asks.

"Ten years ago."

"And you stayed here? You didn't want to move to a town?"

I shrug. "Not really. I have everything I need here."

"Well, not *everything*," she says quickly, maybe more to herself than to me.

When I glance at her over the rim of my cup, I see two spots of red color her cheeks. "What am I missing?"

"Well, um . . ." She laughs softly, averting her eyes. "I mean . . ." She clears her throat. "Companionship?"

"I have Annie and the girls."

"Um . . ." She chuckles again. "That's not what I mean." She takes a deep breath. "I mean . . . a girlfriend. A wife? Unless . . ." She cocks her head.

"Unless what?"

"Unless you don't want that."

We stare at each other, deadlocked for a moment. Finally I look away. It's easier to lie when you're not looking someone in the eyes.

"I'm content with things the way they are."

"But you're so . . ."

My neck snaps up. "So *what*?"

She takes a deep breath, holds it, then lets it go. "Aren't you lonely, Cass?"

I shrug, looking out at Katahdin as the setting sun streaks the sky with purple and gold. I'm getting upset because her questions are hitting way too close to the truth, and I'm a bad liar.

"I'm just not much of a people person, I guess."

"But—"

"But *what?* I don't *need* anyone!" I bark, the strain of lying to her and talking about my past finally getting to me.

I'm instantly sorry for yelling. I can feel her hurt and disappointment, flat and awful in the air between us, even though I'm not looking at her. I hold my breath and tell myself it's better this way. The fewer conversations we have about my past, the better it will be for both of us.

After a long silence, she speaks again. "When do you think I'll be ready to go home?"

Her question slices through my heart like a hot, sharp knife. I let it bleed for a moment before answering.

"You're healing well. I should be able to take the stitches out this weekend," I say. "But the only way out of here is hiking or taking the ATV over four miles of rough ground. Either way, you're going to need another week or two for those incisions to heal."

"So two or three more weeks," she says softly.

Her voice is so sad, I can't help myself. I turn to face her. With tears brimming in her eyes, she looks back at me, and it hurts so bad that I upset her, I almost don't know how to bear it.

"Brynn—"

"I . . . I don't mean to be such a b-burden to you," she whispers, looking away as she reaches up to swipe at a tear.

A burden? *A . . . burden?* It reverberates in my head like a dirty word because nothing could be further from the truth.

"I'm sorry," she says, trying to pull her feet off my lap.

But I drop my hands to them, holding them where they are, my breath catching as I feel the skin of my palm press deliberately flush with the skin of her feet. I sink into the feeling of touching her—the warmth of her, of those busy blue veins moving her blood, of the birdlike bones and soft skin cradled in my rough, calloused hands. She is an angel, while I harbor the devil inside. But in this moment—in this finite, stolen moment when I should push her away—all I can feel is reverence and gratitude.

A burden?

The minutes I've spent with her are the greatest gift my quiet life has ever known.

I draw her foot up to my face, closing my eyes and pressing my lips to the arc of the soft instep. I rest there for a moment, ignoring the burn in my eyes, surrendering to worship. Her sole. My soul.

"I wish things were different," I murmur before placing her foot back on my lap. When I open my eyes to look at her, she's staring back at me, her lips parted, her eyes shocked.

"Cassidy," she says, her voice breaking on my name.

Gently I lift her feet, place them back on the old, nubby couch, stand up, and walk alone into the dark, cold night.

Chapter Twenty-One

<u>Brynn</u>

Here is what I know for certain:

I am falling hard for Cassidy Porter.

When tears sprang to my eyes last night, it wasn't because he'd yelled at me and pushed me away—it was because I have only two or three weeks left with him. Being here, in his rustic hideaway, I can feel myself healing, strengthening, the pieces of my jigsawed life coming back together. In the quiet hours while he is working outside, I read his books, yes, but I have had more space, peace, and time to think than I have ever had before. And in this retreat-like sanctuary, with no modern distractions, I am finding myself all over again.

I think about my life before Jem, and my life with him. I think about the pain of losing him, and I think about my decision to come here and say goodbye. I think about everything Hope said, and I think about my parents and my friends back in San Francisco. I think about the future and what I want out of life. And I think about Cassidy.

No matter how hard I try to impose order on my thoughts, in fact, they *always* return to Cassidy.

I am in awe of him in a way that I can't seem to compartmentalize. If I was sixteen, I'd call it a crush. But I'm a fully grown woman, and I know it's more than that. I'd be lying if I tried to paint it as less.

So I can't get him out of my head, and I've just about stopped trying.

There is just so much about him that speaks to me, that draws me to him, that I like, that makes my toes curl.

There's the way he *carried me down a fucking mountain* and sewed up my wounds. And the way he consumes books the way other men consume sports statistics. There's the way he plays the guitar, so soulfully, you'd swear he was twice his twenty-seven years. Or the way he spent an entire night hiking through darkness to find a phone with a little smudge of blood just because he thought it would help give me closure. He says so little, but still manages to make my heart go berserk with a word or touch.

And then—a warm pooling sensation in my stomach makes me moan softly as my eyes flutter closed—there's the way his body looks while he's chopping wood. His back muscles in motion are mesmerizing: the way they flex and bunch, stretch and release. I want to lay my palms flat on them as they move so I can feel the power underneath. He's brutally, scorchingly hot—an actual, real-life Adonis—and my long-neglected girl parts go a little wild watching the sun shine down on his tan, sweat-soaked skin.

I've been here for over a week, and I know I'm not ready to go. I don't even want to talk about leaving. If anything, I want to tell Stu at Stu's Pools to go fuck himself, have Milo shipped out here, put my house on the market, and just . . . stay. For a while. Indefinitely. I don't know how long. Maybe forever.

There's something about this place—and about Cassidy Porter—that heals the roughest, jagged, most wounded parts of me, and I'm desperately unhappy when I think of leaving him and going back to the "real" world. Why can't *this* be real?

Last night, when he picked up my foot and kissed it, I was so shocked and so aroused, my panties—oh, God, his *mother's* panties!—were flooded with warm wetness, something that hasn't happened to me in over two years. The hairs on my arms stood straight up. My breath caught. My eyes would have been black if I'd looked at them in a mirror.

But then, as suddenly as it happened, it was over. He got up and walked away, leaving every cell in my body longing for more, and my mind knotted with confusion.

He's attracted to me—I know he is. I can feel it in my toes when his eyes catch mine. I felt it in the way he touched me last night, and a few nights before that, when he pressed his lips to my head. His eyes scan my legs, rest on my breasts, trace the curve of my hips. He licks his lips when he gazes at mine like he's hungry and thirsty at once. His eyes darken. His breathing gets shallow and fast.

And he's not taken—he's lived here since he was nine years old. He hasn't had access to another woman. He's free to do whatever he wants with whomever he wants.

We're young, but of age.

We're untethered to others and attracted to each other.

We're all alone out here in the middle of nowhere.

If anything, as soon as my stitches come out, it's the perfect setup for two or three weeks of nonstop sex in every thinkable position. And whatever feelings we might develop for each other? Well, while it scares me a little to open myself up to love again, I've *missed* loving someone. I've missed *being* loved. I want to *be* with someone again. I feel like I'm almost ready to put myself out there again, and Cassidy, my sweet, hot protector, seems like the perfect partner.

And yet Cassidy, a lone mountain man with no responsibilities except to himself, doesn't seem ready at all.

Why does he "wish things were different"? *What* needs to be different?

Does he fear that his lack of experience will turn me off? Because nothing could be further from the truth. I don't care if he's never been with anyone else. We could spend all summer learning about each other together.

Or maybe he was telling the truth when he said that he didn't need anyone. Maybe he *isn't* lonely. Maybe he truly is happy living off the grid, far from the complications of the outside world—from the mass shootings and the people who disrespected veterans like his grandfather.

Maybe these two or three weeks is all we have because it *won't* hurt Cassidy to say goodbye to me the way it will hurt me to say goodbye to him. His life will just go back to normal, while I already know I will desperately yearn for this place, and for him.

My head starts to ache, so I push the covers down, swing my legs out of bed, and walk down the hallway, to the bathroom. The floor is wet, which means that Cassidy has taken an indoor shower today, and my mind wanders to dirty places, thinking about what he must look like naked.

His body is long and lean, chiseled with muscle. I know this both from sleeping against his chest and surreptitiously watching him swing an ax from the corner of my window. I close my eyes and think back to yesterday afternoon, when he chopped wood for an hour with his shirt off. His hips taper into a sharp V that slides into his jeans, and damn, but that V keeps me awake some nights. I know what it leads to, but I still wonder what the zipper of his jeans is hiding.

Opening my eyes with an unfulfilled sigh, I stand up

and crank the toilet. Then I wash my armpits, hands, and face in the icy cold water that I'm still not used to.

For the first time, as I head back to my room, I realize that I'm not tired, and I don't want to go back to bed. My incisions don't ache anymore, and my face looks almost normal again but for some light yellow discoloration here and there.

I'd like to learn more about Cassidy's unusual home, and, if he'll let me, I'd like to help out a little too.

I open the top drawer of the bureau against the right wall in my room and find two neat stacks of cotton underwear and bras on one side of the drawer, and a pile of rolled, white cotton socks on the other. Choosing a faded, light blue pair of undies and a matching bra, I slip out of my sleeping clothes and pull on the clean undergarments.

Opening the second drawer, I find T-shirts, also carefully folded in two piles. The one on top is light pink—a V-neck with some frayed threads around the neckline. It looks worn but soft, and I slip it over my head. Cassidy's mother must have been a bit smaller on top than me because it pulls across my breasts a little, but a quick check through labels on the rest of the shirts tells me that I'm out of luck for a medium. Good thing cotton stretches. Besides, what other options do I have?

I pull open the third drawer to find jeans and denim shorts, all with the elastic waistbands favored by grannies the world over. Again, however, beggars can't be choosers, so I slip a pair of shorts over my legs and tug them up. They fit loosely, doing nothing for my figure, but I'm able to pull them up under my breasts so that the elastic doesn't press against my bandages. What they lack in fashion, they make up for in function, I guess.

The fourth and final drawer holds sweatshirts and

cardigans, and I pull out a hot pink, zip-up sweatshirt that reads "Maine: The Way Life Should Be," and shrug into it.

On top of the bureau is a hairbrush with a black elastic twisted around the handle. I brush out a week's worth of snarls, almost grateful for the disgusting buildup of oil that acts as a detangler. I need to ask Cassidy about taking a bath or shower sometime soon.

There isn't a mirror in the room for me to check my appearance, but Cassidy has seen me at my worst, so I figure this is at least an improvement on how I've looked since he met me. How I wish I had a little concealer and lipgloss, but I don't think Mrs. Porter was much of one for beauty products. Either that, or they're long gone by now.

Padding barefoot across the living room and into the kitchen, I open the tiny refrigerator and take a bowl of eggs from the cool, dark interior. There are only four, so I beat them all in the same bowl, then look around for a frying pan. I find one in the drying rack beside the sink and place it on one of two stovetop burners, but now I'm stumped. I have no idea how to turn it on.

"Battery ignition."

I turn at the sound of his voice, a wide smile forming on my face in the moment between hearing him and facing him.

"Hi," I say, sounding like a middle school girl who just caught a glimpse of her crush in the hall.

"Mornin'," he says, checking out my outfit. "You're dressed."

"I hope it's okay that I borrowed a few things."

His eyes, which linger on my breasts for a second, eventually slide up to my face. It's got to be pink because I feel my cheeks flush with warmth from the look in his eyes.

He nods slowly. "Sure."

"I didn't want to be useless today."

"You're not useless. You're healing."

"I feel good, Cass. I want to help . . . to contribute. I don't want to be a burden to you. I figured I could do the cooking."

"One, you're not a burden." His lips quirk up in a slight grin. "Two, *can* you cook?"

"Yeah," I say, grinning back at him. "I'm not bad."

"Really?" he asks, his smile widening, his eyes sparkling. "I haven't . . . I mean, no one's cooked here but me in a long time. And before that, it was Gramp, and he was just as happy with a can of beans warmed up over an open fire."

I cringe. "Yuck?"

"Double yuck," he confirms. "What's your specialty?"

"I thought we'd start easy, with scrambled eggs," I say, holding out the bowl of beaten eggs. "I can get more fancy, but I don't know what you have to work with yet."

"We could . . . I mean, if you wanted to, we could go fishing later. If you're up to it." His tongue darts out to lick his lips, and I'm mesmerized by them for a moment. "Pond's not far."

I clear my throat and look up. "I make a mean brown sugar salmon."

"Ahhh," he sighs, and my insides clench. Damn it, but everything he does turns me on! "I don't have brown sugar, but I've got lots of maple syrup. And I can't get you salmon around here, but we've got yellow perch and brook trout."

"I think I can work with that," I say, feeling lighthearted. "Whatever you fish, I'll fix. Deal?"

"Yeah," he says, stepping forward and reaching around me to turn on the burner under the frying pan. "Deal."

His knuckles graze my hip as he withdraws his hand, and I feel it all the way to my toes.

"I . . . I want to be useful," I say, my voice sounding husky in my ears.

"You already said that," he rumbles, not moving away.

My mouth waters. "It's . . . it's true."

"Well, okay," he says, standing so close to me, I can smell the soap he uses and the sweat on his skin from whatever chores he was doing this morning. "But don't go too fast, huh?"

"I'll take it slow," I murmur, and for a split second, holding his eyes as I am, I wonder if we're talking about my recovery or something else entirely.

"Slow's good," he says. Then, suddenly, he lowers his head and backs away. "I'll wash up outside."

My heart is racing so fast, I feel dizzy. But giddy too. I guess I feel *gizzy*.

Turning to face the stove, I grab a wooden spoon hanging from a nail on the wall before pouring the eggs into the pan.

***

The walk to the nearby pond, which Cassidy tells me is called Harrington and is about a tenth of a mile from his homestead, is tougher than I expect.

I'm out of breath quickly, and my stitches pull uncomfortably even though it's a flat, relatively well-worn path and Cassidy walks slowly and carefully in front of me. But just when I'm about to tell him that I think we should turn back, there it is: a small pond, sparkling and cool under the summer sun.

I freeze, taking in the loveliness of it.

Barkless trees and high grasses surround the water's edge, and a buzz of cicadas makes for a summer symphony. I breathe deeply as Cassidy turns around to face me.

"You want to stop?"

"I'm just . . . it's really pretty."

He looks over his shoulder at the pond, then back at me. "Small, as ponds go."

On his other shoulder rests a fishing pole, and he carries a bucket and a tackle box in his hand.

"I don't care. I like it," I say, looking back at the little water hole.

"You were out of breath as we walked," he notes.

I nod. There's no use denying it. "I guess I'm still healing."

"Why don't you take a nap?" he suggests, gesturing to a large glacial rock with his chin. The flat gray surface, bathed in sunshine, is oddly inviting. I bet it's warm. "I'll wake you up after I've caught a dozen."

"A dozen," I scoff, taking a couple of steps through high grass to reach the rock.

"Well, well!" exclaims Cassidy, who is squatting over his open tackle box and pulling out what appears to be a fly lure. "Do I detect a challenge, Miz Cadogan?"

I lower myself to the rock, six or seven feet away from him, and stretch my legs out before me, leaning back on my palms. My eyes zone in on the bare strip of tan skin where his T-shirt has ridden up.

Damn, but he is all man.

"You think you can catch twelve fish in this little pond?" I say.

"My record's twenty-six at this spot," he says, grinning at me as he stands up to cast his line. "So yeah, I think less than half that is possible."

He's bragging and it's adorable, but he's also sexy as hell standing there at the water's edge, casting and reeling. For real? I could watch him forever, except that I feel a huge yawn coming on, and my eyes feel so heavy, I can barely keep them open.

The sun is high and strong, so I shrug out of the hot pink sweatshirt, rolling it into a makeshift pillow.

"I'll believe it when I see it," I tease him, lying back on the rock, the sweatshirt heaven under my head.

"What was our deal again, sassy-pants?" he asks.

Sassy-pants. I chuckle softly, eyes closed, "You catch 'em; I cook 'em."

"You better get some sleep, then," he says, all cocky, "'cause you're going to have a heap of cookin' to do later, angel."

The shines down on my face like a blessing, and I fall asleep smiling.

Chapter Twenty-Two

<u>Cassidy</u>

It takes me about two hours, but I'm not about to stop until I have an even dozen. And then, just for the hell of it, I catch one more. Maybe to show off a little.

I took an hour-long walk in the dark last night, just to cool down after kissing her foot like that. I don't know why I did it. I guess because I felt this desperate, insane urge to prove to her that her presence was an honor, not a burden.

But the feelings it conjured up? The way my blood started rushing so hot and fast, my heart pumping it like crazy? The way my pecker stiffened almost painfully? I've never felt these feelings before, but I recognize them instinctively. I'm wildly attracted to her. If we were animals, I'd want to mate with her. Because we're humans, I want to make love to her.

Love.

A word that keeps entering my mind lately.

And I know it's not possible, because of promises I intend to keep, but I can't help the way I feel.

With my thirteen fish swimming around in the bucket, I reel in my line and remove my favorite lure, tucking it back into a safe place in the tackle box. I close and latch the top, then lean the rod against a tree trunk.

Moving as quietly as possible, I step through the high grass to the rock where Brynn is sleeping.

Since I've known her, I've probably seen Brynn asleep more than awake. I've had a lot of opportunities to watch her sleep. But not like this. Not with her face turned up to the sunshine, her freckles on full display, her lips slightly parted and tilted upward just a touch. Like she's happy. Like maybe being here with me *makes* her happy.

This is an image that will torture me when she's gone, but I can't force myself to look away because, in my whole life, I've never seen anything as beautiful as this woman. If I didn't know better, and if it was allowed, I might even think that I love her.

And there's that word again, I think. I trace the lines of Brynn's face, finally resting on her mouth. I wonder what it would be like to kiss her, to press my lips to hers. They'd be warm from the sun, and soft. What would she taste like? How would her body feel in my arms if I clasped her to me as our lips touched? Would I be able to stop after a single kiss? Or would I need more?

A terrible thought occurs to me, and I wonder if my father ever looked at my mother like this. In fact, Mama could have been wearing that very T-shirt and jean shorts, and my father could have looked at *her* with desire, with want. I don't know if he loved my mother or not. When I think back, it feels like he did. It feels like they loved each other, as unbelievable as that sounds. Because how could he feel one way for my mother and still do what he did to other women? How could he feel love for *her* but a few days later, go kill someone else? It scares me. God, it scares me so bad that I lean away from Brynn, searching my mind for indications that my appetites run similar to his. I search and search, but I can't find anything but protectiveness and tenderness for the small, sleeping woman in front of me.

"I'd never hurt you," I murmur, the words so soft, I can barely hear them. *I'd never hurt anyone.* But there is that tiny part of me that isn't convinced, that reminds me of who I am. I don't know what genes lurk inside me, biding their time to make themselves known.

Sighing with the bleak unfairness of it all, I reach for her shoulder and shake it gently.

"Hey, angel," I whisper. "Time to wake up."

***

For two days we eat all manner of brook trout, cooked up in so many mouthwatering and creative ways, I swear I never knew how delicious fresh fish could be.

Brynn wasn't kidding when she said she wasn't a bad cook.

We've had fillets with a maple syrup reduction, the whole fish dredged in eggs and flour and fried with fresh herbs, and tonight she made some sort of spicy tomato sauce that caught my mouth on fire, but tasted so danged good on the flaky white meat, I couldn't stop eating.

She's taken over my greenhouse, babying the tomatoes and trussing up overgrown herbs. It's come alive under her care and makes me smile every time I step inside.

Speaking of smiles, I live for hers. As if on cue, she looks up at me and grins.

"You okay? I might have gone overboard with the horseradish."

"Is that what's burnin' my mouth?" I ask, reaching for my glass of water.

". . . he asks after three helpings," she says, winking at me.

"It was good," I say, leaning back and patting my

stomach. "You're going to make me fat."

"Impossible. You work too hard to get fat."

"How do you stay so little if you eat like this at home?" I ask, replacing my glass.

"I don't eat like this at home," she says. "Eating like this is only fun if you're sharing it with someone."

I nod, realizing that she learned to cook like this for Jem, probably, then stopped when she lost him. That she would share her skills with me sends a shock of something wonderful through my body.

"Thank you," I say, leaning forward to take her empty plate.

She cooks and I clean up. It's become our tacit agreement since she took over cooking, the day before yesterday.

"Are you still taking out my stitches tonight?" she asks.

I stand up and walk the dishes to the sink, where I add them to the bucket of water that holds the soaking pans and bowls Brynn used for cooking.

"Yeah," I say, turning to look at her over my shoulder. "Everything looked good this morning. I think it's time."

"Will it hurt? I've never had stitches. In or out. And thank God I don't remember most of what happened when they went in."

"Nah. You won't even feel them come out. Shouldn't, anyway."

"And then I'm finishing *Owen Meany*." She sighs. "Are you starting a new book tonight?"

Those D batteries have been burning a hole in my bureau drawer because I've been wanting to suggest a movie night for a few days now. The idea of sitting next to her, *close to her*, on the couch while we watch the small TV has my stomach in good knots. I've read books where a guy and a girl go out on a date to the movies and always wondered what it was like. It's not like I have a right to put my arm around her or anything—I know we wouldn't actually *be* on a date, just watching a movie. It still gets me a little excited. And I can't decide if that's okay or not. Is it okay to want to sit next to a pretty girl in the dark and watch a movie? I guess it is. As long as it doesn't go anywhere.

"How about a movie?" I ask, staring down at the dishes in the sink, which I wash with a sponge, then rinse in the clean-water bucket.

She laughs, and I love the sound of Brynn's laughter, but I'm not sure if she's laughing at me or not this time, so I keep my back to her, concealing my flushed cheeks.

"Wait. Really? Can we?" she asks, and my shoulders, which are rigid, relax because I can hear the excitement in her voice.

"Sure. I have a portable VHS player. A little TV to hook it up to. Batteries."

"I saw your collection of movies, but I assumed you kept them out of nostalgia."

I shake my head and glance around at her. "Nope. We can watch one . . . if you want."

"Yeah," she says. "I'd love it. A little technology fix!"

I rinse another plate and add it to the drying rack. She's told me a lot about the internet since she's been here, and though it's hard for me to completely get my head around it, I love the notion of information at my fingertips. Someday I'd like to give it a try, all this technology she talks about.

"Do you have one in mind?" I ask. "A movie?"

"*You're killin' me, Smalls!*" she says, giggling softly behind me.

I feel a smile split my face and whip my head around to look at her. "*The Sandlot*! You know it?"

204

"Cass, we're only three years apart. Of course I know it. Every kid in our generation knows it." She blinks at me. "Even *you!*"

"I played baseball when I was little."

"Oh, yeah?"

I nod, remembering the day I hit a home run for my Little League team. It was the summer before my father was arrested, before my whole world changed. And it was— before the day I met Brynn Cadogan—the best day of my life.

"Yeah. Little League."

"Before you moved here."

The pan she used to make the tomato sauce needs a little more elbow grease, and I lay into it with a Brillo Pad, remembering Mama's face as I rounded the bases. My father was out on the road, as usual, but she sat in the bleachers watching. She was so proud of me—her "winning little man." And then the whole team hoisted me on their shoulders, and we got our picture taken for the *North Country Register*. We didn't end up winning any more games, but for that day, we were champions.

"Yeah," I say, realizing that she's waiting for an answer. "When we lived in town."

"When your dad was still alive?"

I clench my teeth and swallow hard, transferring the pan into the rinse water. I hate the way she calls him my dad, so casually. He was never, ever my dad. He was, unfortunately, my biological father.

"Um, yeah."

"You are not a man of many words, Cassidy Porter," she says, her voice exasperated. "Don't you have any good stories to tell me?"

Good stories?

205

No. Not many, sweet Brynn.

Finished with the dishes, I pour the soapy water down the drain and put the bucket on the floor. I'll take it outside and dump it later. Then I slide the rinse-water bucket over to where the soap bucket was. I add a little soap to it so it's ready for tomorrow's dirty dishes, then I turn to Brynn.

"Some stories have really bad endings."

She stares at me from where she's still sitting at the square, four-person table. "Do you have a bad story inside of you?"

She has no idea how close her words come to the truth. I flinch.

"Oh. But, Cassidy, we *all* have bad stories inside of us," she says, her voice gentle as she stands up and takes a step toward me.

Not like mine. Not as bad as mine.

She searches my eyes and takes another step toward me, reading my gaze astutely. "Yes, we do. Jem was murdered. That night the cops came to my door? To tell me? One of the worst nights of my life. A horror story if there ever was one."

It's on the tip of my tongue to say that the night the cops came to my door was the worst night of my life too. But I'd be opening a can of worms that I don't ever want to open with my Brynn.

My hands are on my hips, but she reaches out for one of them, curling her small fingers around mine and pulling my hand into hers. As always, her touch sends longing galloping through my body like a herd of wild horses, making my heart thunder, making every nerve ending in my body clamor for more.

"I know something bad must have happened," she says quietly, her green eyes boring into mine. "A mother doesn't just uproot her son from a small town and move out to the middle of nowhere if everything's happy. But whatever it was . . ." She pauses, her fingers clasping mine. ". . . it wasn't your fault. You were just a little boy. Whatever happened with your father or your mother, whatever *they did*, or whatever happened *to them*, you were just a child. It wasn't *your* fault. You know that, right?"

In a roundabout way, I *do* know that.

It's not my fault that my father killed those girls, but the fact remains that they're dead.

It's not my fault that the townsfolk of Millinocket were frightened of my mother and me, but we couldn't live there anymore.

It's not my fault that my blood, my genes, are half Porter, but it doesn't change the fact that my grandfather worried for the monster inside me.

"Whatever it is . . . tell me you know it's not your fault," she says, her sweet voice pleading.

Not my fault?

It doesn't matter.

It doesn't change anything.

I am who I am.

Brynn's eyes narrow as they focus on mine. Her voice is soft when she asks, "What happened to you, Cassidy?"

Would it be a relief to tell her?

My father was a sociopath who killed a dozen women or more. I found out on my eighth birthday. He was tried and convicted and killed in prison ten months later by a group of angry inmates. It became unbearable for my mother and me to live in town, so we moved here.

That's what happened to me.

I look into her beautiful bright eyes that stare up at me with hope and compassion, and my heart swells with yearning to unload my tangled past. But I'm distracted by

207

another emotion shining in her eyes—something deeper and utterly impossible. Impossible, even though I'm *looking* at it, even though I'm *seeing* it stare back at me:

Love.

The deep and impossible emotion brightening Brynn's eyes is *love*.

A jolt of realization makes my breath catch and my head swim. I jerk my hand away and take a step back from her, dropping her eyes and staring desperately down at my toes.

We cannot love each other.

It is not allowed.

"I can't . . ."

"You can't what?" she murmurs, still standing close to me.

So close.

I can't breathe.

I can't do this.

I can't love you.

I can't let you love me.

"It's okay," she says, talking fast, an out-of-control quality entering into her rising tone. "We're adults. We're free. You're here . . . and me. Alone. And . . . we're . . . um, we've been spending a lot of time together. And, um, you know that people who meet during traumatic experiences bond faster? So it makes sense that our feelings would grow into—"

"Stop!" I bark.

The room goes still and somehow spins at the same time. My heart is pounding so loudly in my ears, I bet I'm wincing.

"Cass," she gasps.

"No," I bite out. "Just . . . *stop. Please.*"

"I'm . . . I'm sorry," she says, and it's like someone reaches into my chest and fists my heart. A single, bereft sound that makes me want to die because it is full of so much sadness, so much longing. "I thought . . ."

Her voice drifts off.

I clear my throat, then take a deep breath and hold it.

Do something. Say something.

"Let's get those stitches out," I mutter, finally looking up at her.

Her eyes are glistening because she's about to cry, which makes me feel like a demon. She tugs her top lip between her teeth, gnawing on it for a second before turning her back to me and taking a seat at the table.

"Okay," she says, averting her eyes, her voice defeated.

I reach over the fridge for the first aid box and place it on the table. Without looking at her, I open it and take out a small scissors that I sterilized after using them last time, and a pair of tweezers.

"Should I take off my shirt?"

Yes.

No.

Definitely no.

"No," I say, pulling out the bottle of alcohol and a clean gauze pad. "Just lift it a little."

Her fingers drop to the hem, and she pulls up the shirt, still looking away from me. When I glance at her face, she's blinking rapidly, her jaw clenched tightly like she's desperately trying not to cry.

"Brynn," I say, pulling out the chair beside her and sitting down. "I'm sorry for yelling."

I don't look at her face. I focus on the first of the six incisions, swabbing it with alcohol first, then leaning forward to carefully cut through the middle of each stitch with the small scissors.

"I feel like . . . an idiot," she says, sniffling softly.

Snip. Snip. Snip. Snip. Snip.

"Don't," I say, resting the scissors on the gauze pad.

"I . . . I thought we were . . ."

I tug the stitches from each side with the tweezers, placing each half on the table. The small pile grows as I tug on the tenth knot, relieved when it slides easily from the tiny needle hole. I reach for the Steri-Strip and rip off three small pieces, which I place over the healing incision.

"What?" I ask, moving to the next incision and swabbing it clean before cutting.

"I thought you liked me."

I gulp, taking a deep breath as I pick up the scissors again. "I do."

"But not . . . like *that*," she says.

I'm not totally sure what she means, but I assume she's talking about attraction, and she has no idea how very wrong she is.

Snip. Snip. Snip.

"It's not a matter of liking you. It would be impossible not to like you," I say honestly, finding it far easier to talk about this when I'm concentrating on something other than her eyes. I reach for the tweezers. "But we're very different."

"How?"

"Well, for one thing, my life is here. Yours is in California."

"Lives can change," she says.

"Not that much. My life works. I'm not looking to change it."

The second half of the third stitch doesn't want to come out, and when I force it, she bleeds a little. I take a clean gauze pad and press it to a bright red blood droplet.

"Hold this."

She is holding up her shirt with one hand and can't see what I'm doing, so I reach for her fingers and guide them to the gauze, pressing them gently. My fingers linger over hers for a moment before I pull away.

I can take care of one more incision from this angle and get to work. It's the one that became infected last week, but now it looks good. It's healing well.

Snip. Snip. Snip. Snip. Snip. Snip. Snip.

"So you *do* like me," she says, her voice less upset than it was before.

"Of course," I answer softly.

"And we're trapped here together for two more weeks."

"Mm-hm," I murmur, tugging on another stitch, grateful when it slides out without bleeding. I release the tweezers and add the tiny knot to the pile.

"What if . . .?"

"That's three," I say, interrupting her. "Can you turn a little on the seat? Put your back to me?"

She follows my instructions, giving me her back, which I believe emboldens her to state, "Fourteen days."

"What?"

"We have fourteen days together."

My heart thunders, and I focus on keeping my hands from shaking.

"Today is July 6," she says, her voice soft and nervous. "I'll leave on July 20, no matter what. I won't ask anything of you, Cass. I won't try to change your life. I won't try to stay. I won't ask you to go. I'll never come back, if that's what you want. I promise. I just . . ."

Snip. Snip. Snip.

I swallow, not daring to say a word, desperately wanting to hear the rest of what she has to say, but fearing that it will be too wonderful to refuse, even though I should.

"And, um, if feelings bother you, we can take them out of the equation. No, um, no feelings. No declarations. We like each other. That's enough for me," she says softly, her voice a little brave and a little sad as she finishes.

I pick up the tweezers, and she takes my silence as permission to continue.

"But for the next two weeks, we could, um, *enjoy* each other. *All* of each other."

Snip. Snip. Snip . . . Snip.

I don't realize I've been holding my breath until I exhale. My hot breath streaks across her exposed skin. The tiny blond hairs on her hip stand up, and I stare at them for a moment, blinking with growing realization.

Although I've never been with a woman, my mind skates easily back to those old, beat-up magazines lying under my mattress. I may not know much, but I know what she's suggesting: she's temporarily offering me her body in exchange for mine. I don't know exactly to what extent, but I'm fairly certain she's offering me sex.

I know that it might be the only chance I ever get to experience what she's suggesting, and my blood surges, my body hardening everywhere at the idea.

She's come dangerously close to offering me something I might actually be able to accept—no-strings-attached physical intimacy *with* an expiration date.

No commitment.

No marriage or children or forever.

No chance of infecting the world with my father's genes.

Without realizing it, she's giving me the opportunity to love her without breaking my promises.

Snip. Snip. Snip. Snip. Snip.

I cut through the last of her stitches, then place the scissors on the table.

"Do you understand what I'm saying?" she asks, her back to me, her voice breathless and low. "Do you understand what I want . . . what I'm suggesting?"

"Mm-hm," I hum, surprised I'm able to make any sound at all.

"Is that something you want too?"

I pull out the last of the stitches, then place the tweezers beside the scissors on the table, grazing her bare hip with my wrist as I withdraw it. I stare at her ponytail, at the back of her neck, my eyes sliding down her bunched shirt and resting on her skin. It's white and soft over the waistband of her shorts, and I know if I say yes, I will have the right to touch it, to learn the contours of her body, to love her. Maybe enough to last me a lifetime.

She exhales, saying my name as her breath passes through her lips. "Cass? Please answer."

My heart pounds.

I suck in a breath and hold it for what feels like eternity.

"Yes," I hear myself answer, letting my forehead drop to the back of her neck in surrender. "I want it too."

Chapter Twenty-Three

<u>Brynn</u>

I want it too.

In an instant, my world has color like it's never had before.

I don't know where my proposition came from, other than the fact that my longing for him—my base *desire* for him—has been bubbling up for days and won't be denied anymore.

I lied to him when I said that we would take feelings out of the equation because I am already falling in love with him. But I am willing to keep those feelings to myself if it means we will belong to each other physically for the next two weeks. I will love him through the way that I touch him and kiss him and speak to him. But I will force myself not to say it, no matter how strongly I feel it.

And how will I leave him at the end? After I know the warmth of his body covering mine? The heat of him between my thighs? The way his breath will catch when I arch against him, my inmost muscles sheathing his hardness like a glove for the very first time in his life?

I don't know.

But I will. I will because I promised. I will because I

want this more than I dread our inevitable goodbye. And I will because I have a feeling he will insist on it.

I want it too.

I have no idea how this will work or when it will actually start.

What if he reaches for me right this second and carries me to his bed? Tells me to strip so he can bury himself inside me? Am I ready? Because I've talked a pretty big fucking game at this point, and he's agreed to play.

I am so nervous with him sitting behind me, I can barely breathe. I feel the strength of him—the heat of his forehead against my neck as I drop the hem of my shirt and let it fall over my taped wounds. I am aware of every breath I take, of the way my breasts rise and fall, following the fullness and emptiness of my lungs. I am aware of his breathing too—it's short and shallow and choppy against the back of my throat and makes me dizzy.

He wants me as much as I want him.

Please let it be enough.

"We could . . ." His voice is gravel, husky and low, and I close my eyes, waiting to hear his suggestion, part of me afraid, though I will do whatever he asks. ". . . watch that movie now . . . if you want."

A short laugh escapes my lips. It's a relieved and joyful sound. As much as I want Cassidy, maybe I'm *not* ready to jump into bed with him tonight. I need a little wooing, it turns out, regardless of my bold words.

"Y-yes!" I say, laughing again as he lifts his head, and I peek at him over my shoulder.

His eyes are dark and he licks his lips, but if I'm not mistaken, there's a little smile tugging at the corners.

"*The Sandlot*, right?"

I nod. "Uh-huh. Yeah. Sounds good."

"How about, um, you make us some popcorn while I get it set up?"

"Popcorn? Really?"

"Don't people still eat popcorn when they watch a movie?"

"Of course," I say, realizing that this is something he probably remembers from his short time living in town.

He gestures to the cabinet over the sink with a flick of his chin. "There's kernels, oil, and salt in there."

"Okay."

His eyes linger on my lips for one more second before he stands up, leaning over the table to tidy his first aid supplies and gather the leftover stitches into a pile, which he takes to the garbage.

Still reeling from our conversation and wondering how our agreement will play out, I take out a pot and cover the bottom with a thin coat of olive oil. I place it on the stove, ignite the burner, and throw two kernels into the bottom of the pot, waiting for them to pop. Behind me, in the living room, Cassidy is sitting on the couch, loading batteries into the VHS player for our movie night.

For the most part, I've let the men in my life do the pursuing, so tonight I'm in uncharted territory. I guess I knew—or sensed—that if I didn't break open the conversation, it might not happen. And *not* being physical with Cassidy made me feel so desperate, so hollow, I knew I'd regret it for the rest of my life. Over the decades ahead, without him, I'd remember these days with him, and I'd grieve not having lived them to the fullest.

The kernels pop, and I add two more handfuls of corn to the crackling oil, covering the pot with a lid and listening to the rat-a-tat-tat of the corn.

"Ready when you are," calls Cassidy, who is sitting on

the couch, hunched over our makeshift cinema.

"Two more minutes," I say, feeling a rush of excitement and nerves, which makes my stomach flutter with anticipation as if I were a teenager on her first date.

And then it occurs to me that for Cassidy, tonight *is* his first date. As the last of the kernels pop, I marvel at this fact, embracing it, silently promising to make it the best first date that any twenty-seven-year-old guy ever had.

I pour the popcorn into a bowl, turn off the overhead kitchen light, and head into the living room, taking a seat on the couch beside Cass. I put the bowl between us because, I figure, whether a guy is in his midteens or midtwenties, it's up to him to make the first move. It's not dark yet, but the sky behind Katahdin is streaked with lavender and purple, and without any other lights on, the glow from the small TV screen is bright and clear even though the movie is old and there's a bit of static on the top, no doubt from hundreds of viewings.

"Ready?" he asks.

"Yep."

"Okay, then."

He leans forward and presses the Play button on the player, and the 20th Century Fox logo unfreezes as nineties-style synthesizer music accompanies a voice-over about the 1932 World Series and Babe Ruth's called shot.

I've watched this movie a few times in my life. Along with *Rudy* and *Miracle*, it's one of my father's all-time favorites, and without a son with whom to watch his beloved sports movies, the job fell to me. Truth told? I loved a rainy afternoon watching movies with my dad, and I relax into Cassidy's couch as the movie flashes back to the 1960s, showing a neighborhood baseball scene on the small screen.

I'm so into the movie for the first fifteen or twenty

minutes, in fact, taking handfuls of popcorn on autopilot, that when my hand brushes against Cassidy's in the bowl, I'm jolted back to the reality of where I am . . . and with whom.

My heart flutters as I yank my hand away. "Sorry."

"It's okay," he says, and when I glance over at him, his lips are trembling in the bluish glow of the TV, like maybe he's trying not to laugh.

"What?"

"Are you nervous?"

"A little," I admit.

He gives me side eyes. "Which one of us has never been on a date to the movies? You or me?"

"Don't overestimate me," I say. "This all feels pretty new to me right about now."

"Good," he says, picking up the bowl and putting it on his left side so there's nothing between us anymore. "Because I have no idea what I'm doing." He slides next to me until our hips are flush. "I've seen the yawn-stretch-arm-around-the-shoulder move in other movies, you know. I guess I could give it a try."

"Unless you're actually tired," I say, grinning up at him, "you can skip the yawn."

On one hand, I'm accustomed to him touching me. I mean, Cassidy and I have already *been* physically intimate to a certain degree. He carried me on his back. He's undressed me, bathed me, stitched me, and slept beside me . . . but this is different, and we both know it. This is deliberate. Any time we touch each other from now isn't about caregiving or comfort. It's about want. It's about need. It's about sex.

So when he raises his arm and settles it around my shoulders? My breath hitches.

And as the warm, heavy weight of his palm lands on my

shoulder, I am so turned-on, suddenly I wish we weren't at the beginning of the movie. Damn it, but I wish we were at the end. He squeezes just a little, pulling me closer, and I shift left on the nubby brown couch so that I'm leaning against him. I draw my feet up onto the cushion and put my head on his chest, just below his shoulder. When I glance up at him, he's completely focused on the movie, so I look back at the small screen, forcing myself to calm down and concentrate on the movie.

And little by little, I do, until my heart's beating normally, and my attention is focused on the story of a little boy who moves to a new neighborhood and makes friends playing baseball.

Well, until the pool scene.

As I realize what's coming, I'm hyperaware of Cassidy sitting beside me.

We're about to watch the scene where one of the boys fakes drowning so that the lifeguard he's crushing on will give him CPR and he can steal his first kiss.

"I love this part," he says, reaching for the popcorn bowl and offering it to me.

"No, thanks," I whisper, staring at the TV, my entire body on high alert.

"Do you remember your first kiss?"

I nod. "Of course."

"When was it?"

"I was fourteen. He walked me home after a track meet."

"And kissed you."

I realize that Cassidy's staring at me, his gaze searing as I continue to watch the movie.

"Mm-hm."

"They say you never forget your first kiss."

"You don't," I murmur.

My skin is flushing everywhere, and I can't hear the movie anymore. I can't concentrate on it. I can't concentrate on anything except for Cassidy beside me and what's about to happen between us.

"Brynn," he says. "Look at me."

I do.

I turn my neck to look up at him, and his eyes are so wide and so dark, they look black in the soft ambient light. They drop to my mouth, holding there for a long moment before sliding back up my face. He searches my eyes, as though giving me a final chance to push him away, then pulls me closer so that the tips of my breasts brush against his chest.

"I'm calling my shot," he says.

I whimper softly, my lips parting in invitation.

He looks back at my mouth, wetting his lips with his tongue, then leans closer, his nose brushing mine as he bends his head to claim my bottom lip between his. I close my eyes, arching my back to be closer to him as one of his hands reaches up to cup my jaw, his thumb under my ear, holding my face to his. His lips alternate between kissing my top, then bottom, lip, claiming them each individually, sucking, kissing, stealing my breath as the arm around my waist holds me tighter.

His lips depart, but his forehead rests on mine and his nose nuzzles mine gently. I breathe him in, delirious with his taste and touch, with the smell of him, the almost-unbridled strength of him. For a moment, I think we're done, but he surprises me by leaning forward and pressing his lips to mine again.

I moan into his mouth, relieved because I want more. Gently, I swipe my tongue over his lips, and I feel him jolt against me, a low groan rumbling in his throat as his tongue slides against mine. The pressure of his thumb under my ear increases, his fingers curling into the base of my skull as I seal my lips over his, sliding onto his lap and threading my fingers into his hair. My knees dig into the couch on either side of his hips, and behind me I can hear the song "This Magic Moment" playing in the movie, which is the perfect soundtrack for what's happened between us. Deep inside, something that had almost given up on life knows for sure that it's completely, vibrantly alive again, and my heart laughs because I barely remember happiness like this, but it's here, and it's now, and it's Cassidy holding me in his arms and kissing me for the first time.

His tongue dances with mine—touching, sliding, warm and wet—setting off fireworks inside me as I arch my breasts into his chest, and feel his erection between us, hard and throbbing at the apex of my shorts, straining against his jeans.

We should stop.

I know we should stop because this is his first experience with a woman, and this kiss has gone much farther than most first kisses go. But we're not kids walking home from a track meet. He's a man and I'm a woman, and every cell in my body screams for more of him. So I kiss him some more, swallowing his groans of pleasure, the hairs on my arm at attention when he growls into my mouth, his hands dropping to my ass and pushing my groin flush against his hardness.

And finally, finally, finally, when we've missed twenty minutes of the movie, I wrap my arms around his neck and slide my cheek against his until my forehead rests in the curve of his collarbone.

His breathing is fierce and choppy in my ear, and I

smile as tears well in my eyes. My last kiss for so long was with Jem. Now my last kiss belongs to Cassidy. His arms move to clasp me against him, and he holds me as we catch our breath, our hearts flush and pounding relentlessly.

"Brynn . . . Brynn . . . Brynn . . .," he murmurs, his breath kissing my throat.

I laugh softly, pressing my lips to his neck before leaning up to look into his eyes.

They are spellbound and tender, aching with something so beautiful, so inexplicable, all I can do is stare back. All I can hope is that he looks at me like this every day for the next two weeks so that when I am back in my lonely home, I remember what it felt like to be loved by Cassidy.

"Now you've had your first kiss," I say, grinning at his slick, pouty lips.

"And I'll never forget it," he says, but his tone is different from mine—less playful, more like a vow, like he's promising me something important.

Suddenly my self-consciousness kicks in as I realize I'm straddling his lap, pressing my breasts against his chest with rock-hard, beaded nipples digging into his abs. I lean to the left and let gravity pull my leg back over, sitting back on the couch and settling into his side where I was watching the movie before we got carried away.

"Are you sleeping in my bed tonight?" I ask him as I stare at the screen.

"No."

I whip my neck to look up at him, and he glances down at me, gesturing to the prominent bulge under the zipper of his jeans.

"I've got no self-control with you, Brynn. I want everything now." I'm about to tell him that's fine with me when he continues speaking. "But I'm not getting you pregnant, and I don't have . . . protection."

Part of me is shocked that he knows about condoms. I don't know why, because I'm sure his mother or grandfather taught him the basics of sex ed, but still . . . it surprises me that he should be so thoughtful.

"You could pull out," I suggest, instantly embarrassed by the words because they sound so desperate in my ears.

"No," he says, shaking his head and looking away from me, back at the movie. His jaw is tight and his face drawn, like he's angry with me or in some serious discomfort. "That's not an option."

I nod, wanting to respect his decision regardless of the ache between my legs. I could feel him pressing against me, thick and hard, when I was straddling him.

The practical side of my brain reminds me that I haven't been with anyone since Jem, and what's waiting for me behind Cassidy's zipper didn't feel average-size. Maybe a few days to get better acquainted isn't such a bad idea, after all.

Still, I feel a little deprived, and I cross my arms over my chest and huff out a breath as we sit side by side, hot and bothered, pretending to watch the movie.

"Brynn."

"Hmm?"

"I said I wasn't going to sleep with you tonight."

"I heard you."

"But, angel . . ."

I look up at him because the way he calls me angel makes me want to die a little, it's so reverent and tender.

"What?"

"I plan on kissing you until this movie's over."

My mouth opens to an O, and I stare at him as he slips his hands under my arms and pulls me back onto his lap, cradling me there.

"Any objections?" he asks, locking his eyes with mine as his lips draw closer.

"None," I sigh, letting my Cass have his way with me.

Chapter Twenty-Four

Cassidy

Whatever I thought it would be like to kiss a woman, it's all been blown to bits with two nights of Brynn straddling my lap on the couch while we devour each other's mouths, our bodies pressed close and our breath mingling.

She belongs to me in ways now that I couldn't possibly fathom. She owns a part of me that is already gone—that I can never, ever reclaim again.

Exploring the sweet, soft recesses of her mouth while her fingers curl into my scalp, I have claimed her and surrendered to her at once.

Everything is Brynn.

And I am addicted to everything.

She is air. And water. Smiles and soft sighs as she falls asleep in my arms. She is heat and warmth. She is promise and hope. She is normalcy and company and my temporary talisman against loneliness. She moves like the air or the dark, surrounding me, inside me, of the world and yet belonging intimately and particularly to me. She is everything I want that I can't have, more and more necessary for survival, which means it will destroy me when I let her go. I know this. And yet, I cannot slow down or take less.

I love her.

I will love her until the sky falls.

Until the sun and moon fail to rise.

Until Katahdin crumbles.

I will love her forever.

She grins at me over her shoulder as she collects eggs from the girls, and though I am milking Annie, it occurs to me to leap over the stool I'm sitting on and grab her around the waist, hauling her against my body to kiss her until she's limp and sighing. When she smiles, even I, damned from my very conception, cursed from the cradle, feel my heart soar. That's how it is with angels, I'm learning. I bet the devil couldn't stay away if he tried.

I watch her.

I memorize her.

I drink her in—the way her dark hair caresses her cheek until she sweeps it behind her ear . . . the way her eyes sparkle when she peeks up at me and giggles . . . the way her breasts rise and fall with every breath she takes. Her bare feet crackle softly on the hay that covers the hard wooden floor of the barn, and I am drawn even to them, in love with them, jealous of them, hating them a little because they will take her away from me.

Except I can't hate her or anything about her.

I would die to keep one of those toes safe.

My broken Brynn, in pieces when I found her, seems to be more and more whole every day, and I fall harder and deeper for this sweet, gentle woman every moment I spend with her.

"What?"

"Huh?" I mutter, grinning at her because I am a man in love, foolish with tenderness, unable to help himself.

"You're just staring at me like crazy."

I tug on Annie's teat, and a stream of milk spits into my metal bucket.

"Maybe 'cause I'm crazy about you, angel."

She freezes, and her eyes widen as she stares at me. "You are?"

I give her a look. "You know I am."

"Then why can't we . . .?"

She is about to ask me why our days together must be finite, but she catches herself before the words leave her mouth.

Over the past two days, my Brynn has more than once wanted to push our agreed-on boundaries to include a discussion of our feelings for each other or an extension on our time together, but she has stopped herself every time.

I clench my jaw, telling myself that I shouldn't lead her on with statements like "I'm crazy about you," no matter how right they feel falling from my lips. We have agreed to a physical relationship with each other. Nothing else.

"Are you still . . . going to the store tomorrow?" she asks, her cheeks pinkening as she finds an egg under Stacey and places it gingerly in the wire basket.

The store.

The store, where I will buy a box of condoms for the rest of our time together.

"Yeah," I say, my voice tight as I stand up abruptly, eliciting an annoyed "mahhh" from Annie.

Sex.

Aside from Brynn, it's all I think about lately.

When we finally untangle our fully clothed bodies from each other every night, heading to our separate rooms, my body aches for hers so painfully, I've had to get myself off outside under a freezing-cold midnight shower. It barely helps though. My entire being is a magnet drawn to hers, and nothing will feed the hunger until I am buried inside her.

Twice since *The Sandlot*, I've looked at the pictures in my magazines, not to appease my longing or slake my thirst, but because I want to be sure I understand what to do.

I can't lie, I'm nervous about my lack of experience, and the bounty of hers. I can't promise that I'll be smooth when we finally make love, but damn it, I want to get it as right as possible. For her. And, frankly, for me. So that when she compares me with other men, years and years from now, I will have some small chance of holding my own in her memories.

It's wrong, I know.

But I am desperate that she remember me.

Sometimes it's the only thought that gives me strength when contemplating my lonely future—that after the time we've spent together, I will always be a part of her.

"You know," she says, her voice warm and flirtatious as she leans her elbows on the split rail that separates Annie's stall from the girls' coop. "We should have a picnic at the pond today."

"Yeah?"

She nods, a smile, possibly a little forced, brightening her beautiful face. "Doesn't that sound nice? Sunshine? Warm day? Soft blanket? Willing woman?"

Willing woman.

She's going to kill me.

I put my hands on the rail, on either side of her elbows. "Do you swim, Miz Cadogan?"

"Swim? Of course!"

"You been complainin' about your hair for a few days now," I say, so close to her that I could drop my lips to hers. "How about you let me wash it?"

She gasps, her eyes widening. "Cass, I'd give anything."

"*Anything?*" I grind out.

"Anything, but . . ." Her lips close, but lightly, and she tilts her head. "Don't you see? Everything's already yours."

Kill me. Dead.

I reach for her cheeks, cupping her face as I find her lips with mine.

It's not that I'm *used* to the taste and texture of them, but she is familiar to me now, and I sink into the feeling of her, irritated by the fence between us. Instinctively, I want to feel the heat of her body pressed against mine as my tongue tangles with hers. She moans, and the sound shoots straight to my groin, where my pecker swells with a rush of blood, hardening in my jeans. I try to pull her closer but can't, and finally I break off the kiss out of frustration.

"The pond," I pant.

She nods, her green eyes black.

"The pond."

***

As we walk through the meadow, to the pond, holding hands, I think about what I found in the back of my closet while looking for the swim trunks I haven't used in years.

It's a camera—my mother's old Polaroid—and it has three pictures left inside.

I put it in the bottom of a bag holding a blanket, two towels, and a bottle of shampoo, and now I'm wondering how smart an idea that was. I mean, of course I want a picture of Brynn, but will that picture drive me to madness once she's gone? Wouldn't it be better just to live on faded memories?

"Your mom was smaller than me."

The sun is high in the sky, and the tall grasses sway in a lazy afternoon breeze as Brynn looks up at me.

"Huh?" I glance down at her, wearing my mother's old

navy blue bathing suit and a pair of denim shorts. The stretchy material strains over her breasts, dipping so low, it barely covers her nipples. *It's a good thing we're all alone out here*, I think, because what's under that suit is mine, and I wouldn't want another man ogling her.

"Up top," says Brynn, patting her chest with her free palm. "She was smaller than me."

"Yeah." I nod. "She was tiny."

"Was she sick for a long time?"

I think back to the way she kept to her bed more and more, always tired, that worried look in her eyes increasing as the months went on. "For about a year. It went fast."

"Did you take care of her?"

"Gramp and I both did."

"She never stayed at a hospital?"

"No. She went to a doctor toward the end, but it was too late to do much for her by then."

"Cancer, right?"

I nod.

"How did your dad—"

"Almost there," I say, cutting her off. "Did I mention I found a camera?"

"What? A camera? You did?"

"Uh-huh," I say, squeezing her hand, grateful her attention's been diverted. "An old Polaroid."

"Ha! They're back in style now, you know."

"Really?"

"Yeah. Teens love them. They're smaller now and come in all different colors, but yeah, they're really popular. Everything old becomes new again, doesn't it?"

I wouldn't know. Everything old just . . . is.

"There's not much film left in it," I say.

"Enough for a selfie?"

"A . . . *selfie*?"

"You know!" she says, grinning up at me. "We put our cheeks together, hold the camera away from our faces, smile, and click. Voilà!"

"A selfie," I say, nodding now that I understand. "Yeah. I guess we do. There are three pictures left."

"One of Cass, one of Brynn, one selfie," she says in a singsong voice.

Brynn has a pretty voice. Once or twice, while I was playing the Beatles on Gramp's old guitar, she'd hum along, and I tried to sing softer so I could hear her.

"We could have a campfire tomorrow night," I suggest. "I'll get out my guitar."

"Sounds good."

"Will you sing?"

She nods. "If you play the Beatles, I will."

"Then I'll play the Beatles," I say as we clear the woods and find ourselves at Harrington Pond. "Why don't we spread out the blanket on your rock?"

"*My* rock?" she says, smiling up at me, squinting her eyes at the sun.

I kiss her sweet lips, once, twice, three times before kissing the tip of her nose. "Brynn's Rock."

"Brynn's Cass," she murmurs, her voice husky, her lips moving against my cheek.

The two simple words make something inside me clench hard, and it's almost painful, like a swift kick to the gut.

Not for long.

Not for long.

"Yeah," I mumble. I drop her hand and walk through the tall grass, over to the large, flat rock. I spread out Mama's favorite red plaid wool blanket. "Want to have lunch first?"

She lifts the picnic basket and hands it to me. "No."

"Not hungry?"

"Since you mentioned washing my hair this morning, I can barely think about anything else. *Please* . . ." She sighs with longing, and my pecker jumps in my swim trunks.

"Yeah," I say, turning back to the bag to take out the shampoo. "Let's wash it."

When I turn around, she's pulling Mama's shorts down her creamy white legs. She steps out of them and throws them to me. "Last one in is a rotten egg!"

Giggling, she runs into the pond, jumping in and submerging her head almost immediately, though I know it's got to be cold. Glacier-made ponds in northern Maine are rarely warm, even in July. When her head bobs up, she's gasping, but still laughing. I reach behind my neck and tug my T-shirt over my head, then, holding the bottle of shampoo in my hand, I jump from the rock into the pond. It's cold as heck, but refreshing on such a sunny day, and I rise to the surface laughing, just like Brynn.

From where we are, still relatively close to the shore, we can both stand. I hold up the bottle. "Ready?"

Droplets of water cling to her lashes as she walks toward me. "Bottom's squishy."

Turning away, she backs up against me, no doubt feeling the push of my erection in her back. I can't help feeling turned-on. She's practically naked, and I'm about to touch her.

"Oh," she hums, her voice merry as she rubs her bottom against me. "*Someone's* not very affected by the cold."

I clench my jaw, put one hand on her shoulder to make her stop. "You want your hair washed or not?"

She giggles again, taking a step forward so I'm no longer fondling her back with my jutting length. "Yes,

Cassidy. I want my hair washed."

I pour shampoo into my hand, tuck the bottle under my arm, then reach for her scalp, working the soap into a small lather. She leans her head back, moaning softly. I put another handful of soap into my palms and rub it into her hair, taking care to pull it through the strands, gently digging my fingers into her scalp and behind her ears.

"*Cassssss*," she hums, her eyes closed, her face drinking in the sun.

I pull the bottle from under my arm and toss it onto the shore, then I go back to work gathering her dark hair in my hands and massaging her scalp with my fingers.

"Mmmm," she sighs, the soft moan of pleasure competing with a gentle ripple of water and the summer song of the cicadas.

I lean down close to her ear and murmur, "Time to rinse."

She leans back, her neck straining, and I guide her head into the water, running my fingers through the clean hair from her forehead to the tips then back again.

There's something incredibly intimate about servicing her like this, knowing that her gasps and moans of pleasure are because of me—that I am bringing that sort of satisfaction to her. Knowing that I can pleasure her makes me feel a little godlike, frankly, because she is my angel, the closest thing to Heaven I have ever encountered.

The last of the soap floats away, and she leans up slowly, finally standing in front of me, her back to my chest. I watch, holding my breath, as she skims her hands up to her shoulders. She hooks her fingers under the straps of the bathing suit, then slides them down her arms, over her elbows, pulling her hands through the openings, first one, then the other. The suit is peeled down to her waist, hidden under the water, leaving her back naked to me.

She reaches behind, feeling through the water to find my hands at my sides. Taking them in hers, she steps back, her lower back flush against my throbbing erection. My breath catches as she leans her head on my chest, then raises my hands to her breasts, covering her flesh with my palms. Her nipples are hard, like little pebbles covered in velvet, and I move my hands experimentally, cupping the soft, wet mounds of sweet flesh as she closes her eyes and exhales on a soft moan.

Her breath is ragged and choppy as she reaches up with one arm to pull my head down to hers, but when she leans up and our lips connect, she steals all my breath to fill her lungs. Turning slowly in my arms until her chest presses against mine, she kisses me hungrily. I slide my hands down her wet skin, over the bunched up fabric of her bathing suit to her backside, lifting her up. As she does on the couch every night, she straddles my waist, locking her feet above my hip bone and cradling my hard length between her thighs. The stiff points of her naked breasts rub against my chest as she winds her arms around my neck and holds on.

My penis throbs between us, pressure building as she arches against me, moving her hips rhythmically against my arousal, the silken slide of her warm, wet tongue unbelievably erotic against mine. Every nerve ending in my body is firing as this sweet woman moans into my mouth, and suddenly I can't hold back anymore. I let go.

My orgasm rocks through my body, making me growl in release as I clasp her against me, as ribbons of my hot release jet from my body in spurts, gathering in my swim trunks. I am shuddering against her even as I hold her, and she nuzzles my face tenderly.

"Good?" she asks softly.

"*So* good," I answer, the last of my shudders fading. I open my eyes to find her smiling at me.

"Sleep in my bed tonight?" she asks.

I shake my head. If anything, what just happened is proof that I have zero control around her. I won't risk it. I can't.

"Tomorrow."

She unclasps her feet from my waist and lowers them back to the pond bottom, looking up at me, her green eyes deep and lovely, if a little disappointed.

"Thank you for washing my hair."

"Thank you for . . ."

My eyes drop to her breasts, and though I peeked at them a couple of weeks ago, now I stare at them hungrily, with permission, without shame. They are full and pert, with pink nipples that beckon to me. I want to taste them, to kiss them like I do her lips. Lowering my head, I cup the right breast, plumping it between my hands, then dip my lips to taste her.

Her skin is warm from the sun, but cool from the lake, and the already hardened nipple puckers between my lips. I lave it with my tongue, letting instinct take over as she plunges her hands into my hair, drawing me closer with a gasp and groan. Swirling my tongue around the erect bud, I run my thumb back and forth over its twin before skimming my lips across her chest and sucking it into my mouth too.

"Cass," she cries softly.

I experiment with a little more pressure, sucking greedily, and she whimpers sharply, pushing my head away. I rest my forehead in the curve of her neck, opening my eyes, not certain if I've done something wrong.

"No more," she murmurs, out of breath, her pulse hammering in her throat. She forces my head up and kisses my lips, then speaks against them. "It can be . . . too much."

"Bad?" I whisper, frozen, worried that I might have hurt her.

"No, love. Wonderful," she says, drawing back to look up at me. Her lips are puffy from kissing, and her eyes are dilated and wide. I don't know if she's ever looked so beautiful. "But I want more."

Ah. This I understand.

"Tomorrow?" I say.

"Tomorrow." With a nod of her head, she gestures to our blanket on the rock as she pulls up the straps of the bathing suit, covering herself. "Hungry?"

Always, Brynn. Always.

As though reading my mind, she shakes her head and grins at me like I'm being naughty. I've never experienced this sort of flirting before, and I laugh at her expression because I love it.

She takes my hand and pulls me back to shore.

And I follow.

Chapter Twenty-Five

<u>Brynn</u>

After yesterday's hot frolic in the pond, I felt Cassidy's hungry eyes on me for the rest of the afternoon and today over breakfast too.

As he drives away on his ATV after his morning chores, headed for the store, my heart grows tendrils unfurling toward him, straining to be with him even as the sound of the motor fades into the distance. Finally I turn around and climb up the steps to sit on one of the three rockers on the front porch.

Maybe I'll just rock here until he returns and try to process everything going on between us.

My mind is spinning.

We want each other with a longing that's starting to border on desperation, and for the first time in my life, I'm wondering why there isn't a female counterpart of blue balls. I love the attention, of course—the way he makes me feel like the most delectable, desirable woman in creation, and I have certainly never wanted a man so much in my entire life as I want Cassidy Porter.

That said, my poor heart is counting down the days.

With only ten left, I'm not sure how I can bear it.

Losing Jem almost broke me, but Jem is gone, and

there's no way he'll ever be back. He isn't alive somewhere on the earth, living his life without me. He isn't an option, and making my life a shrine to him isn't what he would have wanted.

It isn't what I want either.

I want to live and I want love.

I want Cassidy.

When I leave him in a week and a half, in the back of my mind I'll know that he's alive—he's living and breathing somewhere on the earth without me. *Without me.* Little by little, day by day, *that's* what will break me: knowing he's out there, alive and well, and I can't have him.

And . . . why not?

Why can't I have him?

I push off from the floor, rocking the chair angrily and thinking back to the two times that Cassidy has ever yelled at me.

The first was when we were reading on the couch and I asked him if he was lonely, if he wanted a girlfriend or a wife. His answer hadn't been ambiguous, nor did it leave room for interpretation.

I'm just not much of a people person, I guess, he said. And when I pressed, he snapped at me: *I don't need anyone!*

My mind segues to our conversation in the kitchen, when he removed my stitches.

Not unlike the other time, he totally shut down when I tried to talk about feelings, yelling at me to stop. Later in the conversation, he made it clear that, although he liked me, he wasn't interested in changing his life, that he liked his life the way it was—essentially the same sentiment he'd shared before.

It's a hot button for sure, Cassidy allowing someone into his life. We can't even talk about it without him yelling at me and shutting down.

And that vehemence should convince me he's telling the truth, right? Except it doesn't, because I've always believed that actions speak louder than words. And Cassidy's actions speak about him caring for me, enjoying me, maybe even starting to love me a little. He claims to feel one way about his solitary life, but he sinks into my company, seeking out my presence, spending all his time with me, holding me like I'm the most precious person in his world. So I'm confused by the disconnect. He says he doesn't need anyone, doesn't want anyone . . . but it seems like—it *feels* like—he needs and wants, well, me.

I keep rocking, the movement soothing and good for thinking.

Why would he say something that wasn't true?

Why must I leave when I am well and able? Why can't we be together for a little longer? Or a lot longer if that's what we want?

I can't help but wonder if his reluctance to be with me, or, indeed, to change his life, has something to do with why he and his mother left the town and moved out here in the first place.

Frustrated that I don't have access to the internet, where I could surf their names, birth records, death records, and newspaper articles, I decide to get a little old-fashioned. Maybe I can piece together Cassidy's history a different way. There's got to be *something* inside the cabin that could tell me why he and his mother left town, why he chooses to live this lonely existence, so far from humanity.

I head into the house. He won't be back for a few hours, so I beeline to his room, at the end of the hall. It's small and tidy, with a twin bed, a nightstand, a bureau, a closet, and a door to the outside. I lean down, opening the first drawer of his bureau, then the second, then the third . . . but even when I carefully push around his neatly folded clothes, I don't find anything hidden in the backs of the drawers.

Turning to his closet, I realize that I can't reach the top shelf, so I get a chair from the kitchen and drag it back to his room. I step up on it and look at the top shelf, where, presumably, he found his mother's Polaroid camera. There are winter clothes—a neatly folded parka and snow pants, plus all manner of gloves, mittens, and hats—in a plastic laundry basket. Feeling around behind the clothes, I find nothing out of the ordinary until my fingers touch a metal box. I pull it gently from the piles of clothes and carefully step down from the chair to take a better look.

I sit on Cass's bed and open the top, peering down at the contents. On top is a folded piece of paper, which, when I unfold it, reveals a set of four photo booth pictures of a little boy and a thirtysomething woman, cheek to cheek and all smiles. I recognize Cassidy and his mother instantly and stare at his mom's kind blue eyes and frizzy blonde hair. She is homely. Her front teeth are badly bucked, and she doesn't wear any makeup, but her smile tells me how much she loves her son, and his smile tells me how much he loves her back.

Setting the photo aside, I pluck a leather bracelet from the box and hold it up. Burned into the leather is the name CASSIDY, uneven and jagged, like he made it by himself.

Under the bracelet, I find another photo, this time of a little boy and a grown man standing side by side in a park, about a foot from each other. The man, who is different from the man I saw in the portrait over the sofa, towers over the boy. He stares intently into the camera with his arms crossed over his chest. The little boy does the same, his mouth a flat, grim line. Neither looks especially happy or comfortable.

I flip over the picture and read "Paul and Cass. Father-Son Cookout. 1995."

Paul.

His father.

About whom he never speaks. Who died when he was nine.

I flip over the picture again and look at the man more carefully—the way he wears his hair slicked to the side and his heavy black-rimmed glasses. His shirt is buttoned all the way to the top and tucked into belted jeans. As I squint at his face, something about him feels familiar, though I don't necessarily note a resemblance between father and son. Then again, I think, tilting my head, Cassidy is very tall like his father. But his father appears to have had brown eyes, while Cassidy's are blue and green. I stare at the photo for an extra moment, feeling unsettled, then add it to the strip of photos and the bracelet beside me on the bed.

I find a few more things in the bottom of the box: three marbles, some dirty coins, an empty turtle shell, a Lego sheriff holding a revolver, and a Lego Indian chief with a scratched face. Nothing out of the ordinary, just little-boy things that any normal child might keep in a box of treasures.

Carefully placing the keepsakes back where I found them, I put the top back on the box and step on the chair to return it to its spot in the back of the closet.

I am no closer to answers than before I went snooping.

I close the closet door and leave Cass's room, putting the chair back at the kitchen table and feeling a little ashamed of myself for violating his privacy.

And I must consider, as painful as it is to contemplate, that there *isn't* some major traumatic reason for Cassidy's lack of interest in a relationship with me.

As tears blur my eyes, I think about his words over the several weeks we've been together:

I'm content with things the way they are.

My life works.

I'm not looking to change it.

He's been honest with me from the very start.

He doesn't want a girlfriend or a wife.

And while he might welcome my company temporarily, he doesn't want me in any sort of *real* way.

Feeling quietly miserable, I walk through the living room, to my bedroom, and crawl under the covers. Sometimes, when I look into his eyes, I feel like I see love there, *but it's not love, Brynn.* It's care. It's kindness. Momentary tenderness. Desire.

But don't fool yourself: it's not permanent. It's about now, not forever.

Stupid girl that I am, I have fallen in love with him.

Utterly, totally, completely in love with him.

And all I want is a forever that I cannot have.

***

"Brynn? I'm back."

My eyes are still heavy and burn from the tears I cried before falling asleep. I open them to find Cassidy's face close to mine, and the light in the room fading. It must be late afternoon, which means I've been asleep for hours.

"Hi," I say.

"You okay?" he asks, his brows furrowing as he places the back of his hand on my forehead. "You look a little . . . funny."

"I'm fine," I say. "I was just feeling a little emotional about everything."

"Everything?"

"Being with you." I smile sadly. "Leaving you."

He flinches, and it's a tiny movement, but I catch it.

Confusion darts through me, scrambling the equations I thought I had worked out before. Does the idea of me leaving hurt him? He drops my eyes, turning away, looking up at Katahdin through the picture windows. Apparently we're not going to discuss it. And if I lie here pouting, I will ruin the time we have left together. I'm not willing to do that, so I sit up and muster a smile.

"Did you get everything?"

He looks at me and nods.

"Also . . ." He reaches into his pocket and pulls out a strip of leather. "I got you this."

I reach for it, staring down at the simple braided bracelet in cinnamon-colored leather. It has two drawstring cords sticking out from the ends that will tighten it on my wrist when pulled at the same time. I love it at first sight.

"For me?"

He reaches for my wrist, then takes the bracelet and slips it over my hand, pulling the cords until it's snug. Then he looks up at me.

"I never bought a present for a girl before."

"You did good," I say, cupping his cheek. "Lots of firsts for you lately."

His eyes, so different and singular, scan my face, finally dropping to my lips. He leans forward, pressing his mouth to mine gently. I pull him down to me, thanking him for the bracelet and trying to let him know how grateful I am for everything he's done for me, and, yes, how much I wish there was the possibility of a future for us.

I swipe the seam of our lips with the tip of my tongue, and he jolts, wrapping his arms around me and hauling me onto his lap. Cradled against his chest, I meet his tongue with mine, my thoughts starting to scatter as instinct takes over. My muscles tense and release, longing for his thickness within me, priming themselves to grip him as he slides inside.

Cassidy breaks off the kiss and leans his forehead against mine, panting softly.

"I sort of wanted . . ."

I open my eyes, ignoring the throbbing deep inside and focusing on what he's about to say.

"What?"

"I was thinking I could take you on a date tonight."

"A date? You mean . . . go out?"

He kisses my nose, then leans away. "No. Here. Have a date here."

"What did you have in mind?"

"Do you trust me?"

And the thing is? I do. Completely. Even with my stupid heart, which will be shattered beyond repair two weeks from now, I trust him. I still hope that there will be a happy ending for us, even though I can't fathom it now.

"You saved my life."

He grins at me and nods. "I did."

"More than once."

"It's one of my specialties."

I giggle because the cocky, playful side of Cassidy is adorable. "Okay. So . . . you didn't answer my question: what did you have in mind?"

"Oh, no. You didn't answer *me*. Do you trust me?"

"Yes." I pout. "But I still want to know!"

He takes a deep breath and purses his lips, like he's considering telling me. But at the last minute he shakes his head. "Nope. You're just going to have to wait."

"For what?"

"I guess you better get ready," he tells me in a singsong voice that I sometimes use with him.

I can't help it. I feel excited, wondering what he's got planned. Another movie? Skinny-dipping after dark? My mind segues to the condoms he bought. Surely sex is figuring into the equation, right?

"Are you romancing me to get in my pants, Cassidy Porter?" I ask, grinning at him.

He shrugs, smiling down at me, two pink spots appearing in his cheeks. "Maybe."

"You don't have to," I say simply, because it's true. This man owns my heart and my body, and, I suspect, before I leave him he will own my soul as well. Jem's is up on Katahdin. Mine will be forever with Cassidy.

"I *want* to," he says, his eyes serious. "You *deserve* to be romanced."

Oh, my heart.

"Okay, then. What do I need to do?"

"Um . . ." He looks around the room, his eyes resting for a moment on the trunk beside the bureau. I've ignored it, assuming it held extra blankets like the trunk at the foot of my bed at home, but now I wonder if there's something more inside. "Choose something to wear and get ready. I'll pick you up in an hour."

"Pick me up?"

"At your door, er, curtain. I'm a gentleman."

I chuckle, nodding at him. "And we're just staying here?"

He nods, looking around the room, his eyes serious when they land on mine. "We're staying here, angel. All night long."

He kisses the top of my head and leaves me alone, and I know that the days are dwindling, and I know my heart is going to hurt when it's over, but I refuse to kill the now grieving an unlikely forever.

I smile to myself, excited for our date, and jump out of bed to open Mrs. Porter's trunk to see what's inside.

Chapter Twenty-Six

<u>Cassidy</u>

I've read enough books and seen enough TV shows and movies to know that a first date is a big deal, and though nothing about our relationship has been conventional, this is one thing that I'd really like to get right.

When I was at the store today, aside from picking up a ridiculous number of condom boxes (six, to be exact, which was all they had in stock), I bought some citronella candles, wine, cheese, two steaks, and batteries for my transistor radio. I can pick up WSYY-FM in Millinocket on a clear night, and this one is going to be about as clear as it gets. I also picked up some marshmallows, chocolate bars, and graham crackers because I promised Brynn a campfire, and it would be a shame to have one without s'mores.

I moved the kitchen table outside, on the grass, and I've covered it with an old tablecloth and set it proper-like, with plates, napkins, and wineglasses. It's Blues Night on the radio, which is fine with me, and the candles flicker cheerfully in the evening breeze. I took an outdoor shower and shaved my beard, then slipped in through the outside door of my room to get dressed. I'm wearing clean jeans, a white T-shirt, and a plaid flannel, because there's a nip in the air tonight.

There's still a little time before I have to "pick up" Brynn, so I pour the wine and uncover the sliced Cheddar I bought at the store. Mostly I'm feeling excited, but the way I'm bouncing around tells me that I've got some nervous energy going on too. I *want* to sleep with Brynn tonight. I'm ready to give my virginity to her. But I want it to be good for her too. I can't tell her I love her, because I can't keep her here, and sharing feelings like that would make it harder for her to go. But when we sleep together later tonight, that's exactly what it will be: lovemaking. I've never loved anyone—not Mama, not Gramp, not anyone—as much as I love her.

I turn away from the house and face Katahdin.

Behind the summit, the sky is a riot of color, which airbrushes the clouds in a way that feels otherwordly. Garish orange. Intense purple. Delicate lavender.

Baxter Peak isn't a pitched peak like you'd see in a child's drawing of a mountain. It's smoothed out and mellow, the highest point at a little over 5,200 feet. Compare this with jagged Everest, which stands at almost 30,000 feet. But Katahdin's been around for 400 million years, created when an archipelago collided with the continent of North America, whereas young'un Everest was formed a mere sixty million years ago. Katahdin might be an old lady, but she holds her own. The most experienced climbers in the world have come away from Katahdin calling her a beast, and for whatever reason, that makes me proud.

Most important of all, she brought Brynn to me, and for that I will be forever grateful. That said, however, lately I've started to wonder how I will bear living here once Brynn is gone.

As I drove to and from the store this morning, I thought that, when she leaves, maybe it's time for me to leave for a while too. Maybe not forever, but for a few seasons. I have more than enough money to start over somewhere else or just travel around for a while. Not only have I lived frugally, but I've got a complete skill set for off-grid living. I could just . . . disappear.

But there will be a lifetime of hours to ponder these thoughts later.

Not tonight.

Tonight there's a beautiful girl inside my house, and she's waiting for me to pick her up for our date.

Running a hand through my still-damp hair, I grab the bouquet of wildflowers I've collected and take the porch steps in a single leap, opening the front door and striding through the living room. At the curtain that separates her room from the rest of the house, I pause, acknowledging the bubbles in my belly before knocking on the doorframe.

"Anyone home?"

"Come in."

Her voice makes me smile, and I sweep open the curtain to find her sitting on the edge of the bed, looking up at me. She's wearing a light blue denim sundress that dips just over her full breasts and ends right above her knees, and an open white cardigan sweater. She wears the braided bracelet on her slim wrist, and it makes my heart swell a little because I gave it to her. Her shiny, chestnut hair has been gathered in a ponytail over one shoulder and tied with a light blue ribbon, and her feet are bare.

Christ, how I wish I never, ever had to let her go.

"Hi," she says, grinning up at me.

I offer her the flowers. "You look beautiful."

"Thank you." She leans down to smell them, then looks up at me with sparkling eyes and upturned lips. *Aw, Brynn, Brynn, how I love you.*

"I've got a vase somewhere," I hear myself say. "I'll track it down for you."

She lays the small bouquet on the end table, stands up, and spins around. "I had no idea your mom had a few more things in the trunk. Most of her dresses were too small, but I thought I could get away with this one if I wore a sweater."

I take a step toward her and drink her in. "I've never seen a woman as pretty as you, Brynn Cadogan."

She blushes, and for just a second I feel like the king of the world because my actions and my words somehow manage to touch her. I'm not worthy of her, but she's here, with me, her cheeks pink and her eyes tender.

"You shaved," she says.

"Gramp's old straight razor," I say, rubbing my soft jaw.

"You're crazy handsome, Cass."

"Right." No one's ever called me handsome before. Well, Mama. But mamas don't count—they *have* to think their sons are handsome.

She laughs, shaking her head. "*Scorching* hot."

Though I've never heard this expression before, the darkening of her eyes tells me it's a good thing to be scorching hot, and I can't help grinning down at her, my blush likely matching hers. "Okay. Um, thanks, I guess."

"I thought I heard music," she says, looking over my shoulder.

"You did. I got batteries for my radio."

"And was that candlelight I saw through the curtains?"

"Yes, ma'am."

"And if I'm not mistaken, I heard a cork popping."

"I can't vouch for the vintage, but yes, I got us some wine."

"A candlelight dinner with music and wine," she sighs,

her eyes soft and tender. "Now you're spoiling me."

It's because I love you, I think, but I just nod, offering her my arm. "Shall we?"

She takes my arm with a soft chuckle, placing her hand in the crook of my elbow.

"Tonight is my first date," I say as I escort her across the living room and through the front door. "I've been waiting for it for a long time." We step out on the porch together. "I hope I got it right."

She gasps when she sees our candlelit table, with the blazing campfire just beyond and Katahdin in the distance.

"Wow," she murmurs. "You nailed it."

It's my turn to laugh with pleasure, loving her reaction. "Yeah?"

"Y-yeah." She nods, then sniffles, reaching up to swipe at her eyes. "It's really b-beautiful. Thank you."

"Hey. You're crying," I say, putting my hands on her shoulders and turning her to face me. "Why are you crying, angel?"

"*You're* the angel," she leans forward, sobbing against my chest, resting her cheek on my shoulder. "You saved me. You breathed life back into me. I . . . I . . . oh, Cass . . ."

Her shoulders shake under my hands, and I don't know why she's so sad, but I hate it, even though sadness is a part of the Brynn I love. Her trust in the world was stolen when her fiancé was shot, and again when she was attacked on the mountain. She has a right to her tears, and I am honored to be the person she turns to when she needs to cry.

"Shhhh, sweet girl," I murmur, sweeping her into my arms and sitting down on one of the porch rockers with her cradled on my lap. "It's okay. It's gonna be all right."

"It *won't* be," she whispers, her breath teasing my neck. "I'm t-trying to be b-brave. But it will b-break me in h-half to say goodbye to you."

I force myself to swallow the sudden lump in my throat because her words mirror my feelings. Oh, God, if only we could run away.

But there's no running from what I am, from *who* I am. It's selfish enough that I am taking these two weeks from her. I can't take more. I *won't*.

But I don't want to hurt her either.

I clear my throat, grimacing because the words I'm about to say taste bitter. "Maybe . . . maybe we should stop here."

"What do you mean?"

"Well . . . we don't have to go any further, or make this any harder. We could, you know, end it now. This. Us."

"No!"

"Brynn—"

"No! We agreed to two weeks."

"I don't want to hurt you," I say, reaching up to rub away the burning in my eyes and wishing I wasn't who I am.

She has been cuddled on my lap, but now she sits up and leans away from me, staring out at the mountain that was here long before us and will still be standing long after we're gone.

"I'm going to be a little sad now and then," she says, "because it aches to think of leaving you."

"Which is why—"

"But I want you any way I can have you, Cassidy Porter," she says, plowing over my words as she turns on my lap to look at me and raises her hands to palm my cheeks. "I don't know why you can't see the same future with me that I can imagine with you. I don't know what secrets you hold that make you think we need to be temporary. But I know that every beat of my heart happens *now* because you saved me, so, in a way, it belongs to you as much as it belongs to me. And whatever time I can have with you, Cass, I will not surrender it."

She kisses me passionately after this short speech, her silken tongue gliding between my lips as her fingers curl into my hair. When she pulls away, her breasts rise and fall rapidly with her panted breaths, and her eyes are as black as night.

"I want the candles and the wine and the fire, but first," she says, sliding from my lap and standing before me, "I want you."

Backlit by the sunset behind Katahdin, she reaches for the sweater and pushes it over her shoulders, letting it glide down her arms. Reaching behind, she unzips the dress, pulling her arms from the straps and letting it whoosh softly to the floor. She isn't wearing a bra, only white panties, and she slips her thumbs into the waistband and tugs. I watch as they sluice down her legs. She steps out of them and stands before me, naked in the dying sun.

"Cass," she murmurs, her voice ragged and deep as she holds out her hand. "I need you. Come with me."

I haven't dared to breathe since she said, *I want you*, but I fill my lungs as I take her hand and stand up, following her back into the house.

Her fingers twine through mine as we cross the living room and enter her room. The light of the sunset bathes the small room with ethereal warmth as she turns to face me and backs up to the bed. Holding my eyes, her hands rise to my shoulders, and she slips her fingers under my flannel shirt, smoothing her palms over my skin to slide it down my arms. Her hands flatten on my chest, then drop to the hem of my T-shirt, which she pulls up to my neck. I reach for the bunched cotton and pull it over my head, my heart racing with love and anticipation as I stare down at her.

Her lips twitch with a grin as her hands skate slowly, side by side, over the ripples of my abdominal muscles. They part ways at my pelvis, and she follows the V-shaped lines of muscle and bone to the waistband of my jeans. Raising her chin just a touch, she reaches for the button at my waist and unsnaps it, then unzips my jeans.

As she pushes the denim over my hips, she looks down, gasping in surprise to discover that I don't wear underwear. When I step out of my jeans, I'm as naked as she is.

Without touching, we stand facing each other, our dark eyes locked. In my peripheral vision, I can see her breasts rise and fall with her breathing. No doubt she can see my erection, thick and straining, pointing straight up between us and pulsing with every beat of my heart.

She is beautiful.

She is offering herself to me.

She is giving me something I never even allowed myself to hope for.

I hear a low, guttural sob fill the room, and at first I don't realize it's me, because I'm not crying.

I'm just . . . in awe, and that's how awe sounds.

I don't know how to feel this much love for someone.

It hurts to love her this much.

And yet I wouldn't trade this moment even to cleanse my blood of my father's poison. Every second of my life, every step and misstep, every breath, every choice, every bit of luck and grace and mercy, has led me to this sacred space. If I have to be me—if I have to be Cassidy Porter, Paul Isaac Porter's son—in order to find myself here, in this beautiful moment, with this sweet, stunning woman, then I will own who I am. And for the very first time in my life, I am grateful to be me.

"Cass," she whispers, "do you trust me?"

I nod once. Slowly. "Completely."

"Stay still," she murmurs, smoothing her hands down my arms and lowering herself to her knees before me, her back against the bed.

Lowering my gaze, I watch as she gently winds her fingers around the base of my erection, then licks a trail from base to tip before taking me into the warm, wet heaven of her mouth.

I cry out, my fingers fisting and releasing air, looking for somewhere to hold on. I reach for her dark hair, winding it through my fingers as I close my eyes.

Her lips move slowly over the ridges of my throbbing skin, and I can feel every swipe of her tongue, every swirl, every lick. In all my life, I've never experienced anything nearly as erotic or half as sensual, as this woman bathing my sex with her mouth. I close my eyes, still running my fingers through her hair, as I feel the pressure in my balls building.

And suddenly I realize that I don't know what I'm supposed to do next. My eyes flare open, and I take a step back, pulling back my hips, my pecker disconnecting from her gorgeous lips with a loud pop.

Her neck snaps back, and she looks up at me with wide, worried eyes. "Not good?"

"W-what?"

"It wasn't good? Too much? I can—"

"N-no. It was . . . it was the . . . the b-best thing I've ever . . ." I run my hands through my hair. "I'm about to . . ."

Her mouth opens to an O, and she grins at me, nodding with understanding. "Oh." She pauses, then grins at me again. "It's okay."

"I didn't want to . . . I mean . . ."

Still on her knees, she cocks her head. "Cass, it felt good?"

"G-God, yes. Yes. You're . . ."

"Then come back here."

I feel my brows crease, but I take a step forward, and she reaches for my rigid sex, stroking it gently.

"Cass?"

"Hmm?" I mumble, trying to keep my eyes open while her touch creates a gathering, an awesome tornado of swirling sensation picking up speed inside me.

"I want you to come in my mouth," she says, clamping her lips over the head of my erection.

That's all it takes.

I roar my pleasure, the sound starting as a low growl and growing to a sharp clap of animalistic thunder that fills the room. I rise to my tiptoes as I let go, releasing my tribute into her mouth in pulsing jets of unspeakable pleasure that make my ass clench and fingernails draw blood from my palms.

With my eyes tightly closed, I don't see her stand up and sit on the side of the bed, but when her fingers thread through mine, I force my eyes open and look down at her. She smiles, widely, her lips bee-stung and slick in the twilight.

"Hi," she says, her expression teasing. "You're back."

It's my turn to drop to my knees in gratitude and reverence, and I do, kneeling before her in absolute devotion and utter fealty. I search her beautiful face, feeling my heart swell so painfully full, I almost can't speak.

"Brynn, I . . . I . . ."

"What?"

I reach for her face, cradling her cheeks in my palms, staring intently into her eyes, wishing I could tell her how desperately I love her.

"Thank you."

She smiles, twisting her neck slightly to kiss my palm. "My pleasure."

"How . . . how do I make *you* feel like that?" I ask.

She leans forward and presses her lips to mine, then takes a deep breath. "The same way."

Still perched on the edge of the bed, she doesn't look away from me as she spreads her legs and lies back. I can smell her scent as I lean my head forward and find I'm anxious to taste her the way she tasted me. Unlike the women in my magazines, who are shaved, Brynn has a soft triangle of dark hair at the apex of her thighs. I flatten my hand over it, reveling in the softness before spreading her lips to seek out her clit.

Bright pink and glistening, I assume that it will feel as good when my tongue touches it as it did when her tongue touched me. I lean forward and place a gentle kiss on the slick skin, and I am instantly rewarded with a moan of pleasure that sends a bolt of heat from my lips to my groin, making me stiffen all over again.

With my shoulders keeping her thighs open, I lap at her sex, reveling in the noises of bliss—moans, whimpers, sighs, and cries—that fill the room. When her thighs clamp my shoulders and she screams out my name, her whole body stiffens for a split second before it loses control, writhing in rhythmic ripples as she pants through her orgasm.

I lean away from her as the tension in her thighs recedes, and I stand up, looking down at her on the bed. Her head lolls back and forth, and her eyes are clenched tightly closed. I love her so desperately, I lower myself to the bed, pulling her against my chest and pressing my lips to hers.

We taste of each other's most sacred parts blended

together, sweet and salty, and a potent reminder of the intimacy we've just shared. We kiss fiercely, our teeth colliding and tongues entwining as I roll her to her back and shift my body over hers, bracing my weight on my elbows so I don't crush her.

Her fingers tangle in my hair, pulling sharply, and it brings me back to reality—to the fact that my pecker, throbbing with readiness for her, has lined up at the entrance to her body, and she has raised her knees to welcome me in.

"Brynn. Angel. Wait. Wait for me."

I roll off her, my feet landing on the floor with a thud. The plastic bag from the store is in my room, and I race down the hall, grabbing it from my bed and running back to her. When I get back to her room, she's lying on her side, elbow planted on the bed, propping up her head.

"I wouldn't have stopped," she confesses. "I would have kept going."

"I can't do that," I say, taking a box of condoms from the bag before placing it on the rocking chair.

She takes a deep breath and lets it go slowly as she rolls onto her back, staring up at the ceiling. "I know."

I sense her disappointment, and it makes me hate myself. The last thing I want to do is make her feel anything less than perfect, anything less than beautiful.

Placing the condom box on the bedside table, I sit down on the edge of the bed, with my back to her, then look at her over my shoulder.

"Do you want to stop?"

Chapter Twenty-Seven

<u>Brynn</u>

Do I want to stop? No.

Am I a little disappointed not to feel him huge and bare inside me? Yes.

Did I actually consider letting him come inside me and get me pregnant so we'd never be free of each other? Absolutely.

But . . . do I want to stop? Absolutely *not*.

"No," I say, sitting up behind him. I spread my legs and press my front flush against his back, wrapping my legs around his waist and my arms around his torso. I lay my cheek against his warm, strong back and say, "That's the thing, Cass. I *never* want to stop."

I know he's been holding his breath because his lungs release in a sigh of relief.

"Then help me with this," he says, reaching for the box of condoms and putting a thin foil packet between my fingers.

"Turn around."

I press a kiss to his back and untangle my legs from his body as he shifts on the bed to face me. His cock stands tall and hard, and my breath catches when I consider that it's been over two years since I've had sex. I gulp softly and hope that he's slow and gentle, or that my body remembers how to do this. I don't want it to hurt. That said, I'm also hoping that the blow job I gave Cass a few minutes ago helps him last because I've been in a state of intense arousal for days, and I'm dying for release.

I stare into his eyes as I raise the packet to my mouth and bite it open with my teeth. Peeling the halves away, I pull out the condom and look back up at him. "Ready?"

For a split second, I wonder if we should talk for a few minutes before he loses his virginity to me, but one look in his eyes tells me that the time for talking is over. This is happening. As soon as possible. And we're both more than ready.

He pulls my hand to his cock.

I pinch the tip of the condom and cover the strong, slick crest of his erection with latex, using my fingers to roll the sheath over his straining skin.

"I know you don't want to hear it," I say, placing my hands on his shoulders to sit on his lap, positioning myself over him, "but, Cassidy, I lo—"

"I know," he says, his voice an urgent and strangled whisper as he cuts me off. "And I want you to know that if things were different for me, Brynn . . . if they were different, I swear . . . "

His voice trails off as I lower my body onto his, impaling myself on his throbbing sex with a sharp gasp, followed by a blissful sigh. He is big inside me—thick and hot—but I stretch to accommodate him, and we are an exquisite fit. I don't know how he has this much self-control, but his eyes remain open the entire time, thin circles of blue and green framing wide black pupils as he willingly spears me, making me his, if not forever, then definitely for now.

"You are . . .," he murmurs breathily, moving his hips

up experimentally as his tongue darts out to wet his lips, "the greatest . . . treasure . . . of my entire life."

Tears collect in my eyes, gathering until his face is a beautiful blur and I feel them course down my cheeks. These words are dear to me, so beloved, in fact, that I clench my muscles around him as hard as I can, willing him deeper, wanting him as close to me as he can possibly be. I wrap my arms around his neck, rocking into him, pressing my breasts against him as he thrusts up again.

I am crying and I am laughing at once as he finds a rhythm. To feel such profound love for him in my heart and to *feel* him, hot and pulsing, deep within me, has my climax speeding up, drawing near with every pump of his hips. His erection massages the walls of my sex with every thrust, and I whimper close to his ear, biting blindly until the soft flesh of his lobe is between my teeth. He gasps, then groans, the sound deep and heavy. His hands clasp my hips firmly, careful to avoid my injuries, as he thrusts up within me.

He is panting against my throat, and I suck on his ear before releasing it. I skim my lips over the smooth skin of his cheek to his mouth, demanding his lips with mine, shifting my hands to cradle the back of his skull and spreading my fingers through his hair.

"I want this," I whisper in a breathless rush, leaning back to look into his eyes just before my orgasm crashes around me. "All I want . . . all I w-want, Cassidy . . . is *you.*"

I scream in pleasure, tight, frenetic contractions starting in my sex and spreading out all over my body, making me shudder against him as he thrusts up inside me again and again, faster and faster. I am floating. I am limp. I only exist because of the man making passionate love to me.

"Brynn!" he cries, his arms clasping me to him like I am his salvation, his only savior, and he calls out my name like it is the only prayer that has ever existed, ever mattered. "Brynn! Brynn! Bryyyyyyyyyyyynn!" And then he adds, his voice ragged and destroyed: "GOD, *PLEEEEASE!*"

A desperate plea.

An anguished, almost despairing entreaty.

I don't know why he screams in supplication to God, maybe for the imminent release that he's never known before this moment. I only know that there is me and there is Cass and there must be God too because only God could have imagined our unlikely pairing, because only a God who loves us could have led us to each other.

His body jerks sharply against mine with a sob, before the contractions inside me, filling the condom, become pulsing waves. His forehead falls forward, resting on my shoulder, his lips brushing against my throat mindlessly, instinctively.

We are so close, we are one person, our hearts pounding against each other, our bodies still shuddering, though we clutch one another fiercely, desperately, still intimately joined together. He takes a deep, ragged breath, then groans against my sweaty neck, his breath hot.

I have known love in my life, but I have *never* felt like this before, and I *never* want to leave the sanctuary of Cassidy's arms.

I press my lips to his neck and close my eyes.

I love this man, and I am his treasure.

I must figure out, in the days ahead, how to keep us together.

It's the only thing that matters now.

***

A week goes by in the blink of an eye.

A happy week goes by even faster than that.

When I was in college, I kept a diary, and as I longed

for whatever boy my heart had seized on, my entries were steady, many, and verbose. But when I reread those diaries, years later, I noticed a trend. I could tell the moment he looked my way or asked me out because the entries would cease. During those times, I was too busy to write. I was too happy to pause and evaluate my life in any real way because I'd gotten what I wanted the most and was walking on air for a while.

But sooner or later, something would pull me back down to earth, and I'd return to my diary because *real life*, blunt and heavy, had reemerged. We recognize certain days as the happiest, after all, only because we have something else to compare them with. And because they are finite.

Somehow able to suspend my sadness about our eventual separation, I have lived in the moment this week with Cassidy, and these precious days have been the happiest of my life.

We have had sex in my bed and in his.

On the couch and on the coffee table.

In the outdoor shower under the stars.

Wrapped up in a blanket on Brynn's Rock, beside Harrington Pond.

We've loved each other's bodies well, reaching for one another at any moment, at all moments, wrapped up around one another until it is impossible to tell where he ends and I begin.

We have slept tangled together every night, our dreams mingling, our breath shared, clasping each other until dawn.

We've gardened and collected eggs and boiled water to wash our clothes.

Our mothers sang the Beatles to us as children, and we sing the same songs to each other while Cass thrums his guitar, and we watch the orange sparks of a campfire ascend to heaven.

He's rocked me to sleep while the cicadas chirp their lullaby.

And I've traced the peaks and valleys of his face while he sleeps peacefully beside me.

All the while, we've ignored the ticking down of the days, letting one run into another, into another. Almost by tacit agreement, we've managed not to discuss leaving each other. I wonder, sometimes, if it's slipped his mind. Maybe he hopes it's slipped mine too.

But just as in college, real life always intrudes eventually. My happy days come to a crashing halt on the morning of July 18. The only way I know that it's July 18 is because my period is like clockwork. When it arrives, I know the date and am suddenly unable to ignore it.

There are two days until July 20, our agreed-on farewell.

If I mean to keep my promise to Cassidy, we have only forty-eight hours left together.

He is asleep in my bed, naked in the half-light of dawn while I sit on the toilet, staring down at the pink streaks on the toilet paper.

I love him, and I am certain he loves me, though neither of us has said the actual words. I straighten my back. Certainly we will figure out a way to stay together, won't we? What we have is special—we need to give it a chance. Things like where we live or my job or his dislike of society don't matter as much as our feelings for each other, do they? They shouldn't. They can't.

And yet, I remember that he only acquiesced to a relationship with me when I made it clear that it would be temporary and devoid of communicated feelings.

But would he give me up now? After so many perfect hours in each other's arms? It breaks my heart to think he would, but another question crowds that one out: *are* you *ready to give up the life you had before you knew Cassidy?*

Yes, I think resolutely. *I love him. Of course I would give up anything to be with him. I will sell my house. I will pack up my favorite clothes, put Milo in his carrier, and return to Maine. Return to Cass. I can make a life here. I can be happy here as long as I'm with Cassidy. Right?*

Except . . .

I wipe again, then ball up some toilet paper and slip back into my bedroom, taking a fresh pair of underwear from the bureau and padding the crotch with tissue before pulling them on. I glance at Cassidy, who snores softly, then take a blanket from the foot of the bed and wrap it around my bare shoulders. I slip out the front door and sit in my favorite rocking chair, watching the sun rise over Katahdin and twisting the leather bracelet on my wrist.

Except what, Brynn?

Except . . .

I miss some of my creature comforts, like my cell phone and satellite TV. I miss plentiful electricity that doesn't depend on sunny days, a generator, or a propane tank, and unlimited hot running water that doesn't have to be boiled first.

I miss being able to walk down the street to the market, and putting a load of clothes in a dryer and having them ready in an hour. I miss movies at theaters. I miss the internet. I miss choosing what kind of music I want to listen to and having it at my fingertips. I miss Amazon Prime. I miss takeout.

I don't like my thoughts. I don't want them, but they continue.

Though Cassidy is a capable paramedic, his mother died out here without medical care. What if something happened to one of us and we couldn't get to a hospital in time? What if we had a child and the child got sick? Would I ever forgive myself if that child died because we had chosen a lifestyle that imperiled us all?

I huddle into the chair and pull the blanket tighter because daydreams are lovely, uncomplicated things and crashing back to earth hurts.

Are you really *ready to give up your life?*

It's a question I ponder as I stir our clothes in a cauldron of boiling water after lunch, while I let them cool, and when I am hanging them on a clothesline one by one.

It nags at me while I am cranking the toilet later in the day and taking the refuse to the fertilizer pile.

It pops up again when I peruse Cassidy's books before dinner, already knowing the collection by heart.

But when I watch him cutting wood, and talking gently to Annie, and replacing a rotted board on the side of the barn, my fears are trounced. Because *I want* Cassidy. I know that to my very soul.

Maybe what I want, I begin to realize, is Cassidy, but *not* his entire lifestyle.

Would it be possible, I wonder, for us to compromise? For us to blend our lifestyles to create a new life together? I don't want Cassidy to give up sustainable living, but if we lived on the grid, we could have reliable electricity to power my laptop, a satellite dish, a hot water heater, and other modern amenities. We could still grow fresh vegetables in a garden of our own, but we could also jump in our car or truck and drive to town if we wanted something.

Would it be possible to still live a quiet life without being quite so isolated? Without being so hidden? Would it be possible to have a place where our privacy was at a premium, but not quite so far away from society?

Because that, I think to myself as I wash the vegetables I've harvested today, could be a plan for life. Such a plan makes me feel hopeful and determined, like if Cassidy would just agree to consider it, we could call our shot at happily ever after.

I look up as Cassidy opens the front door and walks into the kitchen, leaning against the wall to watch me.

"Those carrots are mighty pretty, Miz Cadogan," he says.

I grin at him, feeling buoyant, wanting to share my thoughts with him and hoping he likes them as much as I do. "You think so, huh?"

"Uh-huh," he says, sauntering over to me.

Sexually, he is both instinctive and insatiable, and I've watched his confidence double every day. He knows how to make me come quick and hard with his fingers and mouth; he knows how to hold himself back while he's deep inside me, forcing us both to wait for the intense pleasure of release. He's good at sex—no, for someone who just had sex for the first time a week ago, he's *great* at it—and I can't get enough of him.

His flannel shirt is unbuttoned, showing his tan, washboard abs underneath, and my internal muscles clench. I want him. I *always* want him, and we are almost finished with our eighteen condoms. Yet *another* reason to be closer to town. Certainly he won't argue with that one.

He comes up behind me while I dunk a carrot into the second bucket of water. I use the first to scrub the mud off. The second gets them clean. Set up at the small kitchen table, this system has the unfortunate side effect of getting the table and floor soaked, but it's not a big deal. I'll mop it up when I'm done, and we'll have a delicious, fresh salad with dinner tonight.

I pick up another carrot and submerge it in the first bucket, which is brown and cloudy. When I take it out, it's free of mud clumps, but still needs to be rinsed. I switch it to the other bucket, where Cassidy can see my hands in the light tan water, and I rub the carrot suggestively, feeling his eyes on me. He chuckles softly near my ear and reaches for my hips, pulling me back against him, and I can feel his erection bulging through the denim of his jeans. It's straining against his zipper in a bid to get inside me, and that's exactly where I want him to be.

"You're giving me ideas, angel."

"Is that right?" I ask him, grinning as I pluck another dirty carrot from the pile and rub my ass against his cock.

"Heck, yes."

I want to talk to him about everything going on in my head, but first I want him to make love to me so we're both relaxed and open. I'm wearing another one of the sundresses I found in the trunk, and my period should still be light enough not to matter.

I reach under the skirt for my underwear and bunch them up in the middle as I pull them down, stepping out of them and throwing them under the table. Then I lean forward and reach back again to flip my skirt up so that my ass is bared to him.

I hear him hiss through his teeth, and it's one of those visceral, animalistic sounds that makes the moment even hotter. I hear the button of his jeans pop open, followed by the opening of his zipper. My eyes are closed, but I hear the crinkle of a condom packet being pulled from his back pocket and wait as he rolls it on. When his hands land on my hips, I flatten my forearms on the table, spilling more water from the buckets with my movement. Through the sundress, my breasts are instantly soaked, and Cassidy reaches forward, slipping his hands inside the fabric to cup them.

His rigid cock strains against the crack in my ass as he flicks my nipples with his fingers, tugging on them, squeezing them, rolling them, until they're as hard as he is.

"Please, Cass," I beg him, looking over my shoulder and spreading my legs a little wider.

I feel him probing for the right place, and then, without warning, he thrusts forward, burying himself the hilt with one smooth lunge.

I cry out, half in surprise and half in pleasure. I am so full of his thick, throbbing flesh, I can barely think of anything except what's going on between us. My fingers grip the table, and I hold on as he withdraws, then pushes back inside. His hands are on my hips, holding me steady, and he pants in ragged puffs that I feel on the back of my neck. Again he leans away, again the slap of skin as he rams his cock inside me, making more water slosh onto the table, cold against my straining nipples.

One hand slides from my hip to my pussy, and two fingers find my clit. He massages the turgid bud, pumping into me again and again until my body tenses into one glorious, rigid knot, then explodes with pleasure. He thrusts once more, then stills, holding his breath until he growls my name, coming inside the condom, his hips slowing with his release.

The hand holding my hip slips around my waist, and he rests, lightly, on my back, supporting most of his weight on his feet. His voice is close to my ear when he says between pants, "Brynn. My . . . angel. My . . . greatest . . . treasure."

He is still deeply imbedded inside me.

He lives in my heart, and I know—in the most profound reaches of my soul—that he always will.

My eyes fill with tears as I rest my cheek on the wet table, and I whisper, in total and complete surrender, "I love you, Cass. I want to stay together."

Chapter Twenty-Eight

<u>Cassidy</u>

I freeze as the words I've simultaneously wanted and dreaded fall from her lips.

I love you, Cass.

I love you, Cass.

I love you, Cass.

For one world-stopping moment, I let them sink in. I feel her love for me in the curl of my toes and in the tips of my fingers and with every throbbing beat of my unworthy heart.

Then I clench my eyes shut and force myself to reject it. Because I love her too—for that reason more than any other—I cannot accept or return it.

Kissing the back of her neck, I lean away from her, carefully withdrawing from her body and turning away to pull off the condom. I tie a knot in the top and throw it in the garbage. I zip up and button my pants, then turn back around to look at her.

She is facing me, the front of her dress soaked, her underwear balled up in her hand, her face hopeful and worried at the same time.

"I can't take it back," she blurts out, lifting her chin.

"Brynn, please . . ."

"I need to change," she says quickly, fingering the

bracelet she never takes off. "And then we need to talk."

I watch her go—the gentle sway of her hips, the soft touch of her bare feet on the floor. She loves me.

Which means she's got to go, Cass.

You know who you are, whose son you are.

You've lived this fantasy for long enough.

It's time to say goodbye.

When she comes back to the kitchen, she's dressed in jeans and a tight T-shirt, her feet still bare, her hair back in a ponytail. She stands on the edge of the carpet between the living room and the kitchen, arms crossed over her chest, looking at me with an expression that's breaking my damned heart.

"I know I said I wouldn't fall in love with you and that we wouldn't discuss our feelings . . . but I can't help it. I love you, Cassidy. You're the best man I've ever known. And when I see my future, I see you in it. I *want* you in it."

Me too, sweet Brynn. I see you in my dreams too . . .

I clench my teeth.

. . . but this has gone far enough.

It's time to wake up and face reality.

"I've been counting down the days," I lie, resting my palm on the back of a kitchen chair, unable to look her in the eyes. "In two days I drive you back to civilization or we hike out of here. But either way, it needs to end, Brynn. We agreed that—"

"No!" she yells, shaking her head as she advances on me, stepping behind the other chair at the table. "No! It's *not* over. You can't mean that, Cass!"

"I *do* mean it," I say, forcing these words to be said because the worst possible fate for my Brynn would be to saddle her with me. "We *can't* be together. I made that clear from the very—"

"*Why not?*" she cries, slapping her palm on the table. "Maybe you don't love me yet, but you *care* for me! I *know* you do! Don't lie to me and tell me you don't, because I know you do, Cassidy!"

"I can't love you!" I yell back at her, running my hands through my hair. "I just . . . I *can't*. I can't be with . . . with anyone."

She steps around the chair, closer to me.

"Why not? What happened to you? Why did you move out here? Why did your mother die without medical treatment? Where are the pictures of your family? Why do you change the subject whenever I ask about your father? *Why can't you love me?*"

She screams this deluge of questions at me, and they make me tremble because the answers add up to a truth I must conceal. Those answers remind me, fully and thoroughly, of every reason why I can't have Brynn Cadogan. She thinks that if we share our pasts and sort through these questions, we might find answers that will help us. But she's wrong. Answering these questions won't help her figure us out. They'll only confirm what I already know—that there is absolutely no future for us.

I stare at her, my jaw clenched and my eyes burning.

She takes another step toward me, within reaching distance now, and gentles her voice when she speaks.

"I don't care what happened," she sobs, with tears running down her face. "The past doesn't matter. Only now. I want to be with you. I love you . . . just the way you are." She takes a ragged breath, reaching for my arm, but I step back instinctively, out of her reach. Her touch, which I crave, could shatter my resolve, and I can't allow that to happen. "*P-please, C-Cass.*"

"No."

My tears are getting the better of me, so I look away from her, dropping my gaze to the floor in misery.

"Cassidy," she whimpers.

"*It's . . . just . . . not . . . possible*," I grind out softly.

"Please," she begs. "P-please listen. We could . . . we could get a little p-place closer to town, b-b-but with lots of . . . of privacy. We could have a . . . a l-life together. R-read and m-make love. We c-could have a c-couple of kids . . ."

A couple of kids . . . a couple of kids . . . a couple of kids . . .

The words clang around in my head like bullets fired into a metal barrel, and I can't breathe, because having children would be wrong, would be evil, would be breaking old promises that are still essential and must be kept.

Everything in me rebels against what she's saying, and a swirling storm of panic whirls up. My fists ball at my sides in protest, and she's still standing in front of me, talking about little places and privacy and children—everything I want so goddamned desperately and can never have. The world is spinning too fast and there isn't enough time and I hate who I am and I hear a roar of anguish rise from inside me.

"Noooooo!" I bellow at the top of my lungs, advancing on her like a maniac as she stops talking. *"Never! Ever! Ever!"* I raise my shaking fist and hold it in front of me. *"SHUT UP!"*

She gasps, her eyes widening in fear, and lunges backward, away from me, her feet stepping in a puddle on the floor. I watch as she tries, almost in slow motion, to regain her balance, but she can't. She slips and falls, crying out as her wrist slams to the floor first, breaking her fall.

She screams, then whimpers, curling into herself on the floor and cradling her wrist against her chest as she sobs.

I am standing over her.

I am standing over my beloved, broken girl with fisted hands while she cries.

And suddenly time and space flex and loosen, and I feel the spirit of my father pass through me. And in that split second, I know that there were many, many times that he stood over a woman he had just hurt, watching her cry.

Just like me.

Just like him.

What I have always dreaded, always feared, is happening, is coming true.

I am turning into him.

I blink at her lying there on the floor, my heart racing, my lungs unable to fill. I can't breathe. I can't look away. I am so filled with horror and revulsion and self-hate, I want to die.

It was only a matter of time.

My fingers unfurl, and my hands are shaking uncontrollably. I want to reach for her, to help her, to bandage her wrist and apologize for frightening her, for yelling at her, but I don't trust myself. If I am turning into my father, next time I might do worse than just *raise* my fist—I might actually *use* it.

The best thing I can do—the *only* thing I can do—is leave her, put as much distance as possible between her and me.

I leap over her huddled body, bolt out the front door, barefoot, into the dark night, and start running.

***

It's a while before I stop, and I do only because my feet don't have calluses sufficient for running through the woods at night. They are cut up and bleeding from rocks and twigs and uneven ground. They hurt. I deserve it.

I don't know where that violent, beastly scream came

from, but I know it scared her enough to cause her to slip and fall and hurt herself. I know I am the cause of her injury, and I hate myself for it.

I'm not sure where I am, but I was going southeast, toward Baxter Park, when I left the house, so I assume I've come up on Daicey Pond at this point. I wade in, letting my feet squish into the cold mud. It eases the sharp physical pain in my soles, but nothing can lessen the anguish in my heart.

I have hurt someone.

For the first time in my quiet life, I have *hurt* someone.

And worst of all . . . I have hurt someone *I love*.

Looking up at the dark sky, I consider my options now.

Not that she still wants me after what I did, but I definitely don't trust myself around her now. If she should mention being together or—*God forbid*—having children who might inherit and carry the genes of my insane father, I can't guarantee that I won't lose it again. My God, I raised my fist to her. If she'd kept talking, would I have actually hit her? I feel sick at the thought. I want to believe that nothing could ever lead me to harm her. But I know what lives inside me. I don't—I *cannot*—trust myself.

Live quiet, and no matter what happens inside of you, you won't never be able to hurt someone, Cassidy. It's what yore mama would want.

Gramp's words come back to me, as right and true as the day he said them.

I allowed Brynn to get too close to me.

I allowed myself to get too close to her.

I have put her in jeopardy.

The very thought makes me sob. Tears stream down my face as I throw my head back and scream to the dark, unforgiving heavens, "I'm sorry! I'm so goddamned sorry!"

A drop of water plops on my forehead.

It's joined by another and another and another, dotting my face and wetting my shirt, mixing with my tears and washing me clean.

And the answer comes to me quickly:

To keep her safe, send her away.

If you love her, let her go.

There is redemption only through action.

There is peace only through righteousness.

I know what I have to do.

***

I take my time hiking back to the homestead because I need Brynn to be asleep when I get there.

Gramp kept a glass bottle of ether in the root cellar, mostly for the animals. He'd use it if they were injured or, once, for a cow during the breech birth of her calf. At the end of her life, when Mama was in terrible pain and the fentanyl prescribed by her doctor wasn't helping anymore, Gramp would apply a bit of ether to a rag and set it over her nose and mouth so she could sleep easier. I know how to use it.

Brynn must leave, and she can't come back looking for me. I need to get her away from me, somewhere safe, as soon as possible.

On its own, a fight in the kitchen like ours—an intense, emotional conflict between an otherwise loving young couple—might not warrant more than cursory concern. In fact, between two *normal* people, such anger without name-calling, threats, or actual physical violence might even be chalked up to passionate argument. But *I* am not normal. Now that it's begun, it's only a matter of time before my behavior will escalate. And Brynn must be far away from me when that happens.

My plan is to use the ether to drug her while she sleeps so she stays unconscious, bundle her up in a blanket on my lap, and drive her to Millinocket under cover of night. I'll find somewhere safe to leave her, and then I'll return home to start packing up.

I'll shut up my house as best I can and disappear into the wilderness. I will find somewhere else to live quiet, and this time, I won't allow myself to diverge from that course. And if the madness gets bad enough—I gulp with the heaviness of my thoughts—then I will take my own life.

When I get home, I detour to the barn, then head to the house. It's quiet, and the clock in the tidy kitchen reads 1:10. I move soundlessly across the living room carpet, to Brynn's room, and step through the doorway. I swallow back the meager contents of my stomach when I see the state of her room and my sweet girl.

She is sleeping on her side, tissues littering the floor by the bed, her wrist wrapped in a dish towel. Hurt and sad, she must have cried herself to sleep, and my heart aches with love and sorrow and regret. It never, ever should have come to this.

You did this to her.

You, Cassidy.

My fingers tighten around the ether bottle and rag by my side.

Now do what's right.

Make it right.

So I do.

***

It's a slow ride from my place into Millinocket, and it takes a little over two hours.

The roads are mostly empty—they're often quiet anyway, but from two to four on a weekday morning, almost no one is around, which is good. I know where the police station is from my very occasional visits to town. It's behind the post office, where Gramp used to collect his government checks. My plan is to park close by and carry Brynn to the entrance. I'll leave her there and drive home.

When I stop the quad in the far corner of the parking lot, near the road, I don't see anyone around. Brynn hasn't stirred much during our trip, though I've re-dosed her twice just to be sure she didn't wake up. I stopped feeling my arms halfway through the trip since she was lying across my lap. Now I cut the engine, looking down at her face.

I love you, I wish I could say.

And if things were different, I'd love you forever, my sweet angel.

Thank you for giving me the happiest days of my sorry life.

Thank you for seeing the good in me when I know there is so much bad deep inside.

Thank you for loving me when I was certain I'd spend the rest of my life unloved.

I promise—I give you my most sacred vow—that I will never come looking for you again. I will leave you alone to find happiness. I will leave you alone so that I know you're safe.

You are, and will forever be, my life's greatest treasure, and I will still be loving you on the day I die, Brynn Cadogan.

I clutch her against me, clenching my leaking eyes closed as I lean my forehead against hers and breathe her in one final time.

"Don't come looking for me," I beg her. "If I ever see you again, I'll never be able to let you go."

I gather her into my arms and stand up, pressing my lips to her forehead and holding them there for a long moment.

It is a certain kind of death march as I walk slowly across the dark parking lot, to the nondescript brick building before me, because my life will be colorless and loveless when I leave her and go. But still my feet move forward in their labor because I love her and I suspect my descent into madness has already begun

Finally I am near the door, where I find a bench. I can place her on it, and she'll be just to the left of the police station door. Someone will find her quickly. Or when she wakes up, she'll figure out where she is right away. Certainly no one will bother her this close to the station entrance. It's my best chance at leaving her somewhere safe.

Standing behind the back of the bench, I lower her gently before taking a step away. To my right, there is a bulletin board, and a notice behind the glass catches my eye.

TIP LINE OPEN – MISSING WOMAN / DEAD MAN

The Millinocket Police Department is seeking information about the disappearance of a woman from the Chimney Pond Trail on June 19 In conjunction, police seek information regarding the stabbing death of a man found in an Appalachian Trail lean-to one quarter mile west of the Chimney Pond ranger station on June 21.

Events possibly related.

Any details can be forwarded to the MPD.

My held breath burns my lungs as I read and reread the notice once, twice, three horrifying times.

It cannot be a coincidence.

Brynn is the missing woman.

Wayne, her attacker, is the dead man.

My mind flashes back to that afternoon. To hearing Brynn scream. To finding Wayne stabbing her. To throwing him across the lean-to, where he remained unconscious until I left with her.

No. Not unconscious.

Dead.

I . . . oh, my God . . . oh, my God, no . . . I *killed* him.

I killed a human being.

Brynn stirs in her sleep, whimpering softly, but I turn away from her, and I don't look back. I turn over my quad and zoom out of the parking lot like the devil's on my heels.

She will be safe now. And that's all that matters.

As for me?

I am damned.

I am a murderer now . . . just like my father.

Chapter Twenty-Nine

<u>Brynn</u>

I don't know where I am. I just know that I'm not in bed, because it's hard and cold. If I was in bed, Cassidy would be keeping me warm.

I blink my eyes open and try to orient myself, but I have no idea what I'm looking at. Pushing myself into a sitting position, I realize that I'm fully dressed, outdoors, on a bench, beside a red brick building.

Where the hell am I?

As I twist my head to look around, it throbs like crazy, and I wince, pressing my fingers to my temples.

What happened?

The last thing I remember is crying myself to sleep after our fight—our *terrible* fight in the kitchen when I pressured Cassidy to imagine a life with me, and he rejected me without exception, then left me hurting and alone on the floor.

A sob rises in my throat, but I swallow it back. My head aches and my eyes burn. I have no idea where I am, but hysterics won't help me figure it out.

I reach for my wrist and find it wrapped carefully with an Ace bandage, my braided bracelet moved to my other wrist. Did Cassidy do that while I was sleeping? Did he bring me to town to have it checked out? Surely not. He treated my stab wounds himself. Where *is* he?

"Cass?" I call weakly, looking around at the parking lot behind me. There are only three cars parked and no ATV.

I look up at the sky, noting that the sun is on the rise. I'm guessing it's about six o'clock. The world is still waking up.

"Cassidy?" I call again, standing up.

This is when I realize I have shoes on.

I haven't worn shoes in weeks, so the hiking boots I wore to hike Katahdin feel heavy and confining on my feet. I didn't even realize that Cassidy had saved them, but feeling them on my feet feels wrong, feels like bad news that I don't want to hear.

I scan the parking area for Cassidy's ATV because there's no other way I could have gotten here. But I don't see him. I don't hear the quad's motor nearby either.

Looking down, I realize there is a note pinned to my shirt, and I unpin it, holding it up.

Sweet Brynn. This was the only way. You asked if I love you, and the answer is yes. So much that I have to let you go. You will __always__ be my treasure, and I will never, ever forget you. But you are better off without me, I promise. For both our sakes, please don't come looking for me. Cass. P.S. Your wrist is sprained. Ice it when you wake up.

I inhale sharply, my fingers shaking as I read and reread the short message, its stark and horrible meaning sinking in. I stare at the beautiful, ruthless letters that have severed my life from his. He loves me, but he has gone to drastic measures to keep us apart, and it rips my heart in two.

He's left me here.

He's gone.

My stomach clenches and my knees weaken, forcing me back down on the bench. I lean forward on my knees, afraid I'm going to be sick.

"Miss? Miss? I just seen you out here. Can I help you?"

Turning to look behind me, I see a glass door being held open by a portly, uniformed officer.

"Miss? Are you okay?"

No. No, I am not okay. Not at all.

"I don't . . . I don't know. Where am I?"

"You're in Millinocket, Maine. At the police station," he says, gesturing to the words on the door. "Why don't you come on in? I have a pot of hot coffee brewin'."

"No. I have to find . . ."

Who? Cassidy? No, Brynn. Cassidy's gone. No matter how much he claims to love you, it wasn't enough to want a future with you.

"Miss, you don't look too good. What's your name?"

"Brynn Cadogan."

"Brynn *Elizabeth* Cadogan?"

I nod, distracted from the pain in my heart by the fact that this person knows my middle name.

"Well, good Lord," he says, opening the door a little wider. "We been lookin' everywhere for you."

"For *me*?"

"Ayuh, miss. For you."

I tilt my head to the side and walk into the small police department, watching as he opens a leaf in the countertop and rounds the counter to sit behind the desk. "Brynn Cadogan. Yore parents been sick 'bout you. They been stayin' over at the Ferguson Lake Lodge on Route 11. Been up that mountain 'bout a hundred times lookin' for you, don't you know."

"My parents?" I gasp. "They're . . . *here*?"

"Ayuh. At the Ferguson Lake Lodge."

"How long have they been here?"

"Two weeks? Three, maybe? Don't know exactly, but we see Colin 'n' Jenny least every other day. They come by lookin' for leads." The officer cocks his head. "If you don't mind my askin', what in sam hell *happened* to you?"

I place my palms on the reception desk between us, my fingers white and rigid. "I was hiking Katahdin a few weeks ago. I was attacked. In an AT lean-to."

"Yep." He nods, like he knows, unaccountably, that this is so. "On June 19"

"That's right." I rub my forehead, the bruising headache getting worse and my stomach still roiling, though I haven't eaten anything since lunch yesterday. "I was, um . . . a little bit west of the Chimney Pond-Saddle merge when a man named . . . um, named Wayne attacked me."

"Huh," he murmurs, squinting his eyes and pursing his lips like something isn't quite adding up. "You say his name was . . . *Wayne*?"

"Yes. Wayne. He . . . he stabbed me."

I hear the front door open behind me, and the officer I'm speaking to makes eye contact with someone over my shoulder. "Mornin', Marty. I think you're gonna want to hear this."

Hee-uh this.

Another officer, dressed in street clothes and slightly younger than the first, opens the leaf in the counter and faces me. He looks me over, his brown eyes keen, before nodding slowly.

"Brynn Elizabeth Cadogan," he says, staring at my face.

"Yes, sir."

"Where you been?"

The first officer clears his throat and nods. "Go ahead and tell Marty what you just told me."

"I was attacked on the . . . the, uh, Saddle Trail. A little ways up from the Chimney Pond merge. I had s-skinned my knee and wanted to bandage it up. I stopped in at a lean-to, and . . . and . . ."

The relentless rain.

Wayne's smile.

Want me to take a look-see at your kneesie?

It all comes rushing back, and the room spins so I clench my eyes shut.

"Take your time," says Marty. "Lou, get her a cup of water, eh?"

I take a deep, shaking breath and open my eyes. "There was a man there. Named W-Wayne. He . . . he threw me against the wall . . . and he . . ." My hand falls to my hip. ". . . he stabbed me. He s-stabbed me six times."

Marty tilts his head to the side, then rubs his chin. "*Wayne*, you say."

"Wayne." I nod, twisting the braided bracelet that Cassidy gave to me. "He said his name was Wayne."

"Huh." Marty is perched on the side of Lou's desk with a cup of coffee in one hand and a laptop bag on his other shoulder. He points to a nondescript gray metal desk a few feet behind him. "I think we better sit down to sort this out. Come with me, miss?"

He opens the leaf in the counter, and I follow him to his desk. He gestures to a beat-up, padded chair, and I sit down, gratefully taking the cup of water that Lou offers. I take a sip, letting the coolness sluice down my throat, and suddenly my eyes fill with tears.

Cassidy brought me here.

He *left* me here.

He is gone and believes I am better off without him even though he loves me . . . even after I told him I loved him. Even though we love each other, he isn't willing to give us a chance.

A sudden pain in my chest makes me cover my heart with my palm. I whimper softly, and I think I'm going to be sick. I close my eyes, leaning my chin on my chest.

"Just breathe a minute, miss," says Marty. "I'll get some fresh air in here."

I hear the sound of a window opening, and suddenly the sounds of humanity fill the room—the hum of a car engine, the footfalls of a jogger, the buzz of a cell phone.

I am so far from Cassidy now.

He has abandoned me here.

I am all alone.

Yore parents been sick 'bout you. They been stayin' over at the Ferguson Lake Lodge on Route 11.

As tears roll down my face, I am overwhelmed with a longing to see my parents.

"I want my mom and dad."

"Of course. But first, Miss Cadogan, we really need to hear your story," says Marty, sitting back down at the desk. "Do you think you could just tell me what happened out there?"

I take a deep breath and look up. "And then I can go see them?"

"After we get your statement, I'll drive you over there myself." He clicks the top of a pen and positions it over a notepad. "Let's go back to that day. You were hikin' the AT . . ."

"Not the AT. J-just Katahdin."

"Alone."

"No." I shake my head. "With a group, at first. Two girls from Williams. They turned back because of the rain."

"But you kept goin'."

I gulp, remembering the girls trying to get me to go back with them. At the time, I was determined to keep walking for Jem. And if I hadn't, I never would have met Cass.

My broken heart weeps. Will I ever see Cass again?

"Miss Cadogan? You kept walkin' . . . and then what?"

"The rain was coming down hard, and I slipped. I skinned my knee."

"Then what? Take your time."

"We had . . . we had met a man named Wayne at Roaring Brook. He was . . . aggressive with us. Called us names. He was . . ." *You're just tourists in my dreams.* I shake my head. "He was *off*. We knew he was off from the start. Something wasn't right about him, and we sensed it. He wanted to hike with us, but we said no and he got angry. And then these guys from . . . from, um . . . um . . ."

"Bennington College?" asks Marty.

My neck jerks up, and I search his face. "Yeah. Bennington. How did you . . .?"

"We've talked to them a few times. Them and the girls. They were the last to see you that day." He grimaces. "You skinned your knee. What happened next?"

"I saw the lean-to through the rain, so I walked over to it, thinking I could patch up my knee and wait out the storm. But . . . but Wayne . . . Wayne was . . ."

Well, if it ain't Grandmaw.

My heart is racing like crazy.

"I . . . oh, God . . ." I sob, the events of that terrible day closing in around me.

"Slow down, now," says Marty. "Easy. Breathe in."

I close my eyes and take a deep breath, opening them as I exhale.

"That's right," says Marty. "Now back to this . . .

Wayne."

"Yes. Wayne. He drank some . . . um, some tea and alcohol. S-scotch, I think. He was still angry that we didn't let him walk with us. He threw me against th-the wall, and . . . and . . ."

"And he stabbed you."

My hand has moved to my hip, and I slide up my shirt a little, looking down at two of the pink scars that are still healing. "Six times."

"All we ever found was your backpack. Nothin' else," says Marty. "How'd you fight him off?"

"I didn't." *I was dying.*

"How'd you get away?" asked Lou, who is standing behind Marty, staring at me intently.

"I was saved," I whisper, bowing my head as tears stream down my cheeks.

"By who?"

I look up at the officers and gulp over the lump in my throat. "A man named . . . Cassidy Porter."

Marty and Lou snap their necks around to face each other so fast, I'm surprised I don't hear twin cracking sounds.

"*Porter*?" confirms Lou, eyeing me like I've said something completely crazy.

I nod. "Cassidy Porter."

Marty clears his throat, leaning away from me, his face a mixture of disbelief and confusion. He looks down at his notepad, then back up at me, tapping his pen between his fingers. "Let me be sure I got this straight. You say you were *attacked* by a guy named Wayne and *rescued* by a guy called Cassidy Porter."

"Yes," I whisper, looking at Marty's stunned expression.

"Miss Cadogan," says Marty, rubbing his chin before dropping the pen on his notepad and looking back up at me. "That's impossible."

"I'm telling the truth."

"You can't be," he says evenly.

"I . . . I am. A man named Wayne attacked me. A man named Cass—"

"Miss Cadogan, Cassidy Porter is dead."

With those four words, all the air is sucked out of the room, and I am like a fish on the carpet, flip-flopping like crazy, trying to breathe.

"Calm down, now. Miss Cadogan. Breathe deep."

Marty is pushing the cup of water into my hands, and I raise it to my mouth with a shaking hand, taking a messy sip.

"What are you talking about?" I rasp, my voice breathy and breaking. "That's . . . that's . . . no! No, no, no! I was just *with* him! Just last night. What do you—"

"Slow down." Marty holds a hand up, turning slightly to Lou. "We got a blanket back there? I think she's in shock."

"I'm *not* in shock! Cassidy Porter is *not* dead! He's . . . he's . . ."

Marty backs his chair away from the desk and rolls it over to me until we are almost knee to knee. His voice is gentle. "You've been through a tough time."

"Cassidy Porter *isn't* dead," I sob, circling my thumb and forefinger around the bracelet he gave to me.

But honestly? I can't account for the time between falling asleep last night and waking up here. Something could have happened to him. Maybe that's how I ended up here.

"He is," says Marty. "I can say that with one hundred percent certainty."

My heart drops like it's made of lead.

"This happened last night?" I shake my head as more

tears blur my vision. "What happened to him? Oh, my God. Please, no. Please, please, no. I don't understand!"

Lou returns with the blanket and puts it around my shoulders. Although I didn't want it, I pull it around myself. My hands are shaking and my mind is racing.

"*Please* . . . tell me." I beg, looking up at Marty.

Marty nods, sliding a folder from a mesh basket to his desktop and opening it. His fingers trace neatly typed details, finally stopping at a paragraph midpage. "You were reported missing on June 25. Your parents received a call from an anonymous source who left them a voice message saying you had been injured but you were okay. With no other information, they were understandably concerned. They reported you missing and arrived here on June 26 to look for you."

I don't care about any of this. I need to know what happened to Cass.

"Cassidy Porter! What happened to Cass?" I sob.

"Just follow me here, Miss Cadogan," says Marty. He drops his eyes back to the typed page. "We found a man in the lean-to you're talking about. He was found dead on the morning of June 20th, reported by a couple of early-morning hikers. He was found on his stomach, and there was a knife through his heart. He'd been dead for about eighteen hours by the time we recovered his body. We found your backpack nearby and your, well, a good concentration of your blood in one corner of the lean-to. What we found was a match to your parents, so we know you were attacked there. But a week of bloodhounds searching the mountain turned up nothing. You were in the wind."

"Because Cassidy carried me home on his back."

"*Cassidy*," Marty mumbles, shaking his head. "Well, I don't know about that. What I *do* know is that the dead man didn't have any ID on him, so we ran a DNA test to see if there were any matches in the system." He pauses, and I brace myself because I can sense that something terrible is coming. "There was one parental match, with a 99.9 percent certainty. The man who attacked you . . . the dead man you keep callin' Wayne . . . was born Cassidy Porter, the only son of Paul Isaac Porter."

My mind flashes back.

Paul and Cass. Father-Son Cookout. 1995.

"You know who he was? Paul Isaac Porter?"

"Paul," I say. "Cassidy's father."

"Er, um, yes." Marty is staring at me like he's afraid my head might explode. "But he was also—"

"Wait. So you're saying . . ." I clear my throat. "You're saying that *Wayne*, the man who attacked me . . ." My aching brain is desperately trying to keep up. "You're saying that Wayne's real name was Cassidy Porter?"

Marty nods slowly. "Yes. I am sayin' that I am *positive*, beyond any shadow of a doubt, that the man who attacked you in a lean-to on June 19, and *died* in that lean-to on June 19, was born Cassidy Porter. His DNA was a match to Paul Isaac Porter, who only had one son, Cassidy, born at Millinocket General Hospital on Sunday, April 15, 1990."

"But . . . that makes no sense! I was *saved* by a man named Cassidy Porter."

"I don't see how that's possible," says Marty, flipping through the file until he comes to a DNA test, "unless there are two Cassidy Porters, which feels mighty unlikely. The man who attacked you had a birth record on file. The DNA match was definitive. Father was Paul Isaac Porter." Marty flips through a few pages in the file and stops at the results of an official DNA test. "And just to be absolutely certain of his identity, we compared the DNA to his only living relative, a great-uncle on his mother's side named, uh . . . Lou, you remember the uncle's name . . .?"

"Name of Bert Cleary," says Lou, over his shoulder. He's sitting back at the reception desk, listening to our conversation.

"Right. Bert Cleary. Lives over in, uh, Wolfeboro, New Hampshire. Matched up perfect. Rosemary Cleary was his mama; Paul Isaac Porter was his daddy. Just like on his birth certificate. Open-and-shut case. The man who attacked you, who died in that lean-to, was Cassidy Porter."

"Why did he call himself Wayne?"

Marty shrugs. "Maybe an alias? I don't know, miss." He pauses, staring at me with narrowed eyes, his voice level but heavy. "Miss Cadogan, have you ever *heard* of Paul Isaac Porter? I mean, aside from his being Cassidy Porter's daddy?"

I shake my head, a sixth sense telling me that I am about to hear something very bad.

He looks sorry for a minute, then pulls a black-and-white photograph of a man from the back of the folder. He spins it to face me, and I recognize the face immediately as the same man from the photo of Cass and his dad at the father-son cookout. *Hair slicked to the side. Heavy black-rimmed glasses. Shirt buttoned all the way to the top.*

A few seconds ago, I wondered if there were two totally different Cassidy Porters who coincidentally lived in this area of Maine—one who attacked me and one who saved me. But now I know that's not probable, because *this* man is connected to one by DNA and the other by a photo I've seen with my own eyes. It's *all* somehow connected, though I haven't the slightest idea how to unravel it.

"Miss Cadogan?"

"I recognize him," I murmur.

Marty sighs heavily. "Ain't no good way to say this, I guess, but that man right there, Paul Isaac Porter, was a convicted serial killer. Killed over a dozen women. Arrested in 1998. Tried and convicted back in 1999. Killed in a prison fight in 2000 while awaiting execution."

"You're . . . you're saying . . ."

"Cassidy Porter's father was a serial killer."

My entire motherfucking universe spins out of control as my feeble, overworked, aching mind tries to process what *the fuck* is going on here, what *the actual, ever loving fuck* is being said to me.

Paul Isaac Porter was a convicted serial killer. Killed over a dozen women.

Cassidy Porter's father was a serial killer.

My stomach heaves, surprising us all by emptying its meager contents onto Officer Marty's shoes. I retch and sputter, my tears falling endlessly as I vomit water and bile onto the police station floor.

"Christ, Lou! Get the mop! She's sick!"

I feel a hand on my shoulder, and a moment later someone puts an ice pack on the back of my neck. A mop appears by my feet, sopping up the mess, and another cup of cold water is shoved into my hands. I drink cautiously to get rid of the taste in my mouth, then take a handful of tissues from Lou to wipe my face.

When I look up at Lou and Marty, I find them staring down at me with concern.

"You, uh . . . you okay, now?" asks Lou with a kindly grimace.

My shoulders are still shaking from the retching and crying. My head is still throbbing, and I can't begin to process the information I've been given. *Cassidy's father was a serial killer. And Cassidy isn't Cassidy. Then who . . . who . . .*

It's too much.

All I want is a hot shower and to fall asleep wrapped up in my mother's arms.

"I need my mom," I sob. "Please."

"Yeah. Of course," says Marty. He turns to Lou, throwing him a set of keys. "Will you bring my car around to the front?" Lou hustles off, and Marty looks at me. "It'll just be a minute."

"Thank you."

He sits down across from me again. "To be honest, it wasn't such a huge surprise that the son of a serial killer would get into some trouble of his own. We heard from the Bennington and Williams kids that Cassidy Porter was harassing hikers that day down at Roaring Brook. We figured he got into it with someone on the AT and ended up falling on his own knife."

"No," I whisper, recalling Cassidy's retelling of what happened after I blacked out. "He was thrown."

"Thrown?"

I nod slowly. "Cassid—" I look up at Marty and blink twice. "I mean, *the man who saved me* . . . he . . . he caught my attacker stabbing me and threw him off my body. Wayne, uh, *the dead man* . . ." I cannot bear to call him Cassidy. ". . . must have landed on his knife."

"Hmm. Well, no other prints on the knife but his, so you're probably right. It's a closed case now. He attacked you. Fell on his knife. Thrown. Whatever. Ask me, he got what was comin' to him. Just glad that other fella come along when he did. He's a hero for saving you."

That other fella. A hero.

Cassidy. My Cass.

Except he isn't my Cass. His name might not be Cassidy at all. I have no idea who he is, and I wonder if *he* even knows who he is.

I look up at Marty.

"Who saved me?" I ask in a whisper, more to myself, maybe, than to him.

Marty shuts the folder on his desk and picks up his pen again, holding it over the notepad for a moment before drawing a large question mark.

"I think we've got a bit of a mystery there. You say that the man who attacked you was called Wayne, and that Cassidy Porter saved you. Only that's scientifically impossible. I can't rightly say who saved you, or why in the world he goes by the name of Cassidy Porter." He shrugs. "Just count your lucky stars he found you when he did."

I gulp, staring up at him, letting tears of exhaustion, confusion, and sorrow slide down my face.

"I guess you have a guardian angel," he says, giving me a kind smile as Lou returns to tell us that the car is waiting.

I follow Marty through the station, to the waiting car, letting him open the rear door, and slump into the back seat as I look out the window. More useless tears stream from my eyes.

I have a beautiful, nameless guardian angel hero whom I love.

Who left me here.

Who doesn't know who he really is.

Who is as lost to himself as he is to me.

Chapter Thirty

Brynn

"Brynn, sweetheart, do you need anything?" my mom asks through the bathroom door.

She's hovering.

Not that I blame her, but I need a little bit of alone time after: 1.) Being abandoned by Cassidy, 2.) My disturbing, illuminating conversation with Officer Marty, and 3.) The intense reunion I just had with my parents.

"I'm okay, Mom. I'll be out soon."

"Your dad got back with the clothes. He found, uh, some shorts and a T-shirt at the gift shop."

"Okay," I say. "Thank you."

"Well, sweetheart, take your time. We'll be right out here. Call out if you need something."

"Thanks, Mom."

I've been soaking in their hotel tub for about twenty minutes, keeping my bandaged wrist out of the water. The rest of my tired, aching body feels like it could stay in the hot water for days.

Officer Marty called ahead to the Ferguson Lake Lodge as he drove me over, and my parents were waiting at the front door. I fell into their arms the moment I exited the police car, all of us crying and my mother leaning back again and again to cradle my face in her palms and assure herself that I was here and alive.

We feared the worst . . . back from the dead . . . what happened?

I returned the blanket to Officer Marty, who advised, again, that I make a stop at Millinocket General Hospital to have a checkup, but I don't believe that's necessary. My stab wounds are healing nicely, and I feel fine. I mean, my *body* feels fine. My heart is broken. And my mind? My God. My mind can't stop spinning. I can't seem to fit all the pieces together on one hand, but on the other, so many of my questions have suddenly been answered.

No matter who my Cassidy is, I know one thing for certain: he *believes* that he is Cassidy Porter, the son of convicted serial killer Paul Isaac Porter.

Perhaps he *is* a second son of Paul Porter? It's possible, but it doesn't feel right. Cassidy was the exact opposite of evil: he was all goodness, through and through. I can't imagine even a cell of Paul Porter's evil nature alive in Cass. More likely, I think he might be a second son of Rosemary Cleary Porter, the mother for whom he felt a real, strong, and genuine affection.

But why would she name two of her sons Cassidy? It doesn't make any sense.

What does make sense, suddenly, is the way Cassidy refused to talk about his father, always changing the subject when I tried to mention him. That father-son picture was of my Cassidy standing beside his "father," a serial killer. No wonder I sensed uneasiness in his posture. Did he know what his father was? My God, he lived for years with a monster. Did he sense it? When did he find out?

I take a shaking breath, wondering what he has seen in his life, the horror he has possibly known. Because I can't bear it, I switch gears and put together the pieces of his timeline that were missing.

He was born in 1990, and the picture at the cookout was taken in 1995, the same year as the portrait of him with his mother and grandfather. The newspaper photo from the Little League game was in 1997, and from the normal, everyday way it referred to his parents, I think it's safe to assume that Paul Isaac Porter was keeping his crimes under wraps at that point.

He was arrested in 1998, convicted in 1999, and killed in a prison fight in 2000. But Cassidy moved to the cabin in 1999 without his father. *My mother didn't feel comfortable living alone in town.* He and his mother likely never returned to civilization because his surname was feared and notorious.

So many things make sense now: how he changed the subject every time I asked about his father, why he doesn't want to be around people, why he isolates himself from society. I can only imagine the weight of the name Porter on an innocent little boy's shoulders.

Innocent.

A terrible thought occurs to me, and I let it take shape in my mind because it makes sense to me, though it also breaks my heart.

You are better off without me, I promise. For both our sakes, please don't come looking for me.

Does Cassidy bear some guilt for his father's choices?

Surely he knows that he is innocent of his father's terrible crimes?

My mind segues to the dozens of books on DNA and genetics in his living room. I remember asking if one of his parents was a geneticist, but he said no. And since his father never lived at the homestead, those books belonged to someone else. His grandfather? His mother? One of them was obsessed with DNA and genetics. Why?

I whimper with growing understanding and profound, twisting sorrow as puzzle pieces snap together, giving me a more complete picture of Cassidy's upbringing.

When your son/grandson has a serial killer for a father, you can't help but wonder how he's going to turn out.

I flip through different moments with Cassidy in my mind:

I trust you, I said to him on the first day I was fully conscious at his house. *You probably shouldn't*, he grimly answered.

And in the beginning, he reassured me endlessly that he wouldn't hurt me—it was almost a mantra. At one point he even said: *I just like living out here, is all. I won't hurt you, Brynn. I'm not some psycho. Not yet, anyway. I promise.* That curious "not yet" has new meaning to me now.

Some stories have really bad endings, he said when I asked if he had a story to tell me. He meant *his* story. The story of him and his parents.

And the way he always said that he wished things were different makes sense now too.

He wouldn't have sex with me without a condom. He was adamant about it, and when I asked why, he bluntly said, *I'm not getting you pregnant.*

And during our horrible, blistering fight in the kitchen, he practically screamed, *We can't be together. I can't love you! I can't be with anyone!*

Even the reason he finally flipped out, yelling at me and raising his shaking fist between us . . . I was talking about having kids. *That's* what made him snap.

Oh, my God.

It's all connected, I realize in a startling burst of clarity: the DNA books, his promises not to hurt me, wishing things were different, not risking impregnating me, the conviction that he couldn't be with anyone, and the fierce and furious panic at the notion of having children.

"Oh, Cass," I murmur as my tired eyes blur with tears. "Who told you that you had to stay unloved? Who made you believe that you would make the same choices your father did? And who told you that any children you had would be poisoned too?"

The answer? Someone traumatized by the true nature of her husband or his son-in-law had taken it upon themselves to inject this venom into Cassidy's mind, to make him believe that the son of a serial killer had no right to happiness and barely any right to life.

The stark, cruel, brutal unfairness of it makes my heart stutter.

"Cass," I sob, understanding why he fought his feelings for me, knowing why he pushed me away. I think—my God, this is so sad, I can't keep from crying—but I think he did it to keep me safe. From himself. The one man who I know, in the depths of my heart, would never hurt me.

You asked if I love you, and the answer is yes. So much that I have to let you go . . . you are better off without me, I promise. For both our sakes, please don't come looking for me.

I wipe away my tears, lift my chin, and lean forward to drain the bath.

Except I know things about my Cassidy now that *he* doesn't even know.

The first is that I am *not* better off without him.

And the second is that I am damn well going to start looking for him as soon as I figure out who he really is.

***

"So you're saying that the man who attacked you and the man who saved you are the same person?" asks my mother,

her eyebrows deeply furrowed, her voice terse and confused.

"No," I say, shaking my head. I am sitting on their king-size hotel bed cross-legged in a bathrobe, facing my parents, to whom I've been trying to explain this crazy story for about an hour. "No. Follow me, Mom. The man who attacked me was *born* Cassidy Porter, but we're going to call him Wayne, okay? *Wayne* was the biological son of a serial killer."

". . . which makes a certain amount of sense, considering he tried to kill you, bug."

"That's right, Dad."

"What about Jem?" my mother asks, her voice perturbed. "You say you love this mountain man . . . this s-serial killer's son, but you've been grieving *Jem* for two years, worrying us sick! I can't keep up with—"

"Mom," I say gently, "I know it's a lot to process. Of course I loved Jem. And part of me always will. But Jem's been gone for years. Meeting Cassidy and falling in love with him . . ." I sigh, trying to organize my thoughts so I can catch her up to where I am. "In a weird way, I feel like Jem was part of the journey to Cass. If I hadn't loved him so much, I never would have come here. I never would have met Cassidy. He saved my life. He made me want to live. He . . . he is such a *good* man, and he understands me in ways that are so deep and unexpected, I'm scared of losing him. I'm terrified I'll never find anyone else who will complete me like he does. I love him. I want to be with him, and if he knew who he really was, I think he'd want to be with me too."

My dad pats my leg. "I'm following, bug. And I have to say, I haven't seen you this fired up, this *alive*, since, well, since before you lost Jem. Whoever this Cassidy is, I want to meet him. I want to thank the man who saved my girl."

My father has always gotten me, and I give him a grateful smile, then turn to my mom. "I'm sorry I worried you, but the way Jem died was so shocking, so violent, it took years for me to process it. And I had to do that my own way. The thing is, though, by the time I finally said goodbye to Jem, I realized I'd already said goodbye to him in my heart a while ago. It just took coming here to realize that . . . to realize that my heart was ready for someone new. For Cassidy."

"Sweetheart," says my mom after a long dismissive sigh, "this is just all so sad and upsetting. Listen, how about we order some room service and catch up a little? Your cousin Bel's boyfriend didn't work out. She's got a new one now. Keith or . . . no, that's not it. Anyway, I could catch you up . . . and, oh! We could watch an episode of *Keeping Up with the Kardashians* maybe! We love them! Sweetheart, we were so worried about you, and then we got that strange phone message. And now you're here, safe and sound. Can we just—"

"No, Mom," I say, reaching out to put my hand on her arm and curling my fingers gently around her wrist. "I *have* to get to the bottom of this. I want—no, I *need* your help. But if you can't give it, I understand. Either way, I need to figure this out. Now. Today."

She yanks her wrist away. "We traveled here all the way from Scottsdale, Brynn. We have been worried sick for three weeks, wondering if you were dead or alive! I am *not* outdoorsy, as you *well* know, but I have climbed that goddamned, god-awful mountain *six times* in three weeks! Is it so much to ask that we take a moment or two to catch our breath and *enjoy* one another before we have to hear stories about stabbing attacks and serial killers and this . . . this *Cassidy* person?" She jumps off the bed, standing at the foot with her arms crossed. "I don't think I'm being unreasonable!"

I share a look with my dad, silently begging him for help. I love my parents, and truly, I am so grateful that they're here. But I feel like the clock is ticking down on figuring out who Cassidy is *and* finding him, which is going to be a challenge of its own. But I definitely don't want to sit around watching *The Kardashians* and eating chicken salad croissants when the love of my life has based his entire existence on lies, and has probably pushed me away because he is convinced that he isn't worthy of my love.

"Muffin," says my dad, standing up and pulling my mother's stiff body awkwardly into his arms. "You go on down to the dining room and have a nice lunch now. Maybe a cold Chardonnay too. Come back when you're ready. I'm going to stay here and listen to what Brynn-bug's got to say."

"I'm not letting her out of my sight!" my mother screeches.

"Then, muffin," he says gently as he plops a kiss on her forehead, "I think you're going to have to get on board with solving this mystery because our girl seems determined."

My mother takes a deep breath and huffs. "Well, may I *at least* order us some room service?"

"I'd love it, Mom. Thank you." I smile at her back as she heads into the living room of the suite, then turn to my father. "Thanks, Dad."

He waves away my thanks. "So let me make sure I understand: Wayne attacked you and is dead. Cassidy saved you and is alive."

"Yes." *Thank God.*

"Further, Wayne was the biological son of this Paul Porter, but Cassidy . . . is? Is not?"

I shrug my shoulders. "I don't know. I don't know if

Paul Porter and my Cassidy were blood related, but I do know that Cassidy believed that Paul, the serial killer, was his father. I saw a picture of them together at a cookout back in 1995. Plus, Cassidy was really cagey about his father. Didn't want to discuss him. Changed the subject every time I tried."

"Bug," says my dad, his eyes worried, "you sure you want to go digging around in this? Could be you find something you don't want to."

"Like what?"

"Like . . ." He takes a deep breath, his lips grim. "What if he *is* the son of a serial killer?"

It's a good question. And maybe, for another woman, the answer wouldn't come easily. But I know my heart. I don't skip a beat before answering.

"I don't care," I say, the words rushed and breathless because I want my dad to hear them. "He's still the man who saved me. He's still the man who took care of me. He's still the man I love. I don't care who his father was. Dad, if you knew him, how selfless he is, how smart and capable, how he makes me feel—"

"I get it, bug. I just . . . I want the best for you," he says, his eyes worried as he runs a hand through his still-dashing silver hair.

"I love him, Dad," I murmur again, staring into green eyes so similar to my own as I finger the bracelet on my wrist.

"Your mom made a good point," he says, the eagle-eyed gaze that has served him so well in the courtroom pinning me now. "You loved *Jem* the last time we talked to you. How do you know this isn't some . . . infatuation?"

I try not to feel defensive, because I know that my feelings for Cassidy are real, but my parents deserve a little bit of time to catch up with how drastically my heart has changed in a matter of weeks.

I keep my voice measured and gentle. "Like I said, I'll *always* love Jem. He was a good man and we . . ." Hope's musings about the relative happiness of Jem's and my union come rushing back. "I *think* we would have been happy. But Jem is gone." I pause for a moment to let my words sink in before I continue. "But Dad, I'm a thirty-year-old woman. I *know* myself. I'm *in love* with Cassidy. I've got to give us a real chance. I'll never be able to move on from this if I don't. I'll be stuck here, wondering about him for the rest of my life."

"Okay." My dad nods, and I can see in his eyes that I've won him over. "I hear you, bug. I'm in. Tell me more."

"Three pancake platters and a pot of coffee on the way," says my mom, rejoining us in the bedroom.

"That's just fine, muffin," says my dad as she sits back down beside him on the bed. "Now, Jenny, you read all those mystery stories. What do you make of all this?"

She shrugs, then purses her lips. "Why did your attacker call himself Wayne?"

I stare at her for a moment, blinking, feeling annoyed. With all the questions that could be asked, she's focusing on *Wayne's alias?*

"Mom, I really think there are more—"

"I mean," she continues, deep in thought, "your Cassidy really believes he's Cassidy, right? Did Wayne really believe he was Wayne?"

All of the wind in my sails of indignation flits away.

She's right.

It's a damn good question.

"Where did that officer say that Cassidy Porter was born?" Dad asks.

"Here. In Millinocket."

"I wonder . . . hmm," hums my mother.

"What?"

"Well, if there's a birth record on file for Cassidy Porter, you might stop in and see if there's a birth record for someone named Wayne," she says. "After breakfast, of course."

I lean forward and kiss her cheek, feeling hopeful for the first time since waking up this morning at the Millinocket Police Department. "You're brilliant, Mom."

"Nice work, muffin," adds my dad, squeezing her shoulders.

She blushes, happy to have helped, then tells me to go get dressed.

"And while we're having breakfast, I want to hear more about this man who saved you," she calls as I head into the bathroom. "I'm uneasy about his parentage, of course. But no matter who they were, he *did* save your life."

"Yes, indeed," says my father. "We want to know everything about your Cassidy."

Chapter Thirty-One

Brynn

While I get dressed, my father opens up his laptop and learns that Millinocket doesn't have a Town Hall, but it does have a Town Office that is open today from nine until four. My mother sets up our breakfast in the living room, and we eat quickly, anxious to get started.

The hotel where my parents are staying is the best in the area, but it isn't directly in town, so it's a bit of a drive back over to Penobscot Avenue, and I am jittery with a combination of anticipation and nerves.

I don't know why I feel so strongly that the clock is ticking down on Cassidy's and my chance for a happy ending, but I do. In his note, Cassidy warned me not to come looking for him. It won't be easy for me to find him anyway, hidden as he is. I will need to look at maps of the area and recall everything he told me about where we were located in order to piece together a general location. That said, if he truly believes he's a danger to me, and in an effort to keep me safe from him, I can imagine him picking up and leaving. Maybe not forever. But Cassidy knows how to fend for himself. I suppose he could live in the Maine wilderness for years undetected. I am frightened of losing my window to find him again.

It hurts that he wouldn't share his history with me.

I am so in love with him, but we were also friends.

I wish he had trusted me.

I wish he had *known* that he could trust me, because I saw the colors of his heart and I loved them all.

But for someone as broken as Cassidy, I will need to prove it. And that's exactly what I intend to do: *show him* how much I love him. No matter who his parents were, it doesn't change my feelings for him, and it doesn't change my dreams for a future with him.

"Here we are, bug," says my dad, pulling into a parking spot.

To my surprise, I'm back where I found myself earlier this morning—at the Millinocket Police Department. "The police station?"

"Town clerk's located in the front of the building."

We leave the car, enter the brick building, and find the correct office on the first floor to the left.

An older woman looks up from a reception desk. "Afternoon."

"Hi," I say, holding out my hand. "I'm . . . Brynn Cadogan."

"Hi, there. Janice Dolby," she says, shaking my hand and darting a glance to my mom and dad.

"These are my parents, Colin and Jenny."

"Pleased to know you," she says, standing up and shaking their hands in turn.

"I was wondering if you keep a log, or a ledger of some kind, of birth records."

"You mean birth certificates?"

"No. No, I'm specifically looking for . . ." I scan her face, deciding to go a different route. "Ma'am, have you lived a long time here in Millinocket?"

"Sixty-two years," she says proudly. "Born and raised."

"Do you remember the Porters?"

She raises her eyebrows, her expression closing. "Are you reporters?"

"No! No, ma'am," I say. "But I am curious about Cassidy Porter."

"He was found dead, you know. In June."

"Yes, ma'am." I nod, lifting my T-shirt enough to show my healing wounds. "I know. I was his victim."

"Ohhh, my!" She gasps, looking at my scars, then back at my face. "Land's sake! You're the missin' girl!"

"Yes, ma'am."

"Our Brynn was saved by a man who lives up in the woods," shares my father.

"You don't say . . ."

"Yes." I nod. "And I know this is going to sound strange, but the man who saved me was *also* called Cassidy Porter."

Her eyes widen. "My goodness."

"Ma'am, were there two Cassidy Porters born in Millinocket? Two Cassidy Porters living here?"

"No," she says. "No, not that I recall. Only one. Little Cassidy with different-colored eyes." My stomach drops because she's definitely talking about *my* Cass, not Wayne, and I nod for her to continue. "Him and his mama moved away soon after the trial. Never saw them again."

"Never?"

She shakes her head. "His grandfather Cleary—Frank Cleary—would come into town from time to time to collect his check from the government—he was injured over in Vietnam, don't you know—but I don't much remember seein' Cassidy."

"Where did his grandfather Cleary live?"

"Lord only knows," she answers, shaking her head and sighing. "Folks said he built a cabin way up in the north woods and lived there. Kept to himself. He owned over 2,000 acres up against Baxter Park."

My eyes widen in disbelief. "Two *thousand* acres?"

She nods. "I can show you the survey from the sale if you want."

I nod eagerly, and she gestures to a four-person table in the center of the room. "Take a seat. It's quiet today. I'll see what I can dig up."

As we sit down, I notice my dad's eyebrows scrunched up, like he's figuring something out in his head.

"Brynn," he says, "that's a lot of land."

"I know," I say, but actually, I don't have a very good idea of how much it is.

My father breaks it down. "I'm not positive how much land up here costs, but I'm going to guess it's around $600 an acre, which means your Cassidy is sitting on well over a million dollars' worth."

"Whoa."

"Here we go," says Ms. Dolby, holding a dog-eared manila folder. "Was filed right there under *C* for Cleary." She opens it on the table, unfolding a map tucked inside and smoothing it with her palms. "Yep, 2,160 acres abutting Baxter State Park, bought for $135,000 back in 1972. Sold to Francis and Bertram Cleary." She pauses, humming softly, then grabs a Post-it Note. "Need to contact Mr. Cleary— Bert, that is—let him know that the land's vacant now that Cassidy's passed."

I'm about to say that it isn't vacant and Cassidy hasn't passed, but I'm not sure what claim my Cassidy has to Cleary land, so I swallow my words. If he's not related to the Clearys by blood, he may have no claim to that land at all.

"Ms. Dolby," I say, "is there any chance I could get a copy of this map?"

She glances at my hip, where I showed her the scars from my attack, gives me a sympathetic look, and shrugs. "Can't hurt anything, I guess."

She takes the file and trudges off with it, presumably to a copy machine.

"Why do you need the survey?" whispers my mother across the table.

"I need to study it to try to figure out where Cassidy's cabin is located."

"You don't know?" she asks, seeming surprised.

I shake my head. "I don't. He carried me there from Katahdin, and once I was there, I never left except to go to a local pond."

"When you were driven here to town this morning, you didn't see anything?"

I haven't wanted to think about this very much, but I am fairly certain that Cassidy drugged me so that I'd stay asleep during the drive this morning. It accounts for the bruising headache I had when I woke up, in addition to vomiting in the police station. The thing is, I understand why he did it. He didn't want to fight with me about leaving, and he didn't want me to know how to get back. That said, I'm not sure my mother would understand, so I keep it to myself.

"I was asleep the whole time."

"You don't sleep that deeply, Brynn. The doorbell wakes you up."

"I sprained my wrist last night," I explain, cobbling together a feasible story. "I took a painkiller before bed. Must have knocked me out."

I am saved from having to say any more by the return

of Ms. Dolby, who puts a finger in front of her lips and slides a copy of the survey map to me. I wink at her, fold it up, and hand it to my mother, who stuffs it in her purse.

"Did you have any other questions about Cassidy?" she asks, glancing at the front desk, which remains quiet.

"I do." I take a deep breath. "Could we look up his birth date?"

She sits down at the table with us. "Don't need to. Cassidy Porter was born on the same weekend as the Great White Easter Storm of 1990. Won't never forget it. We got thirty-six feet in forty-eight hours. Sunday, April 15, 1990."

"My goodness!" says my mother. "What a memory you have!"

"More deaths than births that weekend." Ms. Dolby shakes her head sadly. "Includin' my youngest son, Willie."

"Oh, no!" gasps my mother, reaching across the table to take Ms. Dolby's hand and squeeze it.

Ms. Dolby sniffles. "Ayuh. It was the spring thaw, don't you know. He went up Katahdin after church on Sunday mornin' with a friend. Aimin' to be home by supper. No one knew we were gettin' that kind of snow a few hours later. Those boys were wearin' shorts and T-shirts when they left. Didn't have anything they needed for a whiteout like that. Got caught in it and never made it down."

"I'm so sorry," I say.

"I thought we'd lost Brynn on Katahdin," my mother says. "I hate that mountain!"

"Don't hate the hill," says Ms. Dolby, patting my mother's hand. "Ain't its fault that fools want to climb it." She darts a glance to me. "No offense, miss."

"None taken," I say.

She releases my mother's hand and turns to me. "Weren't many born that weekend if mem'ry serves. Cassidy

Porter, of course. And the preacher's son. Hard to forget that. Preacher's wife, Nora, broke her bag o' waters in the middle of 'Jesus Christ Is Risen Today.' Like a waterfall all over the first pew. Her friend gave her a ride to the hospital while Pastor Wayne finished up the service."

Pastor Wayne.

My blood runs cold, and I blink at her in shock.

"W-what did you say? What was the pastor's name?"

"Jackson Wayne."

Oh, my God.

Ms. Dolby continues, "Pastor Wayne finished the sermon and stayed for coffee afterward because it was Easter and all, and everyone knows first-time labor takes an age. Walked over to his house to change clothes 'bout noon, but by the time he was ready to follow Nora to the hospital, the snow was fallin' at a clip. Roads impassable. I don't think he saw baby Jackson until Tuesday mornin'."

"Jackson Wayne," I murmur, pieces of a massive puzzle snapping together in my head as I flash back to the first time I met "Wayne."

They call me Wayne.

I know this mountain.

I'm local, born over in Millinocket.

I could help you.

"Jackson Wayne *Jr.* Called him J.J.," says Ms. Dolby, tapping on her chin in thought. "Strange occurrence in retrospect."

"Why is that?"

"Well . . . the son of the Methodist pastor and the son of a serial killer born on the same night, in the same place, during one of the worst storms of the century."

"Jackson Wayne Jr.," I say feeling breathless. "Um, J.J.—he was the pastor's son?"

She looks up at me and sighs. "Ayuh. But, oh my, you'd never know it. He was a real hell-raiser." Her face sours. "You know what they say about pastors' kids, right? Well, this one was the worst I ever seen."

"How so?"

She shakes her head like she's warding off a bad memory. "Lots of animals went missin' in the Waynes' neighborhood. Kids bloodied up, scared like the devil was chasin' them by the time they got home, but wouldn't say who done it. J.J. was always in trouble, but his parents were such good people, no one knew what to do. He was manipulative, don't you know, puttin' on one face for his parents and another for the world. Let's just say when the Waynes moved on to a parish down south, we were sorry to say goodbye to Jackson and Nora, but no one felt sad watchin' J.J. go."

I look at my father, sitting across from me, and he raises his eyebrows. "It would have . . . it would have been . . . *chaotic* at the hospital that weekend."

"That's the truth," confirms Ms. Dolby, oblivious to the meaningful exchange between me and my father. "We got the I-95 interstate nearby. Folks out and about, visitin' kin for the holiday. Car crashes right and left. People slippin' on the ice. Frostbite. It would've been a doozy."

"We don't want to keep you from your work," says my mother smoothly, patting Ms. Dolby's arm. "We are so terribly sorry about your son. About Willie."

Ms. Dolby nods. "He was a good boy. Only fifteen when I lost him that Easter Day."

"I'm very sorry," says my father.

We all stand up, shaking Ms. Dolby's hand to say goodbye, when I ask, "You said the Waynes moved on. But did they keep any property here?"

"Hmm. Yep. Now that you mention it, they did. A fishin' cabin on a lake out by Katahdin. But I haven't seen any of them in town for ten years at least. Wouldn't recognize J.J. if I bumped into him." She shivers. "That child always gave me the creeps. Somethin' . . . oh, I don't know . . . *off* 'bout him, I suppose. You ever met anyone like that? A little *off?*"

"Yes." I nod at her retreating form. "Yes, I have."

My father takes my arm, leading me and my mother back out of the room and into the hallway.

"Switched at birth," whispers my mother.

I gulp because it is at once outlandish and obvious.

"How is that *possible?*" I ask.

My father sighs. "Unexpected blizzard on a holiday. Chaotic hospital. People traveling to visit family. Car wrecks. Power outages. Two little babies born under such circumstances? Anything could have happened."

"Come on," I tell them, beelining for the front door.

"Where now?" asks my mother.

"The hospital."

***

When we arrive at Millinocket General Hospital, we follow the signs to the information desk.

"Afternoon," says the young woman sitting at the desk. "Here for visitin' hours?"

"No," says my dad, surprising me by stepping forward and grinning warmly. "Actually, we're trying to solve a little bit of a mystery."

"Is that right?" asks the receptionist, smiling up at my dad. He's always been charming.

"Yes, indeed. My daughter, here, Brynn, was born in this very hospital back in 1987."

"Oh, my! Welcome back!"

"We were traveling down from Portage Lake, where we have a summer house, when my wife . . ." My father puts his arm around my mother and pulls her against his side. ". . . went into labor. Well, I pulled off the highway, and thank God this hospital was here waiting for us."

"Amen!" offers the receptionist.

My father chuckles and nods. "Amen, indeed!"

"Then what?"

"Well, we were here for two nights and had the most amazing nurse looking after us. And you know? All these years later, here we are, back up in this neck of the woods, and thought we'd take a chance on swinging in and saying thank you to her."

"O-m-gosh! That is so, so, so sweet!"

My father leans his elbow on the counter and gives her the thousand-megawatt smile that used to win all of his toughest court cases. "Do you think you could give us a hand?"

"Of course!" she says, grinning conspiratorially at each of us. "What can I do?"

"Do you know the name of that nurse up in maternity who's been here for—"

"Like, a hundred years?" the young woman asks earnestly.

I swear I see my mother covertly roll her eyes, but to her credit she nods and smiles. "Just thirty, dear."

"Betty Landon's been there for a long while," says the receptionist.

"You sure, now?" asks my dad. "Betty. Hmm. Betty *does* feel right."

The young woman whispers, "She delivered my mama, and she's *thirty-eight!*"

"Then Betty's our gal!" says my dad.

"She's here today. Want me to see if she's free to come down and say a quick hello?"

"Aw," he says, "would you?"

"Sure!"

I watch as the receptionist picks up the phone, asks to speak with Betty, relates our story, and smiles at my dad triumphantly. "You all go sit over there at that table. I'll send her over when she gets down here, okay?"

"Who's the best?" asks my dad.

"Me?" she asks him with a giggle.

He nods, pointing at her with both index fingers. "You!"

My mother takes my arm and leads me to the table, smothering a chuckle. "He's incorrigible."

"You're lucky he's devoted to you," I say.

"Yes," she says, squeezing me tighter. "And to you."

We sit down, and my dad joins us a second later. "More bees with honey, huh?"

"You could charm the whole hive," I say.

A moment later, an older black woman stops by the reception desk, then looks in our direction, smiling at us as she approaches the table and stands behind the only open chair.

"I'm Betty Landon. I understand you're lookin' for me?"

"Ms. Landon," I say, standing up. "Will you join us for a minute?"

She nods, sitting down in the chair and straightening her light blue cardigan. "Chilly down here. We keep it warm up there for the little 'uns, don't you know."

"Of course," says my mother.

"You wanted to talk to me?" asks Betty, looking at my dad.

"Under false pretenses, I'm afraid," says my father. "Brynn?"

"I wasn't born here," I say, feeling a little bad when Ms. Landon's smile fades. "But I don't mean any harm. I just had a couple of questions, and I was hoping you could help me."

She clears her throat, leaning away from us, her eyes wary. "Questions about what?"

"There were two babies born here on Sunday, April 15, 1990: Jackson Wayne Jr. and Cassidy Porter. Is there any chance you were working that night?"

"The Great White Easter Storm," she says, sitting back in her seat. She takes a deep breath and nods. "Bad time. Yes, I was here. I remember."

"Bad time?" I ask.

"No trucks could get through for days." She shakes her head again. "If the injured could get here, we helped them. But the staff that was here when the storm hit was trapped. We stayed for, oh, I think it was three straight days."

"That must have been exhausting," my mother observes.

"Very," says Ms. Landon.

I reach for her hand, desperate to find out what I can about Jackson and Cassidy. "Those two little boys. They were born that Sunday."

"Yes. I remember we had two boys born during that storm, because later, they found two local boys dead up on Katahdin, and everyone said that nature had balanced itself out." I know she's talking about Willie Dolby and his friend, and I flinch with the terribleness of platitudes. After a breath, she continues. "I wasn't present at either birth. I was mindin' a little 'un in the NICU that was strugglin'. He didn't make it either."

"I'm sorry," I say, waiting a beat before asking, "Do

318

you remember who else was working that night? That weekend? Specifically, who would have been involved in delivery?"

"Would've been . . . ah . . . hmm." She nods, her lips turning down.

"Who? Who was here?"

"Well, Dr. Gordon. And Dr. Maxwell."

I get the feeling we haven't come to the "ah . . . hmm" yet. "Who else?"

"Nurse Humphreys. Theresa Humphreys. She was the nurse on duty that night. Head nurse of maternity, in fact. She stayed all three days."

"Do you mind my asking why you said 'ah' that way when you remembered her?"

Ms. Landon sighs, looking up at me with sad eyes. "She's gone now, of course. She was almost seventy back then."

"Was there something troubling about Nurse Humphreys?"

"Why are you askin' about these boys?" she counters, her face growing cool. "Because I really need to get back to w—"

"Is it possible they were switched?" I blurt out. "Is it possible that at some point between their birth and discharge that the babies were switched?"

Her eyes widen, and she shakes her head, pushing her chair away from the table and standing up. "I'm sorry, folks, but nursin' unions don't look kindly on these types of conversations. I need to head back upstairs."

I stand too, reaching for her arm, which I hold gently. "*Please*, Ms. Landon, I can't begin to tell you how desperately I need this information. I'm begging you . . ."

The nurse looks at me, her eyes conflicted. She leans

close to me, her voice soft. "Theresa Humphreys died in May 1990. Look into it."

She offers me a sad smile, turns, and leaves.

I need the internet, I think, as I leave the table and head to the car without a word, my parents following at my heels, asking about Betty Landon's parting words.

Wait for me, Cass. I'm coming, my love.

I promise you, I'm coming.

Chapter Thirty-Two

Cassidy

Dropping off Brynn at the Millinocket Police Department was the hardest thing I have ever done in my life, but now that I know the truth about myself—that I hurt people like my father did, that I am a killer like him—I take some small comfort in the notion that I got her away from me in time.

It's the *only* comfort left in my wretched life, now that I have lost Brynn.

I had a long two-hour drive to think about Wayne, and I can't say I'm sorry for killing him, which bothers me a lot. Taking a human life would tear apart a good man. But I'm *not* a good man. I don't care that I killed him. Truth told? I'd kill him a hundred times if it meant keeping my Brynn safe.

But my stark lack of regret—of any shred of guilt or remorse—worries me. I took a human life. Shouldn't I feel bad about that? That I don't feels like another step into the hell that is my transformation into Paul Isaac Porter, another indicator that the change has begun.

When I get home, the sun is rising, but I can't bear to witness its glory. I park the ATV in its stall, then climb off, stumbling blindly into Annie's adjacent stall.

I am home and Brynn is gone.

And I will never love—or be loved—again.

I slump down the wall, onto the hay, pull my knees to my chest, and lower my head, letting my rage and fear and sorrow and sheer exhaustion roar up from within me in endless bellows of fury. I scream and yell, my worthless heart bleeding out in the darkest corner of my miserable world. I scare Annie half to death, and she bleats her worry until I stop, curling into a ball by my side and crying like a baby, my body shuddering with sobs until I finally fall asleep.

When I wake up, it's late afternoon. Annie needs to be milked, and the girls need to be fed. Otherwise the place can go to hell. I don't care about it anymore. Anywhere I look, I'll see Brynn now. I'll remember her smiles and sighs, the way she hummed the Beatles and giggled at me, the way her sweet body curved into mine, so trusting, and the way she said she loved me. For a sweet, short moment, she filled my bleak, sorry, unworthy life with color and tenderness.

This homestead, which was once my sanctuary, then my heaven, is my hell now. I can't bear to stay, not that it's even an option.

I need to move on. Immediately.

I'm a murderer now. The murdering son of a serial killer. It's only a matter of time until they come for me, and when they do, there's no way in hell they'll believe I killed that guy accidentally. They'll take one look at my last name, and I'll be sent to prison.

Unless I run.

I am going to pack up what I need, including the rest of Gramp's paper money, and I'm heading north. It's still July, which means I have two months of fair weather. I should be able to find a new place to build my own cabin. Four walls with a makeshift fireplace and chimney by the end of September. I'll wait out the winter, killing whatever I need to survive—a moose for meat, a bear for its skin, geese for their fat and feathers. I've never killed mammals before, but what does it matter now? I've killed a man, a human being. I've given up the only woman who could ever love me. I feel dead inside. The moral code I lived with all my life may as well be dead too.

As far as Annie and the girls go, I can either pack them up on my ATV and drop them off at the store, or I can set them free, knowing they probably won't be able to fend for themselves in the wild for more than a day or two. They were my only friends before Brynn. I owe them more than death at the claws of a bobcat or a black bear, so I decide to take them into town tonight. I'll tie up Annie at the store entrance. I'll leave the girls in a covered crate by the door. Hopefully the people who work there will find homes for them. At least they'll have a shot at survival.

I don't want to risk being seen, so I'll leave at one a.m., when the world is darkest. In the meantime, I can get myself ready to go, to leave this place behind.

Annie nudges me with her head, bleating softly, and I grab the metal bucket from the wall, placing it under her teats and kneeling beside her.

"I'll take you to the store later," I tell her. "I'm sure someone there will find a home for you. Hope so." The only sound is the patter of milk hitting the metal bucket.

"I let Brynn go," I confess to Annie, my heart still beating, even though it's dying. "I had to. I'm no good for her."

I hope no one bothered her. I hope a kind police officer woke her up and helped her figure out where she was. I debated leaving the note pinned to her shirt, but in the end, I decided to do it. I know how hard it was for her to say goodbye to Jem. She's the sort of woman who loves long and hard, and if I didn't at least attempt to give her some closure, she might waste time grieving us. I hope my note tells her just enough to let me go and gives her a jump start moving on from our month together.

A month.

It took only a month to change my entire life.

When it started, I was lonesome, but I knew who I was.

Now? I know what it is to love someone. I know what it is to be loved in return. And I know that I'm turning into a monster, just like I always feared.

I'm not one for self-pity, but damn if I don't feel a little sorry for myself right this minute. I wasn't born to a happy fate. I know that. But how I longed for it. And with Brynn, I almost tricked myself into believing that it was possible.

But it wasn't.

It was *never* possible.

The sons of murderers don't deserve to be happy.

They are born paying for the sins of their fathers.

I finish up with Annie and take the bucket of milk outside, dumping it into the woods. No need for it anymore since I'll be leaving sometime tomorrow.

I usually take the bucket, rinse it out, and put it back on the hook in the barn, but there's no point in doing that either, so I drop-kick it away.

Walking toward the cabin, I keep my head down until I get to the steps, stupidly hoping to avoid memories of Brynn as I step up onto the porch. But she is

everywhere.

I see her in the rocking chair, naked under a blanket, holding a cup of tea as the sun rises over Katahdin. I see her nestled on my lap, her hair tickling my throat as we watch the sunset together. I hear her sigh when I catch her peeking at me while I chop wood, and licking her lips to tell me she wants another kiss.

I open the door and step inside, and there she is again, watching *The Sandlot* beside me on the couch, walking through the living room barefoot, her small feet soft on the carpet. She's in the kitchen, rinsing dishes and frying brook trout and turning to smile at me from the stove. She's choosing a book from the shelves under the window, and she's jumping into my arms to cover my face with kisses, and she's . . . she's . . . she's . . .

nowhere.

A choking sob explodes from my throat, and I grab the first thing I see—Gramp's wooden walking stick leaning by the front door—and I attack the room. I smash little knickknacks that belonged to my mother and overturn the coffee table with my foot. I throw a lamp and hardcover books into the plate glass windows until they shatter, and then I pulverize larger chunks of glass into tiny shards by beating them with the stick. I stalk into the kitchen and throw chairs against the cabinets, destroying both. I lift the table and hurl it into the living room, watching as two legs snap off when it crashes down on the upside-down coffee table.

I *hate* this house where I have hidden for most of my life.

It will never, ever be a home again.

Panting with exertion, I throw the walking stick away from me and brace my hands on the sink, bowing my head as a desperate, keening noise rises from my throat. My body shakes with a sorrow so profound and so complete, I can't think of a single reason to keep on living.

Brynn is everywhere.

Brynn is nowhere.

I am lost.

Chapter Thirty-Three

<u>Brynn</u>

When we get back from the hospital, it's afternoon, and I ask my father if I can use his laptop to do some research. He sits with my mom in the living room of the suite, watching TV, while I open the doors to the deck overlooking Ferguson Lake and do a little cyberinvestigating of my own.

I am almost certain that Cassidy Porter and Jackson Wayne Jr. were switched at birth, but while I know for certain that "Wayne" was the son of Paul Isaac and Rosemary Cleary Porter, I don't have any proof that "Cassidy" (*my* Cass) is the son of Jackson and Nora Wayne. I *need* that proof before I return to him.

My wrist bothers me as I type, but nothing's getting in the way of my search. I take an Advil, powering through the ache of the sprain.

I start with Theresa Humphreys, searching the web for any information I can find on her. An obituary comes up readily in the *North Country Register*. Theresa (Daario) Humphreys was born in Bangor and moving to Millinocket with her husband, Gabe, in 1962. She worked as head nurse in the maternity ward of Millinocket General Hospital until April 30, 1990, and died on May 22, 1990.

I pause here for a moment, looking at the dates

carefully and wishing the obituary offered more information about the cause of death. She retired only twenty-two days before she died? Was she sick? Or was it a coincidence that the two events were so close together?

Frustrated, I scan the rest of the obituary quickly, my eyes locking on the very last sentence: *In lieu of flowers, the family requests that donations are made in Mrs. Humphreys's name to the National Brain Tumor Foundation.*

My lips part as I reread the short sentence, and Betty Landon's warning returns to me: *Theresa Humphreys died in May 1990. Look into it.*

A brain tumor.

Theresa Humphreys must have had a brain tumor, and Betty Landon knew it.

I open a new internet session and type in "brain tumor symptoms."

The Mayo Clinic lists several symptoms for a brain tumor, including headaches and nausea, which Theresa Humphreys could have been explained away as one of a thousand other benign conditions. But the most troubling symptom for me is "confusion in everyday matters." For someone like Nurse Humphreys, who'd been trusted with the lives of babies for almost three decades, caring for infants would have been an "everyday matter." But switching them on an especially chaotic evening could have been a result of "confusion."

It's a small victory and makes my baby switching theory more plausible, but I still don't have proof. How could I get proof? I wonder. That's what I need before I go to Cassidy with all this information. Cold, hard proof that he's not Paul Isaac Porter's son.

Opening up a new internet window, I type in "Nora and Jackson Wayne." If the Waynes were willing to give a

DNA sample that could be compared to Cassidy's, I could get definitive proof.

A web page for the United Methodist Church of Windsor, Rhode Island, comes up immediately, and I click on it, leaning forward in my seat. A New England–style white clapboard church decorates the home page, and I click on the "About" tab, then on the "Our Ministry Team" tab. And when Pastor Jackson Wayne's face comes up on the screen, I gasp.

Sudden tears blur my vision as my fingers rise from the keys to trace the lines of Jackson Wayne Sr.'s face.

It is Cassidy's face thirty years from now.

The blond hair is white, and the skin is weathered, but this face is a carbon copy of my Cass's, right down to the three mesmerizing moles on the pastor's left cheek.

"Oh, my God," I murmur, staring back at an aged version of the face I love more than any other in the world, something galvanizing within me.

I have zero doubts in my mind that Pastor Wayne is Cassidy's biological father, and if there is no other way to prove it, I will drive down to Rhode Island myself. But that would take a full day away from getting back to Cassidy, when I was hoping to scour the survey map this afternoon and evening for an approximate location of his cabin. My father has already rented me an ATV tomorrow from the Golden Bridge Store that Cassidy mentioned once or twice.

Before frustration gets the better of me, I remember that I never did see birth records for the two boys. Maybe I can start there tomorrow.

In the meantime, I need to go downstairs, to the hotel business center, and print everything out: information about the 1990 storm, Nurse Humphreys's obituary, and this picture of Pastor Jackson Wayne. Tomorrow I'll stop by the police station and ask Marty or Lou for a copy of the DNA report proving that Cassidy Porter was the name of my attacker.

I still need solid proof that my Cassidy was born Jackson Wayne Jr., but I feel like I'm getting closer.

Wait for me, Cass.

I'm coming.

***

I am at the town clerk's office at nine o'clock on the dot the next morning with my growing folder of information, and to my great relief, Ms. Dolby is working at the desk again.

Today I'm hoping to get copies of Theresa Humphreys's death certificate, plus birth certificates for Cassidy Porter and Jackson Wayne Jr. I have looked up the requirements for requesting duplicates of such documents, and technically I am supposed to be related to these people in order to ask for their vital records. However, Ms. Dolby was so helpful and sympathetic yesterday, I am desperately hoping she will prove as amenable today.

Her warm smile tells me I might just get lucky.

"Miss Cadogan. You're lookin' well this morning!"

"Thank you, Ms. Dolby. Please call me Brynn."

"Well, then, you're lookin' well, *Brynn*." She raises her eyebrows. "What can I do you for today?"

I decide not to beat around the bush. "I was hoping to get copies of the birth certificates of Jackson Wayne Jr. and Cassidy Porter."

"Hmm," she says, pursing her lips. "Cassidy Porter ain't a problem, 'cause he's dead. But Jackson Wayne Jr.? I don't know. You ain't kin, are you?"

I take a deep breath. "What if I was?"

"Well, then, I couldn't stand in the way of you seekin' out your kin, could I?" she answers shrewdly.

I smile. "Ms. Dolby, I'm looking for the birth records of my cousins Jackson Wayne Jr. and Cassidy Porter. Also, if possible, the death record of my aunt Theresa Humphreys."

She nods at me. "Just fill out this form, Brynn. I'll go make copies for you."

I fill out the form, checking "cousin," "cousin," and "aunt" on the records, and wait against the counter for Ms. Dolby to return with the copies.

The birth certificates will show that the boys were born on the same day, and Theresa Humphreys's death certificate should show that she died of a brain tumor, corroborated by the detail in the obituary. My next stop will be the police station, to get a copy of the DNA test on Cassidy Porter, and then I need my parents to drive me to the Golden Bridge Store, where I will collect my ATV. My father and I spent about two hours leaning over the survey map last night, and if my calculations are correct, it's about fourteen miles to Harrington Pond from the store. I was there twice. I'm going to circle the pond, looking for Brynn's Rock, and try to walk from there to Cassidy's homestead by memory.

And then? Oh, God. My heart races. And then I'll share everything I've learned and hope against hope that our story is just beginning.

"Here you are, now," says Ms. Dolby, placing the three documents on the counter. "Was there anything else?"

"No, thank you," I say, sliding the papers into my manila file folder. "Thank you so much for helping me."

"You didn't even look at them," she says.

"I will. But they're more for someone else than for me."

"Hmm," she hums. "Curious note on J.J.'s birth certificate. Never noticed it before."

I search her eyes before flipping open the file. The first

document is Theresa Humphreys's death certificate, and just as I thought, the cause of death is listed as a brain tumor. If she died only three weeks after her retirement, she probably had been making mistakes for weeks, if not months. No wonder Nurse Landon didn't want to talk about it. But I silently thank her in my heart for leading me in the right direction.

I flip to the next document, the birth record for Cassidy Porter. I review the names of his parents; the location, date, and time of his birth; and his gender and race. Everything looks to be in order, and the document is signed by Elias Maxwell, M.D.

My fingers tingle as I flip to the final document, the birth record of Jackson Wayne Jr., also signed by Elias Maxwell, M.D., placing it beside Cassidy Porter's for comparison. Names of parents, check. Location, date, and time of birth, check, and almost identical to Cassidy Porter's. The boys were born nineteen minutes apart, which only adds to the notion of a chaotic maternity ward.

Gender, male. Race, Caucasian. Check. Check.

Hmm. I squint, leaning closer to the photocopied document.

Next to race, there is something else. A small scribbled note beside the word *Caucasian*. My lips part in amazement and relief as I realize it says "congenital heterochromia iridis."

"Congenital heterochromia iridis," I breathe, looking up at Ms. Dolby with eyes, no doubt, as wide as saucers.

She shrugs. "And ain't that the strangest thing? Because my memory's pretty good, and I remember *Cassidy* as the boy with different-colored eyes, not J.J. Oh, well. Gettin' old, I s'pose." She pats me on the hand as someone enters the office behind me. "You take care now ᛭rynn."

I turn away from her, feeling my smile start in my toes, which curl into the rubber bottoms of my flip-flops. That feeling of elation—of happiness and hope and grace—rises from there, up my legs, to my belly, to my heart, to my head, and I stand there in the Millinocket Town Clerk's Office with happy tears streaming down my face, grinning like I've just won the lottery.

And I have.

This is my proof.

This birth certificate, signed by the doctor who delivered Jackson Wayne Jr., has a scrawled note detailing the unusual color of his eyes. Maybe because it was so rare. Or maybe because he'd noticed that Nurse Humphreys was confused and needed a bit of extra information to tell the babies apart.

I don't care why.

I only care that it's there.

I only care that it gives me and Cass a chance to be together.

***

"Sweetheart, are you certain you're up for this?" asks my mom after the owner of the Golden Bridge Store explains how to work the top-of-the-line 2017 Outlander and gives me a helmet. "You were up at the crack of dawn. And your wrist isn't healed yet. Let your father go instead."

I am already seated on the quad, but I look up at my mom, reaching for her hands. "Thank you for everything. I can't wait for you to meet Cassidy."

"Brynn, *please* let your father—"

"I love you, Mom," I say firmly, dropping her hands and putting on the helmet. "I'm going."

"You *know* where you're going, bug?" asks my dad, putting his hand on my shoulder.

"Not exactly," I say, shaking my head. Then I grin at him, and he hands me the manila folder, which I tuck into the side compartment. "More or less."

"It's noon. When do you think you'll get there?"

"Well, it took him about three hours to get to the store and back. So . . . I have no idea."

"You know where to go?"

I look at the GPS my father picked up at the hardware store. It's strapped onto my wrist with Velcro, and we've loaded the coordinates that we believe correspond with the location of Harrington Pond. From what I can tell from Google Maps, it will be a smooth trip for about ten miles, but there could be a little—*what did Cass call it? oh, yes*—bushwhackin' after that.

I rev the motor like I was shown, looking up at my parents with a smile. "Don't worry. See you tomorrow?"

My father puts his arm around my mother, holding her close as she wipes her eyes and nods. "Be careful, bug."

"We love you, Brynn. See you tomorrow."

I don't wave as I pull out of the parking lot and onto Golden Road. In fact, the wind in my face feels really good, my wrist isn't bothering me (thanks to three Advils), and I have always loved thinking while driving.

I think about Cassidy.

I think about him saving me from Wayne that day up on Katahdin, and carrying me on his back to safety.

I think about him sliding into bed beside me when I asked him to, holding me close all night long, and how I would wake up to him singing.

I think about him hiking back up Katahdin to find Jem's phone, and how he chastised himself so harshly for being unable to find it.

I think about him chopping wood without a shirt on

333

and chatting with Annie while he milked her and fishing for brook trout on sunny days.

I think about kissing him for the first time, cuddled up on the couch watching a movie together.

I think about the way he looked at me, calling me his life's greatest treasure, when he made love to me.

I think that I will love Cassidy until the day I die, and I hope—oh, God, I hope so damned hard—that he meant it when he wrote on that note that he loved me too.

I think that he deserves to know who he is, and I hope that by learning that he's the son of Nora and Jackson Wayne, it will release him from the terrible burden I suspect he's always carried.

I think that one day I'd like to be his wife and the mother of his children. I'd like to fall asleep every night with those strong arms around me, and wake up every morning to those beautiful blue and green eyes.

I think that if Cassidy is my future, I'll be the luckiest girl in the world.

The voice on the GPS tells me to turn onto Telos Road, where I stay for two miles, chasing my thoughts away so I can concentrate on the drive. It's a double-lane dirt road for logging, I think, with thick forest on each side. I almost miss my next turn right, onto a single-lane path that's been used by other ATVs headed to Harrington Pond, which skirts the boundary of the Cleary land. I'm bumping along now, but nothing could make me turn back. I'm doing this. I'm almost there.

I turn right again onto another dirt path, my heart thrumming with excitement to share everything I've learned with Cassidy. What will he say? What will he think? Will he believe me? And after I've shared everything with him, will there be a place for me in his life? Will he want to take a chance on us? To explore the possibility of building a life together? I hope so. Oh, God, I hope so.

Finally I come to a fork in the road, and the GPS tells me to turn left to reach the pond, but there's no path in sight. *Bushwhackin'.* I look to my left, where there's nothing but thin woods and high grass. I take off my helmet for a second, idling at the end of the trail, and that's when I smell it: smoke.

Looking up, I realize that there's quite a lot of smoke, thick and gray, coming from somewhere ahead of me, a little off to the right.

Wait . . .

"No!" I cry, as my mind quickly puts together that the only thing out here that could burn that big and that hot is Cassidy's home.

Has he abandoned it? Or—*a chilling thought makes my heart clench with agony*—could he somehow be trapped inside?

"NO! PLEASE! Please, Cass! Please wait for me! Please! I'm coming!"

It's a mantra as I jam the helmet back on my head and turn the bike in the direction of the billowing smoke.

I have no idea what I'll find when I get there.

I just pray I won't be too late.

Chapter Thirty-Four

<u>Cassidy</u>

"I packed up what I wanted: some clothes and food, rope and knives. Your rifle, Gramp, and the picture of us three, Mama. I took it out of the frame and rolled it up to keep it safe. I grabbed a few of my favorite books and Gramp's old guitar. I left Annie, the girls, and T. Rex at the store. I reckon they'll find homes for them. Hope so anyway."

I take a deep breath and sigh, looking in the direction of the homestead, where smoke is rising thicker and darker. It's not that I wanted to live there anymore—I don't know how I would have borne it without Brynn. Heck, I couldn't stay even if I wanted to. Lord knows I need to be getting north, far away from this town, as soon as possible, before the sheriff comes knocking on my door, just as he came knocking on my father's.

I look at the smoke again, feeling a little conflicted. Maybe because that homestead offered me sanctuary as a child, or because it was where Mama and Gramp died. It was my home for so long, maybe it's just a bit of misguided sentiment.

I look down at Gramp's grave marker.

It was *his* place to do with what he wanted. All I did was carry out his wishes. I squat down beside the stone, gently pushing away the leaves, then I lay my palm flat over it.

"Gramp, I burned it like you told me to. The house, the greenhouse, and the barn. It won't fall into the wrong hands now. No kids out here doing drugs. No government agencies coming out here to look around at what you built. You can rest easy, Gramp," I say, my voice breaking a little because I know I won't be back here for a long time, if ever. "I took care of everything, just like you asked."

I look over at the smoke again. It's been a wet summer, and the nights are already cooling down into the high forties. Situated as it is between Harrington and McKenna Ponds, the homestead should be a controlled burn and not rage into a wildfire. It was always part of Gramp's plan to burn it when he didn't need it anymore, and I find there's peace in carrying out his will.

I pivot on my heels and face Mama's grave.

"Mama," I say, picturing her frizzy blonde hair and sweet blue eyes, "I met someone." I blink rapidly as my mother's face is replaced by Brynn's. "She was . . ." I gulp. ". . . everything to me." The breath I take is uneven, and I inhale through my nose to keep from sniffling. "But you were right to worry. I think . . . I think I might be changing. So I let her go. Couldn't saddle her with someone like me." I place my palm flat on Mama's stone as I did with Gramp's. "I love her, Mama. I suspect I'll always love her, but I did what was right. I just want you to know that."

After destroying the kitchen and living room last night, I packed up a few things in preparation for today. As long as I worked toward the goal of leaving, I allowed my mind to indulge in fantasy.

I thought about Brynn's words: *I want to be with you. I love you just the way you are.* And her plan about getting a little place closer to town with lots of privacy. Read books and make love. Have a couple of kids. A merging of two lives that

337

probably never should have collided, into one.

And damn if it doesn't make my chest ache like someone's driving a hammer into it because I can't think of a better way to spend the rest of my life. Brynn. Me. A place of our own. A *family* of our own.

I burned all of my family's pictures, letters, and documents in the campfire. I punched a hole in the cistern and let the water drain out so it wouldn't douse the fire. I siphoned the diesel from the generator so I could use it this morning to get the fire started.

When everything that needed to be done was finished, I lay my weary body down in the bed where my Brynn had slept, burying my face in her pillow. It still smelled of her— of us—and I thought again of what that sweet life in an alternate universe, in an alternate life, might have looked like. I knew one thing for certain: there would never be a man on the face of the earth as grateful as I would have been. And I would have lived every day of my life knowing I'd been *pardoned*, knowing I'd been *spared*, knowing what it felt like to have a dark fate swapped with a bright and glorious future. Knowing that I'd been blessed with *grace*.

I went to sleep surrounded by memories of my Brynn, dreaming about a forever that could never be.

Today I start over.

I stand up from the graves, looking back and forth between them and knowing I might never be down this way again.

"Bye, Mama. Bye, Gramp. You did your best for me, and I will always be grateful for your care. I will always try to honor you. I will fight against it for as long as I can. But I promise, when the time comes, I will join *you* before I give in to being *him*."

I take one last look at each of the stones and turn the

Unloved

ATV north.

Chapter Thirty-Five

When I arrive at the homestead, it's an inferno.

Flames lick the structures of the barn and the cabin, and the roof has fallen in on both. I keep my distance, standing knee-deep in meadow grass and screaming Cassidy's name, my voice filled with terror and a sadness so profound, I don't know how I remain standing. Over and over, I scream his name until I am hoarse and exhausted, tears running down my face as I stare at the destruction of his home—a place where I rediscovered my will to live and met the love of my life.

"Cassidy!" I shriek through sobs, knowing I'll never find him now that he's gone.

I wish things were different.

"Come back!" I scream, terrified that I have now lost a second man I loved.

You are the greatest treasure of my entire life.

"Heeeeeeelp!" I wail to the sky, to the God who seems to have abandoned me again.

You asked if I love you, and the answer is yes.

Depleted of strength, I slump to the ground against a tree at the edge of the meadow, several yards from the burning house. I am limp and devastated, utterly spent after two days of racing against the clock. I bow my head, resting my forehead on my knees and weep, because I am at the end of the race now, and I have lost.

I have lost everything.

"Angel? Brynn?"

I hear his voice, urgent and panting, and yank my head up to look at a man backlit by the sun, his strong body and wild hair instantly recognizable to me, even in silhouette. "Cass. Oh, Cass," I murmur, but I don't trust myself. The vision is ethereal, and I am drained and bleary. I can't trust myself. I don't know if he's real.

But suddenly he kneels before me, his mismatched eyes looking directly into mine. His hands reach for my unbandaged hand, gripping it gently but firmly between his. He brings it to his face, closing his eyes and pressing his lips to my fingers. And with that soft, familiar touch, I know it's him.

It's my Cassidy.

I launch myself against him, winding my arm around his neck and inhaling the goodness of him. Tears stream from my eyes as I feel his arms wrap around me and hold me close. He stands up, lifting me into his arms.

I am being carried. My face is buried in the warm skin of his neck, and I won't let go. I don't care where he's going, I care only that we're together again, and I silently promise that I will never, ever let him go. No matter how long it takes to convince him, Cassidy will be my life's work, my heart's only desire. And I will never give up on the love we share or the future we can have together.

"Why, Brynn?" he says raggedly, still walking with sure strides, holding me safely in his arms. "Why did you come back?"

I don't answer him. I nestle into his neck, nuzzling his

throat with my nose. We will talk when he stops walking. For now, I just want to reassure myself that I've found him and he's holding me in his arms. I haven't lost him, after all.

"I begged you not to come back. We can't be together, angel. We *can't*." His voice is agonized, and my plan not to speak goes out the window.

"We *can*," I whisper.

Still walking at a clip over uneven ground, he continues. "No! You don't . . . Brynn, you don't *know* about me. You don't know who I am. You don't know where I come from. I didn't want to tell you, but damn it, Brynn!" he cries, holding me tighter. "Why did you come back?"

"Because I love you," I say near his ear.

He makes a sound halfway between a whimper and a groan, but doesn't argue with me.

When he slows to a stop, without opening my eyes, I know exactly where we are. The cicadas sing, and I hear a fish—probably a brook trout looking for Cass's lure—jump with a light splash.

We're at Brynn's Rock.

Finally I open my eyes, leaning away just a touch to look at the pond, then at Cassidy. His beautiful, familiar, beloved face—the dirty-blond scruff of day-old beard, the full pink lips, the three moles on his left cheek, and his unforgettable eyes—makes me sob, even though I'm smiling at him. When I got to his homestead, I thought I'd never see him again. But he's here. God has not abandoned us, after all.

"Hi," I say.

"Hi." He sighs, his face bereaved. "You should have stayed away. You're not safe with me."

"Yes, I am." Then I say the same words I said to him that terrible night in his kitchen. "I love you. I want you."

"But you don't know—"

"Yes, I do, Cassidy. I know *exactly* who you *think* you are."

Staring at me with an expression of utter shock and horror, his breath catches. His arms loosen, and I drop my feet so I fall to the ground beside him gracefully. His hands droop at his sides, and I take one, leading him to the warm, flat rock where I've slept, where we've made love, where we're going to talk now and figure out a way to bridge the past, to the present, to forever.

"You *know*?" he murmurs, his eyes wide and distraught as he sits across from me on the rock. "*Everything?*"

I nod, speaking slowly and gently. "I know about Paul Isaac Porter. He and Rosemary Cleary had one child, a son, Cassidy. He was born on Easter Sunday, April 15, 1990. There was a freak storm that killed two boys up on Katahdin that day, and two baby boys were born at Millinocket General Hospital that afternoon. You were one of them."

He searches my eyes, then clenches his jaw and lowers his head, staring down at the stone. I think he might be so overwhelmed that he's crying, and I let him. I am the first human being who has spoken to Cassidy about his life, his truth, in over two decades. I cannot imagine what a shock and, maybe, *relief* it must be to share his wounded past with someone he loves. I swipe away my own tears and reach for his hand.

"I love you," I repeat softly, jaggedly, through tears. "I want to be with you."

"How?" he sobs. "How can you want me when you know what I am? When you know the monster I could turn into at any time?"

I whimper softly at the pain—the sheer and profound *anguish*—in his voice. I need to control my emotions. I need to be strong for him when I tell him who he really is and that most of his identity has been built on a lie.

"Because we are so much more than our parents," I say, cupping his cheek and forcing him to look at me. "And because, Cassidy . . . not everything is always as it seems."

"What do you—?"

"Can I tell you a story? And can you promise me that you'll try to listen?"

"Brynn, I don't—"

"*Please.* Please. For me."

He closes his parted lips and nods.

"Do you trust me, Cass?" I whisper.

"You know I do."

I take a deep breath, feeling nervous, wishing I had my manila file folder with me. But maybe it's better to tell him first. Then, if he doubts what I'm saying, we can go get the file for proof.

Holding his eyes hostage and his hand in mine, I begin:

"Easter Sunday 1990 started warm and sunny. It was the spring thaw, and people went to church or got in their cars to join family for brunch. What they didn't know was that just after twelve noon, a blizzard would start. It would be one of the worst whiteouts of the century, and later, they'd call it the Great White Easter Storm.

"That morning, two women in Millinocket went into labor. One was Rosemary Cleary Porter, who was married to Paul Isaac Porter. The other was Nora Wayne, who was married to the Methodist minister, Pastor Jackson Wayne. Both women arrived at Millinocket General Hospital in the late morning, already in early labor, but neither gave birth right away. In fact, they were both in labor for about eight hours. Because of the storm, neither of their husbands could join them at the hospital, and the doctors and nurses on staff had already worked their full shifts. As the hours ticked by, the hospital became more chaotic, and there was no more staff coming to relieve those working. The storm made the roads impossible for passage. More patients kept arriving. The doctors and nurses were exhausted, but they kept working. The two mothers went into delivery that evening."

I lick my lips, searching his face for signs of distress or realization, but I don't find any. I offer him a small smile that he doesn't return, and then I keep going.

"The doctor on duty that night, Dr. Elias Maxwell, probably knew that his head nurse, Theresa Humphreys, wasn't performing as sharply as she had for most of her thirty years on the job, because she'd been suffering for months with a brain tumor that was likely affecting her judgment and job performance. But she was still the head maternity nurse. She was responsible for the two little boys born that night—Cassidy Porter and Jackson Wayne Jr.

"Two weeks later, on April 30, she retired. And three weeks after that, she passed away."

"What are you saying?" he asks, his chest pumping up and down with shallow breaths, his eyes severe.

Gulp. "Stay with me, Cass, okay?"

He nods, but it's not a leisurely gesture. It's curt and impatient, wondering where I'm going with this wild, twisting story. *Oh, Cass. It's coming. I promise.*

"One baby went home with the Porters," I say. "The other went home with the Waynes."

He's still nodding at me, his eyes wide and intense.

"The *wrong* baby went home with the Porters," I say as carefully as I can, "which means the wrong baby went home with the Waynes."

I am holding my breath as he stares at me, without moving, without flinching. The only thing I can see in my peripheral vision is the relentless rise and fall of his chest.

"What are . . . what are you saying?" he asks again. And then he asks a third time, his voice louder and more frantic. "Brynn, what are you saying?"

"I'm saying that your birth name," I swallow quickly, trying to stay calm, squeezing his hand in mine, "is Jackson Wayne Jr."

He releases my hand like it's burning him, and his entire body jerks away from me. His voice is breathy and low. "That's . . . that's not possible. That's crazy."

"Cassidy," I say, forcing myself to regain control of my emotions. "You are *not* the biological son of Paul Isaac Porter. You never were."

"Brynn," he says, wincing as he turns to face me, "I know you want me to be someone else so you can—"

"No, Cass," I interrupt him. "You *are* someone else. I have proof."

"That's impossible. My mother was—"

"Nora Wayne."

"No. No!" he yells, his eyes wide and wild. "Rosemary Cleary was my mother."

"Rosemary Cleary loved you and raised you," I say, "but your biological mother is Nora Wayne."

"The pastor's wife? No. No. No, no, no. No no no no no. I know who I am. I . . . I *know* who I am. I've always known."

"Cassidy," I say gently, reaching for his arm, which—I'm grateful to say—he lets me hold, "I can tell you more."

"This isn't true," he says frantically. And then, more softly, "This *can't* be true."

"It *can* be," I say, my heart breaking for him, "because it is. Can you listen to me? There's a little more."

He runs a hand through his hair and nods, but his voice

is breathless when he says, "W-what? How can there be more?"

"Do you remember the name of the man who attacked me?" I lower my chin and watch his face—I watch as he remembers, as the horror of the truth starts making sense to him.

"Wayne."

"Yes," I say. "*Jackson* Wayne. The man who attacked me, the man who . . . who died that day, *thought* his name was Jackson Wayne, but Cass . . ." I have to keep going now. He needs to hear it all. "He died. He died when you threw him. And when they recovered his body, he had no ID on him, so the police ran a DNA test. There was only one match in the system." I pause before connecting the dots for him. "To Paul Isaac Porter . . . his biological father."

"*Oh . . . God!*" he sobs, his breath coming in uneven fits as he digs his hands into his hair and faces away from me.

"Cass," I say gently, reaching for him, but he shrinks from me, turning away, hiding his tears.

His shoulders are shaking, and he has drawn his knees up against his chest, clasping them with his arms, his back partially turned to me.

Cass. Oh, Cass. If I could take away this pain, I would.

His entire life has been a struggle, a lie, an accident, a terrible conviction.

For a moment I consider leaving him to his tears, but deep inside I know he needs me now more than ever. Spreading out my legs, I scooch up against his back, wrapping my legs and arms around him and resting my clasped hands together over his. I rest my cheek against his strong, broad back, a shock absorber for his tears. His body shakes, and I can hear the gut-wrenching sounds of a grown man sobbing, but I clench my eyes closed and force myself not to cry, no matter how much I want to. How many times was Cassidy strong for me? It's my turn to be strong for him.

Eventually his sobs subside, and his breathing begins to even out.

"If this is true . . ."

"It *is* true. All of it. You are *not* Paul Isaac Porter's son."

"Jackson Wayne was a . . ." His voice breaks. "A mean little kid."

"He was Paul's biological son."

"And I'm . . . I'm . . ." His body shudders again, and he can't speak.

"You're the son of Nora and Jackson Wayne, Cass." I take a deep breath, making sure my voice is strong and even before I say, "You're *not* the son of a serial killer. There is nothing but goodness in you."

"But I yelled at you," he says, turning to face me. "I raised my fist to you."

"Couples fight," I say, searching his eyes. He spreads out his legs on either side of me, and I slide onto his lap, scooting up until our chests are touching and our arms are around each other. "You didn't hit me. You would *never* hit me, Cass. You were only trying to *protect* me."

His face falls, crumpling before my eyes.

"I killed him," he whispers, horror laced in his voice. "I killed Jackson Wayne. I'm a murderer. What if they come for me?"

"Come for you? Oh, Cass," I say, my heart breaking all over again for him. I reach for his face, looking into his eyes. "No. No, you aren't a murderer, and the case is closed. I was attacked, and Wayne fell on his knife. No one's coming for you but me. You saved my life. You're a hero, Cass. *My* hero."

I press my lips to his, then pull him closer, pressing his

forehead onto my shoulder. This time, his sobs are silent, though they rack his entire body and mine too.

I readjust my arms around him.

It's *my* turn to hold *him*.

***

He has a lot of questions after his initial shock wears away, so I take his hand and lead him back to my rented ATV, where the manila file awaits.

"You're sure we were switched?"

"Mm-hm. On the birth certificate of Jackson Wayne Jr., the doctor wrote a note about heterochromia."

"Whoa," he sighs, the puff of breath sharp because he's still processing everything. "You said the nurse had a brain tumor?"

"Yes."

"Do my . . ."

I stop walking and turn to look at him. "What?"

"Do my . . . *parents* . . ." He pauses for a moment, then continues, "know about me?"

"Not yet," I tell him. "But you look exactly like your dad. It's uncanny."

He exhales through his mouth with a *phew* sound. "I've never used that word before."

"What word?"

"*Dad*," he says softly.

I clench my jaw to keep from sobbing. When I can, I respond. "Maybe now you can."

And then we keep walking.

The homestead has burned almost to the ground by the time we return, and after I pull the file from the quad's side pocket, I turn to find Cassidy standing still, staring at the smoking, smoldering destruction before him.

"Do you wish you hadn't burned it down?" I ask.

"No," he answers, turning his head to look at me, his gaze infinitely tender. "I couldn't live here anymore. I would have seen you everywhere."

Oh, my heart.

I nod at him, holding out the folder. "Do you want to go somewhere to look through everything? My parents got me a hotel room in town. We could go there if you want."

He takes a deep breath. "I need time to process this, Brynn."

"Oh." My mind scrambles to understand his meaning, and as I do, I feel like the wind's been knocked out of me. He needs time. Time. Alone. Away from me. Fuck. *Get it together, Brynn. You've just turned his life upside down. If he needs time, give it to him.* I force a smile, swallowing over the lump in my throat. "Okay. Well, I could go, and you could come and find me when you're, I mean, if you—"

"Not time away from *you*," he says in a rush. "It's just . . . hotels, people . . . I don't know if I'm ready to go hang out in town yet."

"Ohh." My relief makes me light-headed. "Right."

"There are cabins at the Golden Bridge Campground," he says. "Maybe we could rent one for a few days and sort this out. I have to get my head around it."

"Definitely," I say, offering him the file. "We can definitely do that, Cass."

"Wait," he says, taking the file and placing it on the ground before looking back at me.

"What?"

"Angel," he says, his voice deep and emotional as he pulls me against him, then puts a finger under my chin, tilting it up so I'm facing him. He captures my eyes with his and holds them steady. "I don't *ever* want *any* time away from you. Understand? Never."

"Never," I whisper back, feeling tears track down my cheeks.

"I love you," he says. "I love you so much, it's been killing me inside not to tell you."

"I love you too. So much. Don't ever leave me again."

"I promise," he says, his palms flush against my cheeks, his thumbs swiping at my tears.

"Say it again," I ask him, leaning my head back and closing my eyes.

"I love you," he says, dropping his lips to my forehead. "I love you," he says again, kissing one eyelid and then the other. "I love you," he says, pressing his lips flush against mine.

I wind my arms around his neck, leaning into his body, into his strength, into his kiss. His tongue meets mine, and I sigh into his mouth, threading my fingers through his hair and arching my back so that my breasts flatten against the ridges of muscles on his chest.

We kiss while the smoke of one life winds around us and the promise of another is finally—finally—within reach. My Cassidy is a phoenix rising from that fire—the same good man he always was, without the burden of a mistaken identity, without cursed blood flowing through his veins.

When he draws away from me, his eyes are dark with arousal, but still somehow lighter than I have ever seen them.

"I'm not Cassidy Porter," he says, a little bemused, a small smile tilting his lips up.

"It's strange. I know that being Cassidy Porter was a burden to you. But to me," I say, keeping my fingers laced behind his neck, "Cassidy Porter was an angel. A *guardian* angel. *My* guardian angel. You gave me back my life in so many ways."

"Then we're even . . . because now you've given me back mine." He searches my eyes before kissing me soundly. When he backs away, his expression is serious. "When I left you at the police station, I told you, 'If I ever see you again, I'll never be able to let you go.' And here you are."

"Here I am," I say, letting my tears fall because they are born of a happiness so complete, I never thought I could feel this way again.

"I'll never let you go," he says fiercely, and it's a promise, a vow that holds with it the promise of a sweet forever: a home we build together, reading books and making love, and children. *Our* children.

"I want kids," I whisper, holding my breath. "*Your* kids. *Ours.*"

His face seizes for a moment, then relaxes little by little. Finally his lips tilt up, and when they do, I realize that his eyes are glistening. He runs his knuckles down my cheek, caressing it.

"Me too. Someday," he says.

I know that processing everything—trusting that what I've said and what he reads is true—will take some time, but I see the hope and promise shining in his eyes, and for me, a woman who was once broken, it's enough.

"Someday," I say, grinning up at him. I reach down for the file and hand it to him. "Hey, in the meantime, what should I call you?"

He tilts his head. "Cassidy, I guess. Not Cassidy *Porter.* Just Cassidy."

"Cassidy," I say, lifting on my tiptoes to touch my lips to his. "*Just* Cassidy . . . you are loved."

Epilogue

<u>Cassidy</u>

Brynn sold her house in San Francisco, and had her cat, Milo, shipped East. From the sale of her house and the money I'd saved from Gramp's pension, we were able to buy forty acres of land just over the border, in Bartlett, New Hampshire, with views of both Black Cap and Cranmore Mountains. Brynn's not interested in climbing them, which I understand. The last mountain she climbed was Katahdin, last summer, with me. I took her up to Baxter Peak so she could bury Jem's cell phone, like she planned. I will always be grateful to him, and to Katahdin. Without them, Brynn and I wouldn't have found each other. But our memories of Maine were a mixed bag, and New Hampshire felt like the fresh start we both needed and deserved.

     Our property's at the end of a lonesome road, surrounded by the White Mountain National Forest, and we built our house ten miles into our land for even greater seclusion. I guess it'd be fair to say that we're the very *last* house on the grid.

     It's a strange thing to have electricity at the flick of a switch, or hot water just because I want it. I don't know if

I'll ever get used to it completely, but I'm man enough to admit that I appreciate the satellite TV, not that I understand why anyone needs that many channels.

It's a twenty-minute drive from our house to the road, but once you're there, it's only fifteen minutes more to North Conway, which has every store and restaurant you can think of, plus Memorial Hospital, which is important to my Brynn.

Especially now.

I glance over at her, reading on a window seat in the sunlight, her belly rounder by the day. She's not due for another four months, but I'm grateful to be closer to town too. Last week I joined her for her doctor's appointment, and I could hear my son's heart beating strong inside her. Grace. Such grace.

This woman, my wife, gave me back my life, and in her body she grows a life that is half her and half me. Together, they are the miracle I longed for, but never thought I could have, and my heart stutters at the thought of anything happening to them. I will protect them and cherish them until the light fades from my soul. I will never, ever take them for granted. I will live my life in reverence and thanks.

"You're looking at me like crazy," Brynn says, glancing my way and grinning.

"That's 'cause I'm crazy about you," I say, walking over to her with two mugs of tea.

She giggles as she accepts the mug and takes a quick sip. "Ooo! Nice and hot."

I nod, looking out the window at the expanse of land and the mountain peaks in the distance.

"You talked to your . . . to Nora?"

In the weeks after Brynn told me about my parents, I reached out to Nora and Jackson Wayne via e-mail, once

Brynn showed me how to use it. I explained that the son they'd known as Jackson Jr. had passed away, explained what had happened back in 1990, and introduced myself as their biological son. Though it took some time to unravel everything for them, once they understood, they were eager to set a time and place to meet in person.

I confessed the whole of my connection to their son, J.J.—that I'd killed him saving Brynn's life—when we met, and I held my breath, wondering if they'd still want a relationship with me after this revelation. But to my surprise, they did. I am sure they grieved the son they knew in their own way, but they bore nothing but open-armed forgiveness and acceptance for me.

Brynn was right: I look exactly like my father, Jackson, whom I call Jack. So much so, in fact, that none of us were surprised when the DNA test we took came back matching us as father and son. Nora, my biological mother, asked me to call her Mom recently, but I can't do it yet. Rosemary Cleary wasn't perfect, but she loved me and I loved her. She was my mother even if we weren't related, and out of respect for her memory, I think she'll be the only woman I ever call Mom. I hope Nora will be okay with that over time.

I couldn't get rid of the name Porter fast enough, but Wayne didn't sit right either. In the end, with Brynn's help, I decided that my name should be Cassidy Cleary, and our baby's name will be Colin Francis Cadogan-Cleary, half the grandfather I knew and half the grandfather who already dotes on him.

We see the Cadogans, who bought a lake house twenty miles south of us, on Conway Lake, often. Their place is pretty grand, with plenty of room to host the Waynes, with whom they have become very close, and who are planning to visit closer to Brynn's due date. This baby sure will be surrounded by love.

My Great-Uncle Bert—my grandfather's brother—got in touch with me a few months ago, and though I hadn't seen him in years, we met halfway between his house and mine, and spent an evening drinking beer and reminiscing about the old homestead. I see it often in my dreams, and when I do, it isn't burning. I remember the days that Brynn and I shared there, and mostly my memories make me happy.

Uncle Bert sold the land up in Maine and gave half the money to me. *I don't need it*, I told him, but he insisted that Gramp would have wanted me to have it. I'll make sure my wife is comfortable and put my son through college with that money, I guess, though it's more than I can ever imagine spending. I was taught to live quiet, and even in our modern house, with electricity and satellite TV, I still like to keep things simple.

"I talked to her," I say, responding to Brynn's question about Nora. "She's staying with your folks at the lake house in October."

"And Jack?"

"He's getting a replacement to take care of things at the church for the months of October and November." I smile at her, remembering Nora's words. "I think they're going to follow that baby all over the hospital to make sure history doesn't repeat itself."

She smiles at me and picks up her feet so I can sit down. When I do, I place my tea on the window ledge, and she puts her feet in my lap, just like she used to when we sat on the couch together reading *A Prayer for Owen Meany* and Kurt Vonnegut. I rub her feet because I know she loves it. And I do it because I love her and never, ever—not for one second in any day between now and the one on which I die—will I forget that she is my life, my beating heart, my angel, and my salvation.

"I love you," I say, pausing to look at her belly with profound pride and happiness before lifting my gaze to her face. "Always."

"I love you too," she says, a twinkle in her ivy-green eyes. "Always."

I don't think too much about Paul Isaac Porter anymore, though I dream about that raccoon now and then. In my favorite dreams, I figure out a way to set it free. I watch as it limps off into the woods, hoping it finds a way to magically heal itself and carry on living.

In a way, that's what happened to me and Brynn, I guess.

Mama and I were broken and scared when we escaped to the woods, and that's how I would have remained if not for Brynn.

She was my magic.

She healed me.

She gave me back my life.

She is, and will forever be, my life's greatest treasure.

Because of her, I am loved.

THE END

UNLOVED PLAYLIST

While My Guitar Gently Weeps The Beatles
While My Guitar Gently Weeps AM and Tina Dico
While My Guitar Gently Weeps Quinn Sullivan
Falling Oh Gravity
If I Fell The Beatles
In My Life The Beatles
My Heart With You The Recues
Ride twenty one pilots
The Greatest Sia
You Were Always On My Mind Renee Isaacs

I probably listened to AM and Tina Dico singing "While My Guitar Gently Weeps" over 1,000 times during the initial writing of *Unloved, a love story*. There is a poignancy to the song that became Cassidy's theme for me, and the words—especially "I don't know why nobody told you how to unfold your love" and "I don't know how someone controlled you/They bought and sold you"—pretty much ripped my heart out from the start.

Thanks to George Harrison, the master, for his deft hand and word mastery. Still in awe. Forever grateful.

ALSO AVAILABLE
from Katy Regnery

a modern fairytale
(A collection)

The Vixen and the Vet
Never Let You Go
Ginger's Heart
Dark Sexy Knight
Don't Speak
Shear Heaven

Fragments of Ash
Coming 2018
Swan Song
Coming 2018
At First Sight
Coming 2018

THE BLUEBERRY LANE SERIES

THE ENGLISH BROTHERS
(Blueberry Lane Books #1–7)

Breaking Up with Barrett
Falling for Fitz
Anyone but Alex
Seduced by Stratton
Wild about Weston
Kiss Me Kate

Marrying Mr. English

THE WINSLOW BROTHERS
(Blueberry Lane Books #8–11)

Bidding on Brooks
Proposing to Preston
Crazy about Cameron
Campaigning for Christopher

THE ROUSSEAUS
(Blueberry Lane Books #12–14)

Jonquils for Jax
Marry Me Mad
J.C. and the Bijoux Jolis

THE STORY SISTERS
(Blueberry Lane Books #15–16)

The Bohemian and the Businessman
The Director and Don Juan

STAND-ALONE BOOKS:

After We Break
(a stand-alone second-chance romance)

Frosted
(a romance novella for mature readers)

Acknowledgments

First and foremost, I owe thanks to my George. You shared the story of *The Devil in the White City* with me on a drive to the airport, and I became obsessed with the idea of a serial killer's child being a hero in one of my stories. Well, now, here we are. Hold tight, my love . . . I'll be back to thank you again later.

Next, I want to thank my Mia. I reached out to you with my first chapter and novel concept while I was on vacation, and you said, "Heck, yes! People need a serial killer's son for a hero! Keep writing!" Okay, you might not have said exactly that, but it was close. Thank you for being my sounding board and writing partner, friend, and cheerleader. I adore you. #NoSpace

To Sejla and Selma, who listened to me prattle on about *Unloved, a love story* on a car ride to a Boston signing, thank you so much for making me feel like my idea could captivate and encouraging me to continue. I still didn't know how to write it, but after sharing my idea with you, I knew I had to keep writing!

To my Radish Readers, who gave *Unloved, a love story* a try from the very beginning: Lena D., Bel M., Allison H., Heather G., Patterson G., Maeve W., Carlotta G., Freja E., Sunshine T., Jackie A., Sharon C., and Candi V. You loved Cass and Brynn from the very first chapter, and it means the WORLD to me to share the finished story with you.

To all my other readers, thank you for reaching out to me to share your excitement about *Unloved, a love story*, and giving this book a chance. I hope you fall in love with Cass and Brynn as much as I did!

To Katy's Ladies and my long, long list of supportive bloggers, who endlessly pimp and support me, you know who you are, and I would not be me without you. Thank you for loving my words and for taking the time out of your busy days to read them. I am so blessed with your kindness and friendship.

To my production team: Marianne (cover; not this one, but all the rest!), Tessa (developmental edits), Chris (developmental edits), Melissa (line and copy edits), Elizabeth (proofreading), Cassie Mae (formatting) and Tanya (graphics), you kick more ass than should be possible! LOL! Thank you for all you do to make my words shine. Writing books is one thing; sharing them with the world requires your finesse. I am grateful for it.

To Heather, Sage, Lydia, and the awesomeness at TRSOR, THANK YOU!! I can't get this book out into the world on my own. You PR dynamos lifted it up and gave it wings!

To my Ridgefield friends—especially Shannon, who supports me in one hundred different ways—thank you. Autumn, Kerry, Joy, Trieste, Maria, Jillian, and Kim, HUGE kisses and thanks for a fun-filled summer! A special shout-out to the folks at Parma Market and Ross Bread + Coffee, in thanks for keeping me caffeinated and fed. To Chris, Nik, Pete, and Tanner at PTP of Ridgefield, thanks for listening to me talk about this book while keeping me (and my kids!) healthy—you guys are the best! #TeamPTP And to Allison, who doesn't live in Ridgefield: whether you are in Hingham or Houston, you're *always* in my heart and cheering me on.

To all the authors who supported this book, especially Mia, Kelly, Ilsa, Annika, Tia, Carey, Leylah and Layla, who asked to read a copy of *Unloved, a love story*, in advance. THANK YOU!! I love our author community, and I am so fucking grateful for/to all of you!

To my mother, father, brother, Henry, and Callie, I

love you all more than words can express. You are always foremost in my mind as I navigate the twists and turns of this crazy career. None of my success would mean a thing without you in my life.

Finally, and again, to George. For your unfailing love and support. For bringing home sandwiches when I'm a lunatic on a deadline. For asking "How's the writing going?" every day. For believing in me more than anyone else in the world. You are my other half, the warm body I reach for in the night, and the reason I will never, ever feel unloved. #AllTheMuch #Forever

About the Author

New York Times and **USA Today** **bestselling author Katy Regnery** started her writing career by enrolling in a short story class in January 2012. One year later, she signed her first contract, and Katy's first novel was published in September 2013.

Thirty books later, Katy claims authorship of the multititled *New York Times* and *USA Today* bestselling Blueberry Lane Series, which follows the English, Winslow, Rousseau, Story, and Ambler families of Philadelphia; the six-book, bestselling ~a modern fairytale~ series; and several other stand-alone novels and novellas.

Katy's first modern fairytale romance, *The Vixen and the Vet*, was nominated for a RITA® in 2015 and won the 2015 Kindle Book Award for romance. Katy's boxed set, *The English Brothers Boxed Set*, Books #1–4, hit the *USA Today* bestseller list in 2015, and her Christmas story, *Marrying Mr. English*, appeared on the list a week later. In May 2016, Katy's Blueberry Lane collection, *The Winslow Brothers Boxed Set*, Books #1–4, became a *New York Times* e-book bestseller.

Katy lives in the relative wilds of northern Fairfield County, Connecticut, where her writing room looks out at the woods, and her husband, two young children, two dogs, and one Blue Tonkinese kitten create just enough cheerful chaos to remind her that the very best love stories begin at home.

Sign up for Katy's newsletter today: www.katyregnery.com!